MICHAEL
CARROLL

STRONGER

a SUPER HUMAN Clash

PHILOMEL BOOKS
AN IMPRINT OF PENGUIN GROUP (USA) INC.

PHILOMEL BOOKS
A division of Penguin Young Readers Group.
Published by The Penguin Group.
Penguin Group (USA) Inc., 375 Hudson Street, New York, NY 10014, U.S.A.
Penguin Group (Canada), 90 Eglinton Avenue East, Suite 700, Toronto, Ontario M4P 2Y3,
Canada (a division of Pearson Penguin Canada Inc.).
Penguin Books Ltd, 80 Strand, London WC2R 0RL, England.
Penguin Ireland, 25 St. Stephen's Green, Dublin 2, Ireland
(a division of Penguin Books Ltd).
Penguin Group (Australia), 250 Camberwell Road, Camberwell, Victoria 3124, Australia
(a division of Pearson Australia Group Pty Ltd).
Penguin Books India Pvt Ltd, 11 Community Centre, Panchsheel Park,
New Delhi—110 017, India.
Penguin Group (NZ), 67 Apollo Drive, Rosedale, Auckland 0632, New Zealand
(a division of Pearson New Zealand Ltd).
Penguin Books (South Africa) (Pty) Ltd, 24 Sturdee Avenue, Rosebank,
Johannesburg 2196, South Africa.
Penguin Books Ltd, Registered Offices: 80 Strand, London WC2R 0RL, England.

Published simultaneously in Canada. Printed in the United States of America.
Edited by Kiffin Steurer. Design by Amy Wu. Text set in 10.5-point Palatino.

Library of Congress Cataloging-in-Publication Data   Carroll, Michael Owen, 1966–
Stronger : a super human clash / Michael Carroll.   p. cm.   Summary: Recounts the
history of the misunderstood villain called Brawn. [1. Science fiction. 2. Adventure and
adventurers—Fiction.] I. Title.   PZ7.C23497St 2012   [Fic]—dc23   2011022436

ISBN 978-0-399-25761-2
1   3   5   7   9   10   8   6   4   2

For Dani

PROLOGUE

THIS MORNING, WHEN ONE of the medics from the U.N. was digging a bullet out of my arm—most of the time they fall out by themselves, but this one was a keeper—he asked me how many times I've been shot.

"I dunno," I said. I was lying on the ground, faceup, as he worked on me. "Forty or fifty?"

"I can see forty or fifty bullet wounds right *now*," he said, looking up and down my body. "I meant, how many times have you been shot in total?"

I couldn't answer that. I'd stopped counting a long time ago.

I've certainly been shot hundreds of times. Maybe thousands. Maybe even *tens* of thousands.

A U.S. Army colonel once said to me, "Whatever doesn't kill ya makes ya stronger."

I guess it means that if you can get through all the bad stuff that life throws in your path, you come out the other side with the experience of having survived and the knowledge of how to get through it again. Or, as my dad always liked to say, "conflict builds character."

Sometimes the conflict we encounter comes from other people, and sometimes it comes from ourselves. We all have weaknesses; we all make bad decisions. We're only human.

Of course, the thing about bad decisions is that most of the time we realize they were bad only in hindsight. At the time, they seem right. I mean, only an idiot would think, "This is a bad decision, but I'm going to do it anyway."

When I was sixteen, I made a decision that I *knew* was right. My friends didn't agree with me, we fell out—to put it mildly—and as a consequence my decision changed not only my life, but the lives of countless others.

Far too many people suffered and died because I tried to do the right thing. And even now, almost a quarter of a century later, the echoes of my decision are still being heard.

My decision was only one link in a long chain of events, but—as another old saying goes—every chain is only as strong as its weakest link. If I hadn't done what I did, the rest of the chain would have fallen apart.

Hardly a day goes by when I don't think, *If I'd known then what I know now* . . . But I *was* trying to do the right thing. I have to keep reminding myself of that. We *can't* know all the consequences of our actions before we take them. We can only act on the knowledge we have at hand.

So even though I sometimes dream about going back to

visit my sixteen-year-old self and slapping him across the back of his head for what he did, I can't blame him.

We have to make our decisions, and whatever the consequences of those decisions may be, we have to accept them. Suck it up. Live with it. Life goes on.

For some of us.

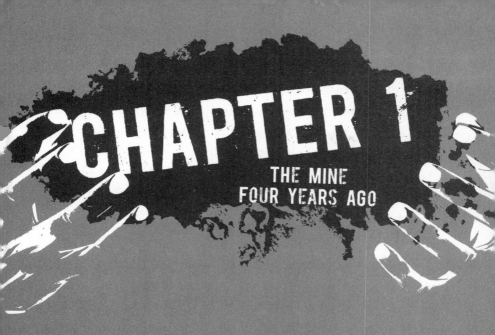

CHAPTER 1
THE MINE
FOUR YEARS AGO

I WAS NEARING THE END of my sixteen-hour shift in the main branch of the platinum mine's oldest and deepest shaft, tunnel D. Because I couldn't easily wield a pick or a drill to extract the ore, my job was to load the loosened chunks into the iron-wheeled cart and, when the cart was full, push it up through the shaft and out to the processing station.

I was on my hands and knees in the deepest part of the mine—the shaft's ceiling was far too low for me to stand upright—using my bare hands to scoop the rubble from around Keegan's feet into a pair of steel buckets. I'd already tossed the larger rocks into the cart behind me.

"Gotta be close to quitting time for you," Keegan said. She was about five foot five, thin but wiry, and she kept her red hair long but tied back. She stepped back from the wall and shifted to the side a little to allow the weak yellow light from the nearest lamp to illuminate her work area.

"Almost," I said. "One more trip up, then I've got to bring down the new rails. Setting them will be tomorrow's job." The rails on which the carts ran were fifteen feet long and had to be set into the ground like railway tracks. It was a tough job made more difficult by the barely adequate ventilation, the poor light, and the shaft's low ceiling. Right now the track ended about thirty feet from the wall on which Keegan and the others were working.

Donald DePaiva—the second-in-command to Thomas Hazlegrove, the mine's overseer—shone his flashlight in Keegan's direction. "What's the delay?" he barked at her.

"I was just—"

"Shut up and dig!"

Keegan examined the calluses on her hands for a moment, then picked up her pickax again and swung it at the wall. A tiny fragment of rock shot back and scratched her upper arm— she didn't even notice. "Might not be worth the effort laying the new tracks," she said to me. "We're running dry here too."

A few months earlier the mine's C shaft had been almost completely abandoned. There was so little ore coming out of it that it was decided that only a skeleton crew was needed. The rails had been removed, and now only eight men, instead of the usual thirty or so, were working to extract the last possible lumps of ore from the shaft. They were bringing out less than four wheelbarrow-loads a day.

I was about to respond when I heard—no, when I *felt*—the ground trembling. We'd all felt it before, far too many times, and we knew what it meant: One of the tunnels was coming down.

"Out!" I shouted. "Move! *Now!*"

Keegan and the others dropped their tools and ran.

I scrambled after them as fast as I could, squeezed past the almost-full cart, and saw that Keegan had stopped to help one of the kids who'd tripped and been left behind. "I'll get her!" I shouted to Keegan. "Just go!"

Keegan hesitated for a moment, then let go of the little girl's hand and ran.

Still on my hands and knees, I reached the girl and saw that it was the daughter of my friends Imyram and Edmond. She was five years old—I remember the day she was born—and her tears had carved clear lines in the dirt on her face.

Without stopping I snagged her up in one hand and kept her tucked under my chest. If the ceiling collapsed on top of us, there was a chance my body would protect her. I could feel her trembling as she clung to my arm, but I didn't have time to offer her any words of comfort. "Just hold tight!"

Ahead, the guard DePaiva was facedown on the ground, pinned beneath a foot-thick wooden support beam. Two more workers rushed past me and leaped over DePaiva without giving him a second glance.

For a moment I was tempted to follow suit, but I couldn't leave a man to be crushed to death if the rest of the ceiling collapsed. I grabbed the nearest end of the beam with my free hand and heaved it upward. DePaiva scrambled free, his flailing hands and feet throwing a fresh cloud of dust in my face.

A group of workers darted out of a side tunnel and skidded

to a stop as they saw DePaiva approaching. "Run!" I roared at them. "We're clear—I'm the last! Get going!"

By the time I emerged from the shaft's exit, almost all of the workers had swarmed out of the other tunnels, their faces tight with panic. Imyram grabbed her daughter from my arms and said, "Thank you, thank you!"

I nodded to her as I looked through the crowd for Keegan, then spotted her standing to the side. "What *was* that?"

She pointed back toward the tunnels. "The C shaft. The ceiling collapsed about fifty or sixty yards in. Only minor damage to D, I think."

Most of the platinum mine was covered by a huge metal dome—steel plates crudely welded together—that shielded us from not only the harsh weather but also the eyes of the rest of the world.

The dome was more than fifty yards high, about three hundred yards across, and easily twice as long. It was painted to match the surrounding landscape. From the ground, of course, it was pretty clear that it was a man-made structure, but from the air it was almost invisible. And being a dome, it didn't cast any unnatural angular shadows that might draw attention.

This is because the mine didn't officially exist.

And the *reason* it didn't officially exist is that it wasn't just a mine. It was a prison camp.

The mine was surrounded by a twenty-foot-high electrified fence, with cameras set on high poles watching everything. Nothing could get in or out without triggering an alarm.

It was home to almost four hundred prisoners and—in the improvised barracks that surrounded the mine shafts—fewer than two hundred beds. That wasn't strictly a problem because there were two shifts every day, twelve hours each. We were not allowed any possessions other than the clothes we'd been wearing when we arrived. There was no segregation of men and women, or adults and children: Every prisoner was there to work, and if we didn't work, we didn't eat.

When I first came to the mine, all I knew about platinum was that it was expensive. I thought it was mostly used for jewelry, but Keegan told me that most of the world's platinum was used in cars as a key component of catalytic converters, which cut way down on pollution. Given the conditions of the mine, it wasn't much of a comfort to know our enslavement was making life a little better for people who didn't even know we existed.

We used picks and drills to extract ore from the four main mine shafts, loaded the ore into iron-wheeled carts, and pushed them up the winding tracks to the processing station, where the platinum was extracted. It was exhausting, debilitating work. Twelve hours a day, seven days a week, and most of it spent in the dark, claustrophobia-inducing shafts.

Another prisoner, Ferdinand Cosby—Cosmo to his friends—approached Keegan and me from the ore-processing station. "Who's down there, do you know?" Cosmo was of average height but stick-thin. And I really *mean* stick-thin; even his bones were thinner than a normal person's. His skin was a patchwork of gray and white, like a piebald horse.

Keegan said, "Jakob's group. They were working alone when it happened—just our luck that none of the guards got caught in it."

I said, "If they were deep enough, they could be just trapped. We have to—" I stopped when I realized that everyone's attention was focused on the tunnel entrance behind me.

I turned to see four guards come staggering out of the B shaft in a cloud of rock dust, one of them half carrying another. Though they were coughing, gasping, and rubbing at their grit-encrusted eyes, they still had the presence of mind to stick together and hold on to their guns.

The man carrying his colleague collapsed to his knees, and I instinctively moved to help him—and found myself facing the raised guns of the other two. "Get away from him!" one of them yelled, his voice rough and wheezing.

From beyond the crowd I saw Hazlegrove coming out of the little prefabricated office that overlooked the mine, accompanied by the rest of the guards. Some of them were half out of uniform, as their shift too was ending. All of them were armed. Hazlegrove raised a bullhorn to his mouth. "Any one of you freaks takes one more step and we *will* open fire!"

Hazlegrove was short—well, to me *everyone* was short—bitter, and pudgy. He thought of himself as "hard but fair," but from our side of things he was most definitely "hard but cruel." He carried a swagger stick tucked under one arm like he was a British army officer in the Second World War.

Hazlegrove lowered his bullhorn and called his two cronies, Elliot Swinden and Donald DePaiva, to his side. As far as I understand it, they'd been his pals in college, and he'd gotten them their jobs. I don't know if it paid well, but most of the time there was little real work for the guards to do.

"What happened, Mr. Swinden?" Hazlegrove asked.

Swinden slapped the dust from his uniform. "Ceiling collapsed. C shaft. Started pretty deep down. Looks like there's no way through—it's completely blocked. The damage to the other tunnels seems to be pretty minor. We'll need to shore up the ceiling in a few places, but it could have been a lot worse."

"The C shaft . . . ," Hazlegrove muttered. He glanced at DePaiva. "What's the yield over the past month?"

DePaiva was using a gray handkerchief to wipe the sweat-caked dust from his face. "*Very* low—we've pretty much exhausted that seam. Probably should have abandoned it a couple of months back."

Hazlegrove nodded, and pursed his lips for a moment. I could see him working it out. . . . It'd take days to clear the blockage—maybe weeks, depending on how deep it was—and Jakob's team was only eight men.

I felt my stomach tighten as Hazlegrove briefly glanced at me. I knew what he was going to say.

"Close it up."

The guards' hands tightened on their weapons as an angry murmur rippled through the rest of the workers.

Hazlegrove looked up at me again. "You got a problem with that?"

"You bet I do. There are *people* trapped down there. Jakob Winquist's team."

"Chances are they're already dead." He squared his shoulders and looked around, staring at the assembled workers. "Everyone who's supposed to be working, get back to it. Now."

Keegan nudged me, and I looked down into her eyes. "Go on," she muttered. "Tell him."

"I was just about to." Louder, I said, "Mr. Hazlegrove, you can't just abandon them. At least let us dig long enough to find out whether they're alive!"

He walked over to me, stopped two yards away, and looked up. Then—trying to appear casual—he took a few steps back so he could better see my reaction. There was the smallest trace of a smirk on his lips. "Go for it. But you'll be wasting *your* time, not mine. Any rescue attempt is to be done off shift." He turned his back on me, addressing the others. "Is that understood? Dig for your friends if you want, but as far as I'm concerned, they're dead. That's *official*. And since they are officially dead, if it happens that any of them are not, then they get no more rations. You feed them out of your own share. However you decide to do that, it's up to you." He jerked his thumb over his shoulder, at me. "So blame the giant Smurf here if you find yourself going hungry."

Back in the day, I could have grabbed him, crushed him into a ball, and thrown him straight through the dome. But although I was still much stronger than an ordinary man, the old days were long gone.

Hazlegrove stalked away without looking at me for my reaction, because he knew me. He knew I was beaten. I've been a beaten man ever since I was first dumped in this place.

For the first few months after I arrived, I worked with some of the other prisoners on a dozen escape plans. And one time three of us almost made it out. But the guards . . . Well, it's fair to say they weren't chosen for their kindness and understanding. They caught us in the act, and shot Diego and Catharina right in front of me. Then they shot *me*, square in the back of my head. But I was a lot luckier than the others in one way: My skin is tough. It's not quite bulletproof, but it's strong enough that even at point-blank range the bullets don't usually penetrate more than a half inch.

So they shot me again, and again. Maybe two dozen times in total, until I collapsed. They gave me a few days to recover—left me chained up in one of the work sheds—and then it was back to work. As punishment, my shift was expanded from twelve hours a day to sixteen.

That was before Hazlegrove came to the mine, of course, when his predecessor DaLemacio was in charge. DaLemacio died a couple of years later when a crossbeam supporting the crushers snapped. One of the steel cables whipped back and caught him in the side of his head, which cracked open like a soft-boiled egg hit with a spoon. That was the closest thing we'd ever had to a vacation.

Hazlegrove was given the job on the grounds that he would cut costs. And he lived up to that promise: He reduced our rations and installed rain barrels to catch the runoff of rainwater from the dome. Rainwater is much cheaper than pumping the water from the river three miles away, and who cares if it's stagnant and filthy? We were prisoners. We didn't deserve clean water.

But those were only minor cuts compared with Hazlegrove's greatest achievement. He'd concluded that the kids were a drain on the mine's resources: They consumed food but didn't give anything back. Hazlegrove's plan was simple: Any children under the age of five had to share their parents' rations. Any kids older than that would receive their own rations—as long as they worked.

The younger kids swept up, dragged buckets of platinum ore to the crushers, and ran messages across the compound from one guard to another. If they didn't work, or if they dropped a bucket once too often, they were beaten. Oh, the guards showed *some* kindness by beating the kids only with their hands and not their truncheons, but the first time I saw it happen . . . I lost control.

I grabbed hold of the guard—a fat man called Vamos—and punched him in the face. That one punch broke his nose and all of his teeth, shattered his jaw, and fractured his skull. Sadly, he lived, but at least he quit the mine soon afterward.

Hazlegrove punished me again for that. He cut my rations by three quarters, and I'm a big guy; I need to eat a lot. When after a few weeks it was clear that starvation hadn't curbed my anger, he picked three of my friends and had the guards beat them within an inch of their lives.

Now, as Hazlegrove walked away from me, I had to suppress the urge to leap up and come down on his head, and keep jumping on him until every one of his bones turned to jelly.

Keegan saw the look on my face, and she reached up and put her hand on my arm. "We'll get them out," she said with a forced smile.

A couple of the others approached. "What's the plan?" Cosmo asked. In the outside world, Cosmo would never have survived. His weak muscles gave him just about enough strength to stand upright. Unable to dig or carry anything, Cosmo had been assigned the task of operating one of the crushers, and he couldn't even do that for very long: He was barely strong enough to pull the machine's levers.

"I don't have a plan," I said, and then added, "yet." I sat down cross-legged and shrugged. "Maybe we can dig a side tunnel through from D?"

Keegan nodded. "Yeah, that might work. If the blockage isn't too heavy, there's a good chance some of Jakob's team is still alive. So we pick a spot about seventy, eighty yards in— that should be past the blockage—and we bore through. The shafts are about twenty yards apart at that depth. It'll take a couple of days, and that's only if we don't hit any bedrock."

Cosmo said, "No, look, here's what we should do. . . . Instead of digging a full-size tunnel from D, we just dig a bore-hole. Wide enough for me. That'll be a lot faster. I can go through, see if there's anyone alive in there."

"Good thinking," Keegan said, and Cosmo beamed at that. He'd had a crush on Keegan since the first day they met. She continued, "If there *is* anyone alive, you can bring them food and water while we work on widening the tunnel."

By now, there were two dozen workers gathered around us. And they were looking at me to give them the go-ahead. They saw me as their leader. They always had. Not because I'm smarter than anyone else—which I'm definitely not—or because I've been here so long. It's because I'm bigger and stronger.

I don't like being a leader. I've *never* liked that. I'm much happier following other people's instructions. Actually, I'm happiest when I'm completely on my own, but it's been a very long time since I was able to indulge in that luxury.

Keegan reached up to my shoulder and casually brushed the dust and tiny flakes of rock from my blue skin. "What do you say, Brawn?"

I nodded. "All right. Let's get to work."

CHAPTER 2

TWENTY-SEVEN YEARS AGO

I WAS TWELVE YEARS OLD when my world ended. Not *the* world, of course. Just *my* world.

It was Sunday morning, and I was in church, in the choir. Not by my own choice, mind you. My mother had made me join a year earlier. I came home from school one day, and when I opened the door, she was waiting for me with Pastor Cullen. "Here's my little darling now, Pastor! Isn't he adorable? Voice like an angel! Go on, sweetheart, sing something for the pastor!"

"Ma, no!" I pleaded.

"No, petal. You have to. Sing 'Always on My Mind'—you love that one!"

That was embarrassing, and made even worse because my best friends Adrian and Jaz were right behind me.

I turned bright red and then Jaz nudged me in the back. "Go ahead, Elvis," he said. "We don't mind waiting."

I spent the next year trying to live that one down. It didn't help that I actually *was* able to sing. Pretty soon Pastor Cullen was giving me solos.

I didn't want to do it, but I couldn't say no to Ma. Well, I *could* have said no, but it wouldn't have made any difference: When she set her mind on something, that was it.

Pastor Cullen was the same: No matter how much you protested, he did things his own way. That was why everyone in the choir had to dress up in a long white vestment. An alb, it's called. Goes from your neck right down to your ankles. Not so embarrassing to be seen in when you're with nineteen other choristers, but it's horrible when you're doing a solo and all your friends come along and sit in the front row just so they can make faces at you and try to get you to crack up, and then they rib you about it for ages. "Dude, how come you're not wearing your *dress* today?"

The only concession Ma made was to allow me to wear my sweatpants and a T-shirt under my alb: It was bad enough to have to wear that thing without having to have a suit on under it.

But when I was twelve . . . It was the last Sunday in September. I was with the rest of the choir, and feeling a little nervous because I had to sing "God's Glory Be the Highest" and wasn't completely confident of the middle eight.

Pastor Cullen was at the pulpit in the middle of his sermon. He was about sixty years old, white haired, red faced, and jowly. He had far too much nose hair and ear hair for one man, and he always smelled of stale sweat and laundry detergent.

The church was an old building, constructed back in the day when it was fashionable to decorate them with all the oak, marble, and gold paint the builders could get their hands on. I was standing off to the side, right next to the marble pulpit, which was a prized spot among the choir because the pastor didn't allow us to have chairs—we had to stand for the whole service—and on really sweltering days we could rest against the pulpit and cool ourselves down a little.

That day Pastor Cullen was on a particularly long and rambling rant. "The spirit of the community is that of its individuals. The Lord tells us, 'Thou shalt love thy neighbor as thyself.' If one person is unhappy, that brings us all down, so we must strive to bolster our community by enhancing the lives of those around us. 'Do unto others as you would have them do unto you.' This is not purely a Christian concept. Hindus, Sikhs, Buddhists, and followers of many other faiths—even some that predate Christianity—subscribe to the idea of karma: You will be repaid in kind for the manner in which you treat others. 'Whatsoever a man soweth, that shall he also reap.' That is as true for matters of the spirit as it is for matters of the community. Good and evil, selfishness and altruism, kindness and greed . . . These are within all of us. We choose the nature of our character, and that choice affects everything we do and infects those around us. We cannot choose our neighbors, but we *can* choose how we treat them."

I knew what was coming next. We all did. Pastor Cullen had been stuck on the same topic for months: "To strengthen our town, we need solidarity. Unity. Faith in our community as a whole and in its individual members. Buy your groceries and gas locally. Instead of going to West Peyton to buy a new car, save money and buy a good-quality used car from a dealer right here in town."

I looked out over the sea of mildly irritated faces. No one had the guts to stand up and tell the pastor to give it a rest: His cousin owned the only secondhand-car dealership in town.

The pastor didn't seem to be getting anywhere near the main point of the sermon—unless the point was "I want to talk and you'd all better listen"—so I found myself growing more and more agitated.

I had to sing as soon as he stepped away from the pulpit, and it was always nervewracking. The longer he talked, the more nervous I became, especially because he didn't always build up to a dramatic ending that we could see coming: Sometimes he just trailed away like he was giving up.

I realized that I was clenching and unclenching my fists, so I forced myself to stop. A thin trickle of sweat ran down my back, even though it wasn't a particularly warm day.

The guy beside me, Chad Farnham, whispered, "You OK?" Chad was in his twenties, but only a couple of inches taller than me. He'd been the number-one soloist until I joined the choir, so he was always looking out for me: If I got sick, he'd have to take my place, and he didn't want to be there any more than I did.

"Just wish he'd get on with it," I whispered back. Anyone who sings in a choir that's led by a gasbag like Pastor Cullen pretty quickly learns the ancient art of ventriloquism.

"Well, just don't mess it up this time," Chad said.

"Once!" I muttered. "*One* time I got the verses mixed up!"

"He kept us all back for extra practice, dude. We all suffered."

"Let it go, Chad."

The pastor was still talking, going all over the place like a blind man trying to mow a football field in a hurricane. Then he started on another of his favorite topics, the fact that the community always donated much more to the local hockey team's fund-raisers than to the church.

I felt my stomach churn like there was a massive belch brewing, the kind you get after downing a whole can of soda in one go, but I hadn't yet had anything to eat or drink that day.

"You look like you're gonna barf. You *sure* you're OK?" Chad whispered out of the corner of his mouth.

"I will be. Back in a minute." Where I was standing I was mostly hidden from the congregation, and the pastor couldn't see me from that angle, so it was easy enough to slip back into the vestry without causing much of a disturbance.

The vestry was small, plainly decorated, and only just big enough for the whole choir to assemble. There was a desk, a single chair, and two other doors, one leading out into the church's rear parking lot and the other to the toilet.

I pushed open the second door and knelt before the bowl. My stomach suddenly spasmed as though I was about to throw up, and at the same time my skin started to itch and sting like the worst case of sunburn ever. My arms and legs began quivering, and I had to clutch the sides of the toilet bowl to steady myself. My brain started pounding, *Boom*, *boom*, *boom* . . . Over and over like a bunch of angry villagers trying to smash through the castle gates with a massive battering ram.

For a second, against the bowl's white porcelain, my hands looked almost blue, but even as I tried to focus on them, the nausea and the headache faded. I took a few deep breaths, then pushed myself to my feet.

OK, I told myself. *You're all right. You're not going to throw up.*

I felt fine, as though nothing had happened. In fact, better than that: There was a sense of clarity that reminded me of the way my ears would sometimes pop a few hours after I went swimming and I'd realize that until then I hadn't been able to hear properly.

I returned to the vestry and quietly opened the door to the church. Pastor Cullen was coming to the end of his sermon—accusing the people of loving hockey more than they loved God—and I was about to squeeze past the rear-most members of the choir and return to my place when it happened.

Something exploded out of me—that's the only way I can think of to describe it: It felt like every square inch of my skin just erupted.

For a while—seconds, maybe minutes—all I knew was the pain. But it began to fade, and I became aware of the screaming, a deep bellowing roar that seemed to vibrate through the floorboards and shake the church's walls.

When I was finally able to open my eyes, when the convulsions and retching eased, all I could see was what looked like a cobweb, black against a white background.

It took me a moment to realize that I was lying on my back, looking up at the church's ceiling, its white plaster now shot through with fresh cracks. The cracks were spreading, growing sporadically as the ceiling shook and shuddered in response to the ongoing screams.

And the screams were coming from me.

CHAPTER 3

I SLAPPED MY HAND over my mouth and missed, hitting myself hard in the cheek instead. Had it not been for the pain still coursing through my body, I might have laughed at that.

But the pain was easing by the second, the all-encompassing cramps and nausea receding like the lake behind a shattered dam, leaving behind clusters of twitching nerves that hopped under my skin like suffocating fish.

I forced my mouth closed—that much at least I was able to do—and tried to sit up, but my arms and legs felt wrong. Too bulky, awkward, and unmanageable, like when you wake up with your arm tucked behind your head and it's gone all numb.

Particles of plaster dropped from the cracks in the ceiling, and I instinctively raised my arms to shield my eyes, then almost yelped when I saw two massive blue-skinned hands racing toward me.

They were *my* hands.

So I lay there for I don't know how long, looking up at my oversized blue hands, clenching them into fists, waggling my fingers, rubbing them together. I would have thought that maybe I was somehow now wearing large rubber gloves if not for the sensation: When I poked the skin, it felt real. I could even feel the pulse in my left wrist.

I raised my head and looked down the length of my body: Powerful-looking blue legs protruded from the shredded remains of my vestments, and all I could think about was how lucky I was to be wearing my sweatpants. They were stretched almost to the limit around my muscular legs, but at least I wasn't naked in church.

My skin was *blue*. It was hard to get that concept to fit inside my head. Blue, and hairless: Even the tiny little hairs on my arms were gone.

I ran one hand over my head and felt my hair fall away from my scalp.

A tiny part of my brain was signaling for attention, like a niggling reminder that I'd forgotten something, and then I realized what it was: No one was saying anything.

I raised my head and looked around. I was next to the pulpit, right in the middle of where the choir should have been, but I was alone.

More able to control my limbs now, I hoisted myself up onto my elbows.

The church was deserted, the doors at the back wide open, some of the pews overturned, open hymnbooks scattered everywhere like a flock of rectangular birds that had all just dropped from the sky at the same time.

I rolled onto my stomach and pushed myself upright, and discovered that the church had shrunk: I could easily have reached up and brushed my hand against the cracked ceiling.

Crouched on the floor, half hidden behind the altar, was Pastor Cullen. He had his head down and was rapidly muttering prayers, his trembling hands gripping his dust-smeared copy of the Bible.

I took a step toward him and my bare left foot collided with the edge of the marble pulpit. I stumbled forward and grabbed the top of the pulpit to steady myself—and it shattered into fist-sized fragments.

Pastor Cullen looked up at me and shrank away, whimpering, then curled himself into a shivering ball, clutching the Good Book to his chest.

Then I was right beside him, looking down, trying to understand. He was either very small or very far away, but I couldn't tell. I reached my hand down to him, and stopped. With my fingers spread, my left hand was large enough to cover his head.

"Please don't kill me!" he screamed, and I jerked my hand back.

"What do you mean?" I asked. Or, at least, I *tried* to ask—but I couldn't speak. All that came out was a series of deep, rumbling growls.

"Not me, not me . . . Take the boys instead!" He whimpered again—he sounded like an injured dog—and I took a step back.

What's happened to me? I wondered. I was still too shocked to fully take it in. Somehow I had changed from an average-sized twelve-year-old to a hairless blue giant.

I tried to say, "Pastor Cullen, please, you've got to help me!" but again my words came out like angry gibberish.

Then a voice from outside, electronically amplified, called, "This is the police. Whoever—*what*ever—you are, come out now! Hands where we can see them!"

I looked toward the rear of the church, at the doors that until a few minutes ago had seemed more than adequate—I'd always wondered why church doors were so large—but now I wasn't actually sure that I *could* get out.

I made my way toward them, my legs awkward and only barely under control, crushing the wooden pews into splinters. Then I had to get down on my knees to peer through the doors.

Six police cars waited directly outside, the officers half crouched behind their open doors, their guns aimed directly at me, and even more police cars were roaring toward the church from both directions.

"Don't shoot!" I yelled, but it came out as a growl.

The police officers shuffled in place, steadying their aim, clearly wanting to be anywhere else.

Beyond them I could see two hundred people: the members of the congregation, the rest of the choir—Chad was there, his face pale with shock—and then I spotted my parents. Pa had his arm wrapped around Ma's shoulders, and I wasn't sure whether he was holding her back or holding her up.

"Ma, it's me!" I called, but my words—rough, guttural, and unintelligible to their ears—did nothing to calm down anyone.

On my hands and knees I squeezed myself out through the doors, then straightened up. The onlookers all backed away even farther.

Everything looked smaller—and weaker—from this perspective.

One of the police officers lowered his gun, but kept it in his hand as he slowly approached me. "Who are you? Why did you attack these people?"

I started trying to tell him that I hadn't attacked anyone, but gave up almost immediately.

The officer stopped a few yards in front of me and swallowed hard. "Look, you have to let us inside to help the wounded, all right?"

I shook my head, trying to tell him that there *were* no wounded inside, but that was clearly the wrong move, because he took a couple of steps back and tightened his grip on his gun.

What happened next was so fast, I guess no one can really be blamed: I stepped to the side so that the officer could see past me into the church, and on the edge of my vision something large and white and flapping rushed straight toward me. I reacted without thinking: I grabbed hold of the attacking thing and threw it.

It was only when it was in the air, soaring over the crowd,

that I realized it had been Pastor Cullen trying to dart past me. Screams burst from the spectators as the pastor crashed down onto the roof of a police car that was screeching to a stop, shattering its windshield and crushing its red and blue lights.

If the police had been waiting for a signal to open fire, this was all they needed. The first bullet struck me in the chest and the next two hit my shoulder. They hurt—no more than a bee sting but enough to make me cry out. And *that* was enough to kick the whole mess into a higher gear.

Bullets ripped into me and into the wall of the church. The screams of the fleeing onlookers were almost loud enough to drown out the gunfire.

A bullet hit me just below my left eye and I instinctively grabbed the nearest thing I could find to shield myself: one of the church's thick wooden doors. I ripped the door from its hinges and held it in front of me. Almost immediately it shattered to splinters: I'd been squeezing it too tightly, and crushed it.

The bullets were still coming, and then there was an even louder *boom* and something heavy struck me in the chest, hard enough to knock me back against the wall.

I looked up long enough to see another cop standing by his car with smoke wafting from the barrel of his shotgun, and then I ducked down through the doorway and back into the church.

OK, all right . . . , I said to myself. *What's happened? Why am I like this? Is this even real?*

I'd heard of lucid dreaming—when you know you're

dreaming but still can't wake up—but I'd never experienced it before.

Even if this *was* a dream, I sure wasn't going to wait around for them to find a weapon powerful enough to kill me. As it was, the whole of my upper body—arms, chest, neck, head, and back—was covered with bullet holes. They didn't hurt much, but there was quite a lot of blood. When I squeezed one of the holes, the bullet popped out, like when you squeeze a zit.

I looked around for something to clean up the blood, but the only thing I could find was the shredded remains of my alb. I used it to wipe down my arms and chest—which dislodged a few more bullets—then tossed the ruined alb aside. Ma was going to give me grief over that—they're not cheap.

The growing wail of approaching sirens echoed through the church, and I knew I had to get out of there. The back door was ordinary sized, and I wasn't sure I'd fit through.

And I also wasn't sure that I *wanted* to run. . . . Where would I go? And how long was I going to be like this? That thought hit me harder than the shotgun blast: *Am I going to be like this forever?*

Why I didn't go insane, I don't know. Maybe it's because kids are more resilient to change than adults. I saw that often enough in the mine.

I sat down next to the front door with my back to the wall and tried to get a handle on what had happened.

Outside, the shooting had stopped and I could hear one cop barking orders: "Get these people out of here—now! You two: around the back. I want all possible exits covered! There's still a kid in there with that thing!"

Why don't I just go out? I asked myself. *If I just stand there and don't do anything to scare them, maybe they'll realize I'm not a threat.*

Right. Like that'll work.

But even if I couldn't talk to them—and I was doing my best to push *that* thought out of my mind—I could still make them understand me.

Over in the corner was the church's visitor's book resting on a little table. I reached out to it and pulled the table closer. The pen was tiny in my massive blue hand, but I was sure I now had enough control of my body to write a message in the book. I was wrong: The pen snapped between my fingers.

All right, I decided as I tossed the pen aside. *Just wait and see what happens.* I looked down at my blue arms and wondered how long it would be before the effect wore off, before I turned back to normal.

I spent I don't know *how* long sitting there with my back to the wall, listening to the panic outside and picturing myself as I had been that morning, concentrating on that image and trying to somehow force myself to change back. I hoped and wished and even begged God to restore me to normal. None of it made the slightest difference.

At the back of my mind, the horrible thought remained that maybe this was permanent. Maybe I was never going to be normal again.

And with that came an even more disturbing thought:

What if I can't make them understand me, and then Pastor Cullen dies and they think I murdered him?

Something outside went *Ptoof! Ptoof!* and two small canisters bounced through the door and came to a stop in the center aisle. For a second I thought they were soda cans, but then they popped and started belching thick white smoke into the air.

Immediately the church was swarming with men: They darted in through the main door two at a time, they smashed in the rear door behind the altar, they came crashing through the big windows on either side, showering the church with fragments of glass. All of the men were wearing black body armor and gas masks.

The smoke from the canisters stung my eyes a little, but not much more than when you're flipping the burgers on a barbecue and the wind suddenly changes direction. Whatever the stuff was—probably tear gas—it didn't affect me as much as the soldiers had hoped. They spread out, surrounding me, each one aiming a wicked-looking gun.

One of them yelled, "On the ground! Now! Facedown, arms spread! Do it!"

They kept their distance as I did what I was told—I figured that the sooner I got to speak to someone in charge, the sooner they could figure out what had happened to me.

For the next few minutes the soldiers remained just out of arm's reach, not doing anything except staring at me. Every time I tried to move, they barked another order to "Freeze!"

When the tear gas cleared, there were more heavy footsteps behind me, and soon the church was fuller than I'd *ever* seen it. Pastor Cullen would have been overjoyed to see that many people on a normal Sunday. There were army guys, cops, and guys in dark suits who looked like they might be with the FBI, all talking softly and slowly walking around me.

In school, we'd read about Gulliver in Lilliput: That's kind of what it felt like.

After what must have been more than an hour of waiting, a tall, dark-haired woman wearing a black suit walked up to me, coming closer than anyone else. She crouched down to look me in the eye. "My name is Harmony Yuan. I'm a Special Agent with the FBI. What *are* you?"

I started to speak, but again it came out as a growl. Everyone except the FBI woman took a step back.

"Can you understand me?"

I nodded.

"But you can't talk?"

I shrugged. Not so easy to do when you're lying facedown with your arms spread.

"All right." Her eyes narrowed as she peered at me for a moment. "We have a lot of questions, but right now there's only one that's important." She raised her hand and snapped her fingers. An army guy passed her a transparent plastic bag that contained my shredded, blood-stained alb. She held it in front of me. "Everyone is accounted for, except for one boy. This is all we can find of him. What have you done with his body?"

CHAPTER 4

THE FIRST CHURCH of Saint Matthew had become a prison with hundreds of guards and one inmate: me.

They didn't quite know what to do with me. I overheard a couple of them who were standing guard near the door:

"He ain't *doin'* anythin'! Why ain't he doin' anythin'?"

"What, you *want* him to do something?"

"Heck no. I'm just sayin' . . . Lookit the *size* of 'im." The man shuddered. "That ain't right. Ain't natural. I'm tellin' ya, Joey, it's creepin' me out."

"Creeping *all* of us out."

Harmony Yuan was the only person in the church who didn't seem to be afraid of me.

She allowed me to sit up, which was a little more comfortable than lying facedown on the floor. "We could put chains on you, but that wouldn't slow you down much, would it?

You probably weigh . . . what? Fourteen hundred pounds? Fifteen?"

I shook my head and shrugged. I'd had no idea of my weight *before* I changed.

"I'm guessing that's in the ballpark. You're more than twice the height of the average adult male. That makes you eight times the mass, at least."

Harmony signaled to two of the army guys to drag one of the pews closer. They scraped it across the floor to just in front of me and quickly backed away. Harmony sat with her left leg crossed over the right, her left elbow on her knee and her chin resting lightly on her hand. A very casual pose probably designed to make me feel more at ease. "The missing boy is Gethin Rao. Twelve years old. His mother and father are understandably upset. What have you done with him? Why are his vestments covered in blood?"

I spread my arms, trying to show that I didn't know what she was talking about. That was the only thing I could think of—there didn't seem to be a universally accepted gesture that meant "I'm the boy you think has been killed."

"The witnesses all say the same thing: The pastor was in the middle of his sermon when there was a sudden flash and a sort of shock wave, like a brief but powerful gust of wind. Everyone in the choir was knocked over, and then, somehow, you were there among them. Everyone panicked and fled. Everyone except the pastor, who was knocked from the pulpit. It was some minutes before anyone realized that Gethin didn't come out with the rest of the choir. So you tell me now: Did you hurt him?"

I shook my head and tried to put on an expression that meant "I'd never hurt anyone!"

"Well, you sure hurt Pastor Cullen. . . . Then where *is* the boy? We know he was here when you appeared. And we found fragments of his sneakers and his T-shirt as well as the blood-stained vestments, and that tells us that he was here *after* you appeared. So where is he? He's not hiding in the church—there's nothing showing up on our thermal scans that shouldn't be there." Harmony sat back and pursed her lips. "And I'd lay odds that's *his* blood under your fingernails."

I sighed and wished I was able to tell her, *Listen, I am Gethin Rao, you stupid woman!*

I put my right thumb and index finger together, and made writing motions in the air.

Harmony shrugged. "What's *that* supposed to mean?"

Oh for Pete's sake! I saw a discarded hymnbook lying open on the ground and pointed to it, then made the writing gesture again.

"You . . . you want to conduct a song?"

"Give me a pen and some paper!" I yelled. Of course, it came out like a string of furious grunts and growls and scared the pants off all the cops and soldiers. I froze as several dozen weapons once again swung in my direction. And then I thought, *Why not keep going? If I've lost the ability to speak, I might have to learn all over again, so the more I talk, the sooner that'll happen.*

So, doing my best to keep my voice calm, I said, "I want something to eat. I'm starving. And I'm thirsty. So don't just sit there all looking shocked and scared—get it through your thick heads that I *am* Gethin Rao. He's not missing—he's me."

Harmony regarded me for a moment. "I'm told that Pastor Cullen is in a bad way. Arms and legs broken, possible fractured skull . . . You also damaged his spine. It'll be some time before the doctors know whether he'll be able to walk again. So even if we find that kid alive and well, we've got you for assault with intent. You understand what that means? Attempted murder."

"Oh, come on!" I said. "That was an accident—I thought something was attacking *me!*"

Moving slowly, Harmony stood up. "Listen up, people! We need to get this creature to the compound in Mussenden, so put your heads together and find a way to transport him out of here. You have two hours. Disperse the crowd outside— and make sure they're not going to talk. Threaten them with the IRS if you have to. And I want a total media blackout, understood? I see one grainy photo of a giant blue man in the newspapers and you'll all be facing charges." She took one last look at me, then walked away.

The other soldiers and police and FBI guys began talking about me as though I wasn't able to understand them, even though Ms. Yuan had clearly demonstrated that I could.

"Elephant shackles," a man in a suit said. "You know? When they need to tie up elephants at the circus. That's what we need."

"Or a bunch of cattle prods," another one suggested. "We use them to herd him into the back of an eighteen-wheeler."

"Heck with *that*," a third said. "He killed that kid—I say we all open fire at once and turn his brain into Swiss cheese!"

That was it for me. I'd heard enough. I stood up—they all backed away again—and walked toward the doors.

"Stop!" someone shouted.

I turned around and looked at them. "No."

They all began to shuffle nervously, fingers tightening on triggers, unsure what to do.

I got down on my hands and knees and passed through the doorway. There was a fresh ripple of gasps and screams from the crowd as I straightened up.

Ahead, Harmony Yuan whirled around to look at me. "Stop! You're under arrest!"

I walked toward her, slowly so she wouldn't panic. But that didn't stop everyone *else* from panicking, and the crowd began to scatter, racing away from the church.

Then I saw my parents standing with a police officer—the same one who'd fired the shotgun at me—and I turned toward them. "Ma, Pa, it's me!"

My mother and father turned and ran, Pa dragging Ma away by the arm. But the policeman held his ground and shouted, "Stay back! Haven't you done enough harm already?"

Then the officer reacted to something behind me. His face paled and he too turned and ran.

I looked to see what had spooked him.

Rumbling slowly along the road was a tank.

I didn't know what kind of tank it was—I'd never been that interested in military hardware—but it was big and heading straight for me.

No way, I said to myself. *They're not going to actually shoot at me with that thing, are they? I haven't done anything wrong!*

An amplified voice bellowed out, "This will be your only warning! Get down on your knees and place your hands behind your head! You have ten seconds to comply!"

"Look, I know you can't understand me, but—"

I noticed the flash from the tank's barrel at the exact moment something slammed into my chest and knocked me back across the church's parking lot.

I crashed straight through the pastor's beloved '65 Mustang and hit the church wall hard enough to crack the bricks.

And then I got up. There was barely a mark on me. The car was ruined, though, and that annoyed me more than the fact that the army had hit me with a shell from a tank. I'd loved that car too. Always wanted one of my own. Now it was just a scattered collection of blackened metal fragments.

I couldn't understand what was wrong with everyone. OK, so I was huge and blue and probably looked quite scary, but I still hadn't actually done anything bad. What had happened with Pastor Cullen was an accident—why couldn't they understand that? If I were a bad guy, wouldn't I have done more? Wouldn't I have attacked the cops when they shot at me?

But this was years before I'd heard of the "arachnid response," the automatic reaction a lot of people have to spiders: They react with fear and revulsion even when they know the spider isn't dangerous. That was what was happening here: They were just terrified of me.

Turning to face the tank again, I yelled, "No way was that ten seconds!"

And then I heard the helicopters.

Three of them, swooping in low over the town, heading straight for the church.

Behind me, all the soldiers and cops and FBI guys were spilling out through the doorway, running like the devil was chasing them.

Ahead, the rest of the cops and the army were pulling back—even the tank had shifted into reverse and was moving in a hurry. It clipped the edge of a parked car and then drove right back over the top of another, flattening it.

Twin streaks of fire erupted from the lead copter, and the concrete in front of me was ripped to shreds.

I did the only sane thing I *could* do: I turned and ran.

With the copter's bullets strafing the ground all around me, I raced around to the back of the church and kept going through the rear parking lot.

The back wall was about fifteen feet high. I jumped for it, expecting to grab the top and pull myself up. Instead I soared much higher, cleared the wall by a good three feet, and came down so hard in the field behind it that I sank to my knees in the dirt.

But even that didn't slow me much: I surged through the soil as easily as someone running through a shallow pond.

I knew the town well, of course. There's hardly a twelve-year-old kid in the world who doesn't know every secret nook and cranny in his hometown. I knew the shortcuts through the housing estates, the barely visible paths through the woods. And I knew the caves: That's where I was heading.

Back in the church, Harmony Yuan had mentioned thermal

scanners. I'd watched enough cop shows and read enough comic books to know what they were: cameras that detected heat instead of light. And I knew that someone of my size would be giving off a *lot* of heat—more than enough for them to be able to track me.

But not in the caves, I was sure. The caves were old and huge and went on for miles. And some of them held deep lakes where, according to the guide when my elementary class was there on a field trip, the temperature was the same all year-round. That would be the perfect place to hide.

All right, God, I prayed. *If you're not going to change me back, at least let me get away from these guys!*

In some respects, that was a clever plan. For a twelve-year-old. But, being only twelve, I hadn't quite learned how to think everything through. Sure, immersing myself in the underground lake masked my heat signature, but it didn't occur to me that the soldiers would simply start looking in the place where the heat signature had suddenly disappeared.

They tracked me, they found me, and they caught me.

When I was about six or seven, Pa saw me kneeling beside my bed praying for a new bike. He'd picked me up, and sat down on the bed with me on his lap. He said, "The thing about prayer, son . . . Well, it doesn't work like that."

I said, "But Ma said that God answers *every* prayer!"

"Yeah, that's right, Gethin. He does. But, sometimes, the answer is no."

CHAPTER 5
THE MINE

WE KNEW THAT HAZLEGROVE was keeping an eye on us as we worked to dig the narrow horizontal passage through to the C shaft. Maybe he was curious to see whether any of Jakob's team had survived. Maybe it was because an event like this had a tendency to bring people together, and the last thing a prison guard wants is his prisoners united in a common cause.

That was one of the reasons the rations were so meager: They fed us just enough to keep us alive and working, plus a little more so that we could argue over who'd received the biggest share. It was almost a science. If they fed us a decent amount, we'd have the strength to fight the guards, and if they starved us, we'd revolt.

But by keeping us on the edge of hunger at all times and allowing some prisoners certain privileges—longer breaks, showers with warm water, the opportunity to wash their clothing, an extra blanket on cold nights—it sparked resentment among the other prisoners.

The guards created factions by spreading rumors. Once, they told us that they had heard the mine was soon to be shut down and that some of us would be released and the others executed. "Not sure when it's happening," they said, "but whichever shift is producing the most ore, well, they're the ones who're going to live." The immediate effect was that everyone started working harder. Just what the guards wanted. But then a *secondary* effect kicked in, something the guards stupidly hadn't anticipated: Certain members of each shift began sabotaging the other shift by blocking the rails or loosening the wheels on the carts as they were finishing their own shifts.

Hazlegrove knew that cruelty had to be tempered with logic: You can torture people, but only to a point. Once past that point the victim will turn on you, so the trick is to always keep a close eye on how far you're pushing them.

As we worked to reach Jakob's team, Hazlegrove sent guards down every hour into the D tunnel to watch our progress. The guards always came in threes, for their own safety.

But it was Hazlegrove himself who caught up with me as I was on my third trip down, followed as ever by Swinden and DePaiva. "You really think they're still alive, Brawn?" He tapped his swagger stick against the side of his leg as he walked.

"I'm hoping they are."

"Hmm . . . Hope. The prisoner's friend. What else are you hoping for, I wonder? Freedom?"

I kept my head down as I pushed the cart ahead of me. Not because I didn't want to look him in the eye, but because the tunnel wasn't big enough for me to stand upright. "Why not?"

Swinden said, "It'll never happen, you know. You'll die here."

"You're assuming that I *can* die. Maybe I'm immortal."

"But you're not superhuman anymore, are you?" Hazlegrove asked. "You people all lost your powers. Maybe once, you could have torn this whole facility apart with your bare hands, but not now. Sure, you're much stronger than a normal person, but that's just because of your size. You're still blue and still thirteen feet tall, but that's all. You're as human as every one of your friends here."

"If you say so."

He sighed. "What's the point of saving them? Even if they survived the tunnel collapsing on top of them, they'll die sooner or later. Malnutrition, another accident, infection, infighting . . . Or they'll just reach the end of their usefulness and we'll execute them."

"Is that how it's going to happen? When we get too old, you'll just shoot us in the head?"

"Probably."

"So what's to stop us from just dropping our tools and refusing to work? If we're going to die anyway, why don't we just let you get it over with?"

He laughed. "That brings us back to the prisoner's friend. Hope."

I said nothing for a moment, just kept pushing the cart. Then I turned my head to face him. In the weak yellow-orange glow cast by the lights fixed to the walls, he looked almost friendly. "Mr. Hazlegrove, you're right, I'm not as strong as I used to be. But you know that I could still crush your skull in one hand, don't you? And I could do it faster than your friends here could react. I just grab, squeeze, and you're dead."

He didn't seem bothered by this. "And my guards would kill you."

"Not easily. I'm not superhuman anymore, but it would take a heck of a lot of bullets to bring me down."

"You won't do it. You know that if you did, the consequences would be severe. Remember?"

I remembered. Four years earlier I had tried my second escape attempt. One night I climbed up onto the dome where I figured there were no cameras, no guards watching. I was right about that—the dome covered almost the entire compound and was far too big to monitor—and I would have made it too except that Hazlegrove's men heard me scrambling across the apex. By the time I reached the other side, he was waiting for me with four guards.

Each of the guards was standing behind another prisoner, holding a gun to the back of the prisoner's head. Not a word was said: I slid down off the dome, landed on my feet, and walked back into the compound. Since then, I'd had a good half-dozen opportunities to get out, but I knew I couldn't do it without someone else paying the price.

When we reached Keegan and the others, I started to empty the buckets back into the cart, two at a time.

Hazlegrove aimed his flashlight into the narrow shaft they'd dug. "You've a long way to go."

"We'll do it," Keegan said.

"I'm sure you will. But for the next sixteen hours you'll have to do it without your blue friend." He looked at me. "Your next shift starts in eleven minutes."

Cosmo, who'd been using his feeble hands to move the chipped-away rock one stone at a time, said, "But that's totally unfair! Brawn's been working twenty-four hours straight!"

Hazlegrove said, "I don't make the rules. Oh, wait, yes I do." He grinned at us, then turned away.

And immediately turned back. He stared at Cosmo. "You. You don't *ever* speak to me in that manner, understood?"

Cosmo nodded, and looked away.

Hazlegrove lashed out with the swagger stick, catching Cosmo across the face, the blow hard enough to send the thin man crashing against the jagged wall of the tunnel.

As Hazlegrove pulled back his arm to strike again, I stepped between them. "Another blow could kill him. You don't want that, do you, Mr. Hazlegrove?"

The tip of the swagger stick was waved menacingly in front of my face. "Are you *threatening* me, freak?"

"Just stating a fact."

He sneered. "If you can work a sixteen-hour shift, then do another three or four hours down here, and still have the strength to *state facts*, Brawn, then it seems to me that we're not making the best use of your talents. From now on, you do *twenty*-hour shifts." He poked me in the chest with the tip of the stick. "Get the message?"

"Loud and clear." I picked up two more buckets and dumped their contents into the cart.

"Good. Because I'm starting to think you're more trouble than you're worth." Hazlegrove stalked away, followed back up the tunnel by his two cronies.

"You should get going," Keegan said to me. "If you're late for the start of your shift . . ."

"I'll make it. You OK, Cosmo?"

He nodded. "Man, we've got to get out of this place."

"What's the word from Jakob?" I asked, glancing at the tunnel.

"They're getting there. It'll be a few more days, though."

I dumped the last of the buckets and tossed them aside. "Good work. See you guys in about twenty hours." I crouched behind the half-full cart and started pushing. Its steel-wrapped wheels screamed under the weight, and I felt like joining in.

The rockfall that had apparently trapped Jakob's team had been no accident. It had taken months of careful planning and subtle manipulation of the rosters to get all of the strongest diggers—except me, of course—on one team. For weeks we'd been storing supplies of food and water in the depths of the shaft where the guards rarely visited.

The narrow tunnel we were digging to connect D shaft and C shaft wasn't really so that Cosmo could squirm through and search for the others. It was a ventilation shaft that would provide fresh air to the sealed portion of C shaft.

Even now, Jakob and his men were working furiously, probably nonstop, doing exactly what years of prison life had trained them to do: They were digging. Heading slowly but steadily to the surface. Tunneling their way out.

CHAPTER 6

TWENTY-SIX
YEARS AGO

ABOUT TWICE A MONTH Harmony Yuan visited me in the cell block. I didn't know *where* the cell block was—somewhere underground, I assumed, because there were no windows—but I guess they treated me pretty well. Three solid meals a day, a TV set that showed two old movies every evening, a dozen new books every month and a bed made from four thick mattresses laid side to side. The cell was a cube, thirty feet on each side—just enough space for me to walk around a little, but not enough for me to build up speed if I decided to take a run at the walls.

All but one of the walls were solid stone: The fourth wall was glass, with a small door that opened into the cell and had beveled sides that prevented me from pushing it out, and nothing on the inside that provided enough grip for me to pull it open.

The very first morning, I woke to find Harmony standing outside the cell. "You're going to try to break out. You'll fail." She rapped on the glass with her knuckles. "This is a metallic glass, one of the toughest substances in the world. It's so new that its inventors haven't even come up with a clever name for it yet. We don't know the limits of your strength, but we'll be very surprised if you can even make a scratch in this."

I tried, of course. Again and again. I slammed into the glass with my shoulder, punched it, kicked it, slammed my oversized steel chair into it so often that by the time I gave up, the chair was nothing but a mangled pile of metal bars.

They'd given me clothes: three pairs of blue jeans, three white T-shirts. Harmony said that they'd been specially made by a guy who worked as a costume designer in Hollywood—he'd been told that they were needed for a new movie adaptation of Richard Matheson's novel *The Shrinking Man*. Harmony even gave me a copy of the book.

Harmony always sat in the same place, on a wooden chair in front of my cell's glass wall. On some visits she spoke, telling me a little of what was going on in the world, but a lot of the time she just sat and looked at me. It made me feel like I was an animal in a zoo.

Occasionally, she would speak about the missing boy, telling me that his parents were sick with worry, that a lot of people were petitioning the governor to have me tried and executed.

She told me that Pastor Cullen was now using a wheelchair and probably would be for the rest of his life, and that Gethin Rao's parents had been utterly broken by the loss of their son.

"There are still search parties every weekend," Harmony told me. "They're hoping that the boy was scared and ran, and that he'll eventually turn up safe and sound."

But they never gave me anything to write with, despite all the different ways to mime "give me a pen!" that I could think of. I figured pretty early on that they knew what I wanted, but just weren't going to give it to me. Once, I even spelled out my name with books on the floor, but no one seemed to care.

My memory of how they'd caught me was a little fuzzy for a long time. I was able to recall lowering myself into one of the deep, cold underground lakes in the caves, and I clearly remember waking up in the cell, but what they did to me in between those events I had no solid idea.

Eventually, Harmony told me that the soldiers had dumped a hundred gallons of liquid nitrogen into the lake. They'd then chipped me out of the ice and were astonished to discover that I was still alive. That, apparently, had changed everything: They had to learn more about me. "And so we brought you here," Harmony had said. But she refused to tell me where "here" was.

Aside from the two guys who brought me my meals and books and once a month herded me into another cell so that mine could be cleaned, and the bunch of guards with guns and gas masks who always accompanied them, Harmony was the only person I saw for months.

Then one day, as she sat watching me in silence, a potbellied middle-aged man wearing tan-colored slacks and jacket came from the corridor carrying a fold-up chair. He set it down next to her and lowered himself into it, then folded his arms and looked at me. "Remarkable. He's clearly intelligent."

Harmony stared at him for a moment. "And *you* are . . . ?"

"Intelligent? Yes, I am. Very. Gordon Tremont, from UCLA. Expert in linguistics, communications, and microprocessor design. Your boss invited me, which is a generous way of saying that I was press-ganged. Threatened with all manner of distasteful events should I refuse, blindfolded and taken in the middle of the night. Two days traveling with not one clue as to where we are. How very paranoid of him. He told me to see if I could, as he put it, 'make some sense outta that creature's language.'"

"I'm not a creature," I said. Or, rather, I growled.

Tremont went, "Hmm . . ." Then he leaned forward with his elbows on his knees and said, "Count for me, please. From one to ten."

I did as he asked. It sounded like growl, bark, growl, snarl, bark-snarl, growl-bark, and so on. Nothing like it should have.

"Let's try again," Tremont said, "from ten down to one."

When I was finished, he nodded. "All the same noises, in correct reverse order. Fascinating. It could just be a form of aphasia."

Harmony asked, "Aphasia?"

"Simply put, a fault in the brain's language center. He knows the words, *thinks* he's saying them, but they're not coming out. He's definitely intelligent. Well, as intelligent as *any* twelve-year-old boy, I expect."

Harmony wet her lips and paused for a moment. "What are you saying, Mr. Tremont?"

"It's *Dr.* Tremont, actually. And I'm saying that young Gethin Rao isn't missing at all." He pointed to me. "Our taciturn cerulean colossus *is* Gethin Rao. Am I right?"

I nodded, and pointed to my chest. I couldn't help grinning—at last, someone understood! I was finally going to get out of here!

Then Harmony said, "You think we don't know that?"

Dr. Tremont and I stared at her.

"We've known from the beginning who he is. But we can't let that knowledge reach the public. Imagine the panic if people thought that at any moment *they* might undergo a spontaneous transformation into, well, something like that."

I roared at her—I can't remember what I said, but I'm sure it wasn't nice—and threw myself at the glass door. I bounced back, landed on my feet, and did it again, and again.

When I'd calmed down a little, Tremont said, "This is inhuman! I demand that you release him—immediately! The boy does not deserve to be locked away. He has committed no crime!"

"He resisted arrest," Harmony said. "*That's* a crime."

"*Reprehensible!* You people . . . How can you sleep at night? What if *your* child was taken away for no reason?"

"I don't have—"

"Shut up!" he roared at her, loud enough that she actually flinched—it was the first time I'd seen her lose her composure. Still looking at Harmony, Tremont pointed to me. "You will release that boy! Immediately! Or, I swear, I will go over your head! I will speak to the president himself!"

"And tell him what, Doctor? That there's a secret base somewhere—you don't *know* where we are, do you?—in which we are keeping prisoner a four-meter-tall blue-skinned boy? Do you think he'd believe you?" She squared her shoulders and glared at him. "You will teach him to talk. And you will not leave this compound until you've achieved that. Understood? We want to know why and how this happened to him."

"Isn't it obvious? He's a superhuman!"

"That's not obvious at all, no."

"Don't you follow the reports? He is not the only one! Maxwell Edwin Dalton, sixteen years old, able to read minds. A young woman who can control any form of energy. A young man who can fly under his own power. Another who can move so fast, the rest of the human race might as well be marble statues. And I know for a *fact* that your people have recruited a seventeen-year-old boy who's been gifted with intelligence that's completely off the charts." Tremont turned away from her, came right up to the glass, and placed his hand on it, looking in at me. "There are even stories of a shapeshifter, did you know that? A man who—at will—can change into another person. Right down to the fingerprints." He paused for a second, then looked back at Harmony. "Is that how you found out your blue prisoner's identity? His fingerprints?"

"No. His DNA."

"You're telling me that he still has the same DNA?"

"Yes. And to save you the trouble of asking, it's human. Completely human. Nothing to indicate how this change occurred. The same with Dalton and the young genius you mentioned. They're all human." Harmony walked up to the glass and stood next to him. "But they're not *just* human. They're more than that. And we have to know why."

After that, Dr. Tremont came to see me every day, morning and afternoon, at least two hours each time.

He always called me by my first name, always treated me like a person, not an animal. He conducted dozens of tests on me. Simple ones at first, like giving me a series of cards with words on them. He'd say a word and I'd hold up the correct card. Then spelling: He gave me a pile of wooden blocks with letters on them—the same blocks you'd give to a preschool kid. I did pretty well on that one too until he got to phrases like *pseudo-mnemonics* that I'd never actually heard before, let alone learned to spell.

After a few weeks, he arranged for an oversized computer keyboard to be installed in my cell. It was connected to a screen that he could read, and for the first time since that day in church, I was able to properly communicate with the world.

"I want to go home." They were the first words I typed.

"I'm sorry, Gethin," he said. "They won't allow that. It's out of my hands."

"How long have I been here?"

"Almost six months, I think."

"They have no right to keep me. I haven't done anything wrong!"

He shrugged. "It seems that they require neither right nor reason. I'm a prisoner here too—they won't let me leave until I can get you to speak again. Or until it's been proven that you'll *never* speak again. But I don't think that'll be the case. Tomorrow we'll begin working on basic phonemes. They're the sounds that make—"

He stopped when I started typing again: "They don't care if I can speak. That's an excuse. They could have brought one of these machines in months ago."

The doctor nodded. "That thought *has* crossed my mind. Gethin. Listen for a few minutes, please?"

"OK."

"Human babies learn to speak by a sort of trial-and-error system. Have you ever heard a child learning to talk? They might know the word *dog*, and they'll say that when they see one. Their parents encourage them. Positive reinforcement. Then they might see a cat but not yet know the name for it. But they will recognize that it has similar attributes to a dog: It's a quadruped, it has a tail, it's covered in fur. So they'll say 'dog' and their mother or father will correct them, tell them that the word for that particular animal is *cat*. Are you following this, Gethin?"

I typed, "Sure."

"Good. Now, when you think about it, by the time children are, say, two years old, they have learned hundreds of words, and most of the time will get them right. They are able to subconsciously identify some very subtle differences. For example, my sister has twin six-year-old girls and a one-year-old boy. The girls are identical. I mean, *I* can't tell them apart—they've played some clever tricks on me, I must say—but their brother always knows who is who."

I sat back and watched him for a moment, wondering where this was going.

"The human brain is a remarkable machine, Gethin. Think about that. My one-year-old nephew, who has practically no experience of anything other than eating and crying, and who still gets confused about which way up a spoon should go, is better at something than I am."

I typed, "He's had more practice."

Dr. Tremont laughed. "Yes, of course. That's the point I'm steering toward. . . . When we're toddlers we're constantly learning. Testing, retesting, experimenting, guessing, and so on. That process of repetition effectively carves pathways into our brain. As we grow, we develop shortcuts. If I ask you to multiply ten and five, you know the answer is fifty. You don't need to calculate it every time."

"But that's just what we call memory," I typed.

"Right. That's how memory works, to a degree. In the brain's language centers we store millions of these shortcuts. I say the word *tiger* and you know exactly what that means. The word brings up a picture of a tiger in your brain, maybe with sound. Or even smell, if you've ever had the good fortune to encounter one up close. And it works the other way. When you want to communicate the word *tiger* to me, you don't have to think about how to make the right sounds.

That's already *hardwired* into your brain. The correct word just comes out."

I nodded, then typed, "And that's the part of me that's gone wrong?"

"I think so, yes. Our tests have shown me that everything else is still working—and working rather well—inside your head. But when you speak, the wrong sounds come out. Now, I mentioned phonemes. . . . They're the basic parts of human speech. What we're going to have to do is work on them one at a time so that when you attempt to make a particular sound, that's the sound we get. We're going to reprogram your brain."

"Will that work?"

The doctor was silent for a moment, then gave me a tight-lipped half smile and shrugged. "I'm . . . hopeful. It's got to be worth a try."

Dr. Tremont and I worked nonstop over the following two months. It was exhausting at first: For the entire first week I had to say "ah" over and over, with the doctor constantly correcting me, until something kicked in and suddenly the "ah" sound was coming out whenever I used a word that required it.

After that, my rate of progress increased, and by the end of the two months I was able to speak whole sentences without a single growl, grunt, or snarl.

I quickly learned that Dr. Gordon Tremont was not the world's foremost expert in linguistics. He admitted that he was good, but not the best. It turned out that he'd been chosen because his psychological profile was very close to Harmony

Yuan's, and it was hoped that—like her—he wouldn't suffer the same reaction to me that most people did.

They were right about that, at least. Whoever "they" were. The doctor and I got along very well. He worked hard, but he was usually happy enough to chat rather than lecture.

On the last morning of the doctor's stay, he approached my cell rather slowly. He just looked at me for a few moments, then cleared his throat. "Good luck, Gethin. I hope . . . I hope they see sense one day."

"Can you do me a favor? Tell my parents I'm still alive."

"I . . . Yeah. Sure. I'll do that."

But I could tell from his expression that he was lying. And he knew that I could tell. My captors were monitoring us, and I had no doubt that if he did try to contact my parents, the penalties would be severe.

Nevertheless, I nodded. "Thanks. For everything."

He gave me a thin-lipped smile, then turned away.

After that, it was back to the old routine: Harmony spending hours each day just watching me.

Despite the situation I had to admire her patience and self-control, because she never seemed to be bothered by the fact that now that I'd relearned to speak, I didn't *stop* talking. I told her thousands of times in the first couple of days that I wanted to go home.

She barely responded, of course. Now and then she would just shake her head, or say, "When we've found out everything we need from you, we'll see what can be done."

Eventually, I gave in. "How are you supposed to find out what you want to know if you don't *ask* me anything?"

"We have a way to go yet. Your cell is rigged with sensors that monitor your heart rate, perspiration, and stress levels. If there was anyone else in there, we'd have begun the interrogation immediately because those sensors act as a very accurate lie detector. But your physiology is so much different from a normal person's, they're practically useless."

"But I *won't* lie. I want to get out of here. I'll tell you whatever you need to hear."

"That's my point, Gethin. Someone in your situation is liable to lie without realizing they're doing so if—"

"That's the first time you've ever used my name."

She stopped, and pursed her lips in thought. "So?"

"So maybe you're finally starting to think of me as a person, not a monster."

Her only response to that was "Hmph."

"Tell me something. . . . When you're talking about me to your bosses, what do you call me? Gethin? The boy? The prisoner? Or maybe it's the monster?"

"The subject," she said.

"Oh. So you're saying that I'm *not* a prisoner?"

But she knew I was just trying to throw her off guard, and she had a lot more experience at that sort of thing than I had. She said, "Want to guess how the guards refer to you? They call you Brawn. You know that word?"

"Yeah. It means 'strength.' As in, 'All brawn and no brains.'"

Harmony nodded. "That's right."

"That's not very fair. I'm not an idiot. I've got brains."

"Yes, but *they* don't see that. They look at you and their immediate reaction is to run away. We're still trying to isolate the reason for that—and the reason that it doesn't affect people like myself and Dr. Tremont—but there's a strong indication that it might be an olfactory reaction. Smell, in other words."

"But I wash every day! Well, most days."

"I know that. Gethin, smell is a much more powerful sense than most humans realize. A sudden whiff of a particular scent can trigger immediate and overwhelming emotional responses."

"So I smell?"

"Not as such. Some scents act only on the subconscious. It's not like you smell of strawberries, or manure, or peanut butter. But whatever it is, it seems to trigger the fight-or-flight reaction in most people. As long as you're like this, you're not going to be making a lot of friends."

"How long *will* I be like this?"

She shrugged.

"When can I go home?"

"You can't. I'm sorry, but that won't be permitted."

"Then I'll get myself out."

Harmony smiled at that. "I really don't think you will, Gethin. No one has ever escaped from this facility. You have to accept that you'll be here for as long as we want you here."

That was one thing she was wrong about.

CHAPTER 7

TWO AND A HALF MONTHS after the first anniversary of my imprisonment, I escaped.

It was surprisingly simple, in the end, and I was annoyed at myself for not thinking of it sooner. It was merely a matter of living up to the beliefs my captors already had about me: I allowed myself to become a monster.

When the two guys let me out of my cell to give it its monthly cleaning, I grabbed hold of both of them. I locked my hands around their little heads and roared at the guards, "You let me go or I'll kill these two men right here and now!"

All of the guard's rifles were instantly raised to shoulder height, aimed at my head. One of them shouted, "Let them go! This is your only warning!"

"No!" I roared back. "You listen—"

Immediately a high-pitched, deafening siren began to

wail. Then a thick white mist came squirting through the ventilators—the two guys immediately went limp, unconscious—and the guards decided not to waste time trying to negotiate with me: They started shooting. I threw the two unconscious guys back behind the glass wall of the cell—I didn't want them to get hit—and took a run at the guards.

A hail of bullets ripped into me, but that didn't slow me down. I grabbed the nearest guard and threw him at his friends like a bowling ball. Took hold of another and used him as a battering ram to force my way to the end of the corridor, where a massive steel door had slammed down.

It took me almost a minute to punch a hole in the door and then tear the hole wide enough for me to climb through.

Another long corridor, this one absolutely *packed* with soldiers. All wearing white protective gear, all aiming their guns at me.

I paused for a moment, wondering whether it was worth the effort. I was pretty sure I'd survive whatever they threw at me, but I was already in a lot of pain: My entire body was covered in bullet holes, my clothes almost torn to shreds.

And then I thought, *They* can't *open fire—they'd hit the guys behind me!*

They opened fire.

It was like being caught in a sudden sandstorm, only with bullets instead of sand. Behind me, five or six soldiers died, shot by their own men, and I finally understood the seriousness of my situation: If they were willing to sacrifice their own people to keep me prisoner, then they were capable of anything.

I tore a large chunk off the steel door, then held it in front of me as I ran.

A crescendo of bullets ricocheted off my makeshift shield as I plowed through the soldiers, knocking them aside, no longer worried about hurting them. If they didn't care about me or each other, why should I care about them?

I'm sure I even stepped on a few as I ran. Probably broke a lot of bones.

To my right, four soldiers rushed from an open doorway. As the doors were closing behind them, I had a quick glimpse of dozens of rows of computer terminals, all manned by scared-looking people bundled up in thick coats, gloves, and fur-lined hats.

The four soldiers immediately opened fire at me, but I was moving fast and protected by my shield. One of them was struck by a ricochet from his own gun, which served him right, but his colleagues didn't try to help him: They just kept shooting.

At the end of this second corridor was another set of steel doors, but as I approached them, they opened, showing me daylight for the first time in a year.

Outside. The air was almost achingly cold, and breathing was already difficult with a hundred bullet wounds in my chest and arms, but the first deep breaths I took were heavenly.

I looked around, saw that I was on the edge of a large flat, open area surrounded by a high ridge, like the inside of a crater. It was maybe a couple of hundred yards across, with the doors at one side and a shallow ramp on the opposite side. Off to the left, three large white half-track trucks were lined up.

The ridge and the ground were dazzlingly white from the sunlight, almost blinding, but I refused to let that stop me.

Behind me, there was a deep rumble as the doors began to close once more, and my first thought was that they had decided it was safer to let me go. . . . And then I saw the massive white-painted anti-aircraft guns fixed to the ridge that encircled the compound. Three of them, all with their barrels turning in my direction.

All three of the anti-aircraft guns fired simultaneously—and uselessly. Maybe it was the frustration of being locked up for so long, or maybe my strength and speed had grown, but I saw the missiles coming, homing in on me as I ran, and at the last second I jumped up and sailed over them so that they detonated against the doors behind me.

At the apex of the jump—which had to be thirty feet at least—I flung my crude shield at the nearest gun. It spun through the air like a giant misshapen Frisbee and crashed into the gun with enough force to shatter it into useless fragments that showered the area, raining down on the two soldiers who'd jumped out of the gun just in time.

The moment I landed, the remaining two guns fired again. I dodged the first shell, but the second slammed into the ground at my feet. The explosion sent me hurtling backward, tumbling head over heels. I crashed face-first into the back of one of the half-track trucks and kept going, straight through the truck's cab.

I landed heavily on my back, the wind knocked out of me.

But I was on my feet again in seconds, running back to the ruined truck.

In the cell I'd read about Vikings going on a berserker rage, where they got so worked up before a battle that practically nothing could stop them. . . . That was what was happening to me: I was getting free and I didn't care what it took.

I honestly believe that if I'd had to kill some of the soldiers, I would have done it without pause.

When I reached the truck, I skidded to a stop, crouched down beside it, and took hold of the chassis. It took very little effort to raise the entire truck over my head and throw it at another of the anti-aircraft guns.

The truck flipped as it arced through the air, coming down roof-first on top of the gun. But I didn't stop to admire what a great shot that had been. I was already running for the third of the guns, racing up the steep embankment.

The guys working the gun had time to fire six shots before they panicked and ran. I dodged the first two shells, leaped over the third, ducked under the fourth. I swatted the fifth shell aside. I caught the sixth in my left hand, and then my face was only inches away from the barrel. On either side, the two soldiers were running like crazy.

"Yeah, you *better* run!" I yelled after them.

I put the shell nose-first into the barrel, drew back my fist, and punched as hard as I could.

The explosion was extremely satisfying, and I hoped that the guns I'd destroyed had cost a fortune.

I pulled the ruined barrel off my hand and looked back down toward the prison doors. There was no sign of activity, except for the six gun operators, all running in different directions.

I poked through the wreckage of the gun for something I could use as a weapon if anyone came after me, and found a small rectangular handheld computer. It was badly scorched, its plastic buttons had melted, and the screen was cracked, but its metal casing seemed to be intact. I was about to toss it aside when I spotted the date and time in the corner of the screen: *23:02 Dec 16*. But I knew that couldn't be right—it was clearly daytime.

Then the time changed to 23:03, and I became aware that something was out of place, something my subconscious had noticed but the rest of me had been too busy to worry about.

Most of the soldiers had been wearing white. The truck and the anti-aircraft guns had also been white.

I looked around. The ground in the crater and the ridge on which I was standing . . . It wasn't rock that seemed white because my eyes weren't used to the light. It was densely packed snow.

I scanned the horizon. It was almost perfectly flat, and there was nothing but snow in all directions. There were no mountains, no trees, no fields or roads.

The sun was above the horizon. If the time and date on the computer were both correct, that meant there was only one place on the planet I could be.

Antarctica.

CHAPTER 8

FROM MY VANTAGE POINT on the edge of the crater I looked back down over the base. The massive doors through which I'd escaped were still closed—though now scorched from the explosions—and I wanted them to stay that way.

But my first task was to round up the six fleeing soldiers. Even though they'd tried to kill me, I wasn't about to leave them out in the open where they might freeze to death.

The first one turned out to be the most difficult to catch: He darted across the packed snow like he was a native. Without slowing, he scrambled over ice ridges, leaped across seemingly bottomless crevasses, skidded down embankments. . . . He was great. I could easily picture him in an action movie, the plucky hero escaping from the giant blue monster. But he was still only human. I could run at more than twice his speed, and—so far—the cold hadn't affected me much.

When I got close enough, I launched myself into the air and came down directly behind him, snagging the fur-lined hood of his parka. He immediately unzipped the parka and darted away, his breath misting in the subzero air.

"Hey!" I roared at him. "How long do you think you'll last out here without your coat? I promise I'm not going to hurt you!" I called. "I'm just going to lock you guys up long enough for me to get away!"

But still he kept running.

I caught him a couple of minutes later. The cold was already slowing him down. His face and neck were almost white enough to match the snow, but shot through with red lines and blotches. Lumps of ice had formed on his beard and eyebrows.

I handed him his parka. "Put that on, you idiot!"

As he struggled into the coat, I looked around to see how far we'd come from the base. It turned out that the guy had been circling around: About five hundred yards to my left I could see the columns of smoke billowing from the ruined guns.

I picked up the guy, slung him over my shoulder, and carried him toward the edge of the crater, and we reached it in time to see the five other gunners rushing across the crater's floor toward the doors, which were now partly open.

"All right," I said to the soldier as I set him down. "I'm letting you go. Go on. Run."

He looked up at me for a moment, then slowly began to back away, as though he didn't trust me. I didn't blame him for that—I figured that Harmony had told the soldiers all sorts of lies about me.

I watched as the soldier skidded down the side of the crater and raced for the open door. Then I slowly followed him.

From inside the base I could hear panicked shouts and the screams and whimpers of the wounded—not my fault—but I ignored them all. There were two more half-track trucks in the crater, as well as a bunch of one-man snowmobiles. They were all piled together in front of the doors—and, suitably crushed so that my captors couldn't use them to follow me or even move them out of the way, they made a pretty good barrier.

For the next hour or two I ran in as straight a line as possible away from the base. With so few landmarks ahead of me, I had to keep checking over my shoulder for the columns of smoke to be sure I wasn't drifting off to one side or the other.

And then the first blizzard hit. Regardless of how big and strong you might be, a snow blizzard is practically impossible to walk through. Not just because of the freezing temperatures, but because of the wind and low visibility. A steady gale, no matter how hard you try to fight it, will eventually push you off course. If you can't see more than a few yards ahead and there aren't any shadows to reveal the position of the sun, you can end up walking in circles.

If I'd been a normal human, the cold would have killed me in minutes, especially since I was wearing only a shirt and a pair of jeans, and they were both riddled with bullet holes.

I don't know how long I walked, but it was probably three

or four days before I heard the dogs. Huskies, dozens of them, their constant barks and growls carrying far over the frozen desert. I kept moving, hoping that something would present itself before they reached me.

I had no plan other than to escape. I tried to remember something useful about Antarctica, but I kept coming back to one thing: a vague sense of relief that I was on the end of the Earth that had penguins and not the one with polar bears.

One of the things I remembered was that the closest other significant landmass to Antarctica was South America, but that would be useful only if I was on the right part of the continent. If I was on the other side, I could be walking for months.

The thought had occurred to me that my captors couldn't have built that place just for me: Clearly it had already been established. So what was it? And why were there so many guys working on computers in a room that—judging by the way they were bundled up and the plumes of misting breath in the air—was kept almost as cold as the weather outside?

On what I figured was probably the fifth day, the hunger pangs pounded on the inside of my stomach like a prisoner with a sledgehammer trying to smash his way out of his cell, and my eyelids were going on strike: I had to stop and get some rest.

I could still hear the dogs, but it was impossible to tell how far away they were. They could have been a day behind me, or only a few minutes. Either way, I had to sleep. I found a shallow depression in the ground and lay down in it. It'd give me a little shelter from the wind, though there was the very strong possibility that I might never wake up.

Something wet and warm pressed at my face, my neck, my arms, and legs, and I woke to find myself literally covered in white and black fur. For a brief moment I thought that this was another change, that whatever it was that had turned me into a blue giant had now made me extremely hairy.

Then I noticed a pair of amber-colored eyes looking at me. And another pair, and another. A dozen dogs were lying across my body.

Voices caught my attention, and I raised my head a little to see three bulky figures silhouetted against the low-lying sun. One of the men was talking to the others: *"Oye, mira! Él está vivo. Y despierto."*

It took me a moment to realize that he was speaking Spanish. There wasn't much I'd been good at in school, but I had always done pretty well in Spanish. He had said, "Hey, look! He's alive. And awake."

"This is the one the Americans were chasing?" another asked.

"Take a guess. Who else is out here?"

"So, what is he?"

The first man shrugged. "Blue."

"That's not a lot of help, Ricardo."

I raised my head a little, and saw three bulky figures silhouetted against the low-lying sun.

The one on the left nudged the one in the middle. "You should talk to him."

"Me? You're the boss."

"Correct. I'm the boss, and I'm telling you to talk to him."

The man in the middle approached. He pushed back the

hood of his parka, removed his tinted goggles, and pulled the scarf away from his mouth. "*¿Hola? ¿Habla usted español?*"

I nodded. "A little, yes. Um . . . *Quién es usted?* Wait, that's not right, is it? Sorry."

"English." The man nodded. "We can do English." He looked me up and down. "*Los perros* . . . The dogs. They found you. They like you, I think. They are trying to keep you warm."

"OK." I didn't really know what else to say.

"Who are you? No, *what* are you? We have never seen a man like you before. You are blue. And very big."

"I know." I sat up, moving slowly in case I startled the dogs. The two on my chest slid off and immediately scampered around behind me, pressing against my back.

The man looked back at his colleagues, who shrugged, then turned to me again. "So . . . Where are you going?"

"Home. America. *North* America."

He nodded at that. "OK. But it is a long walk. And a long swim. And then a much longer walk." His eyes narrowed. "Do you know where you are?"

"Antarctica."

"*La Antártida, sí.* But . . . How did you get here?"

"It's a long story. Can you help me get home?"

"Sure. Well, we can take you to our base. But the Americans might find out. For the past week they have been looking for something. That is you, yes?"

"I guess."

"They have helicopters, men in trucks. . . . But the blizzard must have covered your tracks, because they are looking in the wrong place." He pointed off to the right. "They are one hundred, two hundred kilometers in that direction. My friend, we will make a deal, *sí*? You tell us everything about you— where you come from, how you are . . . like this . . . and why the Americans were keeping you here in this frozen hell—and we will do what we can to get you to Tierra del Fuego— Argentina—without your captors discovering you. Agreed?" He grinned and extended his right hand.

I couldn't see any better option. I shook his hand. Even with the bulky gloves he was wearing, his hand was swallowed up by mine.

CHAPTER 9

THE MINE

COSMO'S PIEBALD SKIN was visible only through long scratches in a thick layer of mud and sweat-soaked rock dust. He was so exhausted that he almost passed out as he squirmed free of the narrow access shaft, and I had to grab him before his head cracked off the floor.

I gently lowered him to the ground, and Keegan passed me her rolled-up jacket to place under his head. She held her water bottle up to his mouth and poured a little in, then splashed some on her free hand and used it to wipe the grime from his face.

Donny DePaiva, Thomas Hazlegrove's number-two man, was watching with three of his fellow guards. DePaiva was in his forties and never seemed particularly interested in the workings of the mine unless Hazlegrove was around, in which

case DePaiva suddenly became the most hands-on and atten-
tive guard you could imagine. "Well? Are they alive in there?"

Cosmo shook his head. "No trace of them. Nothing. They
must have tried to get out when the cave-in started. If they'd
stayed where they were . . ."

"So they got crushed." DePaiva shrugged. "Well, we tried.
All right." He jerked his thumb at the narrow tunnel. "Seal
it up."

Keegan said, "Or we could just leave it. You never know—
we might need to break through again one day."

"Yeah, whatever." DePaiva had already turned away and
was walking back toward the surface with his colleagues.

When they were gone, Cosmo said, "They're making progress, but it's slow going. Jakob reckons it'll take a month,
maybe six weeks."

Keegan said, "That's not good. Their food and water will
run out long before then."

"So we bring them more supplies." Even as I said that,
I knew it wasn't going to be easy. On top of the difficulty
of obtaining more food and water without the guards noticing, there was the secondary problem of actually getting it to
Jakob's team. Cosmo was the only one who was small enough
to squirm through the access shaft, and he really didn't have
the strength to crawl through more than once a day, certainly
not often enough to bring the necessary supplies to Jakob.

There was a solution to that, but I didn't like it. Not one bit.

•   •   •

I crouched down just outside the doorway to the rusting prefabricated cabin that served as Hazlegrove's office. He was sitting with his feet up on the desk, leaning way back with a PneumatoDrill 400 maintenance manual opened in the middle and lying across his face.

I knocked on the door. "Sorry to wake you," I rumbled.

Without moving, he asked, "What do you want, Brawn?"

"I have an idea. It's a good one too. It'll increase productivity quite a lot."

"Go on."

"But in return for the idea, we want better conditions. Bigger rations, new clothes, new bedding. Or at least get the current bedding fumigated. This blasted place is crawling with lice."

"I thought that insects avoided you."

"I think they don't like the taste of my skin. They scurry away from me and make it all worse for everyone else."

"Huh. So what's this idea?"

"Put the kids to work in the mine shafts. Only a couple of hours a day, just to keep them from getting bored. You can assign some of the weaker adults to watch over them. With Jakob's team gone we're eight men down. This'll more than make up for that."

Hazlegrove pulled his feet off the desk, removed his makeshift eye shield, and sat up. "That's a strange suggestion, coming from you."

"Yeah, well, I'm not suggesting that they do anything too dangerous. But they could bring water down to the workers, help with clearing the loose ore. It'll get them used to working in the shafts, and it means their parents won't have to be worried that they're not being supervised."

He stood up and walked to the door. "I'm not scared of you freaks. You know that, right?"

"I never thought you were."

"By rights you shouldn't even exist. In older civilizations people like you would have been put to death."

"OK." I wondered where he was going with this.

"And yet here you are, alive and healthy. Something to think about, eh?" He waved one hand at me, urging me to move away from the door, then stepped out and looked around. "There are three hundred and seventy-two inmates of this mine, almost a hundred of whom are too old, too weak, or too young to be productive enough to cover the cost of feeding them." His lips tightened and his eyes narrowed for a moment. "All right. We'll give your suggestion a go. Any accidents or delays caused as a result will be your fault. But you'll get what you asked for. Except the new bedding and clothing, but we'll delouse everyone's existing clothing at the same time we do the bedding."

"Good." I nodded. "Yeah, that'll work."

"But there'll be a price, Brawn. And you won't like it. I'll need to work on some details, talk to the warden. Agreed?"

"You want me to agree before you tell me what that price is?"

He grinned. "Correct. Agree to my terms and you'll get your extra rations today. It'll take a week or so to get enough lindane to delouse the beds and clothes."

I didn't want to agree, but we needed the extra rations to keep Jakob and his men going, and we needed the kids allowed in the mine shafts because they were small enough to crawl through the access tunnel and bring those rations to the escape team.

We couldn't all escape, we knew that. But now that Jakob and the others were believed to be dead, they wouldn't be missed. If they weren't missed, no one would be looking for them.

But Hazlegrove's price . . . I couldn't even guess what it might be. All I could do was hope that it was a long way off. Long enough for Jakob and the others to tunnel their way to freedom, and—ideally—find someone who could get the rest of us out.

"All right," I said. "It's a deal."

Time passed slowly in the platinum mine, but it passed even more slowly when there was something to hope for.

After two months of round-the-clock digging Jakob and his team broke the surface some hundred yards beyond the perimeter fence. Those of us who knew of the escape plans—and there weren't many: even the kids who assisted had to be sworn to secrecy—crossed our fingers and prayed to any number of deities that the team would find help.

But we knew it was a slim hope. Even though we were all prisoners, not all of us were criminals. Some of us were there simply because we'd proved to be an inconvenience to our governments. My friend Keegan, for example, had never been a superhuman. She had never committed a crime. She was imprisoned because she'd been in a relationship with her country's secretary of defense and he'd been careless enough to leave unprotected documents on his computer. Keegan found the documents by accident and, being naturally curious, read them. The documents proved that a minor election had been rigged. She mentioned it to the secretary, and a few days later she was here, in the mine.

Every new arrival was quizzed mercilessly by the other inmates: We wanted to know what was going on in the outside world. Did they know about us? Where exactly is the mine located?

Keegan, just like the rest of us, knew only that it had taken the best part of a day to reach the mine, and that she had been blindfolded throughout the journey.

But Jakob and the others would find out exactly where we were. As summer approached and the air under the dome became almost too hot to breathe, that was the only thought that kept us going.

In mid-June, the ventilator that pumped clean air into the deepest of the tunnels suddenly stopped working. Hazlegrove decided that it would be too costly to fix or replace, so we had to make do with the second ventilator being switched back and forth every half hour.

A week later, the second ventilator overheated. Sweat-drenched workers emerged from the mine shafts, pale skinned and hollow eyed, gasping for breath.

Within an hour, the last of the mined ore had been put through the crushers, and then no one—not even the guards—

knew what to do. For the first time since I'd arrived at the mine, work was halted.

We had grown accustomed to the constant humming of the ventilators, the whining of the drills, and the relentless growling of the ore crushers. Without them the silence was shocking, almost ghostly.

Hazlegrove found me lifting Loligo into her vat. Loligo was like me, a former superhuman whose powers had come with a physical change. She had tentacles in place of her arms, and gills in the side of her neck. She was a water-breather, and could live in the air for only a few hours at a time. There wasn't a lot of work she could do in the mine, so she helped prepare the meals and looked after any new babies. Loligo was Italian, but unlike most Italians I'd met, she'd never learned to speak any language other than her own.

"You!" Hazlegrove shouted at me. "Get these people organized!"

"Organized doing what, Mr. Hazlegrove?"

"Something. *Anything*." His eyes were wide. "It could be *days* before we can get the ventilators working!"

Loligo said, *"Abbiamo bisogno di riposare."*

He looked at her, his upper lip curled in distaste. "What?"

"She said we need to rest. She's right. A few days off will do us good."

"This is *not* a blasted vacation camp!" He stood there for a moment, seething, his swagger stick slapping furiously against the side of his leg, and for the first time I wondered what it was that drove a man like Thomas Hazlegrove.

Why would any sane person voluntarily work in this

place? Perhaps it was money. I had no idea what platinum was worth, but we extracted quite a lot of it, and the costs were minimal. Maybe the warden paid Hazlegrove hundreds of thousands of dollars to run the mine.

"All right . . . Brawn, spread the word. This time tomorrow I'm going to address the crowd. I want everyone there. Everyone. Understood?"

"Sure. What's this about?"

"You'll find out when everyone else does."

Some of the younger prisoners had never experienced silence. They'd been born in the mine, where there had always been the ever-present rumble of heavy machines. That first night few of them were able to sleep. For the adults, though, there was almost a party atmosphere. We gathered in groups, talking, sometimes even laughing. The night was filled with a sense of hope, a feeling that this one simple change was a harbinger of better days.

And those of us who knew of Jakob's escape were even more certain of that feeling.

I slept well that night, better than I had in more than ten years, and it was luxurious to be allowed to wake of my own accord and not because one of the guards was poking me in the face with the muzzle of his gun.

As I was waiting in line at the water barrel, Keegan called to me from in front of the guards' dens, waving me over. I passed my water bottle to the man behind me. "Fill this for me, will you, Crisanto?"

He nodded and said, *"Tiyak."*

When I reached Keegan, she pointed over to the far side of the shaft entrances. "New people. Eight or nine, I think. Lift me up so I can see."

I reached down and she sat in the crook of my arm, then I hoisted her onto my shoulder. "I see them. Hazlegrove is with them."

"They're not prisoners," Keegan said. "What are those things they're pushing? They look like lawn mowers. Can't be, though. It's been a long time since any grass grew under the dome."

We watched for a while. There were ten of them, all men, in two-man teams. One pushed the lawn-mower-like machine, and the other took notes on a clipboard. They were there for almost two hours, going back and forth over the ground, and when they were finished, they were led out through the northern gate, far from the prisoners.

In the afternoon, every prisoner assembled in a ramshackle cluster in the open space in front of Hazlegrove's office.

Finally, Hazlegrove emerged, bullhorn in hand, DePaiva and Swinden flanking him, and all the other guards watching us carefully.

"Quiet!" Hazlegrove barked into the bullhorn. "All of you . . . Settle down and listen up! The ventilators will be back working in a couple of days. In the meantime, you all get some time off." He paused. "Thank me later. Now, in the past couple of months you've seen some improvements. Larger rations, more water. Healthier conditions. That doesn't come free. Not free at all. When Brawn negotiated the deal, I told him there would be a price. He didn't know what the price was, but he agreed anyway." Hazlegrove barked a harsh laugh. "And this is the man you've chosen as your *leader*?"

A lot of people looked at me, and I shrugged. No one had chosen me, not really. It had just happened. And I didn't care what he had to say about me—I was more concerned with the price he was about to announce.

"Our visitors this morning used ultrasonic probes to scan deep beneath the surface. That technology didn't even exist the last time this mine was silent—and it's only *because* the mine is silent that the probes were able to work." He pointed to a spot past the mine-shaft entrances but still under cover of the dome. "The scans showed two large, and *very* rich, seams of platinum ore right over there. So enjoy your brief rest, because once the ventilators are back online, we're opening up two new shafts. It's going to require a lot more manpower. But since we don't *have* any more manpower, we'll just have to make the most of what we do have. From now on, we're operating on fifteen-hour shifts." Hazlegrove grinned. "Have a nice day. But don't get used to it."

The anger that rippled through the crowd was almost palpable, a wave of hatred that washed over Hazlegrove and was as effective as the wind pushing against a ten-ton steel pylon.

Hazlegrove gestured to me, beckoning me to approach.

As I broke free of the crowd, he also called to Keegan and Cosmo. They came to a stop beside me.

He had to shout to be heard over the noise, but I think that was what he wanted. "Jakob Luke Winquist. Your friend. Remember him?"

I nodded. I had a sick feeling I knew what he was going to say.

"He and his team were caught yesterday morning trying to cross the border into Kazakhstan. The three of you lied to me. You participated in—and covered up—the escape of eight prisoners. I'm sure that others were involved, and I'm equally sure that you won't tell me their names, so I won't bother asking."

Hazlegrove walked slowly around me, staring first at Keegan, then at Cosmo. Then he stopped once more in front of me, looking up. "The escapees are, of course, now dead." He glanced at Keegan, whose eyes were beginning to tear. Either from sorrow or hopelessness. Maybe both. "Don't cry for them. They don't deserve your tears. They broke the rules. Rule breakers must be punished."

He nodded to DePaiva and Swinden. They came forward, their guns held loosely in their arms. "By way of punishment, we are going to shoot two of you, in the head, one shot each. The other one will merely be locked up in the hot box for a week. Because I'm not *completely* without mercy, I'll allow you to advise me which two will be shot."

"Me," I said instantly. "Shoot me twice."

"Twice? No. It doesn't work that way," Hazlegrove said. "Because *you* know you'll probably survive a shot between the eyes." He looked from Keegan to Cosmo. "Brawn and one other."

"Why choose me at all if you know I'll survive?" I asked, even though I knew the answer. I was stalling for time, desperately trying to think of a way out of this.

Hazelgrove said, "The other prisoners look up to you. Seeing you wracked with guilt will help remind them who's boss around here. So choose. The woman or the skinny freak."

"Me, then," Cosmo said. "You know that makes sense, Hazlegrove. I can't work as hard as Keegan. I've probably got only a couple more years left, at most."

Keegan started to speak, but Cosmo said, "No! No, you get to live." He stepped up to her. "You have to live. Brawn and I, we're superhuman—or we were. But you should *never* have been brought to this place. You have to live so that one day you can get free and work to put an end to this."

She put her arms around him and pulled him close—but still she was careful not to crack his fragile ribs. "There has to be another way!"

"You know there isn't." He smiled at her then, and for a moment I thought he was going to tell Keegan that he had always loved her. But he said nothing. Maybe he figured it was better that way. Instead, he just kissed her on the cheek, then stepped back and resumed his place beside me. He reached up and put his hand on my arm. "When you get out . . . Give them hell, big guy. Avenge my death, and all that."

"Yeah, I will. They'll pay for everything that they've done to—"

I stopped: DePaiva and Swinden had cocked their rifles. "No. Not *here*, Hazlegrove! Not in front of the kids!"

"Of course here! How are they supposed to learn the lesson if they don't *see* you being shot?" He nodded to Swinden.

There was a sharp *crack!* and I was staggering backward before the pain of the bullet even registered.

I stumbled, reeling, blinded from the pain, and the second shot rang out as the crowd started screaming, panicking.

I dropped to my knees, gingerly probed my forehead until my fingers brushed against the bullet, then pulled it free.

And then, beside me, Cosmo's voice whispered, "Oh God, no . . ."

I looked up to see Keegan lying on the ground, her lifeless eyes staring up at the inside of the dome.

Hazlegrove was standing over her body, but looking at me. "You can advise me. Doesn't mean I have to listen."

CHAPTER 10

TWENTY-FOUR YEARS AGO

ON THE MORNING OF my fifteenth birthday, I woke up in a tree.

That wasn't unusual, because I'd woken up in a tree every morning for the previous two months. Except for that one time about three weeks earlier when the branch on which I was sleeping proved to be too weak to support my weight: That morning I'd woken up thirty feet above the ground and falling fast.

Something caught my eye, and I saw that a millipede the size of a hot dog was meandering its way up my arm, which struck me as more odd than creepy, because usually insects gave me a wide berth. I picked it up in my other hand, and—for a moment—wondered whether it might be breakfast. But then I thought of all those legs scuttling down my throat and changed my mind. I was hungry, but not *that* hungry.

I put the millipede onto a nearby branch and allowed myself to topple sideways. It was quicker than climbing down, and I was only about forty feet up. I crashed down through the lower branches and landed on my feet.

The jungle was deep in shadow, with the sunlight coming from my right, which told me I was facing the right direction: north. I started walking.

It had taken me two years to walk from Tierra del Fuego in southern Argentina through Bolivia and to my current location, Yapacana National Park in Venezuela.

After rescuing me in the Antarctic, my new Argentinean friends brought me to their base, a weather research station on the Ronne Ice Shelf. There were ten people in their party, all men, all scientists, and for the first week most of them were terrified of me: They kept me in the large shed that housed the dogs, which suited all of us just fine. The dogs seemed to love curling up on top of me and falling asleep.

But gradually the scientists' natural curiosity overcame their fear, and I was accepted into the group.

They were smart and funny, and the sixteen weeks I was with them passed quickly. They put a lot of time into teaching me Spanish and poker, though in truth I wasn't much good at either. I earned my keep by looking after the dogs and helping out around the base.

Of course, the Argentineans wanted to know all about me, but I refused to tell them my real name: I no longer wanted my parents to find out that I was still alive. It had been more than a year since the incident in the First Church of Saint Matthew.

I figured it was better that they continued to believe I was dead, because knowing the truth would put them in danger from my former captors.

After having been held prisoner for so long it came as something of a shock to be with people who treated me like a human being. And I received an even bigger shock the first time I squeezed myself into the bathroom, looked in the mirror, and saw my face for the first time. There hadn't been a mirror in the prison, and the cell had always been too bright for me to properly see my reflection in the glass. I'd already known that I was completely hairless—I didn't even have eyelashes—but I never expected to see pure white eyes looking back at me. Solid white, no iris or pupil.

The leader of the group—a very laid-back and cheerful older man called Enrique—later examined my eyes very closely and declared that he had absolutely no idea why I wasn't blind. "The color white reflects light. There can't be enough light getting in for you to be able to see." He sketched a diagram of an eye on a sheet of paper. "Photons—particles of light—pass through the eye's lens and are focused here, on the retina, which is composed of light-sensitive cells. When the photons strike them, the cells transmit signals to the brain via the optic nerve. If there's no light getting into the eye to trigger those cells . . ." He shrugged. "You should be blind."

Enrique was also fascinated with the color of my skin. "There is a medical condition called argyria that causes skin to take on a blue or gray tint. It's caused by the long-term inhalation of silver compounds. . . . But its effects are nothing like this." As I sat cross-legged before him, he poked my upper arm with his finger. "This *feels* like flesh, but it's much stronger, more resilient." His probing fingers found a scar on my biceps. "This wound . . . When we found you, it was a few days old. Now it has almost completely faded." Enrique patted me on the forearm. "You are a fascinating creature. I'm glad we found you before anyone else did."

I think that was one of the reasons they liked me: Aside from monitoring the weather patterns and occasionally venturing out to drill core samples of the ice, they didn't have a lot to keep themselves busy. But now they had a giant blue kid to exercise their scientific minds. They took samples of my skin and spent days analyzing them. They got me to spit into a beaker to see if my saliva was the same as everyone else's. Everything about me was a puzzle, and scientists love puzzles.

The Argentineans never told their superiors about me. At first, it was because they didn't think they would be believed, but pretty quickly they realized how much danger they would be in if the Americans found out.

At the end of the sixteen weeks, Enrique arranged for a Russian Mi-10 helicopter to come to the base to collect a sealed container of "samples" and deliver it to a research ship waiting off the Palmer Archipelago.

Through a series of called-in favors and, I suspected, one or two hefty bribes, Enrique managed to set everything up so that the container would be unloaded from the ship once it reached Tierra del Fuego, about seven hundred miles to the north, and then left unwatched overnight.

I never saw any of my Argentinean friends again, but in the years that followed it was sometimes very comforting to think that somewhere in Antarctica is a research station that houses a large photo of me laughing and joking with them, surrounded by a dozen huskies who wanted nothing more than to curl up in my lap.

I'd like to be able to say that I spent my two years in South America doing something useful and heroic, like saving impoverished villagers from ruthless gang lords or greedy corporations, but the truth is that most of the time I just stuck to the shelter of the jungles and did my best to avoid anything to do with civilization.

Aside from occasionally encountering a road that I couldn't easily go around—in which case I usually waited until nightfall before crossing—during the first two years I came into contact with people only once, and that was in southern Bolivia, just north of Cañón Seco.

It was early morning, and I was daydreaming as I marched through the forest when I walked straight into a clearing in which there was a ring of six two-man tents around the smoldering remains of the previous night's campfire.

Before I could retrace my steps, I realized that I was only a few yards away from a very sleepy-looking freckle-faced man who was relieving himself behind a tree. When he saw me, his mouth dropped open in shock.

I decided that the best approach would be to act as though I were nothing out of the ordinary. "Morning," I said, and kept walking.

"What . . . ?" He very quickly finished his business and raced after me. "Wait!"

Don't turn around! I said to myself. *Just keep going!*

"Wait, stop!" he yelled.

A woman's voice called from one of the tents. "Andreas? What is it?"

"There's a . . . a giant blue man! You've *got* to see this!"

The sounds of mild panic and confusion came from the other tents, and almost as one, six tent flaps were unzipped and the campers came scrambling out, six men and six women in total.

One of the men screamed when he saw me, and fainted, but most of the rest were more curious than scared.

They rushed up to me, then stopped when I turned to look at them. "Camping, huh?" I asked. I couldn't think of anything else.

The first man—the one with a fresh pee stain on his jeans—said, "You . . . You speak *English*?"

"Sure." I shrugged. "Well, see you later."

I turned to go, but three of them ran in front of me, staring up with open mouths and wide eyes.

"What, you've never seen a giant blue man before?"

"No! How . . . What . . . Where do you *come* from?"

"My tribe," I said, pointing back the way I'd come. "There's, like, forty of us. You should go check it out."

The man made a face of disbelief. "Gimme a break. Where are you *really* from?"

"I'm American. Going back home."

I could see from their expressions that they just didn't know what to make of me. I was bombarded with questions: Who are you? Why are you blue? What do you eat? Are there others like you? How come you're so tall? What's the deal with your eyes? How old are you?

I really should have said my good-byes and walked away, but I was enjoying the attention too much.

"What's your name?"

I wasn't about to tell them my real name, so I said "Barnaby" because it was the first thing I thought of.

One of the women smiled. "Yeah, right. So . . . "—she made air quotes—"Barnaby, what are you doing here in Bolivia?"

"Like I said, trying to get home. It's a long story. And most of it is secret."

The other members of their party had kept their distance, and I didn't give them much thought, until I heard the clicking and whirring of cameras.

I turned back to see that five or six of them had produced expensive-looking cameras complete with huge telephoto lenses.

"Ah, come on! What is this? Who *are* you people?"

"Photographers," the nearest woman said. "There have been sightings of a rare tree frog in this area. It's supposed to be extinct. So we . . ." She smiled. "Forget the frogs, Barnaby— you're *much* more interesting!"

I spent most of the morning begging them not to publish their photos while they continued to take more and deluged me with further questions, all except for one—the first man— who only wanted to talk about the tree frog. One of his friends told me that they'd been in Bolivia for three weeks and that the guy had not once shut up about the frog, driving them nuts.

In the end I had no choice but to walk away from their camp. I had the vague hope that if their photos were published, most people would think they were fake, but my former captors would finally realize that I hadn't died in Antarctica.

After I left the camp, I doubled my speed, but I knew that sooner or later I would be tracked and found.

And a few months later, on the afternoon of my fifteenth birthday, in Yapacana National Park in Venezuela, they found me.

CHAPTER 11

THEY CAME IN LOW over the trees, from all angles, more than twenty helicopters. And not people carriers this time: They were gunships.

I ran, of course, even though I knew there really wasn't anywhere safe to go. But I kept to the jungle and avoided any clearings that might be large enough for the copters to set down.

I passed beneath the north-most copters, and they whirled around to track me as I crashed through the undergrowth, leaped over streams and rivers, vaulted fallen trees. My bare feet churned up the jungle floor, gouging a path that even an idiot could follow. Birds and other animals—usually unperturbed by my presence—scattered ahead of me, the birds taking to the air in great flocks, ruining any possible chance I might have had of hiding.

Just keep going! I told myself over and over. *If they catch you, you'll end up back in Antarctica!* I was not going to let that happen. If I had to, I'd fight back.

But that would be a last resort. I was sure that the crews of those helicopters were only following orders. Unless they actually opened fire on me, I wasn't willing to hurt them.

That thought had barely crossed my mind when they *did* open fire.

The jungle around me was torn apart, a storm of bullets ripping into the trees, killing countless animals, tearing up the ground far more effectively than anything I could do.

I was fast, but the copters were much faster and didn't have to navigate uneven ground. Five of them darted ahead and resumed firing, blocking my path.

They're not actually shooting at me! I thought as I made a ninety-degree turn to the right. *They're just trying to herd me in!*

And then a volley of bullets streaked across my back, and I understood that this was *not* a mission of capture: They were here to kill me.

I was dead if I stopped, and just as dead if I kept running. There was only one other option: I had to fight back.

I snatched up a fallen branch as I ran, but it was rotten and crumbled to damp powder in my hands. I need something stronger. Bigger. I jumped straight at the nearest tree, its trunk the width of my waist, and, using my weight, wrenched it loose from its hold on the forest floor. I stopped just long enough to pull it free, leaves and bark raining down on me.

One of the gunships passed overhead from left to right,

and I threw the tree like a spear: It clipped the copter's rear propeller, causing it to spiral down into the treetops.

Another two copters swooped around ahead of me, their side-mounted guns flaring. Bullets ripped into my right shoulder with enough force to send me spinning. I crashed to the ground—and kept rolling as the forest floor around me was strafed with gunfire.

I collided with a huge manchineel tree and, seeing no other choice, leaped up and grabbed hold of its lowest branches. I pulled myself up and began to climb.

The base of the tree was peppered with gunfire. At first I thought the gunships were working their way up, adjusting their aim to hit me, but I quickly realized that they were trying to bring the tree down.

I reached about thirty feet before the manchineel's branches were too weak to support my weight, and as I was preparing myself to leap to the next tree, one of the gunships cruised by, circling to get a better angle.

That was a mistake: I sprang forward, straight at the copter, and caught on to the stubby wings at the side that housed its guns and external fuel tanks.

The copter bucked and swayed as I pulled myself up. I saw the pilot slam the joystick forward, and the craft immediately pitched forward.

Still holding on to the edge of the wings—with my clenched fingers actually digging into the metal—I flipped my legs forward, braced them against the landing gear, and pushed as hard as I could.

The metal screamed as the entire wing was torn free of the fuselage.

Naturally, without anything keeping me up, I tumbled to the ground, but I knew that I'd survive the fall, and I had the pleasure of watching the copter spin out of control.

But that didn't stop the others from swinging back around to target me again.

When I hit the ground, I immediately jumped to my feet and snatched up the now-leaking fuel tank. It felt sufficiently big and heavy as I hefted it in one hand. And it arced beautifully and made a very satisfying explosion when it struck the blades of one of the other copters.

As the second copter crashed down, the others pulled back. So far, no one had been killed. I felt a little better about that, but to be honest, right then I wouldn't really have cared much if they'd all died: They'd started it.

The crews of the remaining gunships were clearly as angry with me as I was with them. They stayed at a distance but kept pace with me and continued firing. I was hit seven or eight times, maybe more, and though none of the bullets struck anything vital and I healed very quickly, I could feel myself slowing down.

I knew I wasn't going to win, and it was clear that they weren't going to let me go.

Then one of the copters launched a missile at me. I saw it coming and abruptly changed direction . . . And so did the missile. No matter which way I ran, the missile kept adjusting its course.

At the last moment—when the missile was only a couple of yards behind me—I ducked behind a wide-trunked tree. The explosion split the trunk, scattered burning fragments far across the jungle.

The copter passed low overhead—its powerful rotors dispersing the clouds of wood smoke and spreading burning cinders far and wide—and I crashed through the flaming debris in the opposite direction.

I emerged in a small clearing where I saw three new copters waiting for me. As one, they all launched missiles.

I changed direction again, and as I desperately tried to outrun the missiles, the jungle around me was being torn apart by gunfire from the other copters. I was a dead man running. I remember thinking, *This is a lousy way to spend my fifteenth birthday!*

Launching three heat-seeking missiles at the same time turned out to be a mistake: As I ran, and constantly shifted direction, the missiles came closer and closer together . . . Then—I later learned—one of them locked on to the heat signature of another. There was an explosion that tore the jungle apart.

I'd been knocked off my feet, and now quickly scrambled up to see that I was now in the heart of an inferno.

For a second all I could do was stand there, shocked, and then through the smoke and flames I saw the copters again, hovering just above the treetops. As I watched, one by one the copters peeled away.

Within a few minutes, the jungle was almost silent.

As soon as I escaped from the fire, I dropped down next to a tree to catch my breath, and tried to understand what had happened. Had they been ordered to pull out? Maybe they realized I wasn't a bad guy after all. Or maybe the Venezuelan government had learned that a foreign military power was conducting an operation in their country.

That last thought triggered another: Why was I assuming that the gunships were American? For all I knew, they belonged to the Venezuelan military, or some other country.

But whoever they were, they now knew where I was. I pushed myself to my feet, and kept moving.

It was about half an hour before I realized why the gunships had called off the attack. They had been shooting at me almost nonstop for a good five minutes. . . . They had run out of ammunition.

And that told me that they would be back.

Five days passed before the copters came again. This time there were fewer of them—not more than five or six—and they came from the south.

I'd been running since the first attack, always heading north. I figured I'd covered more than a hundred miles—a lot more than I'd usually cover in five days, because I was no longer concerned about being seen, about carefully skirting around villages or waiting until nightfall before I crossed an open area. I was just running like crazy, and if that meant charging straight through a town in the middle of the day, so be it.

My goal was to get back to the USA, but I hadn't decided

exactly what I would do when I got there. The attack had changed that: Now what I wanted above all was revenge on the people who had imprisoned me for a year in Antarctica. I'd made no plans for the form that revenge would take, but I was determined that it would be big, and devastating, and very, very public.

At least this time they kept their distance and hadn't started shooting yet.

Instead, it turned out that they were herding me into another trap. I should have seen it coming, but sometimes—especially when I'm boiling with fury—I find it hard to think past the immediate situation.

The gunships steered me right where they wanted me to go . . . out of the forest and into a huge plowed field that offered nowhere to hide.

Over the field a dozen more copters had set down in a wide semicircle, their rotors slowing to a stop. In front of each one, five or six soldiers stood with machine guns trained on me. And directly in the middle Harmony Yuan was waiting.

The soldiers hadn't opened fire immediately—that was something—and I knew that if I returned to the forest, the gunships would come after me and this time they wouldn't stop.

I slowed to a walk, and tried to look unconcerned and casual as I approached Harmony.

With her expression as dour as ever, she said, "So. Gethin. Or Brawn. Or *Barnaby*, if you prefer . . . You owe us almost eight and a half billion dollars."

"Yeah? How do you figure that?"

"That's what it's cost to find you. Two years we've been searching. Two *years*."

I sat down cross-legged in front of her. "You could have saved yourself all that money if you'd just given up after the first few days."

"It was worth it. We've finally caught you."

I looked down at my wrists, then back at Harmony. "Really? I don't see any handcuffs. You haven't caught me *yet*. As I see it, I'm still free."

"How did you escape from Antarctica?"

"I'm not telling you that."

Harmony pursed her lips. "Did you have help?"

"*Help?* Aside from your goons the only other living creatures I saw were penguins, and all they ever did was make a lot of noise and produce a heck of a lot of poo while doing their best to avoid me."

"Then tell me how you've remained hidden all this time. How did you survive in the jungle?"

"Turns out I've got a stomach as strong as my skin. I can eat just about anything. I can live on grass and ferns if I have to."

"Interesting . . . We'll have to test that."

I shook my head. "No more tests. I'm not going with you. Unless you're just going to give me a lift back to the States."

"Gethin, you don't understand. You're still only a kid. What happened to you is . . . It's enormous. It potentially has incalculable repercussions for the human race. You can't even begin to comprehend the scale of things."

"I don't have to comprehend anything!" I jabbed my index finger in her direction. "You people ruined my life!"

"We didn't make you like this."

"How do I know that? One minute I'm normal, the next I'm like this, and suddenly there's cops and FBI people like you claimed to be and army guys all over the place! How'd you all get there so fast? And who are you *really* working for? There's no way an FBI agent is authorized to smuggle someone out of the States and lock them away in the Antarctic!"

"Gethin, you have to come with me."

"So you can figure out a way to kill me? You're out of your mind!"

"We have no intention of killing you."

"Yeah, well, a few days ago—"

She cut me off: "Things have changed in the past five days. We're not here to kill you, or capture you. The Powers That Be have decided that you're significantly more useful alive than dead. We're giving you a job."

CHAPTER 12

THE MINE

TIME SEEMED TO STOP. All I was aware of was that everyone in the mine was watching me, wondering what I would do next.

I had a strong feeling that Hazlegrove was hoping I'd attack him: That would give him the perfect excuse to kill me right there and then. I wasn't nearly as strong as I had been before my powers disappeared. One bullet to the head would only slow me down, but if all of the guards fired simultaneously . . . I wasn't sure what would happen, and I didn't want to find out.

Keegan was dead. Nothing I did would change that.

The only logical course of action would be to keep my head down and watch for a better opportunity to escape.

"Your fault, Brawn," Hazlegrove said. "You created this situation. No one escapes. You got that? No one."

I felt the fury subside a little as I looked at Keegan. She would want me to remain calm. I could almost hear her voice telling me not to do anything I would regret later.

I climbed to my feet, and slowly walked over to my friend's body. The guards had not taken their eyes off me, nor had their aim faltered. They were ready for anything I might do.

Still moving slowly, I turned to look down at Hazlegrove.

His grin slipped, and I saw a single bead of sweat run down his forehead. He swallowed. "Well?"

"A few minutes ago you told us that we'd have to work harder. This is how you intend to encourage us? What if we drop our tools now, and never work again? Will you kill *all* of us? How would that look to the warden, and to whoever is pulling his strings? Do you think they would be pleased with you, or angry?"

"I don't think you're in any position to lecture—"

"She has to be buried. A proper funeral. Keegan was a Christian, a Catholic. We'll need a priest."

His usual smug composure returned. "That's not going to happen."

"A funeral," I repeated. "With an ordained Catholic priest. And it has to happen within three days."

Hazlegrove shook his head. "Keep dreaming. You can perform your own funeral service, but you are *not* getting a priest."

I took a step back, and looked around at the other prisoners.

Beside me, Cosmo crouched down next to Keegan and gently closed her eyes. "Brawn . . . ," he said softly, so that only I could hear. "We . . . we have to *do* something."

He was right. But what *could* we do? It was taking every ounce of my control not to grab Hazlegrove and rip his spine out through his chest, but I had to hold myself back. If I attacked Hazlegrove, the guards would open fire and a lot more people would die.

I looked back at Hazlegrove. "When the ventilators are repaired, we'll go back to work. Like you said earlier, we work and you feed us. But this back-and-forth power play . . . these petty, cruel actions that you think make you a big man . . . that all ends now. No more games, Hazlegrove. Because this whole place is teetering on the edge, and if you push any harder, it will all come crashing down. Believe me, you do *not* want to be caught in the middle of that."

Hazlegrove sneered. "You think you can get away with threatening—"

"It's not a threat!" I roared, and Hazlegrove jumped back. "It's a *warning*, and unless you're the biggest moron who ever walked the Earth, you'll heed it!"

He paused for a few seconds, looking at me, then nodded once and turned away.

Part of me wished he hadn't, that he had tried one more thing to reinforce his sense of power, because I *would* have snapped. I would have locked my hands around his puny head and crushed it to jelly.

But I saw in his eyes that he knew how close he had come to death, and I hoped that this was a turning point, that some good would come from Keegan's murder.

•   •   •

The following morning Keegan was buried. All of the prisoners gathered in the small patch of ground just outside the dome that served as a cemetery, the last resting place of twenty-seven other prisoners whose lives had been lost while working in the mine.

There was no priest, but we did our best to remember how a funeral should be conducted. Prayers were said, speeches made, and as I lowered my friend's cloth-wrapped body into the grave, Cosmo said, "I've got something to say. Everyone, please . . . If you'll bow your heads for a moment?"

Everyone lowered their heads.

Cosmo cleared his throat. He hesitated for a second, then said, "When someone we love dies, it breaks all of us. We're damaged, fractured, but we're not weakened—never that. Instead, we're united in grief, in love, in hope. That unity gives us strength, and we will need that strength to survive."

Cosmo glanced back over toward the dome, where many of the guards were watching with vague interest, then continued: "Keegan believed that the taking of human life—no matter *what* the reason—is an unforgivable sin. Even in a situation where the only way to survive is to kill another. Even then. Unforgivable. I ask you to honor our friend by living as she would. I know that many of you are filled with rage over our situation here, and that our freedom seems an impossible goal without more blood being shed, but you must never, *never* take the life of another."

He knelt down beside the grave and tossed in a handful of dirt. "Rest in peace."

Cosmo straightened up, looked at me for a moment, then

backed away into the crowd. A line formed, and one by one, everyone present said their good-byes.

I had my head down, my thoughts on Keegan, when I heard one of the guards raise his voice: "Where d'you think you're goin'?"

I looked up to see Cosmo walking past the guards. "I need to talk to Mr. Hazlegrove," he said.

As he passed through the doors, I thought, *Whatever you do, Cosmo, don't be a fool. If you antagonize him, you'll end up in the hot box, or worse.*

I could picture Cosmo marching up to Hazlegrove's office and tried not to think of him as "the Mouse That Roared." A stick-thin figure barely strong enough to stand upright, raging at the man who cared so little about other people that he ordered a woman to be killed and then only grudgingly allowed the woman's friends to use a shovel to dig her grave.

Whatever argument you have with him, Cosmo, you're not going to win, I thought.

And then another thought struck me: *What if he's not going to Hazlegrove to argue with him? What if he's planning to—?*

I was already running, the startled guards darting out of my way and reaching for their guns at the same time.

Normally I had to crouch way down to get through the doors, but on this occasion I didn't have the luxury of taking my time: I made a low jump, throwing my legs forward and my head back, skidding through the open doors like a baseball player sliding into home plate.

Then I rolled forward onto my feet and ran, ignoring the shouts of the guards behind me.

Ahead of me, just outside Hazlegrove's office, Swinden and Donny DePaiva had just grabbed hold of Cosmo, pulling something sharp and metal from his skeletal hands.

"No!" I roared. "Let him go!"

Hazlegrove emerged from his office, and Swinden said, "Caught him, sir. Coming for you. Had this in his hand." Swinden held up the metal object, a small piece of plating from one of the carts that had been sharpened to a point.

I slowed as I reached them. "Let him go—he's not thinking straight! He wouldn't have done it!"

Cosmo turned to look at me. "I would! I was gonna slit that monster's throat!"

Hazlegrove said, "You better talk some sense into your friend, Brawn. Otherwise there's going to be another grave out there before the day is out."

I crouched down in front of Cosmo. "Listen to me, man! This is not the way! All that stuff you said outside about not taking a life . . ."

"That was Keegan's belief, not mine!" Cosmo bared his teeth. "He has to die. He deserves to die!"

"Maybe, but what then? The warden will just bring some-one else in. Someone worse."

"Coward!" he spat. "That's what you are, Brawn. A cow-ard! You're so scared of them that you're *letting* them treat us like dirt!"

"Yeah, I'm scared! But not for *me*. Cosmo, they can't hurt me. But they can hurt you and everyone else. These people . . . They're not human." I looked at DePaiva and Swinden, then at Hazlegrove. "They're scum. And they *know* they're scum.

Swinden's a barely literate moron who in the outside world would have a hard time telling the moon from the sun. De-Paiva is the biggest—and laziest—brownnoser who ever lived. And Hazlegrove . . . he's just a weak-minded, evil, petty little man."

Hazlegrove said, "You mind your words, Brawn. You're not—"

"Shut *up!*" I turned back to Cosmo. "We will get out of this place, all of us. But it's better that we leave on our feet than in a box. So we have to stick together. You said it yourself. We'll need our strength to survive. Because above all, we have to be around to watch these men get the justice they deserve."

Cosmo looked down at his feet. "One day, Hazlegrove. One day it will happen. You'll get what's coming to you."

Hazlegrove said, "Take him away. Two weeks in the hot box."

I stood up. "No, you can't do that. He might not survive that long!"

Hazlegrove considered this. "Hmm . . . You're right. Better make certain, then. A *month* in the hot box."

"That's a death sentence! You might as well shoot me now!" Cosmo yelled.

"If you wish." Hazlegrove reached for his gun and pulled it from its holster.

I grabbed his hand, squeezing my fist around his just as he pulled the trigger.

The gun exploded, and Hazlegrove screamed. He staggered back with blood pumping from his charred, misshapen right hand.

CHAPTER 13

TWENTY-FOUR YEARS AGO

"YOU ARE TO BE our secret weapon, Brawn. Our last resort."

I was, finally, back in America, in a decommissioned military base somewhere in northern Texas. Still far from home, but at least it was the right continent.

Harmony Yuan's people had reconditioned a corner of an old aircraft hangar as my quarters. It wasn't that much different from the cell in Antarctica, but it had the illusion of freedom. And it *was* only an illusion: I was not allowed outside the hangar during the day, and at night I was supervised at all times.

Right now, Harmony was in my quarters talking me through a slide show of other superhumans. Most of the photos were blurred, and sometimes there was nothing but a sketch. In all, more than forty superhumans featured on Harmony's list.

"The rest of the team won't even know about you unless it's absolutely necessary. Now, some of these people we are certain we can trust. They—so far—have worked only for the good of humanity. We're aiming to recruit as many as possible. But there are *others* . . ."

The screen switched to a photo of the ugliest guy I'd ever seen. His skin was completely covered in red and yellow sores, like the world's worst case of acne. "This is Dioxin. He's a few years older than you. The sores on his skin constantly seep a viscous, poisonous acid. His strength and speed are maybe a little above average, but it's the acid you need to watch out for: It can burn through pretty much anything."

Another picture: a woman. Very good-looking, but stern. "Slaughter. We figure she's about twenty-one, but that's only a guess. We know nothing about her background. She can fly under her own power, and she's strong and *very* fast. And utterly ruthless. She's a killer, Brawn. Dioxin has also killed, but Slaughter actually enjoys it."

Another woman's face appeared. "Impervia. As far as we know, she has pretty much the same abilities as Slaughter, although she isn't a bloodthirsty killer. She hasn't yet done anything that puts her on one side of the law or the other, but we're watching her."

The screen changed again, this time showing nothing but a silhouette with a question mark. "This man is potentially one of the most powerful. A telekinetic we call Terrain, because that's what he can control. His ability allows him to move soil and rocks and sand in great quantities. If he put his mind to it, he could sink a continent, or create earthquakes or volcanoes. That's an incredibly potent ability in anybody's hands."

"But you don't know his name or what he looks like?" I asked.

"Not yet."

The next picture showed an extremely thin man with deep-set eyes and mottled gray and white skin. "This man's real name is Ferdinand Nikolai Cosby, known as Cosmo to his friends. Eighteen years old. American born of Russian descent. Like you, he was perfectly normal until he hit puberty. But unlike you, his change was more gradual."

"What powers does he have?"

"None, that we know of."

"Well, what's he done?"

Harmony raised an eyebrow. "Done?"

"If he's one of the bad guys, he must have done something bad, right?"

"So far, he's not done anything. He's on the list because he's a superhuman. And lastly . . ." Again the picture showed only a silhouette. "The shape-shifter. A photo of him would be useless. He can become anyone, and that makes him very hard to find, and potentially very dangerous. All that we know is that he calls himself Façade." Harmony walked over to the screen and tapped it with her forefinger. "He's one we're very eager to find."

"How come?"

"Because he'd be the ultimate spy."

"You really think you can build a team from these people?"

"We do. We have access to almost limitless resources, and we operate totally off the books. We don't cost the taxpayer anything."

For the first few weeks in Texas, Harmony's people thought it would be a good idea to train me. After all, I was still only fifteen and, in their opinion, just a kid. They figured that I ought to receive the same basic training as everyone else in the military.

That quickly proved to be a waste of time: I could already run much faster and for much longer than even the fittest of the instructors, and the weights were a joke to someone who could bench-press a school bus. I demolished the punching bag on my first go, and it was pointless teaching me how to use a gun when my fingers were too large to easily fit the trigger guard.

So Harmony decided that it would be more beneficial to train my mind instead. "It's time to hit the schoolbooks, Brawn. Six hours a day, six days a week," she told me. "English, math, history, geography, the works. You'd be in high school by now, tenth grade, so you've a lot of work ahead of you if you want to catch up."

"Who's going to teach me?"

"We selected an old friend of yours. You'll meet him this evening. Lessons begin tomorrow morning."

The old friend turned out to be Dr. Gordon Tremont, the man who'd taught me how to speak when I was in Antarctica.

In the three years since we'd last met, he'd lost some of the excess weight he used to carry around, and looked stronger and more confident. "Gethin Rao," he said with a broad smile as he entered my quarters. "They didn't tell me that *you* were to be my new pupil! I honestly never thought I'd see you again."

"How are you, Doc?"

"As well as can be expected, young man. How old are you now? Fourteen?"

"Fifteen."

He nodded at that. "Fifteen. Well, well. As they say, time flies like an arrow. And fruit flies like an apple."

"Er, *pardon?*"

"I'll leave that one with you." He sat down on the wooden chair opposite me. "I am now your teacher, so they tell me. Hmm. It's been a long time since I taught anyone of your age, but I'm sure that together we can muddle through. Tell me . . . Did you escape or did they release you?"

"I escaped. About a year after you left."

"A *year?* Dear Lord, what's wrong with these people? But you escaped, that's the key thing. Excellent. I do hope you caused a lot of damage along the way!"

I nodded. "Yep. And it took them another two years to find me."

"And now, here we are, together again." He looked around. "The décor has changed, at least that's something. And your door is open. But I suspect that your movements are still restricted, yes?"

"Well, yeah. But they tell me that's more for my *own* safety than anything else. I don't know how much Harmony's told you, but I'm being kept secret for now."

Dr. Tremont shrugged. "I'm sure they have their reasons. . . .

How's the food here? I recall that it wasn't up to much in Antarctica."

"It's a *lot* better. We even get pizza on Fridays."

"That's good to hear. Even the soldiers in Antarctica had to eat that slop. An operative in the computer room once told me that they had to wolf down their food before it froze."

I grinned. "I don't feel sorry for anyone who was there voluntarily." That triggered a thought that had never occurred to me before. "They *were* volunteers, right?"

"I believe so," the doctor said. "I could name a dozen computer experts who'd jump at the chance to work on cutting-edge microprocessor design, despite having to work in subzero temperatures." Then he added, "Computer processors work faster in the cold, you see."

"Why's that?"

I couldn't help noticing the flash of disappointment across his face. "Ah. You don't know anything about how computers work?"

"You mean, like, on the inside? Not a lot. In school we learned about binary numbers and that computers have got billions of teeny on-off switches inside them, and if a switch is off, that represents zero, and if it's on, it represents one." I shrugged. "That's about it."

"Pity. Computers are what it's all about, Gethin." He raised his eyes to the ceiling and pursed his lips as he thought. "How can I best put this? Computer processors are dumb. All they can really do is count and compare values. But they can do that extremely quickly. Say you want to crack an encrypted file but you don't know the password. All you know is that it's a six-digit number. You could start with all the zeros and work your way up. That's a million combinations, right? Let's say for the sake of argument that you have to go through all the combinations, and each one takes one second. A seven-digit password would take ten times as long, right?"

I nodded. "OK . . ."

"But how long does it take to crack a password that's *thirteen* characters long? Assuming that you have to check every combination."

I had to think about that. "If seven digits is ten seconds, then eight is a hundred, nine is a thousand seconds. . . . A thirteen-digit combination would take ten million seconds."

"Correct. If you'd given any other answer to that, I'd have abandoned this right now! So, ten million seconds is about one hundred and sixteen days. Fourteen digits would take ten times that long, about three-point-two years."

"Wow."

"Wow indeed. But our files here, for example, have *twenty-four*-digit passwords."

I did my best to run this through my head. *Fourteen is three-point-two years, so fifteen would be thirty-two years, sixteen would be three hundred and twenty. . . .* When I got to the end, I said, "That can't be right."

"What answer did you get?"

"Thirty-two trillion years."

The doctor grinned again. "It really messes with your mind, doesn't it?"

"But if you have lots of computers all working on it, they could divide up the numbers to check. You know, each one checks a different range of combinations."

"Ah!" the doctor said, grinning. "But suppose you have a password that's not twenty-four digits long, but *fifty*? Even with a million computers checking, the process would take so much time that the universe would come to an end long before you were finished. What you'd need is a computer that could check all the combinations at the same time."

"That's impossible," I said.

Dr. Tremont leaned forward, resting his elbows on his knees. "With current technology, yes, it's impossible. But not with quantum computing. Quantum theory—nothing to do with the superhuman who uses that name, by the way— basically tells us that all possibilities exist at once." He chewed on his lower lip for a moment. "It's hard to get your head around this, I know, but it's real. Think of it like this: What if an infinite number of universes exist parallel to ours? In each one there's the same computer attempting to decrypt the same file. If you can establish communication between each of those computers, and you assign them a specific code to check, then your answer comes back almost instantly."

This was really making me dizzy. "No . . . But *that's* impossible!"

"That's not actually how quantum computing works, but it's a handy way to visualize it. As for whether it's possible . . . A lot of people seem to think it's not only possible, but inevitable. Right now, there are more than a dozen companies and institutions in the USA trying to develop quantum processors, a hundred more throughout the rest of the world. If anyone *can* get quantum computing to work, the possibilities are endless. People talk about artificial intelligence as the ultimate goal of computer technology. Brawn, those people are thinking *small*. . . . Quantum computing would allow us to create something a lot more exciting: artificial omniscience."

"Omniscience," I said. "That's all-knowing, right?"

"Exactly. An omniscient computer would change the shape of human civilization forever. If you wanted to know the answer to even the most complex problem, you could just ask it and it would tell you." He snapped his fingers. "Just like *that*."

I said, "Wow . . . But wouldn't a truly omniscient computer know that you wanted to know the answer before you asked it?"

Tremont smiled and nodded. "Bingo! Gethin, I've been through many conversations like this with many other students, and you're the first one to make that deduction. Yes, whoever creates the first working quantum processor will instantly become the most powerful person in the world."

"You think that's what they were working on in Antarctica?"

"It's possible. It would certainly explain the large number of computers they had and the extreme cold of some of their labs. It's my guess that they intend to raid every other facility working on quantum processing. They'll use you as muscle to get in, then send in their hackers. . . . But that's a discussion for another day, I think. . . ." His knees cracked as he stood up, and then he stretched and yawned. "Look at that—dark outside already. They've set me up with an office on the far side of the base. It's got a bed, a hot plate, and a TV set. All the comforts of modern life."

I stood up too. "I'll walk back with you. I'm allowed out when it's dark. During the day there's the chance that I'd be spotted by airplanes passing overhead."

He walked ahead of me, moving quite slowly. "Very sensible. Can't have fresh photos of you appearing in the newspapers, can we? Not if you're supposed to be a secret."

I ducked my head as we passed through the hangar doors and out onto the concrete. It was still warm under my bare feet from a day of sunlight. The two soldiers posted at the doors fell into step behind us.

"True. Though if anyone *did* publish new photos, I suppose that they wouldn't be . . ." I stopped walking, and the soldiers almost crashed into me.

Dr. Tremont also stopped, and looked back at me. "Something the matter?"

"I'm not sure. . . . Doc, I always thought that commercial aircraft weren't *allowed* to fly over military bases. So why would Harmony tell me to stay out of sight?"

He looked puzzled for a moment. "But the base was officially decommissioned. I expect that the no-fly restrictions were lifted."

We resumed walking. "Yeah, I guess that makes sense."

"Things have changed, Gethin. I'm sure that Ms. Yuan and her people have only your best interests in mind."

"Ha!"

"You don't agree? You don't trust them?"

"She *says* everything's changed, but after the way they hunted me down? No, I don't trust them. I think they stopped trying to kill me only because I was costing them a fortune. Eight and a half billion dollars, she said. I can't believe it cost *that* much."

"Well, I'm sure that those two helicopters you destroyed weren't cheap," Dr. Tremont said. "It's not like damaging a car. Cars can be repaired, but I can't imagine anyone brave enough to get back into a helicopter that's already crashed!"

I stopped again, and turned to the two soldiers. "Guys, can you give us a minute?"

"We're sposta—" Technically they were disobeying orders by not sticking close to me, but I could tell from their expressions that they were just as scared of me as most people were.

"Just wait over there," I said, pointing back toward the hangar. "I'm not going anywhere."

We watched the soldiers walk away, and then the doctor asked, "What's bothering you, son?"

"It's the whole secrecy thing they've got going on. A huge base in Antarctica, this place here, everything else. I mean, they took you in the middle of the night, right? Blindfolded you so you didn't even know where you were going!"

"That's the way these sorts of people operate, Gethin. They can't trust anyone."

"Can I? Can *I* trust anyone?"

He smiled. "Well, you can trust me."

"Yeah . . . Y'see, Doc, that's what's bugging me. How did you know that we were in Antarctica?"

"Surely you don't suspect me, do you? Gethin, I'm one of

the world's foremost experts in computer technology. I recognized some of the hardware they were using. It was bespoke stuff—handmade, not off the shelf. When I was brought home, I hacked into the manufacturer's files. I found out who paid for it—turned out to be a dummy company—but tracking the hardware itself was rather simple."

I knelt down, and sat back on my heels so that we were almost eye to eye. "How did you know about the helicopters?"

"Gethin, really! You're becoming paranoid!"

"But if she told you about that, why were you so surprised to see me? Your story doesn't add up, Doctor." I leaned closer. "Who are you?"

"You *know* who I am!"

"It's all fake, isn't it? You're working for them, and you have been all along. In Venezuela they discovered that they couldn't kill me, so instead they decided to recruit me. They made up a bunch of lies to get me on their side, and they brought you in because they figured I'd trust you."

Dr. Tremont ran his right hand over his chin as he stared at me. "You've got it all wrong. I swear, I do *not* work for them."

I shook my head. "I don't believe you. It's just another trick."

"You're big, and strong, and fast, Gethin. Powerful enough to kill everyone on this base. But before you go flying off the handle, you have to ask yourself one very important question, OK?"

"What's that?"

"You must ask yourself if you're sure—if you're absolutely

certain—that you are fast enough and strong enough to find and rescue your parents before we kill them."

He turned around, and as he was walking away, he called over his shoulder, "But there is one thing I wasn't lying about, Brawn. I *don't* work for them. They work for me."

CHAPTER 14

I DIDN'T SLEEP THAT NIGHT. I rarely slept much anyway, but that night I lay on the ground just outside the hangar doors and looked up at the stars.

I couldn't think how to get out of the situation. There was no way to know whether Tremont's people had my parents held prisoner somewhere, or if they were just watching them. Whatever the case there didn't seem to be anything I could do to help them.

Harmony came by once, at about two in the morning. "You need your sleep. Lessons start in a few hours."

Without looking at her, I asked, "Is that an order? Are you going to murder my folks if I don't go to bed?"

She didn't respond, and soon the echoing click of her heels on the concrete faded away.

At dawn the guards' shift came to an end, and fresh ones took their place. "Inside," I was told. "You know the rules."

"Make me."

Harmony turned up shortly afterward. "Brawn, if you insist on behaving like this, it's not going to end well."

I yawned and rolled onto my side, my back to her.

She walked around to face me again. "You don't understand what's happening here. You think you do, but you're wrong. The human race is on the edge of a precipice, looking down into oblivion. Two centuries ago there were a billion people on the planet. After one hundred years it had almost doubled. Since then, it's more than tripled to six billion. What do you think it will be like in *another* hundred years? Do you know how to calculate exponential growth?"

"Skip ahead to the bit that you think is going to make me care."

"If the population doubles in the first century and then triples in the next, the pattern suggests that in the following hundred years it will quadruple. That's twenty-four billion people, Brawn. A hundred years after that, and it'll quintuple: one hundred and twenty billion. Another hundred years, we're looking at three quarters of a trillion people. Do you want me to continue?"

"I didn't want you to start."

"The Earth is already overpopulated. We're consuming resources faster than the planet can replenish them. Ninety-nine percent of the world's wealth is controlled by less than one percent of the population. Half the world is starving, and what's the reaction from those of us in the lucky half? We hold rock concerts and telethons to raise enough money to feed the hungry children of the third world. We give them a chance to live, to grow up, and have children of their own. We like to think we're saving them from famine, when what we're really doing is breeding new generations of starving people."

I sat up. *She can't be serious*, I said to myself. *This has to be just a ruse to get me on their side again.* "Do you really believe that?"

"Whether I believe it is not important. What is important is that most people are content to sit back and watch the human race suffocate itself, or just pretend that it's not happening. But some of us are in a position to make things better. What's the solution, Brawn? If you were in charge, what would you do?"

"I don't have to play this game."

"Just humor me. What would you do to reduce the rate of population growth without culling the poor?"

I shrugged. "I don't know. Take the money away from the rich and use it to educate the poor. Teach them how to work the land so that they don't have to rely on handouts."

"But suppose the land's a desert and nothing can grow. What then?"

"Then you bring water to the desert. Most of the planet's surface is covered in water, so there's plenty to go around."

"OK. Suppose you can do that, that you have a way to desalinate the seawater and irrigate the deserts, but the governments of those starving countries won't allow outside interference on that scale. What then?"

"Then you *make* them do it." I knew that I was being manipulated again, but I couldn't help being drawn into the conversation.

"And if they resist? If they'd rather fight than lose their control? What do we do then? Go in anyway and fight them if we have to? Break international laws?"

"If we have to, yes! Because people are more important than governments."

"Well, is there another way? Think, Brawn."

"You want me to say that people like me should take control."

"Shouldn't you?"

"No. Just being stronger than other people doesn't make me better than they are."

"But if you can do something to help others, and you don't, what does that make you? Selfish? Cowardly? Detached?" She raised an eyebrow. "Inhuman?"

"What help would *I* be? Being able to lift several tons isn't going to help irrigate the deserts!"

"Not directly, no. But you're powerful enough to capture Terrain, and *he* could do it quite easily."

Tremont's people were trying to guarantee the survival of the human race. Or so they wanted me to believe. But I had to ask myself why they hadn't mentioned this when they'd caught me three years earlier.

Though I was sure that they were lying, I had no choice but to play along. These people had tried to kill me, and they'd had no qualms about putting their own soldiers into the line of fire: I had no doubt that they *would* kill my parents if I disobeyed them.

Dr. Tremont did not show up for lessons that first day, or any other. Instead, a box of twenty textbooks was delivered, all of my other books were removed, and I was told that my TV set would be operational for only a couple of hours in the evenings.

It was a pretty effective way to get me to study: I didn't have anything else to do.

A month after Dr. Tremont revealed his true colors, I was woken shortly before midnight by the sound of powerful rumbling engines outside the hangar, and I opened my eyes to see Harmony standing at the door to my quarters. "You're going into battle. You leave in five minutes."

The tone in her voice told me that this was not a good time to complain or delay. I quickly dressed in the combat gear that had been specially made for me: fireproof black shorts and T-shirt, and thick leather gloves, but no boots— they hadn't yet found anyone able to make boots strong enough or large enough for me. There was also a leather helmet and a pair of goggles, but the helmet's only purpose was to house a two-way radio transceiver, and the goggles, I was pretty sure, were included as part of the outfit only so my colorless eyes wouldn't freak everyone out.

With the shorts, T-shirt, gloves, leather helmet, and goggles in place I looked like a guy from before the First World War who couldn't make up his mind whether to go swimming or fly his biplane.

Outside the hangar was a Lockheed Hercules, its rear ramp

already down, waiting for me. "Get in and hold on," Harmony said as I passed her. "It's going to be a fast and turbulent ride."

"Where are we going?"

"Not we. Just you. You're going three hundred and sixty miles due west. I'll explain the rest when you're closer to your destination."

I nodded. "All right."

"Brawn . . . Don't mess this up. And don't even *think* about trying to double-cross us."

I crawled into the back of the Hercules and sat down: There wasn't enough room for me to stand. I'd expected a bunch of soldiers there too, but there was just me. The aircraft was taxiing toward the old cracked-concrete runway even before its massive ramp had risen.

The plane juddered along the runway for a while, then suddenly lurched into the air, and I skidded on my butt toward the ramp before I grabbed hold of the straps fixed to the inside of the hull.

Harmony's voice came through the transceiver. "Brawn, do you read me?"

"Like a book."

"The correct response is 'Loud and clear.'"

"Loud and clear, then. But don't call me Brawn. I want a new code name. A proper superhero name."

"What do you suggest?"

"I dunno. . . ." I looked around the plane to see if there was anything that might inspire me. "How about Hercules?"

"Fine. Hercules it is. Your destination is fifty miles west of

Albuquerque, New Mexico. Flying time is a little under one hour. Sit tight and try not to break anything."

Harmony refused to tell me what I'd be up against—"for reasons of security"—so there was nothing for me to do on the plane but sit in the dark and worry.

All too soon Harmony was on the radio again. "Look alive, Brawn. Touchdown in ten minutes."

"It's Hercules, not Brawn. So what am I doing here?"

"U.S. military forces are in a standoff against a man called Norman Misseldine, fifty-eight years old. Misseldine is the leader of a radical survivalist group that claims to be dedicated to bringing about a new world order. There are a couple dozen groups like that scattered throughout the U.S., and normally they're of little concern. They content themselves with fortifying their defenses and broadcasting their anti-establishment rants, but two days ago Misseldine issued a direct and credible threat against the government."

"How credible?" I asked.

"He contacted the authorities in Charleston, South Carolina, and directed their attention to the sea one mile southeast of Sullivan's Island. At the predicted time, a new, small island rose out of the sea. It remained in place for only two minutes, but that was long enough for Misseldine's point to be made. If his demands aren't met, his next target will be Washington, D.C."

"Well, how do they know that the island wasn't just some freak occurrence?"

"Because it happened exactly when and where Misseldine

predicted, and it was perfectly circular. That's not likely to ⸜
happen in nature. We believe that Misseldine hired Terrain to
create—and then destroy—the island."

"So I'm going up against another superhuman?"

"Probably not—no one has entered or left Misseldine's fortress in months, and everything we know about Terrain suggests that he can't trigger seismic activity from a distance—he
has to be present for it to work. The military has cut off all
communication from Misseldine's base so he won't be able to
contact Terrain for help."

"OK, so where do I come in?"

"The army hasn't yet been able to breach Misseldine's defenses, so Dr. Tremont has offered them our help. We've told
them we can get in and capture Misseldine without the loss of
a single life."

The pilot's voice boomed out of a loudspeaker. "Four
minutes."

"OK, then. How do we do this?"

The plane had set me down a mile from the fortress, where I
was picked up by a large flatbed truck driven by a U.S. Army
colonel who didn't seem at all surprised that I was thirteen feet
tall and blue. "In the back," he said. "An' hold tight. I drive fast."

As I climbed in, he popped open the window at the back of
the cab. "Dunno what your people told you, kid," he bellowed
over his shoulder as the jeep bounced and careened over the
ground, "but word's come down the line that you're gonna be
able to get in without causing any casualties along the way."

He gave me a quick glance. "Me, I think that's a buncha horse hockey, but I just do what I'm told."

A minute later I saw lights ahead in the darkness. Driving on the wrong side of the road, we overtook a pair of jeeps, three armored personnel carriers, and a couple dozen soldiers on foot.

"Misseldine's base is a fortress. Literally. Two stories above ground, reinforced walls two feet thick." He looked back at me again. "You think you can get through that?"

"Maybe."

"Maybe?" He was still looking at me. "*Maybe?* What kinda talk is that? How many times you been deployed, son?"

"This is my first time."

The colonel let out a very exaggerated sigh, and finally returned his attention to the road. "Wonderful. The fortress's got strong bars on all the windows, and the walls have got those little slots in them here and there. Y'know, like in an old castle? So Misseldine's goons can shoot out through them. You bulletproof?"

"Sort of."

"Sort of, he says. 'Cause that's *exactly* what we need. We coulda taken the place hours ago. But no, we hadda wait for you. Kid, you don't even know your own specifications, do ya?"

"That's one way of looking at it," I said. "Another way of looking at it is to say that I haven't yet found my limitations."

The colonel laughed. "*That's* more like it. Now, lissen up. The fortress is surrounded by a wall. It's about eighteen feet high an' topped with coils of razor wire. Outside that they got a forty-yard-wide ring of thornbushes. You gotta get through the bushes first, son. There's a narrow road through them leading to the gate, but that's the most heavily guarded."

"Bushes don't seem like the best way to defend—"

"You ain't seen anything like this kinda bush before, kid! It's called Trifoliate Orange an' it grows fast an' it's very dense. I mean, *really* dense. You could near walk on it, if it wasn't covered in razor-sharp five-inch-long thorns. A man gets stuck on that, it's like skydiving into a stiletto factory!" After a second, he added, "That's stilettos as in daggers, not as in shoes."

I saw what he meant when the jeep shuddered to a halt: Portable spotlights blazed out toward the fortress, clearly showing the sprawl of bushes. Off to the side eight or nine soldiers, three jeeps, and another armored personnel carrier were trapped in the bushes as other soldiers tentatively attempted to cut them free.

I tried not to notice that almost all of the other soldiers were watching me as they slowly backed away.

The colonel said, "So how are you planning to do this, son?"

"I have no idea."

He sneered. "Oh, in the name of great lumpy gravy! You really *are* a rookie! Kid, I was told to wait for backup. That's you. Just get in there and capture Misseldine without anyone getting killed. I want this operation done and dusted without having to break the seals on the body bags." He looked me up and down. Mostly up. "Yer strong as ya look, right?"

"I'm strong."

"So you'll probably live." He gestured toward the fortress. "Away you go, then."

"Kill the lights," I said.

"What's that?"

"The lights. I don't want them to see me coming."

"We already shot out all their cameras, but they've got night-vision glasses and infrared scopes. They'll see you anyway."

"All right . . ." I began to walk forward, then spotted another vehicle and turned back to the colonel. "Is that what I think it is?"

"Sure is."

"Nice. I'll go in and check the place out. When I give the word . . ."

He nodded. "Good luck to ya, son. Go in hard an' fast, that's my advice."

There were no signs of life in the fortress, no lights in the windows. When I reached the bushes, I stopped and carefully examined the thorns. They were almost as long as my fingers and very strong, but their points splintered against my skin. The bushes came up to my waist so I could easily see where I was going.

I resumed walking, pushing myself through the dense tangle of tough branches as countless thorns scraped uselessly against me. They snagged the material of my shorts, but it was strong stuff and resisted well.

Harmony's voice came over the radio. "Good work, Brawn. Keep—"

"Hercules," I corrected her. I was getting to like the name more and more.

"We can talk about that later. Ignore what the colonel said—keep the pace down. Slow and steady, make sure they know you're coming. That way they're less likely to start shooting in panic."

The bushes were thicker and taller as I neared the wall, and I could hear muffled voices from inside the fortress.

The wall was composed of large, crudely cut stone blocks, easy enough for anyone to climb, but the razor wire strung along the top was off-putting, even to me. I didn't think it would do me much damage, but I decided not to take the chance: It looked a lot tougher and sharper than the thorns.

So instead I drew back my right fist and slammed it into the wall with all my strength.

That was the first time I'd not held back when using my fists, so I was expecting to shatter a block or two.

I *wasn't* expecting to find that the wall was reinforced with steel girders all along the inside.

And I certainly wasn't expecting my fist to do more than crack a few blocks: It pulverized one of the blocks and hit a girder square-on, smashing it free of its concrete foundation and causing a thirty-foot-wide section of the wall to topple inward, leaving the dense coils of razor wire to dangle ineffectually overhead.

As the dust settled, I heard Harmony's voice whisper over the radio, "Good *Lord* . . . !"

I walked through, stepping over the broken stone blocks. And then gunfire erupted from within the fortress.

I snatched up one of the girders and raced forward: I knew I could survive being shot, but it still stung like crazy.

Bullets plowed into the ground all around me. One clipped my left leg, another two sparked off the girder.

Ahead was a set of large double doors, big enough for me to pass through without having to crouch too much.

But if there was one thing I had learned from watching action movies, it's that when you're storming your enemy's base, you don't go in through the main door. . . . To the left of the door was a window with thick metal bars fixed on both the outside and the inside.

I skidded to a stop next to the window, ducked down beneath it, grabbed hold of the bars, and pulled, tearing them right out of the wall and shattering the glass in the process.

There was a roar of rapid gunfire from inside, and a stream of bullets passed over my head. Then I slammed the girder against the inside bars, knocking them back into the room.

The gunfire stopped, replaced by a series of short, sharp clicks: The gun was empty.

I heard heavy, nervous breathing, shuffled footsteps, the rustle of thick robes. It was easy to picture the shooter desperately trying to change the magazine in his gun with sweat-slicked hands.

I tossed the girder aside and grabbed hold of the window frame, pulling myself up and in with one movement, landing in a crouch right in front of two terrified young men. They were wearing dark gray military fatigues. Their heads were shaved, and they wore beards with no mustaches, which is always weird. I don't care if Abraham Lincoln did it, it's still creepy.

I plucked the machine guns from their trembling hands and threw them out through the window. "Where can I find your boss? Misseldine or whatever his name is."

The one on the left darted for the door, but he was much too slow. I grabbed his arm and pulled him back, then took hold of his companion. I pulled them close so that my head was almost touching theirs, and snarled, "Stay here. Got it?"

They nodded dumbly, and I shoved them over to the corner farthest from the door.

The door was going to be tricky: It was built for average-sized people. There didn't seem to be a way for me to pass through with any dignity.

I was saved from having to worry about it by a burst of gunfire from the corridor and a line of bullet holes instantly puncturing the door. I decided to go through the wall instead.

One kick was all it took and the corridor was a mess of plaster dust and splinters.

Three more guys were waiting, shooting at me. Bullets raked across my chest, and before I could reach the men, they turned and ran.

The corridor was so narrow that my shoulders were brushing pictures off the wall as I raced after them, half running, half crouched. They darted through another door at the end of the corridor and slammed it shut behind them.

I launched myself at the door, crashed through and rolled to my feet, and saw that I was now in a large gymnasium with thirty men and women all aiming their guns at me: It was a trap.

But I didn't think it was a very *good* trap, because rather than instantly opening fire, they all just stared at me in shock.

I took a deep breath and bellowed, *"Drop your weapons!"*

They threw their guns to the floor and stepped back.

"Misseldine—where is he?"

One of the men pointed a trembling finger at a door on the far side of the gymnasium.

"All of you—on the ground. Facedown, hands on your heads! *Now!*" I strode toward the door. "Stay put and stay quiet!"

One hard kick took the door off its hinges—

—and suddenly the floor beneath my feet collapsed.

I plummeted straight down and landed hard, shoulder-first on packed dirt. I looked up to see that I was in a large square pit, and twenty yards above, the men and women gathered around to peer at me.

Then some of the crowd parted, and an older man wearing a white hooded robe was looking down. "The blue giant. I read about you last year. So you're working for the U.S. military now?"

I stood up and looked at the walls. Like the floor, they were made of packed dirt. I figured it wouldn't be hard to punch a few handholds and then climb up. There were already some holes close to the top of the pit.

"I'm Norman Misseldine," the man said. "We figured they'd send in a specialist, and had a feeling it might be a superhuman. Lucky *our* specialist is also a superhuman." He gave a signal to one of his acolytes, who saluted before darting away.

From all around me came the sound of machinery, powerful enough that the walls of the pit started to tremble.

Misseldine shouted over the noise: "Fella called Terrain. Charged me twenty thousand dollars to create that island, but it was worth every penny. And for free, he made that pit for us. Made it happen just like *that*." He snapped his fingers. "The dirt just flowed away like water in the sink when you pull out the plug. And then he told us how to make *this* stuff."

A liquid started to spill out of the series of holes near the top of the pit. It was thick and gray and glistening. With a loud *thump* the first stream of the liquid splattered onto the floor of the pit. It piled up a little before spreading out. The second and third streams hit, and within seconds I was up to my ankles in the viscous fluid.

"Try fighting your way out of that!" Misseldine shouted down to me. "The pit's twenty yards deep, five yards across. That's five hundred cubic yards of concrete. Weighs about one and a half million pounds."

"You think concrete's gonna stop me?" I yelled up at Misseldine.

"See, it's not *just* concrete. It's sand, cement, and gravel, but instead of water, it's mixed with a huge quantity of *Caulobacter crescentus*. You know what that is?"

"Never heard of it."

He smiled. "It's a bacterium. Pretty common stuff, but it produces a natural adhesive that's three times as effective as the strongest superglue. I figure you've got three, maybe four minutes before it sets."

I had to admit, that one *was* a good trap.

CHAPTER 15
THE MINE

THE HOT BOX WAS a small windowless shed made of black-painted sheets of corrugated iron. The sheets were overlapped to eliminate any gaps that might allow a breeze to blow through. Instead, a thin slot in the door, about a foot above the ground, was the only form of ventilation.

The hot box was outside the huge dome that covered the mine, on the south side to catch more of the sun. Even in mild weather the heat inside the box was overwhelming before noon, and it continued to rise throughout the day.

In the depth of winter the name became ironic: It was so cold inside the box that anyone unfortunate enough to be locked inside it had to keep his eyes closed to prevent them from freezing over.

The box was large enough to accommodate six people

standing up, or one blue giant sitting with his knees pulled up to his chest.

I was ordered into the box after the incident in which Hazlegrove's right hand was damaged. Food and water were delivered once a day, in the hottest part of the afternoon, and the guards made sure that I didn't have nearly enough and that the food was always laced with strong spices to make things even more uncomfortable for me.

I could have smashed my way out of the box at any time, but I'd been warned that if I tried anything, the other prisoners would suffer.

DePaiva told me that I should consider myself lucky. Hazlegrove had wanted to kill me for what had happened, but the warden had intervened: I was more useful alive than dead. I was also fairly certain that they didn't know *how* to kill me.

But at least Cosmo was still free. That was the one thought that kept me sane for the four weeks I was locked in the box. If anyone else had been in my place, Hazlegrove would have left him to rot, but with two new shafts being opened, they needed my strength, so I knew I'd be freed eventually.

When my time was up, Hazlegrove himself was waiting for me. His hand had been repaired, but by the looks of things the surgeon had been using a knife and fork. He was missing part of his index finger from just above where the nail should have been, the rest of his fingers were swollen and misshapen, and the skin halfway to his elbow was covered with thick red scars.

As I crawled, blinking, into the sunlight, my arms trembling, my whole body slick with sweat, Hazlegrove said, "You did this to me!"

I didn't have the strength to respond.

"You listening to me, you freak? You nearly cost me my hand!"

I briefly looked at him, then put one hand on the roof of the hot box to push myself up to my feet.

"You think you had it bad before, Brawn? That was nothing! *Nothing!*" he spat. "I'm going to make your life a living hell!"

All I could say was "Why?"

"Why? *Why?* Because you ruined my hand! I can barely even hold a pen now!"

"You pulled the trigger. It wouldn't have happened if you hadn't been trying to shoot Cosmo."

His lips curled in disgust. "Get inside. Hope you got some sleep in the box, because your next shift starts in an hour. If you miss the start of your shift, or if I think you're not working hard enough, I'm going to pick another worker at random and execute them." He leaned closer. "You can't beat the system, Brawn. But the system sure can beat you." Then he raised his ruined hand. "Remember this. Every time you think I'm pushing everyone too hard, you remember what you did. My son is only a year old and he's completely freaked out about it. My own son, and he runs crying to his mother whenever he sees me. That's what you did to me."

That came as a surprise. I'd had no idea that Hazlegrove was even married, let alone had a child. I couldn't imagine any woman being foolish or desperate enough for a husband to choose a monster like him.

But then maybe he was the sort of guy who didn't take his work home with him. Maybe at home he was the kindest husband, the most devoted father, a loyal and generous friend.

Even if he's all that, and more, I said to myself, *that doesn't excuse the way he treats us. It actually makes it worse.*

I knew from my own experiences and from the way others had reacted to me that there are very few people who are truly evil. But there sure are an awful lot of jerks.

I still had hope that Hazlegrove was merely one of the latter. As we walked back to the dome's entrance, I asked, "Mr. Hazlegrove, what would make you happy?"

"What?"

"If we were all dead, would that make you happy?"

He didn't respond.

"I don't think it would, because the mine would then either shut down, or the warden would be forced to get real miners in and pay for them. He'd blame you for that."

"What's the matter with you? Did you lose your mind in the hot box?"

"No, I didn't lose my mind. But I gained some perspective. We will work harder and more efficiently if we receive better treatment. We'll give you less trouble and make your life easier. Everyone wins. It really is that simple."

"The only thing simple around here is you."

"Just think about it, that's all I ask." I smiled. "We don't have to like each other to work well together."

•   •   •

My words to Hazlegrove must have had some effect, because a few days later he called me, Cosmo, and three others to his office. "I'm sick of looking at all you freaks every day, coming to me whining about your dumb problems, so things are going to change. I'm dividing the workforce into five teams. Each one of you will lead a team. That means your people come to you, you sort out their problems, and you come to me only when it's absolutely necessary. It also means that you're responsible for what happens to them, and for what they get up to. You understand me? Brawn?"

"We understand. You're making us trustees."

"Call yourself whatever you like. You can be 'Champions of the Oppressed' if that makes you feel better about it. Just do your job."

"What about rations?" Cosmo asked.

Hazlegrove gestured to his underling, Swinden. "*He'll* talk to you about that. Now get out of my sight."

Swinden followed us back out to the mine, then beckoned us to follow him away from the louder machinery so that he could more easily make himself heard. "From now on, rations will be tied to the yield. The more ore your team extracts, the more food you get to divide between them. Same goes for all the other privileges."

One of the other new trustees, Emily Stanhope—the widow of the supervillain Necroman—asked, "Why us?"

"Because you're the best of a bad bunch," Swinden said. "The other inmates look up to you. You all are the toughest, or the smartest, or the prettiest. Whatever works for you." Then

he glanced at me. "Though maybe not the prettiest." Then at
Cosmo. "Definitely not the toughest."

"Yeah, very funny," Cosmo said.

Swinden laughed and walked away.

Emily watched him go as she spoke to the rest of us. "OK.
The five of us will need to work together. Make sure we meet
at least once a week. There'll be rivalry between our groups,
but we can't let it get in . . . the way . . . of . . ." She stopped.
"He's gone."

We all looked at one another for a moment, and then Ashley Roesler—formerly a political correspondent for a North
Korean media service—broke the silence. "Is it my birthday or
something? Am I dreaming this?"

"Champions of the Oppressed," I said. "I like that." I
looked at Roman Laberis, one of the newer inmates. "What do
you think?"

"I think Hazlegrove is even lazier than before. Now we
have to do all his work for him."

"Roman, you're missing the big picture," Cosmo said.
"We've never had a reason to come together before, and now
we've not only got a reason, but our meetings will actually be
encouraged. What we have here is brains, experience, strength,
and the ability to foster loyalty among the workforce. Hazlegrove has just put together the best escape committee this
prison has ever seen."

CHAPTER 16

TWENTY-FOUR YEARS AGO

IF THE BACTERIA-BASED adhesive in the concrete had been a type that set faster, I would have escaped the pit easier: I'd have just kept on top of it as it poured into the pit. But Misseldine had chosen his glue carefully. The heavy mixture clung to my skin, weighing me down, making me too heavy to jump. I tried to climb up the walls, but the dirt crumbled away in my hands.

Within a minute the concrete was up to my waist.

"It's clear they chose you for your size and strength," Misseldine shouted down. "If you'd had any intelligence, you'd have destroyed enough of the Trifoliate Orange to allow your friends to get through."

Quietly, I said, "Harmony, can you hear me?"

"Just about."

"I'm trapped. I—"

She interrupted me. "I heard. And I can see it too. There's a camera in your goggles. Can you see a way out?"

"No." The concrete was creeping up my chest. Already I could feel its great weight pressing against me from all sides. "Getting harder to breathe!" I had my arms above my head— I knew that if I let them get dragged down into the mixture, then moving them would be close to impossible.

"Stay calm, Brawn. Fill your lungs, then take rapid, shallow breaths. Don't expel all your air at once."

"The colonel who picked me up from the plane . . . Tell him to go ahead."

"Go ahead and do *what?*"

"He knows." I formed the fingers of my right hand into a point, then pushed my hand deep into the packed dirt of the wall. I did the same with my left hand, forcing it through the dirt a couple of inches away from my right. Then, keeping my arms straight and using all of my strength, I pulled my hands apart.

A mini-avalanche of soil and stones collapsed down on top of me, but I kept going. Pushing my hands into the dirt, pulling them apart.

More and more dirt spilled over me, and I was thankful for the goggles keeping it out of my eyes.

The spill of concrete competed with the collapsing wall of dirt, but I was digging faster than the concrete was being poured.

The soil covered my head, and still I kept going. I wasn't making much forward progress, but that wasn't the idea.

Then I could no longer move my feet: The gray mixture

was setting from the ground up. My knees locked next, then my waist. The concrete set around my chest, and I could no longer breathe. Not that I'd have wanted to, because I would have been breathing in dirt.

The soil pressed down on me, but better the soil than Terrain's concrete-and-bacteria mixture.

Harmony kept me informed as I waited. "It's working, Brawn. The colonel's men sprayed a large section of the bushes with the kerosene. It's burning fast. They'll have more than enough room to maneuver now. If you can—"

Then her voice was cut off, but I had no way of knowing whether that was because the signal couldn't get through or because the weight of the concrete and soil had crushed the electronics wired into my leather helmet.

By now the bacteria-concrete mixture had completely solidified. I was still able to move my arms through the soil. If I hadn't knocked all that dirt down on top of myself, I'd have been totally immobilized by the mixture. But I was afraid I'd left it too late. I could feel my lungs burning, felt my head growing light through lack of oxygen.

I jerked my arms down on either side of me, slamming my elbows hard into the concrete. White-hot pain juddered up my arms, and if I hadn't been locked into an upright position, I might have fainted.

I slammed my elbows down again and again.

I don't know how many times I did it. It could have been a dozen, two dozen . . . a hundred times. But eventually the concrete cracked.

With some difficulty I forced my hands into the cracks and pulled. There was no movement at all on my left, but on my right a large chunk of the concrete broke free. Then another, then the section enclosing my chest shattered, and it was all I could do to remain calm and not suck in a deep breath.

I was able to turn to the right a little, enough to allow me to use both hands to pummel the concrete.

When enough had been smashed away, I was able to plant both hands on it, palms down, and push.

With a loud, trembling *crack* the concrete around my legs crumbled, and I was free.

Moving blind, I used my legs to push off against the half-shattered concrete, forcing myself deeper into the soil beneath the gymnasium.

I was moving at a painfully slow speed, swimming up through the dirt, but at least I was moving.

After what felt like forever, my outstretched hands collided with something solid and unyielding. I quickly probed it with my fingers, but couldn't find an edge. No way past.

And then, in the oxygen-starved haze of my brain, I realized that it was the underside of the gymnasium floor.

I pulled back my right fist and punched upward. A second punch and I felt something splinter, but I couldn't tell whether it was the floor or my knuckles.

On the third punch my hand burst through.

I grabbed the edge and pulled, felt the floor brush the top of my head. Two more punches, left and right at the same time, and the floor above me shattered, upward and out, and the blackness beyond my goggles suddenly turned to blinding light.

I heard a voice say, "It's him!" and then a small hand was grabbing mine. In seconds, more hands were on me, taking my arms, pulling me up.

They weren't being nearly as much help as they thought they were, but that wasn't the point.

I collapsed onto the ground, head down, coughing and gasping, filling my lungs over and over with air that tasted sweeter than honey.

"Everyone back, give 'im space!" The colonel crouched down next to me. "Tough day at work, son?"

I coughed. "I've had better."

"Well, we got 'em. Every one. And no fatalities on their side or ours. Misseldine's already on his way to the nearest lockup, and we got some of those hostage-negotiator fellas coming in to talk some sense into his followers."

Slowly, with bursts of pain flaring through every muscle and every joint, I sat up.

The colonel was looking up at me. "Don't feel bad, son. That was a good idea about burning down the bushes. So yer mission ain't a *total* failure."

I pointed down at the hole through which I'd emerged. "Failure? Do you have *any* idea what I've just been through? I had to—"

He raised a hand to cut me off. "Listen, kid, I been in the forces fer thirty years. There's nothing ya can tell me that I ain't heard before. Yer *alive*, ain't ya?" He slapped me on the arm. "Whatever doesn't kill ya makes ya stronger."

· · ·

The following afternoon I was lying on my bed reading when I received a visit from Harmony and Dr. Tremont. It was the first time I'd seen the doctor since I'd discovered that he was controlling the whole operation.

"That was almost a disaster," Tremont said. "They could have killed you."

Harmony said, "Norman Misseldine is talking about bringing charges against you. For trespassing, destruction of property, endangering the lives of his followers."

I threw my history textbook aside. "But you told me to go in!"

"I know. I'm just making a point."

"Which is?"

Tremont said, "Misseldine is smarter than you are, Brawn. He won't be the only one. You have to do better. A *lot* better."

Harmony nodded at that. "We're taking away your TV set. You're going to have to start *really* studying. We'll be setting tests that you had better pass. From now on, you're on basic food. Pizza is for winners. The better you do in the field, the more privileges you'll receive."

I jumped to my feet. "This is totally unfair!"

"Wrong," Tremont said. "It's perfectly reasonable." He reached into his jacket pocket and pulled out a sheet of paper. "Your schedule."

I snatched it out of his hand. According to the schedule I would be getting up at six every morning. Exercise for one hour, then I was allowed fifteen minutes to shower and eat breakfast. This was followed by studying until noon. I had a half-hour lunch break, then more studying until five. I was sure I could handle the basic math, English, history, and geography, but that was just the morning session: The afternoon session covered espionage, military history, world politics, and basic computer skills.

I stopped reading there, and looked up. "I'm not doing all this."

"Yes, you are," Harmony said. "If you refuse, we'll take away your bed. See how you like sleeping on the concrete floor for a few weeks. Brawn, you *have* to catch up. You're way behind everyone else your age."

"And whose fault is that? Yours! You're the ones who locked me away in the Antarctic for a *year!*"

Dr. Tremont shook his head. "Don't blame others for your mistakes and failures, Brawn. That's just pathetic. It's childish."

I knew I was being manipulated again, but I still couldn't quite see how. If you looked at it from their point of view, everything they said almost made sense. Almost.

I had the feeling that no matter what path I chose, it would end up being exactly what they wanted me to do.

"Don't call me Brawn. I have a real name, you know. And if you want to give me a code name, I want it to be Hercules."

"That's not going to happen," Harmony said. "We've discussed it, and the name doesn't track well. Hercules was a demigod, the son of Zeus and Alcmena. He was manipulated by the goddess Hera into killing his wife and children. That's not the sort of image we want to present when we go public.

We feel that the name Brawn works much better. It's simple, it's a word most people already know, and it has no religious or mythological connections. We've been thinking—"

"I've been thinking *too*," I said. "I'm leaving."

Tremont tutted. "That would be unwise. There would be repercussions."

"Right. You'll kill my parents."

"You don't want that to happen, do you?"

I sighed. "No, I don't. But here's something for *you* to think about. If anything happens to my folks, I'll know who to blame."

The silence stretched out as they glared at me.

"What exactly do you mean by that?" Harmony asked.

"What do you think it means? You've got them under surveillance. That's good. You can make sure that no harm comes to them, because your lives depend on their safety."

Tremont took a step closer. "You are actually *threatening* us? Are you insane as well as stupid? Brawn, we control the entire—"

I grabbed hold of his arms and lifted him straight up. "Go on. I'm listening."

"Put me down!"

"Why? Give me a reason I shouldn't just squeeze my hands together and crush you like an empty soda can."

He choked out the words, "Your . . . parents . . ."

"No, you're not getting this, Doctor. If you kill them, there's nothing to stop me from destroying your entire operation, starting with you. You gotta stop thinking of my ma and pa as leverage against me. Think of them as my conscience. They wouldn't want me to tear your head from your shoulders. I can do that. It really wouldn't take much effort." I opened my hands and let him drop to the floor. "How do you like that, huh? Not so much fun being on the other side of a threat, is it?"

As Harmony helped the doctor to his feet, he said, "You wouldn't do it. You're not a killer."

"How do you know? Just because I never *have* killed, that doesn't mean I never will. But maybe you're right. Maybe I wouldn't kill you. But I could very easily *ruin* you. I could go to the newspapers and TV stations, tell them everything you've done. I could explain to them that you spent eight and a half billion dollars of the taxpayers' money tracking down an escaped prisoner who was only thirteen years old at the time."

They jumped aside as I strode toward the oversized door. "Find someone else to do your dirty work for you. I'm leaving. If anything happens to my parents, I'll find you and kill you all."

Then Dr. Tremont suddenly blurted, "We need you! The *world* needs you!"

"Maybe it does," I said. "But it sure doesn't need *you*."

CHAPTER 17

TWENTY-THREE YEARS AGO

IT WAS THREE O'CLOCK in the morning, and I was climbing out through the hole I'd smashed in the wall of a convenience store, carrying two canvas bags stuffed with food, a large bag of tortilla chips between my teeth, when a woman's voice said, "Stealing from the 7-Eleven? That's just pathetic!"

I peered around the barely lit parking lot, but couldn't see anyone.

"Up here, genius." The voice came from above.

I looked up to see a vaguely familiar woman floating down toward me. She was wearing a red-and-purple costume.

I dropped my ill-gotten gains: I wanted to have my hands free just in case she was there to fight me. In the previous five months I'd had four battles with other superhumans: two with Titan, one with Paragon—though that one wasn't really a fight, he just flew away—and one with a skinless strongman who called himself Muscle.

"Still," the woman said, "at least this time you had the sense to choose a store that didn't have an alarm."

"You've been following me?" A few days earlier, in a different store in another town, I'd barely escaped from the cops after the store's alarms brought them running.

"Brawn, you're not hard to find, are you?" She hovered in place about eight feet above the ground, so that we were eye to eye. "It's not like you can disappear into a crowd."

I picked up the bag of chips and opened it. "Sorry. Haven't eaten real food in days." To myself, I added, *and if we're going to fight, I'll need to keep my strength up*. I poured half the bag into my mouth, then opened one of my stolen bottles of cola to wash down the chips.

The woman began to drift away into the darkness. "Come on, before someone sees you."

"I have to find a phone first," I told her.

"What for?"

"To call the cops." I pointed to the hole in the wall. "I don't want someone coming in and completely looting the place."

She raised her eyes. "Even more pathetic."

"I took only about twenty bucks' worth of stuff. That and the cost of repairs won't set the owner back too much. But if he lost *all* his stock . . ."

"Well, the cops are already on the way. I can hear the sirens. Come on."

I scooped up my groceries and followed her out of the parking lot and into a quiet side street. "So why have you been following me?"

"Curiosity, mostly. There aren't a lot of people like us, and most of those I've met are suffering from the delusion that they're special. They want to be heroes."

"And you don't?"

The woman laughed. "I've got enough to do without worrying about public adoration." She looked down at my bags. "So what did you steal? Don't tell me, it's the four Cs, right? Cookies, candy, cola, and chips."

"Yeah. I can eat anything—grass, trees, anything organic—but sometimes you just have to have chocolate, y'know?"

She floated over the wrought-iron fence into a small public park, surrounded on all sides by new apartment blocks. I stepped over the fence and followed, still wondering whether I was going to have to fight her.

She stopped in the middle of a bunch of trees and sat down. "Pass me some of those chips, then."

I tossed her an unopened bag and sat down opposite her.

As she opened the bag, she said, "I might have a job for you, Brawn. It pays well, and you'll have a place to live. Hot food too. When was the last time you had a proper meal?"

"It's been a while."

"I'm guessing you didn't choose to be on the wrong side of the law. Circumstances working against you, is that it?"

I nodded, and fed a handful of cookies into my mouth. "So what's this job?"

She made a face as she flicked crumbs off her costume. "Please don't talk with your mouth full. No, I can't tell you what the job is until you agree to do it."

"Then I'm not interested. I've had enough of that sort of thing. Anything top secret or illegal, or both, can go take a running jump."

"What, you *like* the way you live? Sleeping in forests, eating out of Dumpsters, hiding all the time—that's your ideal life, is it? Get a grip, Brawn. You're bigger and stronger than any human. You shouldn't be hiding from them—they should be lining up to worship you. People like you and me, we're better than everyone else. In another age we would have been *gods!*"

"But this isn't another age. This is now." I finished my third package of cookies and drained the last of my soda, then stood up. "Been nice talking to you, but I think we should go our separate ways. What's your name anyway?"

"The media calls me Slaughter. It's not a name I'd have chosen for myself."

A chill ran down my back. "I've heard of you. You've got every cop in the country searching for you. You're a murderer."

She shrugged. "They were only people." Still sitting with her legs crossed, she floated up into the air. "You're not thinking of trying to turn me in, are you? I'm a lot faster than you are."

I didn't want to get involved, but this woman was a killer— I wouldn't have been able to live with myself if I'd just let her go and then she'd killed again.

I lunged at her, my hands outstretched, but she zipped away.

"Like I said. Pathetic. If you weren't such an idiot, you'd have asked me my name first. Then you might have had a chance to catch me." She began to circle around me. "If you won't join me, then you'd better stay out of my way. You get me? You think you're invulnerable, but you're not. Not against me." Then she threw her head back and let out a long, loud scream.

"What was *that* supposed to do?"

Slaughter smiled. "It's supposed to draw some attention." She screamed again, even louder, and started shouting, "Help! Help! Oh God, he's *killing* them!"

All around the park, lights were coming on in the apartment buildings.

"You're crazy!" I said. "Shut up!"

"Someone call the police!" she yelled. "There's blood everywhere!"

I heard the wail of sirens and the screech of tires. I turned and ran to the far side of the park, jumped over the fence, and narrowly missed landing on a police car.

"It's him!" one of the cops said, grabbing his radio. "Dispatch, we need backup! Now! Send all units!"

I didn't wait around to hear any more. I leaped over the car and pounded down the street as fast as I could.

It took me more than an hour to shake the cops. I spent the rest of the night and all of the following day hiding under a low bridge, my head barely above the ice-cold water.

When I finally emerged the next night, I expected the search to have been called off. After all, I hadn't actually done anything wrong. Apart from breaking into the store, that is. But at least the police would have searched the park and not found any bodies. So far, all they wanted me for was breaking and entering. Murder would be a whole different situation.

So I waded to the riverbank and climbed up onto the street. I rested for a while in the alleyway next to a twenty-four-hour Laundromat, warming myself on the hot air that pumped out of its vent.

I must have dozed off, because the next thing I knew the area was awash with red and blue lights, and there were armed police officers slowly approaching me from either end of the alley.

One of them said, "Aw, no . . . He's waking up!"

For a few moments, no one moved.

One officer took a few steps closer and held out his free hand, palm down. "All right, big fella. OK. Now, take it easy. My name's Ridley. I just want to talk to you."

I started to stand up, and they all backed away. "Relax," I said. "I'm not going to attack you."

"All right," Officer Ridley said. "Why'd you do it?"

"I was hungry. Look, I know it's wrong, but if I *could* pay for it, I would. But I can't. And even if I had the money, who'd let me into their store?"

Ridley was breathing heavily, and it looked to me as though he was trying to figure out the best and safest way to get me into custody. "We're not talking about the store, Brawn. That was wrong, and I'm glad that you realize it was wrong. But that's not what we're talking about." He continued to speak softly, as if a calm voice would keep *me* calm. It wasn't really working. "We're talking about the woman. You remember her? From last night?"

I nodded. "Yeah, I remember. But she's long gone now."

Very slowly and carefully, he said, "Yes, she's gone. Gone to the hospital. Where she's recovering from a broken collarbone, a concussion, and two broken legs, just to name a few of her multiple injuries."

"What are you talking about? She flew away!"

"Right. Flew away, as in 'she flew away in an emergency helicopter.' Is that what you mean?"

"No, she flew away as in 'she flew away.' Up into the air. That's one of her powers. She can fly."

The cop frowned. "Wait, *who* are we talking about?"

"Slaughter. You must have heard of her."

"And you believe the woman in the park was Slaughter?"

"She *was* Slaughter! She saw me, we talked, then when I wouldn't help her out with some job she kept going on about, she flew away. Right after she started screaming for help, like I was attacking her or something. I mean, I never even *touched* her!"

"*I'm* talking about the woman you beat up. Patrol officers found her in the park a few minutes after you were seen running away."

"What? Well, that wasn't me—I'd never attack anyone! It had to have been Slaughter. She set me up. After she flew away, she probably found this other woman and beat her up and left her in the park for you to find."

"So it wasn't you?" Ridley asked.

"No!"

Officer Ridley chewed on his lower lip while he thought about this. "I see. In that case I'm arresting you for criminal damage and theft. We'll sort the rest out after we take you into custody. You have the right to remain silent. Anything you say can and will be used against you in a court of law. You have the right to speak to an attorney—"

"That's it. I'm outta here." I stepped around the policeman, and his colleagues flattened themselves against the alley walls.

Then I heard someone whisper, "National Guardsmen are still a few minutes away. You gotta stall him. Just keep him talking!"

I said, "I can hear you, you know!"

"Come back here!" Ridley shouted. "I'm arresting you!"

"Get lost!" I shouted over my shoulder.

"What about the store owner? How do you think *he* feels about what you did? How are you going to make it up to him?"

"I don't care. Tell him to charge five bucks for people to see the hole I punched through the wall. Or he's got security cameras, right? Maybe he can sell the tape to one of those home video shows. Maybe he'll even make enough money to afford an alarm system."

Ridley actually began to run after me. "You're resisting arrest! You know that means I can use any force I deem necessary to stop you!"

"No it doesn't. Anyway, if you shoot me, all that'll happen is that you'll spend the next week filling out paperwork and

I'll still be gone." I turned and looked down at him. "Do you even have a cell big enough for me?"

"Probably not."

"Then I'd let it go if I were you. I'm not waiting around here long enough for the army. They'd end up destroying half your town and I'd still get away."

He stopped following me then, but he didn't stop talking. "You'd better watch out for yourself, kid. Someone like you, you're liable to get into big trouble one day."

"Been there, done that," I called back. "Have fun explaining this one to your boss."

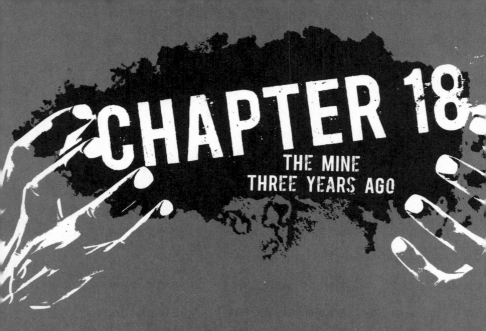

CHAPTER 18

THE MINE
THREE YEARS AGO

IN THE YEAR SINCE Keegan's death, since Hazlegrove established the trustee system, the mine had become considerably more profitable, and not just because of the two new seams of platinum ore.

Cosmo and I worked hard alongside the other trustees to keep everyone's morale strong. It wasn't easy, and we faced a lot of resistance from the prisoners as well as the guards, but little by little the conditions improved.

We insisted that once a month all the machinery be taken off-line for maintenance. Hazlegrove wasn't pleased about that at first, but he stopped complaining when we caught a potentially very serious fault in one of the ore crushers. Had it come to fruition, the crushers would have jammed solid and taken days to repair.

But thanks to us, the process of extracting the crude platinum continued without major interruption. It's a complex and costly procedure, typically producing only a couple of ounces of platinum for every ten tons of ore.

That was why most of the guards were concentrated on the final stages of the process.

Before the trustee system, we were producing no more than ten ounces of platinum a week, but now—thanks to the new seams and more efficient mining—we had almost doubled our output.

I would have been proud, had we not been slaves.

And then the day came when we actually tripled the pre-trustee output. It was mostly happenstance, thanks to a particularly rich vein in one of the new seams, but it was enough to get Hazlegrove out of his office, something that rarely happened in those days.

Not long after this spike in production, he called the trustees together. The others crowded back into his office while I hunched down just outside the door. I could have squeezed my way in through the door, but it wouldn't have been easy and there wouldn't have been enough room for anyone else. "Today was a good day," Hazlegrove said. "Roesler, can we expect many more like this?"

Ashley Roesler shrugged. "Maybe one or two more from the same vein. We got lucky. There could be similarly rich veins under there, but we have no way of knowing until we dig."

"All right," Hazlegrove said. He leaned forward over his

desk so he could see me. "Brawn . . . I looked into your idea of selling the nickel and the iron. Good news and bad news on that one."

Conveyors carried the discarded material outside the mine and dumped it onto huge piles, a decision that had been made long before the mine became a prison and had never been reversed. My idea was that the iron and nickel should be stored separately, as they were considerably more valuable than crushed rock.

"It should be profitable for the nickel, but not the iron," Hazlegrove said. "So we need to find a way to extract one from the other."

I nodded. "All right, but if we're not going to sell the iron, we should still keep it separate from the rest of the slag, just in case it's worth something in the future."

He turned to Cosmo. "What about the nickel and iron already in the slag heaps?"

"That's going to be a messy job," Cosmo said. "I've been talking to the teams that work the electromagnet, and they figure that's the best approach. We rig up some new electromagnets—a lot of them, really powerful ones—and pass every shovelful of slag through them. They figure that should get maybe eighty percent of the iron and nickel. Problem is, there's more than thirty *years'* worth of the stuff out there, and the slag at the bottom has got thousands of tons pressing down on it. Sifting through the whole amount is going to take a lot of work, a lot of manpower. Right now, I can't see it being a viable option."

I said, "Actually, there *is* an easier way. But it's dangerous. Should work, though."

Hazlegrove said, "Go on."

"First we run the new electromagnets over the entire surface to get the easy stuff. That shouldn't take more than a couple of weeks. Once that's done . . . we drill a few boreholes into the slag heaps and set charges."

"Explosives? That's *crazy!*" Cosmo said. "That'd never work!"

Emily Stanhope said, "No, he might be on to something there. . . ." She reached over to Hazlegrove's desk and grabbed a pencil and a sheet of paper, and started working out complex calculations. "The slag heaps are roughly conical, so that's the height times pi times the radius squared, divided by three. . . . Give me a few minutes here." She began to mutter to herself.

"We'd need someone who knows about explosives," Cosmo added. "Though I still don't think it'd work. And even if it did, I'm not sure the yield would be worth the cost."

We discussed it for almost an hour, and then Emily produced the results of her calculations. "Right. I reckon it *can* be done, and it's cost-effective. Using small charges we can blast down through each slag heap a couple of yards at a time. Like strip mining, I suppose. The explosions will spread the slag over a wide area, and then we simply keep running the electromagnets back and forth over it. Then we use a couple of diggers to clear away the loose slag, and move on to the next level."

Hazlegrove drummed the fingers of his good hand on the edge of the desk. "Nickel sells for about twenty-eight thousand dollars per metric ton. How many tons do you think we have out there?"

"It's hard to be sure," Emily said, "and this could be way off, but if you're forcing me to make a guess . . . Could be twenty tons. That would yield more than half a million dollars. And it could be a lot *more* than twenty."

Everyone fell silent for a moment, and then Hazlegrove said, "All right. I need to think this over. You're dismissed."

We left Hazlegrove mulling over Emily's sheets of paper, staring at the calculations we knew he had no way of comprehending.

Roman and Ashley and Emily returned to their teams while Cosmo and I glanced at each other and tried not to grin. Hazlegrove would find a way to make it happen. The platinum that was extracted from the mine was carefully monitored, but everything else was considered waste. No one was watching it because no one cared about it.

We knew that Hazlegrove would spend a lot of time thinking of the half million dollars' worth of effectively free nickel ore that was his for the taking. He would come back to us with an offer: If we could work out a way to set up everything without the warden finding out, he'd increase the rations or allow the workers a few days off, some token gesture of that nature.

But that wasn't the aim of our plan. Over the past year, we had been given more and more responsibility, to the point where we were running almost every aspect of the mine. We now had access to some very useful materials. Hydrochloric acid, sulfuric acid, hundreds of thousands of dollars' worth of crude platinum . . .

And if Hazlegrove did agree to the plan, then pretty soon we would be getting our hands on the one thing a group of inmates should never have: explosives.

CHAPTER 19

TWENTY-THREE YEARS AGO

THE HIGH-PROFILE MANHUNT that followed my encounter with Slaughter made me a little bit famous. That was not a good thing. Though the police were no longer blaming me for attacking that woman, and my version of the events was confirmed by the woman herself when she recovered, the truth somehow didn't seem to matter. The newspaper, radio, and TV reports did mention that Slaughter was the real culprit, but they still kept up their campaign to "end the blue giant's reign of terror."

If all the stories were to be believed, I was responsible for a whole range of crimes throughout the country. . . .

I'd broken into dozens of homes and stores and banks, frequently in places I'd never heard of, let alone visited. It didn't seem to matter to the media that in almost every one of those cases the police immediately ruled out my involvement.

I'd sabotaged a railway line, causing a train crash that "could have caused the deaths of hundreds of passengers." That train did go off the rails, but only at about three miles an hour, no one was injured, and it was quickly discovered that the accident was caused by wear and tear on a poorly maintained stretch of track. Nevertheless, for a couple of weeks I was known as "the train wrecker."

When a suspension bridge collapsed in Arkansas, one of the newspapers ran the story on its front page with a blurry photo of me next to a photo of the bridge. The article itself only named me as "one of the possible causes," but apparently putting me on the cover boosted sales.

In the middle of all the "Brawn Frenzy" I spent a night lying on the roof of an apartment block, listening to a phone-in radio show that came through the open window of one of the tenants. The night's topic was "Brawn: Monster or Villain?" which I felt was more than a little biased, and a bigmouthed local politician was the main guest. His long-winded argument could be summed up something like this: "Brawn is big and blue and has been reported as causing a lot of damage, so therefore you should vote for me." It was all wrapped up in the usual fancy words and false promises, but that was the gist of it.

The show attracted dozens of callers, each with his or her own ax to grind:

"Brawn stole my cat! It must have been him, because I think it probably was."

"I heard that there's more than one of them and they're aliens. That explains why there's so many reports of him all over the country."

"Dude, Brawn is, like, y'know, evil and stuff? If he isn't, then, like, why would people *say* he is? No smoke without fire, dude!"

"Never mind about this man Brawn—I want to know what the police are going to do about that blue giant who's been in all the papers! I'm a taxpayer and I know my rights, and if people don't agree with me, well, then, we might as well be living under a dictatorship!"

"Hello? Am I through? Hello? Yeah, I saw him on TV an' I got scared so that made me forget how many beers I'd had so I kept drinkin' an' then later the cops pulled me over an' I lost my license an' my boss said he hadda let me go. So Brawn cost me my *job*! How am I sposta support my kids now?"

"A creature like that is unnatural. An abomination. We should be doing everything we can to catch him *before he kills again*!"

Then the show's presenter said, "*Riiiight* . . . Well, thanks for that, caller. Folks, near as we can tell, Brawn ain't actually killed anyone yet, so don't go having nightmares. The time is coming up to three fifteen and you're listening to the *Late Hour* with me, Dancin' George Punteri. . . . We're still getting a lot of calls about Brawn and all these other freaks who've been in the news, but if you're sitting there stabbing at the redial button trying to get through, hold off for a few minutes, because we've got a special guest on the line: Pastor Tobias Cullen of the First Church of Saint Matthew in Vermont. Pastor Cullen, you told my producer that you've actually *seen* Brawn, is that right?"

That made me sit up and really pay attention.

"That's right, George. It was almost four years ago, the first time anyone saw him. He attacked my church in the middle of Sunday service."

"Four years," the presenter said. "But Brawn's been in the news for only about a year."

"We were ordered to keep quiet. But there doesn't seem to be any point now—everyone knows about him. He . . ." I heard the pastor swallowing. "He came out of nowhere. There was a flash or something and the creature just appeared in the middle of the choir. There was panic. . . . I did my best to get everyone out. When I tried to escape, he attacked me. He grabbed me and threw me through the air. I crashed into a police car. It was eight months before I could walk again."

"No way! It wasn't like that at all!" I said aloud before I could stop myself.

"He growled and snarled like an animal," Pastor Cullen said. "One of the boys from the choir disappeared that day, and all they found of him were his vestments, covered in blood. The people of the parish spent months searching for him. No other trace was ever found." He paused. "Look, no one's ever said this out loud, but . . . I was *there*. I saw the look in that monster's eyes. I didn't see him do it, but I *know* he killed that boy—"

The presenter interrupted: "But you can't be *certain* of that. If his body was never found—"

"Look, until you've seen him up close, you can't even imagine how big this creature is. You *think* you can grasp the concept of a thirteen-foot-tall man, but, trust me, you can't. Picture a household cat being attacked by a leopard. That's what Brawn is like compared with the average man. The reason the boy's body was never found was that there wasn't anything *left* to find."

"What exactly are you saying, Pastor?"

"Brawn ate him. Killed him, tore him apart, and ate him."

My sixteenth birthday came and went with neither cake nor candles. I spent the day sitting in a cave in South Dakota, reading the first half of a torn-in-two spy novel that I'd found when scouring the local dump. I never did find out whether the brave hero managed to rescue the Serbian ambassador's pretty daughter.

I lived in the cave for a further three weeks. It wasn't a particularly nice cave, but it was reasonably warm and dry.

But I had to venture out eventually: I hadn't eaten anything but leaves and grass for ages, and all I could think about was a large pepperoni pizza. Of course I knew that getting hold of one wasn't an option, but I thought I might find a field of carrots.

I was still careful to travel only at night. I left the cave and strode west through the forest. There were a lot of farms in the county, and I was sure that at least one of them would have crops ripe enough to eat.

But I was out of luck. Most of them turned out to be dairy farms, and the only crop I found was wheat. Dry, rock hard, barely ripe, and tasteless.

Then something happened that I hadn't anticipated. I'd been on the run for so long, rarely staying in the same place for more than a day or two, that it hadn't occurred to me to memorize any landmarks on the way from the cave. I couldn't find my way back.

And I took too long searching for "my" cave when I should have just found the nearest one.

Dawn cracked the horizon as I was walking along a quiet road, and I was so busy noticing how pretty the sunrise was that I almost didn't hear the two black SUVs with opaque windows racing along the road toward me.

They screeched to a stop about fifty yards away, and four men climbed out and marched toward me. Three of them were armed with large-caliber rifles and wearing combat gear. They looked to be in their forties, and from the way they deployed themselves, I could see that they'd had combat training: One stayed on the road, hunched down and aiming his gun at me, while the other two crashed through the hedges on either side of the road, spreading out to cover me from the sides.

The fourth man didn't look to be much older than me. Twenty years old at the most. He was wearing a black two-piece uniform and staring at me intensely.

His stare turned into a frown, and then he briskly shook his head and resumed staring.

I looked at the soldiers on my left and right, then back to the young man. "What are you doing, exactly?"

I heard him say to the third soldier, "It's no good. I can't get through at all."

"Say the word."

The black-clad man nodded. "Take him."

I flinched as all three of the soldiers started shooting, but their shots did no damage whatsoever. It was like being hit by pieces of popcorn fired from a rubber band.

"It's not working!" the man on the left said. "Lash, Ollie— use the Tasers!"

They unclipped their Tasers from their belts and I decided to play along, mostly to see what they were up to.

The Tasers' twin-pronged darts hit me in the chest, and I felt a slight tingle. It wasn't much more debilitating than a warm breeze, but I threw myself backward onto the ground and screamed.

All four of the men cautiously walked up to me as I lay there, twitching.

"This is so weird," said the one in black. "I'm not getting much at all. I mean, there's *something* going on in there, but it's almost alien. Not like anyone else's mind."

"You can't read him?" one of the soldiers asked.

"No."

"Then what do we do? He's not gonna be down for long, and we don't have a way to bring him back with us."

The young man nodded. "True. Ox, call in the chopper."

I said, "Oh great. *More* helicopters."

The four men jumped back. "He's awake!"

I propped myself up on my elbows. "Yep. So, who are you guys and what do you want?"

"My name is Maxwell Dalton," the young man said.

"The mind reader? I've heard of you. Well, don't bother calling your helicopter, because you're not taking me any-where."

He adopted an "I'm in charge here!" pose and tried to look tough. "You're under arrest, Brawn!"

"Don't make me laugh, you little tick! You can't read my mind and your weapons can't hurt me, so you're hardly in a position to arrest me. And what makes you think you have the authority?"

"Simple. You're one of the bad guys, and *my* job is to—"

"Says who? Who put *you* in charge?" I stood up. "Just because you can do things other people can't, that doesn't automatically make you their boss. Tell you what, though, I'll go with you guys if you can give me food and a decent bed and somewhere I can take a shower. I'm getting tired of having to wash in rivers. Otherwise, you're wasting your time and mine."

Dalton took a few steps back and looked up at me, doing the stare-frown thing again.

"Oh please! If that didn't work before, what's changed that it might work now?"

Abruptly, the three soldiers turned away and started to run back to their cars.

"I get it—you were using your telepathy to talk to *them*. So what's it like inside someone else's mind? Do you pick up everything they think? Can you read their memories as well?"

Dalton said, "You're going to be a problem, Brawn. I don't like situations I can't control."

"And since when does what you like have any bearing on the real world? What's your game, Dalton? What are you up to? I mean, with a power like yours you could do pretty much anything you wanted. Is that how you've made your money, by reading people's minds and second-guessing them?" I looked over toward the SUVs. The three soldiers were returning, and for a bizarre moment I thought they were carrying sections of drainpipe.

Dalton turned and ran, racing back toward the cars.

"Yeah, you *better* run!" I yelled. "You're out of your league here, Dalton! You can go . . ."

And then, far too late, I realized that the objects that had looked like drainpipes were shoulder-mounted rocket launchers.

One flared, and I had half a second before it hit me square in the chest. The explosion lifted me off my feet and sent me tumbling backward through the air.

The second rocket hit me while I was still in the air: It slammed into my back and exploded with such force that I was sure that this was it, I was going to die.

I hit the ground hard, headfirst, gouging a deep trench in the road's surface, and before I stopped moving, the third rocket exploded against the side of my head.

With pain coursing through every muscle and burning chunks of asphalt crashing down around me, I forced myself to stand up. *Got to run! Over the fields where they can't follow!*

Through the flames I caught a glimpse of another rocket zooming in. I threw myself to the side, and it missed me by inches.

The fifth and sixth missiles hit me simultaneously, erupting in a fireball that again sent me flying. I landed facedown in a crater of burning tar that clung to my skin as I tried to stand once more.

I really should have fled, but all I could see was Dalton's smirking face, and I desperately wanted to find out what it would look like after I'd smashed it into the road a few times.

So instead I ran *at* them. Another rocket scorched the air as it approached, but I had enough time to see this one coming: I somersaulted over it, came down on my hands, and flipped onto my feet, landing within striking distance of Max Dalton.

But I couldn't do it. Much as I wanted to kick him into the next county, I knew he wasn't strong enough to survive that.

I grabbed hold of him anyway, certain that it would prevent his soldiers from firing again, and bounded back down the road toward his cars. "Gonna be a long walk home for you, Max!"

Still holding on to him I jumped and came down heavily on top of the first SUV, completely crushing it.

As I leaped for the second, one of the rear doors suddenly opened and a fifth black-clad figure dived out.

I landed on the roof and flattened the vehicle. If the passenger hadn't seen me coming . . . My stomach churned at the thought.

I climbed off the ruined SUV and lowered Dalton to the ground as I looked back toward the first car.

Dalton was furious, angrier than I've ever seen anyone. "You idiot! You thundering *maniac*! You could have killed her!"

I stammered out, "You were trying to kill *me*!"

Dalton helped the long-haired girl up from the ground, glaring at me. "She's not even fifteen yet!"

"This is your sister?" I asked. The resemblance between them was strong, except that somehow she was very pretty and he was gangly and gawky.

The girl pulled herself free from Dalton's grip and rounded on him. "You idiot! I told you not to attack him! All those reports about the things he's done, they're all bogus and you knew that!"

"Roz, he could have killed you!"

"You attacked him with rocket launchers! Max . . . You . . ." She ran her hands through her long hair as she let out a low scream of frustration and whirled away. "You tried to *murder* him!"

Softly, he said, "Roz. Roz, listen to me. Just listen. Brawn's dangerous. He's a monster. He hasn't killed anyone yet that we know of, but it's only a matter of time."

Her rapid breathing subsided as she listened.

"He knew you were in the car and he didn't care if you got crushed."

"That's absolute *bull*!" I roared. "How *could* I have known? I couldn't have seen her through the blacked-out windows!"

Then she looked at me, a sneer on her face that mirrored her brother's. "You low-life, filthy *animal*! Everything they say about you is true, isn't it? You don't care about anything or anyone! Max, call Ernie. Tell him to prepare the copter—I don't care what it takes, but we can't let this monster roam free."

I decided I'd heard more than enough. I turned and ran, leaped over the tall fence into the field, and kept going.

That was my first encounter with Maxwell Dalton. My life would have been so much better if it had also been the *last* time I met him.

Something I didn't know for a long time was that after a superhuman's powers kick in, they sort of ebb and flow. There are days when you're at your best and days when you're not that much stronger than a human.

I guess that's because it's less noticeable for those who, like me, undergo a permanent physical change: I always looked the same, so there was no reason for me to suspect that my strength fluctuated.

Max Dalton's men had shot me with live ammunition, but it had had almost no effect on me. The previous time I was shot at, in Norman Misseldine's fortress, the bullets had penetrated my skin.

For some superhumans their powers settle down almost immediately, but for others it can take a very long time. I'd already been a superhuman for four years, and I was still having strong days and weak days.

My encounter with Dalton was on a strong day, possibly one of the strongest. But a couple of weeks later I ran into some trouble, and it was very definitely on one of my weaker days. . . .

I was in a midsized town. It was early morning—dawn was still a couple of hours away—and I had been spotted by a police car.

They chased me, as they usually did. There had been a

couple of occasions when I was spotted by the police and they had done absolutely nothing, though I was never sure whether that was because the officers didn't believe what they were seeing, they just didn't want the hassle, or they were actually on my side.

This time, though, the cops were particularly keen. They gunned the car's engine and roared down the main street after me, sirens blaring. Normally I'd have been able to outrun them pretty easily, but this time I just couldn't seem to get up any speed.

Within minutes three more cars were in pursuit. I darted down an alleyway and saw that the other end was sealed off by a high brick wall.

I made a leap for the wall, and only just caught the top. I pulled myself up and over, and landed on a completely empty street.

I kept running, left down another side street, then right, then left again, trying to put as much distance as possible between myself and the law.

But they knew the town much better than I did. . . . I emerged on a long, narrow road and saw the rapidly approaching blue and red lights at one end, so I turned and raced away. I glanced behind me as I prepared to take another left, and ran headfirst into the back of a garbage truck.

The impact shunted the truck forward a couple of feet and knocked me flat on my back.

Then the garbagemen, at first startled by what had happened, quickly recovered and decided to be heroes: They reversed the truck over me.

Normally I would have had more than enough strength to push the garbage truck aside, but that day I just didn't have the energy. All I could do was lie there and struggle as the police cars screeched to a halt nearby.

And just like that, I was caught.

CHAPTER 20

I SPENT THE DAY IN A CELL in the local jail, watched at all times by at least twenty armed guards. Their handcuffs were too small for my wrists, so they had to use chains and padlocks.

Most of the cops were terrified of me, but they couldn't stop staring at me, like when you find a particularly big spider in the backyard. You don't want to go near it, but you can't help looking.

The officers muttered to each other out of the corners of their mouths, and I caught enough to learn that there was a media frenzy going on outside the jail. It seemed that every newspaper and TV station in the country had shipped their reporters to the town.

I was sitting in the cell, on a steel bunk that had already bowed under my weight, when beyond the bars I saw the door open and a young, pale-skinned woman entered. She stammered that she was my lawyer and that she'd be representing me. She paused, and for a second I thought she was going to turn and run, but she took a deep breath and composed herself.

But she refused to come within twenty feet of the cell's bars, so our conversation was shouted back and forth. "I'm Claudette Rooke, of Bartlett, Fitz, Dear, and Botham," she half yelled, with her pen poised above her notebook. "For the record I, uh, I need to know your real name."

"I can't tell you that," I said. "It would put a lot of people I know in danger. Just call me Brawn. I hate that name, but it's what everyone calls me."

"Address?"

"United States of America, Earth."

"Can you be more specific?"

"Well, what's the address of this jail? Because this is as close as I have to a home."

"Brawn, do you fully understand the reason for your arrest?"

I thought about this for a second. "Actually, no. I don't. No one's told me."

She looked up from her notebook. "You haven't been formally charged?"

"Nope. What *is* the charge, anyway?"

It was her turn to pause. "I'll have to get back to you on that. . . ."

One of the police officers said, "Resisting arrest."

When I looked at him, he went pale and took a step back.

"You arrested me for resisting arrest? That doesn't make sense."

"Well, you were running away."

"You were chasing me."

Another officer said, "You're supposed to stop when asked to do so by a police officer."

"No one asked me."

Ms. Rooke lowered her notebook and the ghost of a smile appeared on her lips. "If you're not going to charge my client, I'll have to ask you to let him go."

The first officer said, "No can do. We've got orders."

"Then tell me why you were chasing him. Is there a warrant out for his arrest?"

"I dunno about that. He, uh . . . Well, everyone knows that he's guilty."

"Guilty of what?" she asked.

"I mean, you just have to *look* at him to know!"

I got up off the bunk and, half crouching under the low ceiling, approached the bars. "You know what this is? Racial profiling. They assumed I must be guilty of something because of the color of my skin."

Some of the officers took great offense at that and shouted their disapproval, while Claudette Rooke slowly turned back to face me, her face grim. "You think that's *funny*?"

I shook my head. "No."

"If you had ever *really* faced racial discrimination, you wouldn't make comments like that."

"And if *you* had ever faced it, you wouldn't automatically assume that I was Caucasian before I changed into this."

"*Were* you?"

"I'm not saying, because it's not important. I was a human, now I'm something else. I'm a superhuman-American. A minority. And that's why I'm being treated like this."

The door behind Ms. Rooke opened, and a well-dressed old man with a pure white comb-over hairstyle walked in. He must have been important, because all the cops suddenly stiffened and pulled in their guts.

He slowly turned on the spot, looking every officer in the eye. "One of you officers has deliberately left his radio on, broadcasting the conversations in this cell to the reporters outside."

From somewhere to my left there was a sharp *click!* and the old man turned in that direction. "Officer Hamblin. You will immediately report to Sergeant Colliver and hand in your shield and sidearm. You are suspended without pay pending a formal investigation."

The officer was shaking and couldn't look anyone in the eye as he slunk past his colleagues.

The man walked right up to the bars and stared at me as he addressed everyone else. "This is a mess, bordering on a fiasco. Charge this man with reckless endangerment, willful destruction of property, burglary, theft, and resisting arrest. In view of the circumstances and the unprecedented media interest, I've requested that Judge Khan convene a special sitting of the county court within the hour."

The white-haired man regarded me for a few seconds, then said, "All right, Mr. Brawn. I know you understand the charges against you. What do you have to say for yourself?"

I moved closer to the bars. "Who are you?"

"District Attorney Philip Olafsson."

"So you know the law inside and out, right?"

"As far as you need be concerned, yes."

"Well, what if I told you a secret that would change everything?"

His eyes narrowed. "Everyone out. Now."

I was impressed: It couldn't have taken the cops more than ten seconds to clear the room.

"You too, Ms. Rooke," Olafsson said to the lawyer, without looking at her.

"My client has the right to have legal representation at all times. . . ." She slowed to a stop when Olafsson turned toward her. "Um . . ." She nervously chewed on her bottom lip for a moment, then left the room, closing the door behind her.

"All right," Olafsson said as he turned back to me. "Surprise me."

"Man, you really *are* one of the bigwigs, aren't you?" I looked at his comb-over. "No offense."

"I never take offense—I don't have the time. What is it you have to tell me?"

I sat down on the floor. "That can wait a second. First I have to ask you something."

He didn't speak, just nodded slightly.

"I get the impression you're a no-nonsense kind of guy. And I'm sure you wouldn't be a district attorney if you weren't smart. On top of that, you've got a lot of guts if you're willing to be alone in a room with me, with only a few flimsy bars separating us."

"You have a point?"

"Yeah. I'm saying that you *know* I'm not a bad guy. So why not let me go and save the taxpayers a whole lot of money?"

"Because you've broken the law. The cost doesn't come into it." Then his expression relaxed a little. "I want you to come with me and talk to Judge Khan. There is a prison in Oak Grove that's recently been modified to house superhumans. Each inmate requires special conditions to render them powerless, but we have an expert who takes care of that. Oak Grove will be your home until we can figure out something more suitable. Brawn, I know you've been running for a long time, so don't look at this as imprisonment. Think of it as an opportunity to slow down, at least for a while. You'll receive good food, a bed, decent treatment. The prison has an extensive library, a good exercise yard, a TV room. It's not a hotel, but it's a darned sight better than sleeping in the woods. This will please the media and get them off your back, so when the time comes to release you, you'll have served your sentence. There's nothing the press loves more than a reformed criminal. It will be a new beginning for you."

"But I haven't even had a *trial* yet!"

"I have no doubts that you'll be found guilty. Do you?"

I sighed. "I could break out of here right now, you know."

"I know you could. Just as I know you won't. I've been in this game a long time. I know the difference between a bad man and a good one who's never had a chance. This is *your* chance, Brawn. Understood?"

"Yeah."

"Now. What was it that you wanted to tell me?"

"It's going to change everything."

"*Nothing* you can tell me will change—"

"I'm sixteen years old."

"A minor." Olafsson's shoulders sagged, and he slumped forward, his forehead pressed against the bars. "Hell."

"Told you."

He remained like that for a few seconds, then straightened up. "Sixteen means that you'd have to go to a juvenile detention center. That would not be a good thing for you. So we stick with Oak Grove. Because of your great size and strength you'll be housed separately from the other prisoners. And because you won't tell us your real name, we can't verify your age. As long as *you* don't tell anyone, we're safe."

I wasn't sure about this at all, but I could see that it made sense. I *was* tired of running, tired of living on clumps of grass or scraps of food scavenged from bins. After my year in the Antarctic and then months on the military base in Texas I wasn't keen on going back to prison, but there was still something to be said for it.

"All right, Mr. Olafsson. If you promise me I won't be there forever, we'll go talk to the judge."

There wasn't any trial. The public believed that there had been, that it was conducted in private for "reasons of security," but instead I was brought to the courthouse where DA Olafsson and Judge Khan just talked to me in her chambers.

Judge Khan was one of those few people who, like the DA, didn't seem to be scared of me. She asked me how I'd been living, whether I had any family, and so on. When she found out I was sixteen, she went very still.

"Now you see the problem," DA Olafsson said.

The judge nodded. "Brawn, you have broken the law on quite a *few* occasions, but clearly there are extenuating circumstances. If you were anyone else, I'd be willing to strike them and clear your record. Effectively, you're a teen runaway."

"Actually, I didn't really run away from home. I was kidnapped. At least, that's how it started."

She went "Hmm . . ." as she flipped through the pages of a thick folder. "The first confirmed sighting of you was four years ago. You allegedly attacked the First Church of Saint Matthew. You materialized in the middle of a service. It was where . . ." She stopped, and looked up. "Where that boy disappeared. I think I understand."

Olafsson said, "Enlighten me."

"Twelve-year-old Gethin Rao went missing on that day. His body was never found. That's you, isn't it, Brawn?"

I nodded.

"Oh, you poor boy! The reports said that you—as Brawn, I mean—were unable to speak at the time. You were chased by members of the armed forces, but they lost you in the mountains."

"That part's a lie. They caught me and brought me to . . ." I stopped myself. "I'd better not say where. I say 'they' but I don't think they're officially part of the government or the army. I don't know who they're working for, but it's all probably very top secret. The thing is, I escaped more than a year later. They caught me again last year and tried to blackmail me into working for them. They said they'd kill my parents."

"How did you get away from them?" the judge asked.

"I told them that if anything happened to my ma and pa, I'd . . ." I stopped, wondering whether it was a crime to threaten to kill someone. "I made it clear that wasn't an option."

"Everything said here is just between us," Olafsson said. "None of this will go on any record. In Oak Grove you can stop running, at least for a while. Take advantage of what the prison has to offer. Learn a trade. The alternative is that you *keep* running, and that's no kind of a life for anyone. Take my advice and accept the offer, son. If you don't, then sooner or later you're going to hurt someone else—accidentally or otherwise—and then a greater authority than the judge here will order that you be hunted down."

Judge Khan asked, "Gethin, what about your parents? Are you certain that you don't want them to know the truth?"

"As far as I know, they think I'm dead. It's better that way. If they knew I was alive, they'd be searching for me, and that would put them in danger. Besides . . . I can't let them see me like this. *Look* at me! I can barely fit in this chair and I have to crawl when I'm going through a door. I know that there are other superhumans, but they're nothing like me. I'm a freak."

"You're certainly unique," Olafsson said. "I guess there's a chance that you'll never have a normal life, that you'll never change back, but my belief is that we should always prepare for the worst and always hope for the best."

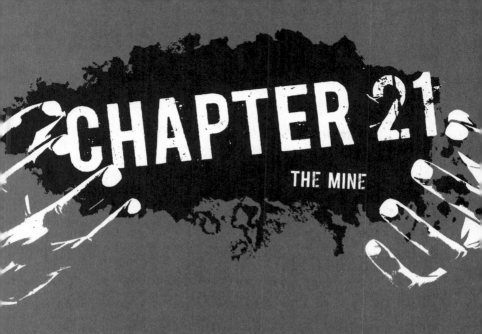

CHAPTER 21

THE MINE

ESCAPE FROM THE MINE wasn't impossible. We'd learned that from Jakob's team. But there was still a problem that we didn't know how to overcome: We couldn't take everyone with us. Not all of us saw that as a problem, though. And that in itself was *another* problem.

At one of our weekly gatherings it became clear that Ashley and Roman had been having meetings of their own. "The five of us," Ashley said. "That's all. The more we take with us, the greater the chance of getting caught."

Cosmo said, "No. Everyone or no one. That's how it's going to be."

"I agree," I said.

Roman smirked. "Yeah, you would. It's different for you, Brawn. You're able to take anything they throw at us, and you've got a champion complex that overrules all logic. You want to save the whole world."

Ashley said, "We cannot take everyone, Brawn! It's as simple as that. Even if there were a way to get everyone out, we don't know where we *are*! Do you really want to lead four hundred people through the mountains without the faintest idea of your destination? We could be out there for months—how would we feed them all?"

"Not to mention that so many people would make for a huge target," Roman said. "It's insane. No, worse than that, it's suicide on a mass scale."

"I think I know a way it can be done," I said. "But not in the way you're thinking. We don't *escape* from the mine. We take it over."

The others glanced at each other, then back to me.

"There are forty-six guards," I said. "They've all got Heckler & Koch P9S handguns, and eighteen of them are armed with Remington 870 shotguns. That's a lot of firepower, especially if concentrated on one target. But not all of the guards are here at the same time. The best time to strike is one hour after their morning shift starts. The night shift will have left by then, and the day shift will only be settling into their routine. We've got four half sticks of dynamite and two liters of hydrochloric acid in the stash. We can do a *lot* of damage with that."

Emily Stanhope had remained silent, but now she said, "No way. It's not going to happen."

I ignored her. "I'll take Hazlegrove in his office. Swinden and DePaiva will be there. Some of the other guards will come running—maybe ten or fifteen if we're lucky. That should leave only a couple of guards on each tunnel, a few on the processing station, two more at each door. It'll be up to the four of you to organize a way to take them out. Once we have control, we should be able to hold the mine long enough to get help. Hazlegrove has a satellite phone and a shortwave radio transmitter in his office."

Cosmo asked, "Who would we call?"

"The United Nations."

"You're assuming that they don't already know we're here. Suppose they do? Suppose that this prison is under *their* control?"

"Then we're screwed no matter what happens," I said. "Jakob's team got out and were captured. That suggests to me that the area is patrolled. So we stay put. Roman's right that the logistics of moving everyone are too complex, too dangerous. We can defend this place for a lot longer than we'd survive in the mountains. We can hold any surviving guards hostage, and if we strike the day after the supply trucks, we'll have enough food and water to keep going for two months, maybe longer."

Ashley said, "Yeah, but the problem with that is that the supply trucks take away the platinum after they deliver the food. I say we attack just *before* they arrive. That way we still have the platinum as a bargaining chip."

"So we'll be rich when we starve to death," Cosmo said. "Not exactly the ideal outcome."

Emily said, "I think you're all wrong. In our situation, escape is just another word for death, and revolution is another word for murder." To Roman and Ashley, she added, "If it were just the five of us who got out, Hazlegrove would come down so hard on the rest of the prisoners, they'd *wish* they were dead." To me, she said, "And your way means that you would certainly be killed. Even if you managed to kill most of the guards, those who survived would start shooting indiscriminately."

"We have to do *something*!" Cosmo said.

"Yes. We have to stay put, and keep working to improve the conditions here. We've already made good progress. We keep Hazlegrove happy and we will all be better off. Escape is impossible, revolt is suicide at best."

"The first duty of every prisoner is to escape," Cosmo said.

Emily shook her head. "No. The first duty is *survival*, and our chances of survival are much, much greater if we maintain the status quo."

We argued for another half hour, and reached no conclusions. I was sure my way was best. Yes, I would very likely be killed in the process, but I was willing to pay that price.

As I worked my shift that night, pushing the cart up and down the tunnel, I had plenty of time to consider my plan, and by the time my sixteen hours were up, I knew that it had to go ahead, even if that meant doing it without the others' help.

Some of the guards would have to die. Certainly Hazlegrove, DePaiva, and Swinden, then whoever else came running. I didn't know if that would make me a murderer, but I didn't care. All I'd ever tried to do was be one of the good guys. Now I was willing to be the villain they'd always wanted me to be.

I would strangle Hazlegrove and use his body as a club to beat Swinden and DePaiva to death. I would take their guns and kill as many of the other guards as I could before they hit me enough times to kill me. I figured that if I was fast, and my own shots were reasonably accurate, I could get to almost all of them.

Then Cosmo and the others would have no choice but to join in. There would only be a couple of guards left standing.

Perhaps Emily was right, perhaps the surviving guards—in fear for their lives—would begin to shoot at random. But that would only inflame the other prisoners, force them into action.

So, yes, it was possible that some of the other prisoners would be killed. Could I live with that on my conscience?

No. But then, I didn't expect to live anyway.

I probably should have taken a few days to prepare, but I knew if I waited any longer, reason might get the better of me. At the end of my shift I managed to get a couple hours' sleep, and then I slowly walked toward Hazlegrove's office.

I tried to look casual as I walked, but I was carefully taking in everything around me. A bunch of the younger kids were chasing each other in the open area between the mine shafts and the guards' quarters, so I stopped them and told them to go find their parents.

As they scurried away, my mind began racing. *Am I really going to do this? Am I actually going to take another man's life?*

I had no doubts that Hazlegrove deserved to pay for the way he treated us, but did he deserve to die?

I tried to force myself to be rational, to remind myself that I should be thinking of him as a slave master, as the man who had ordered Keegan to be shot in the head. But instead the memory of the day he let me out of the hot box kept coming back. He had mentioned his one-year-old son. That was the first time I'd seen Hazlegrove as a real person.

That kid will never understand why his father had to die, I told myself. *Can I do that to him? Leave him fatherless?*

I slowed as I neared Hazlegrove's office. Through the partly open door I saw him talking to Swinden.

There he is. My first murder victim.

No! It's not murder! It's not even revenge! This is justice—and the first step on the road to freedom!

But not for me, I knew. I would never be free, and if I was going to be a killer, then I didn't deserve freedom.

The thought briefly surfaced that I was going to die very soon, but it seemed a minor thing, a blip, compared with the necessity of my actions.

Then Hazlegrove saw me approaching and beckoned to me.

I crouched down outside the door, with my hands on either side of the frame, ready to rip the walls apart so that I would have enough space to get inside.

Hazlegrove said, "Brawn. I was about to send DePaiva to find you."

"Yeah?" I asked. Hazlegrove, Swinden, and DePaiva were gathered around the desk, peering at a dog-eared and age-stained map of the complex.

I took a quick glance behind me. Two guards were on the

gantry just above the main doors, five were standing at the processing station. From the sound of the machinery, it was almost ready to spill the molten platinum into the mold—that was when the guards would be most alert. After a few minutes' cooling, the mold would be lowered into a large vat of water. This solidified the platinum and heated the water at the same time. Already a line of prisoners had formed to take advantage: The first eight or nine would be able to have a quick wash before the water cooled again.

"There's been some good news," Hazlegrove said. "It will mean a few changes around here, however."

I nodded and looked back toward the mine shafts, hoping to see Cosmo, hoping that he'd realize what was happening and get out of the way.

"What sort of changes?" I asked.

When the molten platinum hit the water, it would create great clouds of steam—and that was the moment to strike. The guards would be watching the platinum as best as they could through the steam, and the prisoners would already be jostling each other to get closer to the water.

At the same time, three more guards would be approaching the processing station to take the platinum bar to the vault—one to carry it, two to stand guard—but they'd have their backs to me. "A restructuring of the trustee process."

"OK," I said, not really caring. In a few seconds, I was about to do some restructuring of my own.

The mold was already being lowered toward the water when Hazlegrove said, "So, Brawn . . . Brawn, look at me when I'm talking to you."

Come on! I said to myself. *A couple more seconds . . .* I turned back to face Hazlegrove.

He smiled. It was a smile I'd never seen cross his face. I'd seen many of them, and I couldn't help but wonder what this one meant.

"Is this the part where you try to kill us?"

A knot twisted in my stomach, and Hazlegrove reached down behind the desk and picked up a cloth-wrapped bundle, held it up for me to see. "Recognize this? Dynamite, four half sticks. Two liters of hydrochloric acid. Seven razor-sharp makeshift knives. Almost three ounces of platinum pellets, drops that splashed out when it was poured into the mold."

From behind me came a loud hiss of steam as the mold hit the water, but I barely registered it.

Hazlegrove said, "Taking over the mine. Do you really think the warden didn't anticipate that? Are you that stupid?" He sighed. "Swinden?"

Swinden slapped a sheet of paper down on the desk. "Roman Laberis. Charged with conspiracy to commit murder."

Another sheet. "Ashley Roesler. Same charge." Another. "Ferdinand Cosby, also known as Cosmo. Same charge. Emily Stanhope. Same initial charge, but charges reduced in light of . . . uh . . ."

"Mitigating circumstances," Hazlegrove said. "Stanhope didn't agree with your plans. She told us everything. Her charge was reduced to sedition." He walked around the desk, stopped in front of me, glanced back at DePaiva, and nodded.

DePaiva unclipped his walkie-talkie from his belt and raised it to his mouth. "McDonagh? DePaiva here. Proceed."

From somewhere outside the dome came the sound of a gunshot.

"That was Roesler," DePaiva said.

Another gunshot. "Laberis."

A third. "Cosby."

Hazlegrove poked me in the shoulder with his swagger stick. "*I'm* in control here. Me. Not you. Understand? The penalty for conspiracy to commit murder is immediate execution. Unfortunately, the warden has insisted that I don't execute *you*." His face turned grim. "I was so looking forward to that."

He slapped the stick hard across my face. "But maybe that's a good thing—I've got my own plans for you."

Swinden said, "As a result of your plans to escape, all rations will be halved. Permanently. Any further troublemaking on your part and we will start executing the prisoners. Starting with the least productive, of course."

Hazlegrove said, "You understand what *that* means, don't you?"

I nodded. There was no way I could speak.

"Yes. The children first." Over his shoulder, he said, "DePaiva?"

DePaiva nodded, and into his walkie-talkie he said, "Go for Stanhope."

Another shot rang out.

Hazlegrove said, "The penalty for sedition is also immediate execution." He gave me a thin-lipped smile. "Stupid woman thought she could save her own skin by ratting out her friends."

He slammed me across the face again. "I *trusted* you, and

you betrayed that trust! From now on you will be chained and guarded at all times. The guards watching you will call in every half hour. If they fail to make one of those calls, for whatever reason, people will die. If you attempt to communicate with the other prisoners on matters that don't relate to the work, people will die. When not working you will be kept separate from the other prisoners. But there won't be many times that you're not working, because you are now on duty twenty-three hours every day. After all, we're now down a further four workers. The warden doesn't want you executed, but it's a whole different matter if you die of exhaustion."

CHAPTER 22

TWENTY-THREE YEARS AGO

IN OAK GROVE I WAS GIVEN a cell that looked more like a bank vault from a movie. It was sealed with a large circular metal door, and it took two guards to turn the giant locking wheel.

Inside, four mattresses had been laid side by side, covered with a bunch of different-colored blankets that had been stitched together.

The senior guard, Mr. Chapman, said, "Sorry it's not much. But it's warm and dry, and safe."

I crouched as I entered the room. "It's OK, thanks. It's better than sleeping in a cave, anyway."

Chapman was in his forties, bald with a full gray beard. He always came across as very relaxed and easygoing, but the other guards still respected him.

He followed me into the cell. "My wife made the blankets.

She said to tell you that if they're not comfortable, then you're not to be shy about letting me know." He pointed to a neatly folded orange bundle on the floor beside the bed. "She also made you a new pair of shorts from one of the prison uniforms. They should fit, but if not she can adjust them."

I glanced out to where we'd left the other guard, but he'd already gone.

"A lot of people here—inmates *and* guards—are very nervous about you, Brawn. Until they settle down, it'd be best if you minimize your contact with the general population. But we won't be able to keep you totally isolated. You'll have to mix with them at mealtimes and in the yard. Just keep your head down and it'll be fine."

"Are there any other superhumans here?"

He nodded. "Oh, we do have quite a few. Necroman, Gyrobot, Termite, The Scarlet Slayer, Texanimal, The Waspider, Schizophrenzy . . ."

I sat down on the bed. "I've never heard of the last two."

"Count yourself lucky. Schizophrenzy's a supervillain who has a secret identity that's *also* a supervillain. I'm no expert on criminal psychology, but if you ask me, he's putting it all on. And The Waspider's fast. He can race around the place on his hands and feet, and he really does move like a spider. He can't climb up walls or make cobwebs, but, *man*, he can jump." Chapman smiled. "The 'wasp' part of his name comes from the way he fights his opponents, always darting in, attacking and retreating over and over."

"How do you stop them from escaping?"

"Different ways for each of them. Some are drugged to

keep their power levels down, others are chained at all times. In the case of Gyrobot we just took away his armor and weapons. He's not really a robot, just a guy. But we have to make sure he doesn't get his hands on anything mechanical or electronic, because that guy could turn a kitchen whisk into a death ray."

I must have looked worried or something, because Mr. Chapman reached up and gave me a friendly pat on the shoulder. "Hey, you'll be fine. The DA told me about, you know, your age. I'm the only one who knows. Everyone else thinks you're just an ordinary prisoner. And you really don't have to worry about the other inmates. Chances are they'll be as scared of you as most people are."

"And you're not? Scared of me, I mean."

"I'm told that you give off a scent that triggers people's fear reflex." He tapped the side of his nose. "But not mine. My dad worked in a chemical research lab, and one day I was there visiting him when some idiot messed up one of the experiments, released a cloud of chlorine gas. I got caught in it before my dad got me out."

"Wow . . . So, what, you got superpowers?"

"No, chlorine gas is poison. I inhaled too much of it and it nearly killed me. Pretty much destroyed my sense of smell." He looked around the cell. "So, you've got your radio there— but keep the volume down because none of the other inmates are allowed one—and there's the john. Sure hope it's strong enough to take your weight."

"Yeah, me too."

"There are communal showers, but if you're shy, we can

arrange for you to use them when everyone else is in the exercise yard. Librarian comes around every morning. Officially inmates can read only books on the approved list, but if there's anything in particular you want, just let me know and I can pick it up for you at the bookstore in town."

I nodded. "Thanks. For everything."

"You're welcome. Now, listen . . . Like I said, the other prisoners think you're just one of them, OK? They think your powers have been hobbled like theirs. So whatever happens, don't let them know the truth."

For the first few days, I really enjoyed my vacation in Oak Grove. It was nice to be able to just lie back, listen to the radio, or read without having to worry about being found by a hiker.

But by the end of the second week, I was getting antsy.

"You're gonna have to ride it out," Mr. Chapman told me. "You've not been here nearly long enough."

But he agreed to allow me to spend more time with the other inmates. At least that way I'd never be bored.

I was surprised to discover that I wasn't the only sixteen-year-old in the prison: Pyrokine was a year younger than me, and by all accounts he really *was* a villain. His real name was Fabian something, but I never learned his last name. He had the ability to turn matter into energy, which should have made him incredibly dangerous, but to me he always seemed kind of distant, the way someone gets when they've suddenly lost a loved one.

Mr. Chapman told me that Pyrokine was in Oak Grove because there was nowhere else to put him. He was too powerful to put in a juvenile detention center, and too dangerous to be let loose.

I never spoke to him, though. Pyrokine kept to himself, which suited the other prisoners because they were more scared of him than they were of me.

They were a fascinating collection of oddballs, and I should know. Schizophrenzy was the most entertaining, at first. He had an opinion on everything, and those opinions weren't tied down to anything as mundane as facts or knowledge. But I learned pretty quickly not to engage him in conversation, because no matter what you said, he would go out of his way to prove that you were wrong, even if you agreed with him on something.

The Scarlet Slayer latched on to me as though we'd known each other for years. He was a tall, skinny guy who looked like Ming the Merciless from *Flash Gordon*, if Ming had also been a pirate. He had his head shaved and wore a long beard that was split into two plaits. Of all the superhumans who operated on the bad side of the law, he had been the one who received the most coverage in the press. Not because he was so evil, but because he really *looked* the part.

He was Schizophrenzy's opposite in many ways, because The Slayer almost always agreed with you. It wasn't that he thought you were right, but because he seemed to think that if he agreed with you, you'd shut up and let him take over the conversation.

He was convinced that any day now he'd escape, even though he never actually seemed to be working on an escape plan. "It's gonna happen tomorrow," he told me one Friday during breakfast. "Yeah," he added, nodding for far too long.

His eyes shifted from left to right and back. "You and *me*, man. The Scarlet Slayer and Brawn. Perfect team. They wouldn't be able to stop us. You know who put me in here?"

"Titan," I said. He told me every time we spoke.

"It was Titan," The Slayer said, and spat. "I *hate* that guy! Flying around in his blue pajamas with his little cape and his perfect hair! You know he's *younger* than most of us? Makes you sick, doesn't it? Thinks he's all that, but he isn't. He's not all that at all. So who got you?"

"It was the cops," I said. "They got lucky."

"The cops, wasn't it? Yeah, I could sense that. I have a kind of sixth sense about us superhumans. Met this guy last year. Only about twenty, maybe twenty-one. He's one of us too. But, y'know"—the Slayer tapped a forefinger against the side of his head—"his power's all mental. The guy's smart as a whip and says he knows all about the powers. Like, he knows *why* we have them. He wouldn't tell me that, but he did tell me that he's working on a way to boost everyone's power. Well, not *everyone's*. Just the people he trusts. He reckons he'll be able to give powers to ordinary people, or take them away from the superhumans he doesn't like."

For the first time I was really paying attention to The Slayer. "What's his name?"

"No idea. He found me in Cincinnati. I was hiding out in this apartment for a couple of weeks, lying low, and the guy just showed up at the door. Told me he knew who I was, and that he was working on something big and wanted to put a team together."

"Do you think he was telling the truth? About being able to remove someone's powers, I mean?"

"Sure, yeah." The Slayer nodded. "Like I said, he knew the powers inside and out. Kept mentioning the blue lights."

"The blue lights?"

"Said that it's something to do with the powers, and that not many people can see them. They're like big balls of energy that float around. You ever see anything like that?"

"No."

"Pity. Probably still true, though. Anyway, the guy was supposed to contact me again after a couple of months, but then I got caught." He nudged my arm with his elbow. "Did I ever tell you *who* caught me?"

"No, who was it?"

"Titan. How about that, huh? That shows you the level *I'm* at. Took Titan to bring me down."

The Scarlet Slayer continued talking about Titan for the next ten minutes, which gave me time to think. The young man he talked about . . . I figured it could be the same one that Dr. Tremont had mentioned when he first showed up in Antarctica. The doctor had said, "I know for a *fact* that your people have recruited a seventeen-year-old boy who's been gifted with intelligence that's completely off the charts." If that boy had been seventeen then, that would make him twenty-one now.

Dr. Tremont had proved to be a liar, but maybe not everything he'd said was part of his scheme to manipulate me. Maybe there was some truth to it.

I interrupted The Slayer's story about his battle with Titan. "Listen, that guy who claimed to know all about the powers . . . You're sure he didn't tell you how to get in touch with him?"

The Slayer shrugged. "Not that I recall."

"The team he mentioned, then. Did he name any other superhumans he was talking to?"

He leaned back and squinted into the distance as he thought about that. "Yeah . . . Well, no. He said that he was going to try to find Façade. You know that guy? The one who can change his appearance. Now, that's a power I'd love." The Slayer lifted his right leg onto the table and pointed to the chunky black bracelet fixed around his ankle. "See that? Stops me from flying. If I get more than fifty feet off the ground, it zaps me. I miss flying. It's the *best*, let me tell you, but if I could, I'd trade it for the ability to change my appearance."

"Anyone else?"

"Nah, don't remember him mentioning any other names."

My mind was racing. I knew I had to find that man. If he *had* found a way to remove a superhuman's powers . . .

For the first time in four years, I felt something like hope. Hope that maybe that guy could remove my *own* powers. Maybe he could even turn me back into a normal human.

Three months after I arrived at Oak Grove, I was woken in the middle of the night by the sound of something very heavy crashing into a wall.

I sat up and turned on the light, but the sound didn't come again.

Eventually I drifted back to sleep, and later I woke to find that it was already breakfast time.

Normally, I was woken by the guards an hour earlier.

But that morning, nothing. I wasn't able to open the cell door from the inside, and there were no windows, so I had no idea what was going on. All I could do was wait.

At first I figured that maybe it was the bug going around: The previous day about ten of the guards had called in sick, and Mr. Chapman had said his wife had caught it too.

I turned on the radio, but my usual channel wasn't on the air. I had to go all the way up and down the dial a few times before I found a station that was broadcasting. A woman's voice said, ". . . last we heard, reports were coming in from all over the world of outbreaks of the flu-like plague. So far, it seems to be affecting only adults over the age of twenty." She sneezed a couple of times. "Oh, please don't tell me I've got it too! Hold tight, listeners. I'll come right back."

She didn't come back at all. After a few minutes the silence broke up into static.

The walls of my cell were solid concrete, but I could usually hear some faint sounds echoing through the ventilation system. That morning there was nothing.

Then I remembered the noise that had woken me earlier, and I started to worry. Something had happened. And given that this was a prison housing a lot of superhumans, it probably wasn't something good.

As loudly as I could, I bellowed, "Hey! What's happening out there?!"

There was no response. I called out a few more times, but there was nothing.

I could go through the wall, I told myself. *It's pretty tough, but it shouldn't take too long. Mr. Chapman would understand.*

But I knew I couldn't do that: It would reveal to the other prisoners that my powers were intact, and that would open up a great big can of worms.

So instead I waited. And waited. I decided that if no one showed up by nightfall, I'd go through the wall and to heck with the agreement I'd made with the DA.

After what felt like hours, during which my stomach began to seriously ache with hunger and I started to imagine that everyone else in the prison had died of the mysterious plague and I was the only one left alive, I finally heard something: the crash of metal on metal.

I jumped to my feet. "Hey! In here!"

I paused to listen, then a muffled voice came back: "Hello? Anyone there?"

"Yes! Yes!" I shouted. "In here! Thank God, I thought I was going to starve to death in this place!"

"Where are you?" The voice was louder now, a girl, clear enough to be outside in the corridor.

"Third room on the left. There's a steel door!"

I waited anxiously for the familiar sounds of the door being unlocked, but it was taking too long.

"Hello?" I shouted. "You still there?"

She said, "Um . . . Listen . . . Do you know what's going on?"

"A plague, right?" I said. "Pretty much everyone who's over the age of twenty is infected. It was on the radio before it went off the air. Is that what's happened?"

"Yeah. Look, it was done deliberately. There's an organization called The Helotry who've done this for, well, it's too complicated to get into it now. But I need to stop them, and I can't do it on my own. So I need two things from you before I let you out. First, I don't care what you're in here for, but if you're a superhuman, then I need your help. The Helotry's plague is going to kill millions of people if we can't stop them. So you have to swear that you're going to help me."

"I swear!"

"OK. And the second thing . . . you're definitely a super-human?"

"No doubt about that." I was just about to ask her to find a couple of guys to help her unlock the door when I heard the mechanism begin to ratchet open, so I figured she wasn't on her own.

But when the heavy bolts were drawn back and the door was pulled open, I was surprised to see that she *was* alone.

As soon as she saw me, she backed away. *Why is no one ever pleased to see me?* I wondered. Of course I knew the answer, but just once it would be nice for someone new to smile when they met me.

I did my best not to smile at the girl, though. She was African-American, about fourteen or fifteen years old, and absolutely drop-dead gorgeous. I'd never had any time for girls before I became Brawn, and few opportunities to meet them afterward.

"Remember the deal?" she asked.

"I remember. You know who I am?"

She nodded. "Of course I do. You're Brawn."

For once I didn't hate that name. Not when *she* said it.

Her name was Abigail de Luyando. Though at first we stuck together only because of circumstance, looking back I can see that she was the best friend I ever had. And even to this day, I can't think about her without my heart aching.

CHAPTER 23

FOR A SHORT WHILE—not nearly long enough—we were kind of a team. There was me, Abby, Max Dalton's sister Roz, a guy called Thunder who could control sound waves, and a kid with no powers who somehow just kept tagging along. That was Lance. If he'd had a superhero name, it would have been Big Mouth.

The organization that Abby mentioned—The Helotry— had plans to take over the world. It seemed like that was *every-one's* plan in those days. I remember thinking that anyone who really wanted to take over the world should be locked up for their own safety. I mean, most people can barely organize a dinner party without messing up some part of it.

The Helotry had worked in secret for thousands of years, worshipping a long-dead warrior called Krodin who was apparently the first-ever superhuman. They brought him to our time, and, man, he was one tough opponent.

He was only average sized, but he was as strong as I was and much, much faster. He was a vicious fighter, too, and he was invulnerable. Not in the same way as, say, The Shark, who just couldn't be damaged. Krodin could be hurt, but he healed almost instantly, and anything you did to him usually worked only once. His body could adapt to anything.

The Helotry had recruited Slaughter. Unfortunately I didn't get a chance to take her on, and in light of what happened a few years later, that is my single biggest regret. They'd also recruited Pyrokine—that was why they'd attacked the prison—and used his power to help transport Krodin from the past.

But, with some help from Paragon, Quantum, and Max Dalton, we beat them, and we saved the world. It wasn't without cost: Pyrokine switched sides, and sacrificed himself to destroy Krodin. It was a massive, powerful blast that, we later learned, wasn't simply a big explosion.

After that, I returned to Oak Grove. It wasn't really my choice: Officially I was still a prisoner, and since the whole Krodin situation was kept secret, having me wandering free would have raised far too many questions.

But three weeks later we discovered that Krodin hadn't died in Pyrokine's blast. Instead, he'd been sent back in time about five or six years. Without any of us around to stop him, he began to work his way into a position of power. He recruited Max Dalton, who used his ability to read and control minds to make sure that things went Krodin's way.

Krodin became the chancellor of the United States of America, responsible for the nation's security, and he used that position to build his own army.

Max and Krodin enlisted the help of a young superhuman genius called Casey Duval to create powerful weapons and advanced machines, and it wasn't long before they had sealed off the United States from the rest of the world.

Casey later turned on them, mostly because Krodin kind of brings that out in people, but one of his inventions was a teleporter that would allow Krodin to transport his soldiers instantly to anywhere in the world. The technology was based on the method Pyrokine had used to bring Krodin out of the past.

Of course, *we* didn't know any of this. . . . By sending Krodin back in time, Pyrokine had split the time line in two. In the "real" time line, we carried on as normal, but in the alternate one Krodin materialized five or six years earlier and set about creating his empire.

The first time Krodin's teleporter was used, those of us who'd been present for the battle with Krodin were somehow dragged into that alternate version of Earth.

It was not a nice place. The people lived in constant fear, every aspect of their lives monitored at all times. Almost all of that world's superhumans had either been killed or recruited by Krodin.

At his base in the swamplands of Louisiana, we fought Krodin alongside his former ally Casey Duval, who had taken on the identity of the armored superhero Daedalus. But Casey wasn't fighting Krodin because that was the right thing to do: His plan had been to allow Krodin to build his empire, and then Casey would kill Krodin and take it from him. I guess if you're desperate to rule the world, that's the way to do it: Let someone else do all the work, and then step in at the end.

But Casey's plan didn't take into account the fact that Krodin was much, much tougher than any of us had guessed. . . . After a battle that pretty much tore the base apart—and almost got me killed in the process—Krodin punched his fist straight through Casey's armor, killing him instantly.

In the end, Krodin was defeated by his own technology. Because his body could adapt to anything, we couldn't use the teleporter to send him far away. It had been used on him once, so it wouldn't work again.

Or so we thought . . . But Lance turned out to be smarter than we realized. He set the teleporter's controls to pick Krodin out of the past, from the very moment he materialized after his battle with Pyrokine. Back then, you see, Krodin hadn't experienced the teleporter, so his body had no defense against its effects.

Lance sent him somewhere far away. He wouldn't say where, just that Krodin would not be coming back.

The instant Lance activated the teleporter and pulled Krodin out of the past, the time line was corrected and everything went back to the way it should have been. Krodin's empire vanished, because it never existed.

But, as before, those of us who were caught up in Krodin's blast somehow remained unaffected by the shift in time lines. . . . We stayed in the same place while the world restructured itself around us: We were suddenly stranded in the middle of a swamp in Louisiana.

The fight with Krodin had really taken it out of us. Max was being hailed by the others as the savior of the day, but that really didn't sit well with me. I knew him then for what he really was: a coldhearted manipulator who used his mind control to make everyone think he was a hero. But his power didn't work on me, and I couldn't tell the others. Even if they had believed me, Max would have used his power again to make them forget.

Or he could get them to turn on me, just like he had the first time I met him, when Roz suddenly went from shouting at Max for attacking me to treating me like a monster.

So I knew what Max was really like, and he knew that I knew.

And I also knew he was scared of me, because I was one of the very few people whose mind he couldn't read. Max would never know what I was thinking.

As we walked through the swamp, I carried Abby on my shoulder: She'd been injured, and it didn't make sense for her to walk while I could carry her effortlessly.

This made Lance very, very jealous. It was obvious that he was head over heels in love with Abby. And so was Thunder. That made me feel a little bit sorry for Roz. She was just as cute as Abby, but for some reason neither Lance nor Thunder was interested in her.

Maybe that was Max's influence again, doing what he always does: assuming that he knows best and that there's nothing wrong with controlling people to make sure they act the way he wants.

But I can't say that *I* was in love with Abby, because I don't know what that kind of love feels like.

With Thunder flying and leading the way, and me and Max keeping well apart from each other, our ragtag team began the long, painful walk back to civilization.

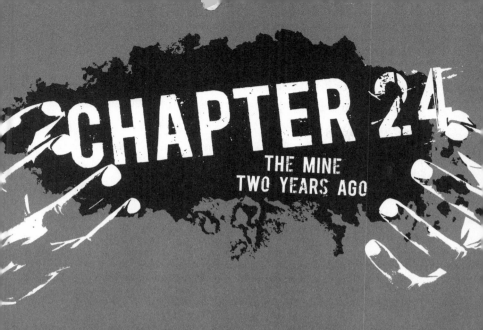

CHAPTER 24

THE MINE
TWO YEARS AGO

I DON'T KNOW FOR CERTAIN whether productivity in the mine decreased after Hazlegrove executed the other trustees, but it's a safe guess that it did.

I also don't know how I kept going. True to his word, Hazlegrove worked me twenty-three hours a day, seven days a week.

More than once I fell asleep as I was pushing the heavy carts of ore and had to be kicked awake by the guards. I lost weight: I had one hour a day in which to eat and sleep, and most of the time sleep hit me the instant my shift was over.

To maximize my sleep time I stayed in the mine shaft. I stopped washing—I just didn't have the time or the energy. Whenever they could, the other prisoners slipped me food and water, and that was probably the only thing that kept me alive and sane.

After the first week I was finding it hard to focus on anything. The guards would issue orders and I would immediately forget them.

By the third week I was starting to hallucinate. This happened so subtly at first that it took me a long time to realize it.

I was reaching the midpoint in my shift, struggling to push the filled cart another couple of yards, when it seemed to me that the walls were starting to move. Not much, just a few inches at a time, and it always happened when I wasn't looking.

But once, a shadow detached itself from the wall and became a woman who smiled and waved at me as I passed. I remember thinking how much the woman looked like Abby, and then realizing that it *was* Abby, that she had come to take me home.

"Keep out of sight," I whispered to her. "If the guards see you, they'll shoot."

"They won't see me," she said. "I know how to hide. Brawn, you're not looking good."

"You missed me, yeah?"

"What do *you* think? Of course I missed you!"

I grinned. "Good to know. It's been a long time. Way too long. Hey, are you and Quinn still together? You two were going to invite me over for dinner, remember? But you never did."

She put her hand on my arm as she walked alongside me. "You would have eaten everything in the apartment."

I passed a group of prisoners heading back down the shaft, and they gave me some strange looks.

"What's with them?" I asked Cosmo.

"Dude, they think you've gone crazy because you're talking to yourself."

"No, I'm talking to Abby," I began, and then realized that she wasn't there. She had never been there. Abby had been dead for years, and I was either dreaming her or talking to a ghost.

"You're suffering from severe sleep deprivation," Cosmo said. "Your mind is playing tricks on you. Earlier you thought you were eating an orange."

"Yeah. I was so sure, I could taste it." I stopped walking, and rubbed my eyes with the heels of my hands. "I think I'm losing my mind here." I looked down at Cosmo. "But, hey, that means I'm not, doesn't it? They say that if you're going mad, you don't *know* you're going mad. So if you think you are, then you're not."

"Yeah, that's supposed to be true."

"Like, just for a second there I started thinking that *you* were dead too! But that was just a dream."

And Cosmo said, "Oh, that was real. *This* is the dream. I died last year, remember?"

I reached my hand out to him and it passed right through his shoulder. "Yeah, of course. I remember."

But even though he wasn't real, he stayed with me for a while, and I was glad for the company.

CHAPTER 25

TWENTY-THREE YEARS AGO

A FEW MILES SOUTH of the border between Louisiana and Arkansas, we waited at a crossroads for Max Dalton's people to come pick us up.

"So everything's back to normal?" Roz asked Max as he stepped out of the old phone booth.

"Seems to be," Max said. "According to Ollie all of us just disappeared from where we were supposed to be. Josh is fine. He's used to me and Roz heading off on missions, so he's none the wiser. From what Ollie says, nothing else has changed. The world is as it should be."

Thunder said, "Yeah, but he didn't sound very happy."

"You should know better than to listen in on other people's conversations," Max said.

Thunder shrugged. He'd been right beside me when Max

ordered Krodin's men to fire at us, but he didn't seem to re-member that.

I was sitting on the edge of the road with Abby on one side and Roz on the other, both pressed up close to me. Not so much because they liked me, but because the mosquitoes al-ways gave me a wide clearance.

Across the street, Lance and Paragon were sitting cross-legged, facing each other and deep in conversation. Paragon's real name was Solomon Cord. He was about Max's age, but we all liked him because he wasn't a self-obsessed jerk.

"Wonder what they're talking about," Roz said.

Abby said, "Probably Lance's family."

A few weeks earlier, after our first battle with Krodin, Slaughter found where Lance lived and killed his parents and brother. Then when the time line changed, he got them back: In the alternative world, Krodin had wiped out The Helotry before they could recruit Slaughter, so she never encountered Lance and thus had no need to kill his family out of revenge.

But when Lance used the teleporter on Krodin and reset the time line, everything was back the way it had been, and Lance's family was still dead.

"I'm not sure I could have done that if I were him," Roz said.

Abby nudged me. "What about you? Do you have a family?"

"Yep. Got a ma and pa back home. They don't know what happened to me. You?"

"Mom, big sister, and four little brothers," Abby said. "My

dad's gone, though. Hey, here's something. I always thought that my mom and dad just separated, but the version of my mom in Krodin's world said that he had an affair and she threw him out."

Roz said, "Wow. So, are you going to mention it to her when you get home?"

Abby stiffened. "Home. Oh, I am going to be *so* grounded! She's probably going mad with worry!" She jumped to her feet and ran for the phone booth.

"How are you going to explain how you got out of Oak Grove?" Roz asked me.

"I haven't given it a minute's thought," I said. "Besides, I don't think I'm going back. Not this time. I've already spent far too much of my life locked up."

"Max won't like that."

"Max isn't my boss. He's not your boss either."

"You don't like him much, do you?"

I sighed. "Roz, your brother can control people's minds. Do you remember what he did when we were fighting Krodin?"

She nodded. "Yeah. He saved us."

"How? What did he *do* to save us?"

She raised her eyes. "Oh please! You were there, remember?"

"I remember Krodin telling Max to put me and Thunder in front of a firing squad, and he did it. And I remember Daedalus attacking him and knocking him out. So how *did* he save us?"

"Well, he . . ." She bit her lip and looked away.

"Stuck, huh? Roz, he's done this before. Back in Windfield

he made you forget about Pyrokine." Out of the corner of my eye I saw Max approaching. "And here he comes now, to make you forget this conversation."

Roz stood up and walked away.

"You're going to have to stop that," Max said to me.

"*I'm* going to have to stop? You're the one messing with people's minds. But you can't mess with mine." I tapped my forehead. "This is a closed book as far as you're concerned."

"I could turn them all against you, you know. I could have the whole world hounding you for the rest of your life."

"Dalton, if you're supposed to be a good guy, why are you doing stuff like this? Why don't you use your powers for good?"

"I do. That's all I do. All of my plans are for the greater good, Brawn. So don't screw things up for me. Keep out of my way. And don't think that I don't know you just because I can't read your mind. I know all your secrets. I know your real name, I know what happened to you when you were twelve. I even know the names of the people who held you prisoner in Antarctica for a year." He tapped his own forehead, mimicking my action. "This is a closed book to *you*, unless you agree to stay out of my business. If you ever want revenge on Harmony Yuan and Gordon Tremont, you'll need my help."

"There *was* a time when revenge was all I could think of, but . . ." I shrugged. "Life's too short for that sort of thing."

"Even after what they put you through?"

"If I wanted revenge on them, I'd already have taken it."

"There's also the matter of your parents," Max said. "I know how to get to them."

"What do you mean by that?"

"You push me the wrong way and I can make them forget that they ever *had* a kid."

I stood up slowly, and looked down at him. "That was a threat, right? You know, for someone who lost his own parents, that's a lousy thing to say. Your true colors are showing, Max. You're a bully. And an idiot. Why do you think I haven't tried to contact my parents? Because I can't let them see me like this. So, yeah, do it. *Make* them forget. You'd be doing them and me a favor!"

I looked over toward the others. They hadn't seemed to notice that I was yelling at Max. I sighed. "Got to say, though . . . That is one very useful ability you have."

He nodded. "It is."

"Aren't you worried that you're going to do permanent damage to someone?"

"I know what I'm doing."

We looked at each other in silence for a moment, and I felt my fury at Dalton start to fade. It seemed to me that we'd reached an understanding. My immunity to Max's control put me in a position that was quite unique for him: He couldn't lie to me as easily as he could to everyone else.

I said, "Krodin was smarter than the other universe's version of you. He manipulated him the same way you manipulate other people. Sooner or later you'll come up against someone else like him."

"Yeah, maybe. But until that happens, I'll stick with my plans."

"And what *are* those plans?"

"Use my powers to build a huge organization to save the human race from destroying itself."

"That's what Tremont told me *he* was doing. He wanted me to raid every place in the country that's developing quantum processors and steal their work. Well, I didn't trust him and I don't trust you. Maybe you should team up with him, so I can distrust the one organization and save myself some time."

"I could actually use you on my side, Brawn. If Tremont's people *can* get a quantum processor to work, they'll be able to take control of every nation on the planet. We have to stop them, and we have to do it before he recruits more superhumans. My experts tell me that right now we're only at the beginning of the bell-shaped curve. In about fifty years there'll be *thousands* of superhumans. Even if Tremont can't persuade any of them to join him, the odds are that a few of them are going to have enough power to wipe out the human race. All it will take is one maniac with that sort of power, and we're done. Hell, there's already a couple I'm scared of. Terrain, for one. He seems to have complete telekinetic control over inorganic matter. If he applied himself, he could crack the Earth in two."

"Maybe so, but is he *likely* to do that?"

"So far he hasn't done anything that suggests he's got the imagination or the desire. But suppose there's another superhuman with *my* abilities. Someone completely unhinged. He could make Terrain do whatever he wanted. *Now* do you understand?"

"I understand your reasons, yes. But not your methods."

"Just . . . Just don't get in my way. For all our sakes. And please stop telling Roz that I'm manipulating her thoughts and feelings. She and Josh are the only family I have. I love them, and I will do anything I think is right to protect them. *Almost* anything: I won't put them—or myself—above the safety of the human race."

I considered this for a moment. "All right. Let's say that you and I make a deal. . . . I'll do as you ask, but in return you have to find someone for me."

I told him of the young man who'd tried to recruit The Scarlet Slayer, and how that man had claimed to know everything about our superhuman abilities, about the strange blue lights that only a few people could see.

When I was finished, Max said, "I know who that was. I've been trying to track him down for the past two years. I'm certain that everything he claims is true. His chief superhuman gift is the ability to see the power in others. With the right resources—which I can provide—he'll be able to manipulate the energy however he sees fit." Max paused for a moment, as though wondering just how much he should tell me. "And now I know his name. We met him, in Krodin's universe. I told you that there were a couple of superhumans I'm scared of. Well, Krodin's one and he's the other one. His name is Casey Duval."

"Daedalus?" I said. "Oh *man* . . . !"

He began to pace back and forth. "In Krodin's world Casey Duval's skills were a lot more advanced than they are in ours. Krodin recognized his abilities and provided him with unlimited resources. That's why we have to find him as soon as possible, before some other group discovers him and starts feeding him what he needs."

"Then we might have a problem," I said. "Because I'm pretty sure that someone else already *has* found him. Gordon Tremont."

Max's face drained of what little color it had. "I pray that's not true."

On the far side of the road, Lance got to his feet and started walking toward us. Max glanced at him, and Lance instantly turned around and went over to Abby instead.

It disturbed me that Max could so easily and so casually mess with someone else's mind, but this wasn't the time to bring that up again. "Look, who *is* Tremont?" I asked him. "What's his organization?"

"Their organization formed three decades ago, a splinter group from The Helotry of the Fifth King. The Helotry believed that the human race could be saved only by bringing Krodin out of the past. Their plague was designed to weaken the humans so that Krodin could rule. But Tremont's people came to believe that their true purpose was to end all human life."

"They want to destroy the world?" I shook my head. "No. Come on, no one's *that* insane!"

"Brawn, you need to get this through your thick skull: The end of the human race wouldn't be the end of the world. Humanity is just *one* species out of millions. Tremont's people want the humans gone so that the superhumans can have the planet to themselves."

"There's not enough superhumans for that to work."

"Not yet. But they were thinking long-term. Krodin was immortal, remember? But the point is that Tremont recruited you because he suspected that *you* would be the instigator of the Armageddon he wanted, that you were very close to their image of the perfect superhuman. Twice as tall as any human, practically invulnerable, inexhaustible, with incredible strength."

I sat down again. "Then they're crazy!"

"I never said they weren't crazy, Brawn. Look . . . You remember your history lessons, the ideal of the perfect Aryan man from Nazi Germany? The concept of the master race? Well, that's what they saw in you. An almost perfect superhuman who was young enough to mold to their will."

"Max, how do you *know* all this?"

"Because once a month a team of Tremont's people visit Manhattan on business, and they always stay in the same hotel suite. I stay in the suite next door, and I read their minds. But they messed up with you. They thought that since you were so young, they could frighten and manipulate you into working with them. Tremont almost lost his mind after you escaped from Antarctica." Max suddenly smiled. "They still don't know how you managed to get to South America, by the way, and that *really* bugs them."

I couldn't help smiling back. "Good. They're never going to find out."

Max finally stopped pacing and sat down opposite me. "You remember how they completely changed their approach when they caught you again in Venezuela? Suddenly they were your friends. Harmony Yuan told you the circumstances had changed. If their resident genius *is* Casey Duval, then I know now that was true. What had changed was that he'd heard about their attack and how you survived it, and he decided that you'd be a good ally."

"I don't see how he made *that* connection."

"It wasn't *because* you survived, it was *how* you did it. You destroyed two helicopter gunships without batting an eyelash. That, and the way you escaped from their base in Antarctica, showed him that you were someone he wanted on his side."

Thunder suddenly called out "Incoming! Copters . . . Three at least, maybe four."

"Finally," Max said. He stood up and stretched. "Look, Brawn, all this is almost as new to me as it is to you. I'm still only putting the pieces together. But after what we saw in Krodin's universe, I'm pretty much convinced that Casey *is* Tremont's genius superhuman. And if so, if Tremont has convinced Casey that the Earth should be wiped clean of ordinary humans, we have to move fast to stop them. Otherwise their organization's name will become a prophecy. If anyone's smart enough to get a quantum processor to work, it's Casey Duval."

"So what *are* they called?"

"When they broke away from The Helotry, they chose a word that summed up exactly what they believe. They wanted something that meant Armageddon. The Apocalypse. The End of Days. They finally settled on an old Norse word. It means 'the final destiny of the gods.' That's how they see us superhumans: as the gods who will inherit the Earth."

"And that word is?"

"Ragnarök."

CHAPTER 26

TWO WEEKS LATER, WE GATHERED in a warehouse on the edge of a small town in northeast New Jersey. The warehouse belonged to one of Max's many companies. From the outside it looked like an ordinary facility owned by a furniture store, but inside, it was equipped with living quarters, meeting rooms, a secure steel-barred cell, a gymnasium, and an armory.

Ox, one of the former U.S. Rangers who worked with Max, drove me to the warehouse in the back of a truck. He reversed the truck in and closed the doors before letting me out. Thunder, Abby, and Lance were already there.

Abby was wearing her homemade armor with her heavy sword slung on her back, and Thunder was in a new costume. This one had the black and green colors of his old wet suit, but looked to be a bit more practical.

"All right, guys," Ox said. "Max and Roz are only a few minutes away. I'll set up the meeting room."

"So where have *you* been?" Abby asked me as I climbed out of the truck.

"Maryland," I said. "Another one of Max's places. What about you? Did you get into trouble with your mom?"

"Yeah, but Max visited her and did his thing to make her forget that I'd disappeared for a few days."

Thunder said, "Same here. But he probably didn't need to use his powers on *my* mom and my stepdad: They were already impressed that Max showed up in an expensive car."

Lance said, "Well, *I've* been living here with the Rangers." He made a face. "I think they've sort of adopted me or something. They wake me up at six in the morning. *Every* morning. And they work out for an hour and then they go for a run. Down to Ridgefield, over to Edgewater, up to Fort Lee, then back here. That's nearly eight miles! All that before breakfast."

"It'll do you good," Abby said.

"Hey, I never said I went *with* them! I go back to bed."

"You should join them," Thunder said. "You're never too young to start a good exercise regimen."

Lance went, "Pfff! It's easy for you guys. You're super-human."

"My powers don't make me any stronger than an ordinary person," Thunder said. "I have to keep fit too."

Abby looked at me. "What about the prison thing? Did Max sort it out for you?"

"Yeah. He persuaded them to release me into his custody."

I explained about my agreement with District Attorney Olafs-son and Judge Khan.

"Cool. So you can be a permanent member of the team, then?"

At the same time, Lance and I asked, "We're a *team*?"

Lance shouted, "Jinx!" and pumped the air with his fist. "Yes! You can't talk until I say your name!"

I was immediately tempted to say, "Oh yeah?" but there was something so childish about being jinxed that I couldn't help smiling. It had been four years since I'd last hung around with people my own age, and I was struck by how much I had missed out on years of silliness, dumb games, and stupid jokes.

Abby thumped Lance in the arm. "Don't do that!"

Thunder said, "Yeah. Superstition brings bad luck, every-one knows that."

Lance grinned as he rubbed his arm. "I *might* say his name if he buys me a soda."

Abby asked me, "Do you even have any money?"

I shook my head.

"Lance, say his name."

Lance faked a cough. "Oh man, I'm real *thirsty* all of a sudden."

From the far side of the warehouse Ox called, "Meeting's on, kids."

Unlike the rest of the warehouse, the ceiling in the meeting room was only average height. I had to sit cross-legged on the floor.

Max and Roz were wearing their black uniforms, which suggested to me that we were going into action.

Max projected a schematic of a large building onto the whitewashed wall. "This is Gordon Tremont's main facility in Pennsylvania, about twenty miles east of Pittsburgh. My sources tell me that Casey Duval is there right now. Security is unknown, but we should expect strong resistance. Certainly live ammunition and very probably a superhuman element. We'll be approaching in silence. Thunder, you can take care of that, right?"

Thunder nodded.

"We need to get close enough that I can scan the minds of the guards, see what we're up against. But regardless of what we find, we're going in. We're the Alpha team. Our primary goal is to get Casey out alive. And we do whatever it takes." He looked around at us. "Abby, Thunder, and I will go in first and punch a hole through their defenses. Roz, Brawn, and the Rangers are our second wave: Once we give the word, they'll come in after us."

Roz said, "But Brawn's the strongest. He should go in first."

Lance said, "No, Max is right. If they see Brawn coming, they'll immediately start locking down everything. We need to already be in there before they even know they're under attack. A mission like this, you have to think of it as surgery. You go in like a scalpel, not like a chain saw." To Max, he said, "And what'll I be doing?"

"Your role is just as vital as everyone else's." Max looked

at his wristwatch. "At precisely nine thirty this evening, you'll
be in the monitoring station here. You will tune the TV set to
channel thirty-one. Are you taking this in, Lance?"

Lance nodded.

"Good. There's a documentary about jet engines. Your mission is to press 'Record' before the show starts, then press
'Stop' when it's over. The timer's broken."

"Oh, very funny! That's all you think I'm good for?"

"That's something I won't know until about ten thirty.
Don't mess it up." Max returned his attention to the image on
the wall. "All joking aside . . . The Beta team's goal is to access
their computers and extract every byte of data they can get
their hands on, then wipe their hard drives and destroy any
backup tapes. It's not enough that *we* have Ragnarök's data:
We have to make sure that *they* can't use it."

Abby asked, "Who's on the Beta team?"

A woman's voice behind me said, "We are."

I turned to see four people standing just inside the door,
one woman and three men. The woman called herself Energy.
She was about twenty, very good-looking, with red-blond hair
and wearing a white-and-green costume. Next to her was
Solomon Cord, now in his full Paragon armor. Beside him
stood Quantum, also wearing white. The last of them was
looking right at me. We'd had a couple of run-ins before.

He nodded to me. "Brawn."

"Titan," I said.

Lance shouted, "Hey, you were jinxed! You're not supposed to talk!" Then he turned bright red when everyone
stared at him. "Uh, sorry."

Max said, "First things first . . . We keep identities secret, understood?" He glanced at Paragon, then back to Lance. "If you know someone's real name, you keep it to yourself unless you're certain that everyone else knows it. Titan?"

Titan said, "Paragon has the hardware and skills to access their computers. Quantum and I will run interference while he does so. Tremont's got a lot of people on call—superhuman and otherwise—and right now we don't know who or what we're going to find there. When we've got what we need, Energy will blast the entire facility with a contained electromagnetic pulse. That'll fry every computer circuit in the place."

Energy said, "Max, I'm not sure that letting the kids go in first is the right move."

"Everyone's got to learn sometime," Max said. "Besides, they might be young but they've seen a *lot* of action. They're good. And they're not much younger than we were when you first came to me, remember?"

Paragon asked, "But Lance stays here, right?"

"Absolutely," Max said. "I'm not putting him anywhere that'll get him into trouble."

Titan said, "There's still a question mark hanging over Brawn." He glanced at me, then back to Max. "Not all of us are convinced he's got the right attitude. We know he's quick to anger, and his reputation is sketchy, at best. He's a known criminal, and I'm not sure it's in our best interest to have any involvement with him."

I asked, "Isn't it customary to add the words *no offense* to the end of a statement like that?"

"If I'd intended no offense, I'd have said that."

"Still annoyed after that last beating, huh?" To the others, I said, "That was in Colorado. He attacked me out of nowhere. Just flew in and started punching me. Titan, remind me again how many times I hit you before you ran away. Once, wasn't it?"

"I didn't run away—there was an emergency that required my attention."

"Yeah, and the emergency was that you had to find a quiet place to have a good cry."

He glowered at me. "No, the emergency was a four-car pileup on the interstate! I saved eight people's lives that day!"

"Or nine, if you include your own."

Paragon said, "That's enough! Titan, Brawn took on Krodin. Twice. If it hadn't been for his help, we'd never have made it. And Brawn . . . You don't get to question Titan's motives, got that? And you *really* don't get to suggest that he's a coward. He's saved my life half a dozen times. I trust him more than I trust anyone in this room."

I nodded. "OK."

Quantum asked, "Max, exactly how much of a threat is this Casey Duval?"

"Potentially . . . he's *very* dangerous. We learned that in Krodin's world. He was able to out-think all of us, planning his moves years in advance. He has a unique understanding of the energy that makes us superhuman, and in Krodin's universe he used that to enhance his own abilities and to turn at least one human into a superhuman. The level of technology they had . . ." Max shook his head. "It was *decades* ahead of ours. Solar cells that worked with almost one hundred percent efficiency, gravity-nullifying engines, advanced alloys, nanotechnology . . . He designed a portable machine that canceled out the powers of any superhuman within an eight-hundred-yard radius. And he created an armor that makes Paragon's look like a tinfoil suit."

"But the Casey Duval in *this* world," Energy said, "well, he hasn't done any of that."

"Not yet."

"We can't arrest someone for something he hasn't done."

"I disagree," Max said. "For the good of the human race, we not only can, but *must*."

Just after sunset Roz and I waited in the copter with Max's team, the former U.S. Rangers Oliver French, Antonio Lashley, and Stephen Oxford.

They seemed like OK guys. Very quiet—they usually spoke only when they had to—and always focused on the task at hand.

Roz was also quiet. I still wasn't sure what she thought of me. Of course, given the way Max was always messing with her mind, I couldn't be sure what Roz thought of anything. But she seemed nice enough.

Max's voice came in over the radio. "Got the facility in sight . . . Possible minor problem: Our plans showed a lot of trees that we were going to use for cover. The trees are gone. There's a good two-hundred-yard perimeter around the main building that's going to be impossible to cross without being spotted. I can't get close enough to read anyone."

Lashley picked up the handset. "Max, this is Lash. Recommend that you hold fire. I can contact the Beta team, send Quantum in ahead of you. He can move fast enough that he won't be seen."

"Negative, Lash. My instruments are showing that they've got the same warning device Termite used in Cádiz. It'll detect Quantum's presence and trigger an alarm."

"He could still—"

"Can't take that chance. We're going in anyway. Thunder, create one of your shock wave force fields around us. I want it to move with us as we run. Abby, you take point, but don't get too far ahead. . . . We're heading for that entrance there. On my mark . . ."

I realized I was clenching my fists. "Man, we should *be* there!" I said to Roz.

"Max knows what he's doing."

"I really hope you're right."

Stephen Oxford—Ox—got out of his seat and called out to the pilot. "Ernie? Take us up. Hold position outside the one-mile perimeter, two thousand feet." As the copter's engines roared to life, Ox turned to me and Roz and shouted, "You two get ready."

Over the noise of the engines we heard Max shout, "Now!"

Then the copter lurched into the air, and we could only guess at what was happening with Abby and the others.

Long minutes passed, and I found myself growing more and more anxious.

Roz shouted, "We should have heard from them by now!"

Lash nodded. "I know. Can't break radio silence, though."

I shifted toward the copter's oversized hatch. "Heck with this—get me in there!"

"Not until Max gives the word," Lash said.

"Look, either they're pinned down and they *can't* give the word, or they've been caught. Either way, I'm going in. And if I have to rip open the side of this copter and jump out, I will."

Lash hesitated for a moment, then shouted to the pilot, "Ernie—go! Pass directly over the facility. One hundred feet minimum. Top speed."

The copter surged forward, and Lash pulled open the hatch. As the wind whipped through, he yelled, "You sure you can do this?"

I grabbed hold of the hull on either side of the hatchway. Ahead, the four-story building was coming up fast. "Warn the pilot!" I yelled back to Lash. "Tell him to expect a sudden loss of balance!"

CHAPTER 27

THE MINE

IN THE INCREASINGLY RARE MOMENTS when my mind was fully alert, I knew that I was dying, just as I knew that I had no choice. If I didn't keep working, Hazlegrove would punish the other prisoners.

But most of the time I wasn't aware of anything other than pushing the full carts of ore up the winding tunnel to the processing station, then returning once the cart was emptied. Over and over, day after day.

Lack of sleep and food combined with the eternal struggle, and I was wasting away. Desperate for sustenance, my strained muscles began to wither. My skin lost its healthy blue pallor and started to turn gray.

Occasionally Hazlegrove stood in the doorway to his office watching me. Sometimes he'd follow me into the shaft, always at a safe distance, just watching in silence.

He wanted me to break, to collapse to the ground and beg him for mercy.

But I couldn't do that. I couldn't let him win.

Two months into the torture, Hazlegrove called me over to him. The hundred-yard distance between his office and the processing station seemed like a hundred miles, but I slowly shuffled over to him.

I stood in front of him, swaying, and hoped that whatever he had to say would take a very long time. This was the first break in the routine I had been granted.

He looked up at me. "You're lasting a lot longer than I ever imagined, Brawn."

I didn't have the energy or the will to reply.

"We had a pool going. All the guards chipped in. Fifty American dollars apiece. I had you down for forty-two days. You beat that. And right up to yesterday, Swinden was looking like the winner. He had sixty-three. But you beat that too." He grinned. "The funny thing is—you'll like this—we had a sort of running joke that if you outlasted all the guesses, the money would be yours. So, well done: You've won two thousand, three hundred dollars!"

In the office behind him, I heard Swinden and DePaiva laughing.

"Of course, you're a prisoner, so we can't actually give you the money. What do you want us to do with it?"

I looked at him for a moment, not quite sure that I understood what he was saying. Then it gradually filtered through that this was all a joke to him.

"Well? Any suggestions?"

"Charity," I said. "Give it to the prison guards' Widows and Orphans Fund. When the time comes, your wife and kid will appreciate that."

His smug grin instantly faded. "Why don't you just die?"

"Because I don't feel like it."

"Yeah? Well, you *will*. DePaiva? Get out here."

I heard the scrape of metal on wood as DePaiva jumped up from his desk.

Hazlegrove pointed past me, to the processing station where two prisoners were about to hook up my cart to the hoist that would tip its contents into the crusher. "Get over there and tell those two to stop what they're doing and leave the cart where it is."

As DePaiva hurried over to the processing station, Hazlegrove said to me, "On my last inspection I noticed that the rails were looking a little loose. They need something heavy to tamp them down into place. Something like a full cart run the entire length of the tunnel. A full cart, from this end of the track to the other. Two hundred times should be a good start. Get to it, Brawn. Come on. Chop-chop!"

I returned to my cart, my feet dragging from the effort.

Behind me, I heard Swinden say, "Boss . . . That's . . . You're not serious, are you? That goes against what you wanted—he won't even be productive now!"

"You have a problem with the way we do things here, Swinden, feel free to quit."

That was all I heard. When I reached the cart, DePaiva was lowering his radio and looking toward Hazlegrove with an expression of disbelief.

The other prisoners were unable to look me in the eye as I started to push it back toward the entrance to the mine shaft.

DePaiva followed me, and into his radio he said, "Boss, are you *sure* about this?"

Hazlegrove's voice came back. "Yes, I'm sure. Don't question me again."

At least going down will be a little easier, I told myself. When I reached the entrance, I ducked my head and kept pushing.

DePaiva caught up with me a minute later. "How long does it take you, usually, to get the cart up from the end of the tracks?"

"Used to be an hour," I said. "Now it's nearer two."

"And how long to bring it back down?"

"Ten, maybe fifteen minutes. Full one will take longer. Forty minutes."

"So that's about two and a half hours," DePaiva said.

I grunted as I pushed the cart past a slight kink in the track that I'd come to think of as The Logjam. "Yeah."

"Then stop. Brawn? I said stop."

I hunched lower, continued pushing. "Hazlegrove said—"

"Hazlegrove is losing his grip. What he was doing before was bad, but this . . . This is torture. It's inhuman. I know I've done some bad things, but I won't be a party to this. So sit down. Get some sleep. I'll wake you in two and a half hours."

DePaiva and Swinden saved my life.

They took turns watching me whenever Hazlegrove was on duty. As far as he was aware, I spent twenty-three hours a day pushing that cart full of ore up and down the mine shaft.

In reality, every two and a half hours I pushed it out of the entrance, up to the processing station, then back down through the entrance and stopped just out of Hazlegrove's sight.

And when he wasn't on duty, Swinden and DePaiva left me alone to do what I wanted. Mostly, that was sleep.

Once, Hazlegrove entered the mine shaft shortly after I sat down. Swinden saw him coming and started kicking me in the side. "Get up! You lousy, lazy pile of trash!"

As I pulled myself up, he said to Hazlegrove, "Collapsed, boss. I think we're pushing too hard even for him."

Hazlegrove said, "Is he still alive, Swinden? Well? Is he?"

"Well, yes, sir."

"Then we're *not* pushing him too hard. Keep watching him. If he collapses again, kick him harder."

After about forty days of this, Hazlegrove stopped me as I emerged from the mine shaft. "Why are you not dead yet? If anything, you look stronger than you did before we started this."

"Second wind," I said. "Or it could be that I'm immortal."

"Productivity is down," Hazlegrove said. "The warden wants to know why."

"Not my problem. You're the one who ordered the murder of the other trustees and halved everyone's rations."

"Productivity will increase by the end of the week, or I will start feeding the weaker prisoners into the crusher. Do you understand?"

"I understand that if you do anything like that, Hazlegrove, you'll suffer a fate that's considerably worse. Don't ever forget that the welfare of the prisoners is the only hold you have on me." I straightened up and stretched, rolling my shoulders back. "You know, one way to increase productivity would be to allow me to get back to work instead of pushing the same bunch of rocks around all the time. And increase the rations again."

"We can't afford that."

"You can't afford *not* to."

He scowled at me for a moment, then turned on his heel and stalked away. He came back a few seconds later with his face red and his teeth clenched. "All right. Let's decide you've taken your punishment. You get the other inmates motivated and things go back the way they were."

It was a minor victory: Hazlegrove hadn't been able to break me, but I'd broken him. "Got it."

"I want productivity up by the end of the week."

"There's one thing I need to know before I can promise that," I said.

"What *now?*"

"What day is today?"

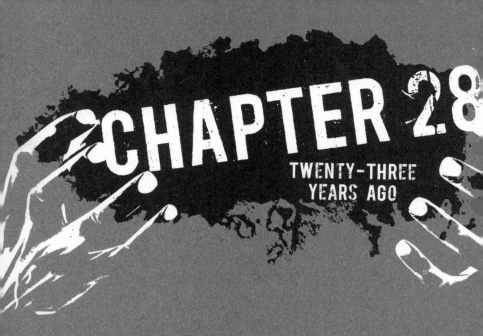

CHAPTER 28

TWENTY-THREE YEARS AGO

THE INSTANT I DROPPED from the copter toward the large, barely lit building, a thought occurred to me: *What if this world's version of Casey Duval has also created a power-nullifying device?*

But I didn't even have time for panic to set in: I crashed down feetfirst onto the roof. For a fraction of a second it held—then it collapsed under me.

I tumbled down into the cavernous room below in a shower of dust, bricks, and crumpled aluminum sheeting, landing in a crouch.

Directly in front of me Abby was swinging her sword at a large, fast-moving, complex piece of machinery. She was standing over Thunder, who was lying facedown on the ground, unmoving.

"Brawn!" Abby shouted. "Need some help here!"

I raced toward her, coming almost within reach of the machine before it sprang into the air and passed over my head in a blur of metal framework, cables, and limbs.

I spun around to face it just as a heavy weight shot out from within the framework and slammed into my head with such ferocity I was almost knocked off my feet. The machine was moving constantly, not on wheels but on three powerful pneumatic legs, the whole device ceaselessly bobbing and weaving, shifting its considerable weight around with all the grace and power of a champion heavyweight boxer in prime condition.

I made another grab for it, and two strong claws instantly locked onto my arm and pulled me forward just as its pneumatic legs launched it up and over me. I pitched forward, stumbled, and it crashed down into my back, flattening me.

Before I could recover, it had tumbled to my left and a claw shot out again, this time with enough precision to grab hold of the tip of my ear and give it a sudden sharp twist. The pain was excruciating, and as I tried to pull myself free, I lashed out blindly with my feet and fists. A lucky kick hit the machine's foremost leg, knocking it aside, and the machine let go of my ear and staggered back as it regained its balance.

As I was pushing myself up, Abby threw herself at the machine, but its many complex arms were just a blur, striking out at her at the apex of her jump. It knocked her to the side and then rushed at me again.

The machine was so intricate and contained so many constantly shifting parts that I couldn't easily tell what shape or size it was. There was no obvious "head" or central mass, nothing specific to aim at.

I crouched, ready to tackle it, and its top half tipped forward and planted its claws and arms on the hard floor. Suddenly it was coming at me upside down, its three massive legs spinning and whirling.

One of the legs clipped my chin at the same instant another slammed into my stomach. I managed to grab the third with both hands, but before I could do anything else, the machine's claws darted out and grabbed hold of my ankles, and its other arms pushed hard against the floor.

Suddenly I realized I was supporting its entire weight.

Another of the legs smashed into the side of my head, so I let go with one hand and grabbed that one just as the remaining leg started to pummel me in the face, a couple dozen short-sharp jabs in a handful of seconds.

Enough! I said to myself. I tightened my grip on the two struggling legs, tensed my arms, and pulled, forcing my arms as far apart as possible.

And then, as though it were learning from me, the machine did the same thing with the heavy claws locked onto my ankles.

Unbalanced, I toppled forward right onto the machine, and it again reconfigured itself: Its arms and legs twisted and shifted, locking onto my own limbs. A thick steel cable shot out of somewhere inside it and snaked around my neck.

I could feel the cable flexing and squirming like it had a mind and purpose of its own. Tiny points of pain scurried across my throat, and I realized that it was not actually one piece, but dozens of thumb-sized machines all locked together, each segment with its own set of clawlike legs, crawling around and around my neck and getting tighter by the second.

A second cable darted across the small of my back, holding me tight as the whole machine began to fold in the middle, its top half forcing my torso up, the rest of it pushing my legs back.

Do something! my brain screamed at me.

I tensed my stomach muscles and tried to force myself forward, pushing against the machine's strength.

Then a third cable blasted out, striking at my face. I flinched, but I was too slow: The cable found its way into my mouth, and I gagged on the sharp metallic taste. Its claws dug into my tongue and the inside of my cheeks as it tried to climb down my throat.

But my enhanced strength wasn't just in my limbs: I bit down. Hard. My teeth pierced one of the cable's segments, crushing it, and the remainder of the cable pulled back.

I had a brief glimpse of sparks bursting from the severed end, but now all I could focus on was the half-dozen segments already in my mouth that had broken apart and continued clawing their way down my gullet.

And that was when I really began to panic. I started to struggle wildly against the machine's grip, my arms and legs flailing. It responded by tightening the cable around my waist and pushing harder against me, trying to snap my spine.

I managed to get one leg free, and as its claws grabbed for

me again, I planted my foot on the ground and kicked out as hard as I could, launching both myself and the machine several feet into the air.

We crashed down hard, and the machine readjusted itself to compensate.

That was the first mistake it made: It loosened its grip on my left arm.

I locked my fingers around the cable at my throat and pulled, severing it from the machine and scattering a dozen segments across the floor.

The claw darted out again, seeking my left arm, but I was able to grab onto it instead. I pushed back against it and heard its powerful motors whining in protest. Then something snapped inside it and the claw went limp. I formed the fingers of my hand into a point, and jabbed down into the mass of whirling metal.

Just as I hoped it would, the machine grabbed onto my hand. I continued pushing, and it continued struggling against me.

I jerked my still-trapped right arm back, and it shifted its weight to compensate.

I pushed my right arm forward and pulled the left back. Again, the machine had to readjust to match my movements. Then I squeezed my left hand into a fist and pulled my arm down toward my side, stretching the machine's arms to their limits.

There was a sharp *ping* as something else inside it snapped, and then the fingers of my right hand touched the ground.

I shifted my own weight onto my right hand, and the machine began to tip over. It reacted by letting go of my legs.

I kicked down, hard against the floor, flipping over so that I landed on my back with the machine above me. I was hoping that this angle would give me an advantage.

But the damage it had sustained wasn't enough to slow it down. Now it was slamming its legs over and over into my head, chest, and stomach.

Two of the legs locked onto my head as the third rose, then came down hard, striking me in the forehead and sending a shock wave of pain through my skull. Dazed, my vision blurring, I saw it coming again, and couldn't even flinch as it struck the same spot.

When it pulled back this time, the sharp, heavy edge was smeared with blood.

Then the leg shifted and its internal mechanisms readjusted, forming the end into a narrow point like the tip of a pickax.

I closed my eyes as it streaked down toward my face.

There was a *swish* of something moving fast through the air, a sharp clash, but nothing hit me.

I heard something heavy and metal crashing to the floor beside me, and opened my eyes to see the sparking stump of the leg flailing.

There was a blur of glistening metal and another sharp clash, and one of the limbs holding my head in place suddenly went limp.

Abby's sword sliced through the cable around my waist,

and I pushed up against the machine, forcing it to my left as I rolled to the right.

I got up onto my knees and looked at the jumble of twitching, sparking metal, and at Abby, now casually poking at it with her sword.

"I think it's dead," she said. "You OK?"

"I will be." I wiped the blood away from my eyes, then felt something rise in my throat.

Abby made a face. "Oh man, you're not going to throw up, are you?"

I pitched forward onto my hands, and felt myself retch and gag. Five of the segments from the cable clattered wetly onto the ground. "I don't think that's all of them. . . ." Another cramp from my stomach. "Nope, here comes the last one. . . ."

My stomach heaved and fresh bile burned my throat as the last of the segments was forced up and into my mouth. I coughed as it passed my tongue, then barfed the bile onto the ground.

"Ew, *gross!*" Abby said.

I started to speak, but my lower lip felt numb.

Abby made a face. "Uh, Brawn . . . It's still there. It's hanging onto your lip."

I pulled the tiny machine free and held it between my thumb and forefinger as it waved its tiny claws uselessly in the air. "Nasty little fellas, aren't they?" I closed my fist around it and crushed it.

But Abby wasn't listening. She had rushed over to Thunder and was moving him into the recovery position.

"What happened here?" I asked. "And where's Max?"

"They were waiting for us," Abby said. "Like they knew we were coming. They hit Max and Thunder with something." She pointed to a cluster of small darts that protruded from the left side of Thunder's neck and face. "They fired at me too, but I saw the darts coming."

"What about Max?"

"They took him. Five guys, maybe six. I was busying fighting Frankenstein's Erector Set over there."

"This doesn't make sense," I said. "Max should have read their minds, and Thunder should have been able to hear them."

"I know. I'm guessing that they had one of those portable power-damping machines that Casey invented in Krodin's world." She held up her two-way radio. "This thing's dead too. Yours?"

"Uh, I think I left mine in the helicopter. So what do we do?"

Before Abby could answer, there was a blur to my left, and Quantum was suddenly crouched next to Thunder, checking his pulse. "Seems OK, just unconscious. No other obvious injuries. Brawn, pick him up. We're out of here."

"They took Max," Abby said.

"I know—Titan and Energy are following them."

I squatted down and scooped up Thunder, and lifted him onto my shoulder. As I straightened up, I heard the familiar whine of Paragon's jetpack approaching from outside.

Quantum looked around the warehouse. "Nothing here . . . And by the looks of the dust, there hasn't been much of anything here for a long time, just that pile of debris."

"That pile of debris was a *robot*," Abby said. "It nearly killed me and Brawn!"

"But it didn't," Quantum said, still looking around. "So it was a ruse. Max was led to believe that this place was Ragnarök's main facility. . . ." He turned to me. "Your part is done, Brawn. Take Abby and Thunder back to the copter, and return to Max's base in New Jersey."

We heard the *thunk* of metal boots on concrete, then Paragon strode through the doorway. "Quantum, you're needed. Northeast, about twenty-two miles. Look for Energy's flare."

Quantum nodded, and then he was gone.

"You kids OK?" Paragon asked.

Abby said, "Yeah, but . . . That's *it*? Our part is over?"

He nodded. "Sucks, I know. But if Titan and Energy had gotten their way, you wouldn't have been here at all." He jerked his thumb over his shoulder. "Let's move. The Rangers are on the way. They'll pick up the pieces and secure the area."

Roz, Thunder, and Abby sat opposite me in the helicopter. Thunder was lying stretched out across the bench with his head resting on Abby's lap and his legs on Roz's. He'd told them he was fine, but they'd insisted he take it easy.

"I can't believe we just got sidelined like that," Abby said.

"I can," Thunder said. "They're older than us. They think they know better."

I said, "They're not *that* much older."

"We need our own helicopter," Abby said. "Roz, are you rich like your brother?"

"Rich? Not even close. It's not like Max inherited anything

from Mom and Dad. He earned everything himself. Are you saying we should have our own team?"

"I am," Abby said. "The four of us, plus Lance."

Thunder sat up. "How? We're all still in school!"

"I'm not," I said. "But you're right. There's no way we can do anything like that without Max's help. Besides, if some supervillain went on the rampage and we were somehow able to get to him, I guarantee you we'd find that Titan and his buddies had got there first. And even if we persuaded them to set us up as junior members of their team, we'd end up, like, bringing them coffee or taking their costumes to the cleaners, or some dumb tasks like that. They don't take us seriously. I mean, Roz, you didn't even get to leave the chopper this time!"

"That's just because Max is so overprotective of me."

"Yeah, but the point remains. They don't think we're good enough."

Abby said, "Well, they're wrong. We're just as good as they are. And we've got a good balance of skills too. Telekinesis, sound control, weapons, and strength. Plus Thunder can fly!"

"You can probably fly too," Thunder said. "We should work on that. In Krodin's world when we were looking for Brawn and we were flying and you were holding my hand . . . I let go for a few seconds, just before we found that freeway sign. It didn't even faze you."

"I don't remember that."

"Well, it's worth looking into. And you too," Thunder said to Roz. "If you can raise other objects into the air, then I see no reason you shouldn't be able to raise yourself." He smiled, then nodded to me. "If we can figure out a way to get *you* flying, then we won't need a helicopter at all."

"Ask Paragon to build you a jetpack," Abby suggested.

"Yeah, I can't see that happening," I said. "The public would love that. They're already terrified of me as it is. Imagine how much fun I'd have when they started blaming me for interfering with air traffic."

Thunder jumped to his feet. "Hold it. . . ." Suddenly the copter was filled with the usual bone-shaking roar of the rotors—he'd had us wrapped in a cocoon of silence so that we could talk. He frowned for a second, listening to something, and then the noise of the copter's engines was again cut off. "They got him. Roz, your brother's fine. Energy was able to trace the residual heat from their transport halfway across the state to another base, then the four of them went in. Quantum went first and took out the guards, and then Paragon grabbed Max while Titan and Energy captured Casey Duval."

"Great," Abby said. "So we got nearly killed, and they get all the glory."

I started to say something, then cut myself off. A thought had occurred to me, and if I said it out loud, then at some stage Max Dalton would be able to read it from the others' minds.

Tremont's people—or Casey Duval's people, depending on who you believed was running the organization—had been waiting for us, which obviously meant that they had known we were coming. Their power-damping machine had enabled them to capture Max and take out Thunder. But that machine hadn't affected me, so clearly it had been gone by the time I'd arrived.

They had to have taken it with them. If that was the case, then how come it hadn't affected the powers of Titan and the others?

There was only one answer that made sense to me: Casey Duval *wanted* to be captured.

CHAPTER 29

"**HOW'D YOU LIKE** my little toy?" Casey Duval asked me, a sly grin spreading across his lips. "Pretty cool, huh?"

"You mean the pile of scrap back in Pittsburgh? Hope it didn't cost you too much."

It was three in the morning, and in Max's base in New Jersey only Casey and I were still awake.

Thunder and Abby had been flown home to Midway, Max and Roz had returned to their Manhattan apartment, and Lance was asleep in his room on the other side of the base.

Casey had been locked in the cell with wrists and ankles chained. He was tall—about six three—with a slim build, broad shoulders, and a very square jaw. His black hair was tight at the sides and back, a little longer on top.

"I like working with machines," Casey said. "People are . . ." He shrugged. "People are unpredictable. It's almost like they have minds of their own. There's an old programming joke I've always liked: A computer is a machine that does what you tell it to do, not what you want it to do. Doesn't apply to me, though. I understand how they work. The robot you destroyed . . . Yes, it cost a lot of money. But mostly what it took was a lot of time and a little ingenuity."

"Which you have, I suppose."

"No. I have a *lot* of ingenuity. The robot was a prototype, based on the tech Tremont's people had been developing. We never got our quantum processor to work, but we did create a lot of very advanced technology along the way, including the self-modifying processor that controlled the robot. . . . You've never seen a machine move and react as fast as that before, have you? When we put it to the test, it was able to analyze every move we made and prepare a counterstrike so quickly, it's like the robot was seeing into the future. . . ." He sighed. "Just a shame it didn't quite live up to my expectations. I really thought I had something there. The trouble with self-modifying processors is that all it takes is one glitch and they change a part of themselves that they really shouldn't change." He leaned back in the plastic lawn chair and peered at me. "You and I would have met before now, if you'd stayed with Tremont's people in Texas. Why *did* you leave?"

"I didn't trust him."

"Very wise. I've never trusted him myself."

"Is that why you allowed yourself to be caught? To get away from him?"

A slight twitch of Casey's eyebrow was enough to tell me that he hadn't been expecting that. "You're smarter than people give you credit for, Brawn." He leaned forward again, resting his elbows on his knees. "This is how it works. . . . Dalton captures me and seizes the assets of the entire Ragnarök organization. Legally, of course, the assets should go to the government, but Dalton will use his ability to persuade the people in power to let him have everything. And the reason *I* want him to have—"

"I don't care," I said. "Seriously. I don't care about you and Max going back and forth with your stupid power play, each of you manipulating the other, playing some dumb cat-and-mouse game."

"Ah, but which of us is the cat and which is—"

"Not interested in *any* of that. Just tell me this: What do you want?"

"Control."

"Of?"

"Same as everyone. I want control of everything. The whole world."

I lay back on the floor and tucked my hands behind my head as I stared up at the ceiling. "Why, though? What good will it do you to control the world? With your brains you could make enough money to live in luxury for the rest of your life, and no one would have to get hurt along the way. You don't *have* to be a supervillain, you know. No one is forcing you."

"Supervillain?" Casey laughed. "What makes you say that?"

"You're superhuman, and you're a villain. It's not complicated."

"Who says I'm a villain? Seriously, Brawn . . . Which laws have I broken?"

He'd got me there. "Well . . . you were working with Gordon Tremont and Harmony Yuan."

"So were you. They lent you out to the military to take down Norman Misseldine and his band of deluded followers. Do you know *why* they did that? Did you even ask?"

"Misseldine was threatening to destroy Washington."

"No, that's why Misseldine had to be stopped. But why did Tremont get involved? It was because he wanted the military to owe him a favor. That favor would have been access to their own research into quantum computing. He used you, just like Max is using you."

"Yeah, but the difference is that I *know* Max is using me."

Again, Casey laughed. "No, you don't know anything of the sort. You know only what he wants you to know. Brawn, Max Dalton is not a particularly smart man, certainly not compared with me, but he's ambitious, and his power allows him to read other people's desires and give them what they want. He can even directly control some people by hiding parts of their memory, or implanting suggestions. One of the first things he does when he meets someone new and important is plant the suggestion that they should trust him. He . . ." Casey stopped himself. "Huh."

I sat up again. "What?"

"Your friends Abigail and Thunder and Lance don't trust Max, but that's because he thinks of them as nothing but cannon fodder. When they're a little older and more experienced, he'll start to see them as potential allies or adversaries, so that's when he'll start directly manipulating their feelings about him. But *you* . . . That's strange. You're already close to the apex of your powers. Max needs you on his side. You're potentially stronger than Titan and you're pretty much invulnerable. Plus you're a tenacious fighter—you keep going long after anyone else would have quit. So why don't you like him?"

"He's a jerk."

Casey raised his eyes. "I know *that*. What I mean is, why hasn't he forced you to like him?" Before I could answer, he said, "Oh my. Oh, that *is* interesting. Max is unable to control you. He can't read your mind." Casey's grin returned. "Until now, I thought that I was one of only two people he couldn't control, the other one being your old sparring partner Krodin. But now I see that there are three of us."

"How do *you* know about Krodin?"

"Tremont's organization is a splinter group from The Helotry. They have quite voluminous files on Krodin. All protected with a bespoke encryption system that's impossible to break." He grinned. "Tremont was an idiot. . . . He put me in charge of their computer division, the primary purpose of which was to crack encrypted files." He grinned again, a faraway look in his eyes. "Now, *that* was a good solution. When you enter a password into a computer, the computer checks the characters one by one to see if they're correct. If they are, it makes a note of that and then checks the next character. I wrote a tiny piece of software that timed the computer's response for each character. We're talking *nanoseconds* here. Correct characters took four-billionths of a second slower to process than incorrect characters. With that, I cracked the encryption on Tremont's files faster than you can blink. He doesn't know that, of course. That's a lesson for you, Brawn: Never show all your cards."

Casey got to his feet and shuffled forward until his forehead was resting against the bars of his cell. "Still . . . If Max can't access your mind, then I can tell you *everything* and he won't be able to pick it out of your brain. You want to know why we're superhuman? Why only some people have these powers? How'd you like to know exactly why your power has made you four meters tall and blue? And I'm sure you'd love to know how to reverse what happened to you, right?"

"Is that possible?"

"I think so. Not with the technology we have today, but maybe in a few years. And that's why I need a quantum processor."

"Go on. . . ."

"One of my gifts is the ability to see and understand the power in others. Your friend Thunder, for example . . . He thinks he controls sound, but that's not quite accurate. What is sound, only vibrations through the air? And there's a young Italian woman who, like you, has undergone a permanent physical transformation. She calls herself Loligo. She's a water-breather. I've seen film of her swimming. . . . It's incredible. She moves through the water just the same way as Thunder flies: She subconsciously commands the water to do whatever she wishes. Let's look at another young woman, the—let's be honest here—staggeringly beautiful Energy. You've seen her produce lightning, and conduct heat. If she could see what *I* see in her powers . . . she'd be terrified, I expect. Energy has the potential to extinguish a star."

I was kneeling in front of his cell now, unable to take my eyes off him.

"All of us have these abilities for a reason, Brawn. Even you."

"Why am I like this? Why did this happen to *me*?"

"Oh, I'm not going to tell you that. Not yet. Max doubtless has this place wired up with dozens of hidden cameras, and he doesn't need to know everything. But where was I? Yes, our superhuman brethren . . . I know *you* can't see the blue lights. Very few of us can. But they're there, spheres of energy floating around, fading into and out of existence. They make us what we are. They provide us with our abilities. I know how to temporarily nullify those abilities, as Abigail, Thunder, and Max discovered in Pittsburgh."

"What are the lights? Where do they come from?"

He shook his head. "That's for another time, Brawn. Like I said, Max is recording. Now, I've got two more superhumans to tell you about. . . . Terrain. I know you've heard of him, and you've seen what he can do. Telekinetic control over inanimate matter. If he weren't such an idiot, he'd really be dangerous. Landslides, earthquakes, volcanoes . . . He could be their master. And then, finally, there's Quantum. The fastest human who ever lived. After Georgina Bergeron's little stunt in Windfield, Quantum took the cure for her plague to every person on the planet. Now, by anyone's standards that's impressive. Pity about what it did to him, though. Quantum was already on the edge of sanity and the strain of visiting almost seven billion people in a little over a day, well—"

"Wait, who's Georgina Bergeron?"

"The old woman who was in charge of The Helotry of the Fifth King. Krodin's followers. You didn't know her name?"

"No one ever said."

"Well, if you ever get the chance to meet her again, ask her about her life. It's as fascinating as it is disturbing. But we're getting away from the point."

"And what *is* the point?"

"The five superhumans I mentioned. Terrain, Thunder, Energy, Loligo, and Quantum. Each one with potentially complete control over the five elements . . . earth, air, fire, and water."

"That's *four* elements. What about Quantum?"

His chains clinking, Casey walked backward to his seat and sat down. "Quantum's power is speed. But what *is* speed?"

I shrugged. "You tell me. I didn't have a lot of schooling, remember?"

"Quantum's ability makes him the most powerful of all superhumans, and therefore the most dangerous. Speed is nothing more than distance over time. Just as Thunder controls not sound but the air in which sound is carried, Quantum has the ability to manipulate not speed but time itself." He smiled. "The Helotry were fools to worship Krodin as a god. If any of us deserve such a lofty title, it's Quantum. The god of time."

CHAPTER 30

THE FOLLOWING EVENING I talked to Max about Casey. "He hasn't done anything wrong. You have to let him go."

"If you knew what I know about him . . . ," Max said.

"Then why don't you *tell* me? What has he done?"

We were in the sectioned-off corner of the warehouse that Max used as his office. Max was behind his desk, sipping coffee as he read something on his computer screen, while I sat on the floor.

"Brawn, let it go. You talked to him for hours last night, right? He got to you. That's what he does. He can be very persuasive."

"Yeah, but what has he done that's a *crime*?"

"For a start, he built a robot that could have killed you and Abby. It's a brilliant piece of work, by the way. I've shipped the wreckage to Cord. Be interesting to see what he makes of it."

"Building the robot wasn't against the law. Max, you can't lock someone up just because he *might* do something bad. That's like arresting anyone who owns a kitchen knife because they might use that knife to murder someone."

Max finally looked away from his computer. "The fact that he wants to rule the world doesn't bother you?"

"It does, but *wanting* to rule the world isn't a crime. What you're doing is much worse than anything Casey has done. You're keeping a man prisoner on nothing more substantial than fear of crimes he might commit in the future."

"So suppose we let him go, and somewhere down the line he ends up killing a hundred people. We would be responsible for those deaths. How are you going to feel then?"

I countered that with, "Suppose we let him go and he *saves* a hundred people?"

"We could argue about this all day," Max said, "but deep down you know I'm right."

That annoyed me. "No, you're not!"

"He told you that his purpose was to manipulate me into capturing him and seizing the assets of the Ragnarök organization. Yes, I *was* recording everything last night. Casey has some bigger game going on here, and I want to know what it is. If that means playing along for now, then that's what I'll do. He wanted to be captured, so why are you so intent on letting him go?"

"If you're so certain he's a bad guy, why are you doing what he wants? And if . . ." I stopped myself. "No, I'm not getting drawn into this!" I crawled back out through the doorway, and stood up.

Lance was waiting outside. "I was listening to that."

"And?"

"And I think you're right."

From his office Max shouted, "No, he's not!"

Lance raised his eyes, and—unnecessarily loudly—said, "We can talk about this later when a certain person isn't here to read our minds!"

We walked over to the gymnasium. I sat on the vaulting horse while Lance attempted to climb one of the ropes suspended from the ceiling. He wasn't able to get very high.

"Never been able to do this," he said, his voice strained.

"You need more upper-body strength."

"Easy for you to say. You don't have to work out." He gave up and dropped the three feet to the floor. "When you were a kid, what did you want to be when you grew up?"

"I don't think I ever gave it much thought. You?"

"I wanted to be the world's greatest con man," Lance said, and then he smiled. "I wanted to be so good that no one would ever know about me. You read about con men getting found out after years of tricking people out of their money, but if they got caught, they can't have been that good at it. I bet there are lots of guys out there ripping people off and no one will ever know."

"So you wanted to be a villain."

Lance lay down on top of a pile of rubber mats. "Ah, now you're sounding like Thunder. What if I was the sort of con man who stole only from bad guys and then donated the money to charity?"

"The Robin Hood trick. Stealing from the rich to give to the poor. Yeah, it's still wrong."

Lance shrugged and said, "Meh. It's not as wrong as ripping off little old ladies. And at the risk of annoying Max,
who's probably listening in right now, it's not as wrong as
using the ability to read minds so that you can make a fortune
in the stock market. Or however he did it. There's only so
much money in the world, so every time some guy makes it
rich, you could say that he's stealing from everyone else."
Lance frowned for a second. "And here's another one . . . The
world's population is growing all the time, but the amount of
money stays the same. So with every new birth the average
person gets poorer. Babies are stealing from us."

I laughed. "Man, you really need to find yourself a hobby!
This is the sort of thing you think about all the time?"

"Sometimes. What about you? What sort of madness oc-
cupies *your* enormous brain?"

"I want to be human," I said, and it struck me that this was
probably the first time I'd said that aloud. But I couldn't stop
myself. "I want to be average sized, and not blue. I'd like to be
able to walk through a crowd and not have anyone notice me."

"Do you think that's even possible?"

"Casey seems to think it might be, someday."

Lance nodded slowly. "Ah . . . Yeah, he tried the same thing
on me. Didn't work, though. I could see what he was up to.
It's an old con-man trick. You want someone to believe something, you say just enough so that the mark fills in the rest for
himself. That way he doesn't think he's being manipulated.
All you really need to con someone is to know what they want
most in life. Usually money. But you have to make it credible.
You don't tell someone that if they invest a thousand dollars

in your scheme, they can make a million. You tell them they can make fifteen hundred. Much more realistic. If you do it the first way, then when it doesn't work, he thinks that he's lost a million bucks. The second way he thinks that he's lost only fifteen hundred."

"But you can't lose what you never had," I said.

"True, but that's not the way people think. And then you can go back to the mark and extract more money out of him. You know what a Ponzi scheme is? That's where you set up a bogus investment company. You get people to invest a hundred bucks and tell them that they can earn twice that in six months. So six months later, you send them a letter saying that their money has doubled. You tell them they can have the two hundred bucks if they want it, or they can leave it with you and in another six months it'll be worth *four* hundred. See how it works? Almost no one ever takes out their money. And if they do decide they want it, then you just pay them out of all the money other people have invested. In the meantime, all the money is sitting in your bank account earning *real* interest. See, Casey could have told you that he can *definitely* change you back to human. That's what you want, so there'd be a part of you that thinks it's too good to be true. But instead he told you that it *might* be possible . . ."

"Which I'm much more inclined to believe."

"Right. Your trust is the investment in Casey's scheme, and he can keep stringing you along for years with the promise that the payoff will be you becoming human, but the truth is, all he'll be doing is using you."

"Wow. Yeah, you could be right." I allowed myself to topple back off the vaulting horse onto the floor. "Remember when the only thing we had to worry about was homework? I miss that."

"Homework *and* girls," Lance said.

"Not me. I was only twelve when I changed. Girls still had cooties back then."

Lance laughed. "You know, you'd think with all the advances in medicine that someone would have found a cure for cooties by now!"

From the doorway, Roz Dalton said, "They've cured girl cooties but not boy cooties." She walked into the room. "What have you guys been doing all day?"

"As little as possible," Lance said.

"Well, Abby and Thunder are on the way. Max said we need to start training together. You included," Roz said to Lance. She grabbed one of the ropes and climbed up, hand over hand, without using her legs, then called down, "Your turn, Lance."

"He can't," I said. "He tried earlier."

Lance gave me a look that said, "Don't tell her that!"

"Hit the weights, then," Roz called down. She was holding on to the rope with one hand, and concentrating hard. "Brawn . . . Drag those mats over, will you? Just in case I can't do it."

"What are you *trying* to do?" Lance asked as I pulled the pile of rubber mats over to Roz and dumped them on the floor beneath her.

"This." Roz let go of the rope, and for a second she remained in place, then wavered and dropped.

I caught her and lowered her to the mats.

"Thanks. Lance, the weights. I'm serious. You need to work out."

Lance grumbled. "But they're too heavy!"

"Start with the lightest and work your way up," I said. I walked over to the large rack of weights and bars and picked the whole thing up. "Where do you want them?"

"Show-off!"

I managed to persuade Lance to try the weights by betting he couldn't even lift *any* of them, and when Thunder and Abby arrived, he was lying on the bench grunting his way through a twenty-rep set. Max followed them into the gym.

"OK," Max said. "What did we learn on yesterday's mission? We learned that we need to keep in top physical condition in case someone else finds a way to nullify our powers. So when the Rangers get back tomorrow, they'll build a personalized training plan for each of you. In the meantime, Roz will keep you on your toes."

"What about you?" Lance asked. "Don't you have to train too?"

"I already *have* a personal trainer." Max looked at his watch. "It's almost seven now. I'll check in on you at nine. No slacking off."

When the doors closed behind him, Lance said, "If we had a TV in here, we could watch movies while we worked out."

"How'd you persuade your mom to let you go?" I asked Abby.

"Max gave me a code phrase to use on her. He said it's like hypnosis. This evening when Ox turned up at the door, all I had to do was say the code phrase to Mom and tell her I'd be away for a few days."

"Same here," Thunder said. "Used it on Rufus and he was all, OK, sure, whatever you say. Man, I wish I'd always had that."

"Rufus?" Lance asked. "It's always weird when people call their parents by their first names."

Thunder didn't look happy at that. "He's *not* my dad. He's my stepdad. You want to know what happened this morning? I was out for a few hours, and when I was on the way back, I could hear Shiho—my little sister—playing in the driveway. She's seven, small for her age. I could tell from the sound of her breathing that she'd been crying, so I ran the rest of the way. I saw her sitting on the gravel beside Rufus's car. She had a plastic beaker of water beside her, and she was dipping an old toothbrush into it and using it to scrub the car's tires. As soon as she saw me, she burst into tears again and said, 'It was my own fault—don't be mad!'"

Abby said, "I *knew* there was something bothering you. What happened?"

"She was playing in the drive, you know, running around like kids do, and she skidded to a stop next to the car and some of the gravel sprayed up and hit the car's fender."

"Wait," I said. "He was punishing her for that by making her wash the tires with a *toothbrush*?"

"Not just the tires. The whole car."

"I see. You're gonna have to introduce me to him someday."

"Thanks, but it's sorted out now."

"What did you do?" Abby asked.

"Picked her up, carried her inside, and told her to go wash up, and that I'd take her to the park. Of course she panicked because she knew Rufus would go mad." Thunder shrugged, then smiled. "He won't be punishing her like that again."

"*What* did you do?" Abby repeated.

"I told him what I thought of him. First time I ever spoke out to him. He swung a punch at me."

I said, "Well, I hope you hit him back."

"No, but I ducked and his fist hit the corner of the kitchen cabinet."

The rest of us went "Ouch!" at the same time.

"Never thought a white guy could go pale so quickly. He was practically *green*. My mom had to take him to the ER." Thunder took a deep breath and let it out slowly. "Man, he's *not* gonna be happy next time he tries to start his car and finds out what I did to it."

"What did you do?" Lance asked. "Glue the wipers to the windshield? Hide a dead fish under the seat? I know, you put a bunch of stink bombs into the air vents, right?"

"No, I put four handfuls of gravel into the gas tank."

Lance and I thought that was hilarious, but Abby and Roz weren't so sure. "He's going to go crazy," Abby said.

Thunder nodded. "Yep. It's going to cost him a fortune."

Eventually, Roz decided that she was in charge, so we had to stop chatting and start working out. Lance and Thunder took turns with the weights, with me spotting them. Even though Thunder was only slightly less skinny than Lance, he could lift almost twice as much, and I could see from his build that he was going to be big.

Roz and Abby thought it would be a good idea to fence. Roz had taken lessons and knew how to use a foil. She showed Abby a few moves, which Abby tried to copy using her own homemade sword. That was cut short when Abby took a playful swing at Roz's very expensive foil and sliced it in two.

We spent the best part of two hours in the gym, mostly working out but occasionally goofing off.

The dynamic between the other four was fascinating to watch. Thunder seriously had the hots for Abby, but she wasn't interested. Roz kept asking Thunder to help her with stuff, so I figured that maybe she had a crush on him. Lance also had a thing for Abby, but I could tell he was holding back. At the time, I thought it was because he didn't think he had a chance against Thunder, and it was years before I realized the truth.

But that was a good evening. When Max finally decided that we could stop, we sent Thunder out for eight pizzas—one each for the others and four for me—and then we spent the rest of the night lying on the mats in the gym and telling jokes.

These guys were my friends. They fully accepted me as one of them even though I was so different. That feeling of belonging was worth more to me than I have ever been able to express.

The only thing that spoils the memory is that other feeling that I tried to keep buried, the ugly sensation that lurked in the pit of my stomach: the knowledge that this would probably be the last time all five of us would be together as friends.

Because I was about to betray them.

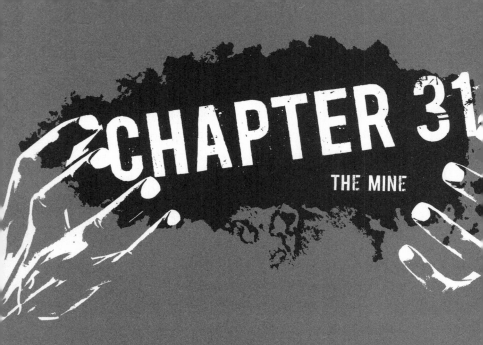

CHAPTER 31

THE MINE

THE YIELD FROM THE PLATINUM MINE had been steady for months. This kept Hazlegrove happy, so he left us alone.

I had almost regained my strength—and was back on sixteen-hour days, which at first seemed like a luxury—when I was summoned to the guards' office. "You get to go outside, Brawn," DePaiva said. "You're getting a visitor."

"Who?"

"No idea. Hazlegrove is waiting at the helipad. He told me to tell you the usual about not trying to escape."

The guards at the doors opened them for me, and for a brief moment I felt important. Then I was outside, shielding my eyes against the sun. The mine's dome had plenty of windows—no glass in them, of course—so I'd seen outside often enough, but this was the first time I'd been out since my stint in the hot box two years earlier.

Hazlegrove was standing with his arms folded on the edge of the helipad. "Someone's come to pick your brains."

"Bit rude not making an appointment," I said.

"Hmph. I don't know who this man is or what he wants, but someone's gone to a lot of trouble to get him access to this place."

A few minutes later we saw it, a black helicopter cruising low over the mountains.

"No markings," Hazlegrove said. "So it's not military."

The copter touched down and its hatch slid open. A young man wearing jeans and a T-shirt jumped out and strode over to us. He couldn't have been more than eighteen. He had close-cropped blond hair and a slim build. "Thomas Hazlegrove?" he asked.

"That's me. Who're you?"

"I'll just need a few minutes of your prisoner's time."

"I *asked* you who you are," Hazlegrove said.

The young man reeled off a long list of numbers. "Recognize that?"

"Should I?"

"That's the number of the Swiss bank account where you deposit the money you've earned by selling the nickel you've stolen from this mine. If you don't want your warden to know about that, you'll do yourself a favor and walk away right now."

Hazlegrove nodded, then turned and left.

The young man looked up at me. "Brawn. Walk with me." He began to stride toward the north side of the dome. "I need your help with something."

I walked alongside him. "Yeah? Well, first you have to tell me where we are."

"You don't know? We're in Lieberstan, formerly part of the USSR. Sandwiched between Kazakhstan, Russia, Mongolia, and China. Now, assuming the past nine years in this place haven't eroded your memory, I need you to tell me everything—"

"Nine years? It's really been that long?"

"It has. I need to know everything about Ragnarök."

"And what'll you do for me?"

"I'll get to that. Tell me about Ragnarök."

I shrugged. "Ragnarök the man, or Ragnarök the organization?"

"Casey Duval is dead. So are Schizophrenzy, Necroman, and The Scarlet Slayer. Terrain's in prison. Slaughter is insane, her memories practically shattered. The Glyph . . . turned out not to be what everyone thought. Ragnarök's henchmen knew nothing—they were hired hands, most of them barely able to do much more than aim a gun. Harmony Yuan has disappeared—even *I* haven't been able to find her—and Senator Gordon Tremont was killed by an unknown assassin eight years ago in Versailles."

"*Senator* Tremont?"

The young man nodded. "He was in office for a little more than two weeks when it happened. After he abandoned his plans to create or steal a quantum processor, he thought he could blackmail and bribe his way into power—you can't keep secrets from a hacker of his skills. Clearly someone took offense to that. The assassination was set up to look like an accident, but my investigation uncovered the truth. Which of course I'm keeping to myself for now. So. You're the only one left, Brawn."

"*Has* anyone ever managed to build a quantum processor, then?"

The man shook his head. "No. It's a pipe dream. For now, anyway. Under Duval's guidance Tremont's people came closer than anyone else. But not close enough." Then he smiled. "It'd be a nice little toy to have, but it's not something I would consider necessary. Now, tell me about Casey Duval."

"He was smart, a bit full of himself. Wanted to control the world and probably would have succeeded if he'd been more careful about choosing his allies. But you don't want to know that, do you? You want to know about the powers."

"I'm told he believed that the source of your powers was the blue lights. What were they, and why could only he see them?"

"I don't know," I said. "He said that he was one of the *few* who could see them, so presumably other people could too. Casey kept most of what he knew very close to his chest. He was the ultimate manipulator. He didn't tell many lies, but he was still a master at covering up the truth."

The blond man kicked at a small pebble and watched it bounce and clatter across the uneven concrete. "Is it true that he believed you were given powers for a reason?"

"So he said."

"Hmm. If so, the obvious implication is that there was

some sort of predestination at work. A plan. And where there's a plan, there's someone who designed it. What do you think? Was he lying about that?"

"I don't think he was lying, but I think he was *wrong*. There's no destiny. There can't be. If there is, then we're only toys that someone else is playing with. I can't accept that."

"But Casey was considerably smarter than you: How could he be wrong and you be right?"

"You're not seriously asking me that, are you?"

He sighed. "No, I guess not. There is one very important thing I—"

"Stop. No more answers until I get something from you."

The man pursed his lips and nodded slightly. "OK. Sure. I'm not going to free you or anyone else from this place, nor will I promise to make things easier, but I can swap you certain pieces of information in exchange for your answers."

"Are my p—"

"Your father died four years ago. Painlessly, if that's any consolation. A sudden brain aneurysm while he slept. The inquest revealed no specific cause—it was just one of those things. Very rare, but it happens."

The strength drained from my body, and I had to sit down. "Oh man . . ."

"Your mother is still alive and healthy. She's now living with her sister's family in Ohio. She has two framed photos of you on her dresser. The first shows you at eight years old, on a red bicycle. The second was clipped from the article in *Newsweek*, taken when you were in Bolivia. She tells visitors that she keeps that second photo to remind her of the monster who

took away her son. She and your father have never told anyone of the time you visited them. They were very proud of
you. Well, for a while. But they always held out hope that one
day you would see sense."

"Who are you?"

"An answer for an answer, Brawn." He glanced at his
watch, then inclined his head back toward the helicopter.
"And our time is nearly up."

As I pushed myself to my feet, I said, "Well, at least I got a
break for a few minutes. You *sure* you can't get me out of
here?"

"Brawn, if you can answer this final question, I promise I
will do everything I can to get you out of here. This really is
important. Important enough for me to fly halfway around
the world to ask you in person. It's related to Casey's frequently unfinished ramblings about the powers. . . . You're the
only one left who could possibly know."

"Know what?"

He stopped walking and looked up at me. "What is The
Chasm?"

"I don't know. He mentioned it a couple of times, implied
that it's where the powers come from. But I never understood
what he actually meant."

"Ah. Disappointing."

"I don't know if it's an actual *place*. I always had a feeling
that The Chasm might just be a state of mind. I think that
Casey didn't really know how to put it into words that other
people could comprehend."

"I once thought that perhaps it was a reference to the incident with Krodin. The Helotry used Pyrokine's power to drill a hole through to the past and pull Krodin forward through time. But obviously that happened *after* the modern wave of superhumans appeared."

"So what difference does that make?" I asked. "When you're dealing with time travel, words like *before* and *after* don't mean so much. If Krodin's arrival in our time caused changes to our reality—and we know *that* can happen—then all the laws of the universe that we take for granted go out the window. Cause no longer has to precede effect. If you throw a rock into a fast-moving river, most of the disturbance to the water will happen downstream. But if the rock is *big* enough . . ."

The man nodded. "Coming from a giant blue bald monster with very little formal education, that's an interesting deduction. . . ." He moved toward the helicopter. "Nice talking to you."

"You still owe me an answer," I said.

"Fire away."

"Who are you, and why did you want to know all of this?"

He smiled. "Ah, but that's two questions. Shame you didn't ask them in the other order, because that would have explained a *lot* more. My name won't mean anything to you."

"Tell me anyway."

"My name is Victor Cross."

CHAPTER 32

TWENTY-THREE YEARS AGO

AT FIVE O'CLOCK IN THE MORNING I was crouched in front of Casey Duval's cell flicking tiny bits of grit at him until he woke up.

Casey's eyes finally opened, and when he saw me, he sat up and started pulling on his boots. "So it's time."

"Time for what?" I asked, but he knew. He'd probably known from the first moment I talked to him.

"I presume you haven't been able to organize any form of transport, or backup. You'll run interference, then?"

I nodded. "I'll hold them off for a few minutes at least."

"This is the right thing to do, you know." He stood up, then moved to the back wall of the cell. "Outer door's unlocked?"

"Yeah."

"I owe you."

"I know. Turn me back to human."

"One day. I promise."

I leaned forward and grabbed hold of the bars. "When you get out of the building, you need to go—"

"I know where I am." He took a deep breath. "Do it."

I planted my feet and strained against the bars. The screech of tearing metal clashed with the cracking of reinforced concrete as the entire barred wall was torn free.

Even as the alarms started to wail, Casey was darting past me and heading for the door.

Five seconds later two of the Rangers—Lash and Ollie— raced out of their quarters, their guns cocked and ready.

"Security breach!" Ollie shouted. He saw me crouched there holding on to the bars. "Duval's gone! Brawn broke him out!"

Lash reduced his speed to a slow walk, moving toward me with his rifle up to his shoulder, peering along its sights at me. "What did you *do*, you giant blue freak?"

I tossed the barred wall aside—it crashed into the front of Ollie's car, totaling it. "What does it look like?"

Ollie was circling around me, also with his gun raised. "Facedown, on the floor! *Now*, Brawn! I swear, I'll open fire!"

Max came running, followed by Lance and Roz.

"No, no, no, no!" Max said. "You *idiot*! What were you thinking!?"

Lance said, "Oh man . . . Why? Why did you *do* that?"

Max shouted, "Roz, get Ernie on the radio. I want the copter here ASAP. And get Ox to call the chief of police—I want a

full sweep of the area. Every cop in the state, every traffic camera!" He strode toward me with his fists clenching and unclenching. "You absolute moron! You've just freed the most
dangerous man in the country!" He scowled at me for a second, then yelled, "Thunder!"

Thunder's voice echoed around the room. "I heard. Everyone's body makes sound all the time. Heartbeat, respiration,
the digestive system, muscles expanding and contracting . . .
Those noises combine to create a sound signature that's completely unique to each person. I'm listening for—"

"I don't want a blasted *lecture*!" Max shouted. "Just find
him!"

I stood up. "Thunder, don't do it. Casey hasn't done anything wrong. We were holding him illegally." I looked at
Lance. "*You* understand, right?"

Lance shrugged. "I dunno. . . ."

Abby came running from her room, her sword in her hand.
"Well, I *do* know. And you shouldn't have done that, Brawn."

Thunder's voice said, "I agree with Abby. Hold on, I think
I've got him. . . ."

Max tried to get in my way as I strode toward Thunder's
quarters. I pushed him aside and roared, "Thunder—don't!
We had no right to hold him!"

Roz ran alongside me. "Brawn, they kidnapped Max! You
know that!"

"*After* we illegally attacked their base. Just because the
people Casey worked with kidnapped Max, that doesn't mean
he was involved."

Roz ran to the door of Thunder's quarters and stood with her back to it, facing me with her hands raised. "Back away. Now."

"Don't fight me on this, Roz. You'd understand that I'm right if Max hadn't been messing with your mind."

The door opened, and Thunder stood there wearing only his jeans. "Casey's on Degraw Avenue, heading west. He's on foot, but he's fast. Abby, Roz—go bring him back. I'll deal with Brawn."

Roz hesitated for a moment, then moved aside and started to run. Thunder glared at me, and I stared back.

Lance began, "Guys, don't . . ."

And then there was nothing but silence, and I realized that Thunder was blocking the sound from reaching me. I suddenly felt dizzy, sick, like I was going to throw up. Something hard and invisible slammed into my chest: one of Thunder's shock waves.

Another hit me in the stomach, then smashed into my face.

Then a wave of pressure hit me, forcing me back, pummeling every part of my body like I was caught in a tidal wave.

It was taking all of my strength just to remain standing.

But I still saw Thunder as a friend—I didn't *want* to hit him, and I knew that if I did, I might kill him.

So I turned and ran. Max and Lance darted clear just before Lash and Ollie opened fire on me.

I felt their shots slam into me: one in my right arm, the other square in my chest. But I kept moving, straight at them.

Ollie fired four more times before he threw himself to the

ground, and each one of his shots hit home: The last one clipped my neck and actually drew blood.

Lash either wasn't fast enough or didn't care about his own safety. He was still shooting at me point-blank as I picked him up and threw him back over my head.

He hit the ground somewhere behind me, but I didn't stop to look.

I jumped as I ran, crashed through the large garage doors, showering the dark street outside with buckled strips of aluminum.

My hearing returned as I raced along Fort Lee Road, heading west toward Degraw Avenue.

I knew that Casey was fast, but Abby was faster. She would catch up with him . . . if I didn't catch her first: My stride was at least twice as long as Abby's, plus I was a lot stronger than she was.

The road wasn't well lit, but I could see a small figure running ahead of me, and I knew from the silhouette that it was Roz.

Before I could reach her, I realized that a wave of sirens was approaching from far behind me. The police.

Oh, this just keeps getting better! I didn't want to fight the police any more than I wanted to fight my friends.

Roz must have heard the sirens—or my bare feet pounding along the road—because she suddenly stopped and turned to face me. "Brawn—no! You don't know what you're doing!"

"Outta my way, Roz! I don't want to have to—"

Again, I was hit by something invisible, but this was different from one of Thunder's shock waves. It was like running into a strong, sticky net that had been strung across the road. It grabbed me, slowed me down, wound itself around my limbs.

It pulled at the back of my knees and pushed against my chest at the same time, toppling me onto my back. Then it started to drag me backward along the road.

I formed my hands into claws and slammed them down, fingers digging deep, gouging rough furrows into the road's surface.

But Roz wasn't able to keep her telekinetic shield up for long. The pressure weakened enough for me to roll to my feet, and soon it was no worse than wading upstream against a fast-flowing river.

Exhausted, Roz collapsed to the ground as I passed her, but she still had enough strength to call out: "Brawn, *please . . .*"

Her hold finally shattered, I was once more able to run at full speed. I reached the junction for the interstate and paused. I knew that Thunder was probably still able to hear Casey, and could well be feeding his location to Abby over the two-way radio, or even directly by throwing his voice so that only she could hear him. *Which way would Casey have gone?*

Ahead the sky was a flickering blue and red: more police cars coming. Those behind me were already racing along Fort Lee Road, less than a minute away.

And then I saw them, on the overpass: Abby had her sword drawn, its point only inches away from Casey's throat. Casey had his arms raised with his back to the high wire-mesh fence. Behind him was a forty-foot drop onto the interstate, which was already heavy with traffic.

"Abby!" I roared. "Don't!"

She didn't alter her position. "Stay back, Brawn!"

I slowed as I reached her, approaching from her left. "Lower the sword. I mean it, Abby!"

The sirens were all around us now, half a dozen police cars stopped at either end of the overpass.

"Shouldn't have come after me, Brawn," Casey said. "I could have handled this. But now that the cops have seen *you*, they'll be more inclined to open fire."

I ignored him. "Abby, please . . . You don't know what you're doing. Max has been tinkering with your mind, making you believe that Casey is one of the bad guys. But he hasn't done anything wrong! Sure, the people he was working for are dangerous, but not him. You have to let him go."

The point of the sword wavered. "Back away! I don't want to have to hurt you too!"

"Neither of us wants that. But you're threatening an innocent man!"

An amplified voice boomed out: "This is the police! You on the bridge—all of you, get down on your knees, hands behind your head!"

"Do as they say, Abby. OK? Let the police sort it out." Even as I said that, I realized it was probably a mistake. If Max got to the police, he could make them believe anything he wanted. But the only other option was for me to attack Abby, and then—I was sure—the police would start shooting.

She nodded. "All right . . . OK. Casey, you first. Slowly."

"Lower the sword first," Casey said. "I don't want that thing anywhere near me! It looks razor sharp."

"It is," Abby said. She took a step back and slipped the sword into the sheath that was slung over her shoulder.

I was already kneeling with my hands behind my head, fingers laced together.

Casey glanced behind him, down through the wire-mesh fence to the interstate below. Then he put his hands behind his head and started to lower himself to the ground.

Abby dropped to her knees—

—And then Casey grabbed the top rail of the fence behind him. In one swift movement he pulled himself up and over, flicking his legs out and clipping Abby across the chin, sending her sprawling onto her back.

I lunged forward, just in time to see him land on the roof of a large truck heading north.

Casey grinned at me, and saluted.

Then the police opened fire.

A bullet struck me in the hip, another hit the side of my head.

I knew that I had no choice now. Even though it had been for the right reason, I had betrayed my friends. They would never trust me again. I vaulted over the fence and landed in a crouch on the interstate. A speeding white Toyota swerved around me, and then I began to run.

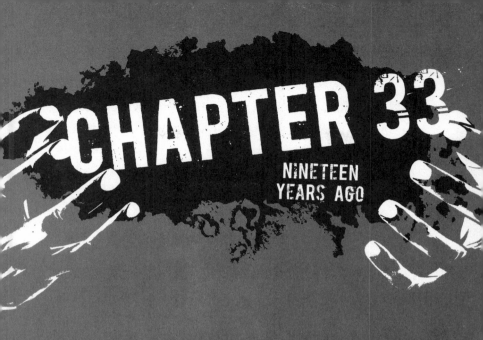

CHAPTER 33

NINETEEN YEARS AGO

I HAD BEEN IN HIDING for almost four years before I met another superhuman.

After I left New Jersey with half of that state's police force chasing me, I traveled north into New York State and lived in the woods next to Meacham Lake.

A young family had a vacation home overlooking the lake, and sometimes in the evenings I would creep up to their house and listen as they watched the news on their TV.

From the news reports, and the papers they left in the recycling bins out back, I learned that Thunder and Abby had parted company with Max Dalton, though I had no way of telling whether that was because they saw him for what he really was or because he dumped them.

Thunder's skills—and his reputation—grew rapidly. Though he mostly kept out of the spotlight and rarely spoke to the press, he was very highly regarded. But most of the public's attention was on what became known as The Big Four: Titan, Energy, Quantum, and Paragon. They worked alongside Dalton occasionally, but I knew what he was really like. Dalton didn't like to share the front pages with anyone other than family.

When Roz and Max's younger brother, Josh, turned fourteen, Max held a big press conference announcing that the three of them would thereafter be known as The High Command. They would operate as a team. This was greeted by the press and public as the greatest news ever, though in the newspaper photos it seemed to me that Roz wasn't comfortable with it.

More and more superheroes appeared, as did more superpowered villains. They clashed frequently, but sometimes the villains were released soon after they were captured, because their lawyers argued that they were innocents who had been targeted by vigilantes.

Casey Duval's name was never made public, but a supervillain using the name Ragnarök became very prominent. He was seemingly impossible to capture, as he was armed with devices that could disable any other superhuman's powers.

I tried to tell myself that I'd done the right thing, but I still didn't feel any better about it. Every time I saw the name Ragnarök, my heart sank. That was my fault. Max Dalton had been right about him.

Ragnarök generally focused his attacks on military bases. Not just in America, but all over the world. There were reports of him in China, Russia, Australia, Mexico, England . . . Each time, he would cause millions of dollars' worth of damage before the target country's superheroes caught up with him, and most of the time he escaped. On those rare occasions when he was caught, he broke free.

Then a new hero appeared, and for a time he really captured the public's imagination: Apex was strong, fast, and incredibly agile. He was also quite brutal in his methods. Crooks and supervillains quickly learned not to even attempt to fight him—they would often just surrender immediately, because if they did run and he caught them, he wouldn't just handcuff them: He'd beat them to a pulp.

The Age of the Superhumans had entered a new phase . . . the rise of the antihero. Apex rarely spoke, and quickly proved to be an equal-opportunities thug: He would use the same force to attack an ordinary mugger as he would a supervillain.

His methods sparked a series of copycats, usually ordinary nonpowered people who thought it would be good fun to be a superhero. After the fifth or sixth copycat was killed, the police started to come down very hard on nonpowered vigilantes.

Like Thunder, Abby kept her head down most of the time. She finally took on a superhero name: Hesperus. She had started using an ax as well as her sword, and was a formidable fighter. One news report showed her taking on thirty of Ragnarök's mercenaries single-handedly, and winning without issuing a fatal blow. Though quite a few hands and feet did get lopped off.

Sometimes my name was mentioned in the papers. Occasionally there were unconfirmed sightings of me in various parts of the world, but there was never anything substantial.

I was careful. I ate only from the forest, and didn't stay in one spot for too long.

But my curiosity kept getting the better of me. I wanted to know what was happening with my former friends. So time and again I returned to the house in the woods.

One particularly cold night, as I was sitting outside with my back against the wall, listening to their TV set, I was so focused on the news report that I didn't realize it had started snowing.

By the time I did notice it, the snow was about three inches deep. I returned to the woods to the makeshift shelter I'd built from branches and leaves. I pulled my old tarpaulin over me—it was my only possession, stolen from a construction site—and fell asleep.

I was woken around dawn by the sound of dogs barking and men shouting. There were flashlight beams bobbing through the trees.

I ran, but it's hard to be stealthy when you're thirteen feet tall, and hard to blend into the green-and-brown forest when your skin is blue. They spotted me, and set the dogs loose.

I knew the forest well, knew the rivers and ravines I could cross where the dogs couldn't follow.

As I ran, I tried to figure out how they had found me. Then I darted across a small, snow-covered clearing and the answer struck me like a sledgehammer: When I walked away from the house, I'd left a trail of giant footprints in the snow.

Maybe some hiker had seen a glimpse of me before, or perhaps there had always been rumors that I was in the forest and the footprints were enough to lead them right to me. I didn't have time to wonder about it.

I leaped over a fast-running stream, scrambled up the steep bank on the other side, crashed through the undergrowth and up a sharper incline, then skirted the rock-topped hill just below the tree line.

I half ran, half skidded down the other side, heading north.

After a solid fifteen minutes, I slowed down and stopped. I could no longer hear the dogs. *Too close,* I said to myself. *Gonna have to be more careful in the future.*

I started to walk, and stopped again. *Oh no . . .*

My feet had made no sound on the forest floor, and I could no longer hear my own breath.

Slowly, I turned in a full circle, scanning the trees for any sign of movement. Nothing.

Aloud, I said, "I know you're there, Thunder. Show yourself." At least, that's what I tried to say, but I couldn't hear my own voice.

Then to my left, on the edge of my vision, something moved, darting between the trees. When I turned to look, it was gone. Seconds later, another movement, this time to my right. And much closer—close enough for me to see the brown leaves falling in its wake.

I had been too long without the company of other superhumans: I'd forgotten one very important thing about my own kind. . . . Some of us were not restricted by gravity.

I looked up.

Two figures were floating above me, silhouetted against the morning sky, not more than twenty feet above my head.

Then the sound returned, and a deep voice said, "Tag. You're it."

I squinted at them. "Who . . . ?"

They moved apart and drifted down, one on either side of me. A man and a woman, both African-American. The man was large, very muscular, and wearing a green-and-black costume. The woman was toned, wearing a silver helmet that put most of her face in shadow, plates of silver armor, and carrying a sword in one hand and an ax in the other.

"We've been looking for you for four years," the woman said.

"Abby? Is that you?"

She stabbed her sword into the ground point-first, and removed her helmet. Her hair was in cornrows in neat, intricate patterns, and her face was leaner than I remembered but no less beautiful. It was certainly Abigail de Luyando.

Behind me, the man said, "You betrayed us, Brawn."

"And that has to be you, Thunder. Figured it was when everything went silent." I turned to face him. "You're a lot bigger than I remembered. Been working out?"

Abby said, "We don't want to do this, but you've left us no choice." She replaced her helmet and grabbed her sword.

"What have I done?"

"You freed Ragnarök!" Thunder said. "Do you *know* how many people have died because of that? That's *your* fault, Brawn. You're responsible for their deaths!"

I shook my head. "No way. I freed him because it was the right thing to do. And because I was the only one who could see the truth. Max Dalton was messing with your minds, making you hate and fear Casey Duval for no reason. What had he done that was against the law? Nothing!"

"Don't you feel *anything* for the people he's killed?" Abby asked. "Or have you really become the monster everyone believed you to be?"

"Of course I feel something! I let him go. And if I could go back in time to that day, I'd do it again! You don't imprison someone for something he *might* do! How do you know that it wasn't the way we treated Casey that turned him bad? Look at it from his point of view: He gets locked up without any hope of a trial, then hounded as a criminal when he escapes. Is it any wonder that he has no faith in the law? Yes, he's done a lot of cruel, vicious things since. I won't deny that. But we locked up an innocent man. And we were supposed to be *heroes*."

"We're taking you in," Thunder said. "It's up to you whether you want to do it the easy way or the hard way. And before you decide, bear in mind that we're not kids anymore. If you don't leave us any choice, we can and we *will* hurt you."

I looked at Abby. "What about you, Abby? You feel the same way?"

Her lips narrowed. "Don't call me that. You lost the right to use my real name a long time ago. As far as you're concerned, my name is Hesperus."

"Hesperus. Yeah, I read that in the paper a few months back. They said that in Greek mythology Hesperus was the son of the Dawn Goddess."

"I like the way it sounds."

I sighed. "So that's who you are now." I turned back to face Thunder. "Do you really think you can beat me?"

His face grim, he said, "I know we can."

"I see. Just out of curiosity, how much punishment can you take? So I'll know when to stop hitting you."

"Actually, it's not me you should be worried about," Thunder said. "Hesperus is the dangerous one."

I took a glance at Abby just as the flat side of her ax was swinging at my head: Her sounds muffled by Thunder, she had taken a leap at me.

I ducked my head and lashed out with my left arm at the same time, grabbed her wrist, and pulled her down out of the air, slamming her heavily into the ground in a shower of dirt and snow and dead leaves.

Thunder hit me in the back with a sonic blast so powerful, it sent me tumbling.

But I held my grip on Abby's arm, dragging her along with me. I rolled to my feet and started to run—

—Then was suddenly jerked back. Abby had slashed her ax at a tree, burying its head deep into the trunk.

She twisted her trapped arm around, and suddenly she was holding on to me, her small fingers biting deep into my forearm.

As I tried to pull free, Thunder hit me again, from the front and rear at the same time. The twin sonic blasts shuddered through me, and I could feel my entire skeleton vibrate.

Abby let go of her ax and freed her sword from its scabbard

on her back. She slashed down at my left arm, aiming for the elbow.

I leaped forward, crashing into her and ruining her aim: The edge of the blade bit deep into my right upper arm.

Still holding on to my left wrist, she pulled the blade free— I felt it scraping off the bone—and kicked out at the same time, planting her heavy left boot into my stomach with much more force than I would have thought possible for someone so small.

I doubled over, then—*wham!*—there was a pinpoint blow to the back of my head, so sharp and precise that I was certain Abby had hit me with the point at the tip of her ax.

But even through my dazed vision I could see that her free hand was still by her side. That could only mean that Thunder's accuracy had greatly increased.

Another piercing pinpoint blow, this one to the nerve cluster in my left upper arm, causing a dam-burst of pain to surge through my body and rendering my arm useless at the same time.

Abby jerked my now-deadened arm forward again and lashed out with another kick, this one to my throat.

Gasping for breath, I collapsed to the ground.

"You had enough yet?" Thunder asked.

Abby finally let go, and stepped back to join Thunder.

Unable to push myself to my feet with one arm numbed and the other severely wounded, I rolled onto my back.

"Give . . . me a . . . minute," I choked.

"While you've been hiding these past four years," Abby

said, "we've been out in the world. Fighting. Training. Either one of us could beat you. So give it up, Brawn. It's over."

"Not over yet," I said. The feeling was starting to return to my left arm, and the wound in my right had stopped bleeding. Slowly, I sat up.

Thunder said, "Then it's only fair to warn you that we were not trying hard. That wasn't our best stuff. If you want to continue this fight, you have to take that into consideration."

I pushed myself to my feet and looked down at them. "In that case, I should point out something you might not have noticed."

"And what's that?" Abby asked.

"You called that a fight," I said. "But that wasn't a fight. A fight is when your opponent hits back. So . . . If you *really* want a fight, let's see how far you're willing to go."

CHAPTER 34

IT WAS NOT A FAIR FIGHT. Hesperus and Thunder were more experienced, had received much more training, and had the advantage of being able to fly out of my reach. Plus there were two of them.

It's often said that you should use your opponents' strengths against them. Me, I prefer to use their weaknesses.

Abby attacked first, swinging her sword and ax at the same time, a whirlwind of razor-sharp metal before her as she launched herself at me.

I dropped to the ground and she passed overhead, the edge of her ax missing me by inches. She instantly pivoted about, darted back down at me, threw her sword directly at me, and—I noticed at the last moment—threw her ax straight into the spot where I had been about to jump.

Instead, I dodged to the right, putting a thick-trunked tree between us.

Thunder blasted the tree from above, shattering the entire thing into a cloud of splinters. Which was exactly what I'd hoped he'd do.

The air was dense with slowly drifting fragments of bark, leaves, and wood, obscuring Abby's vision as she pulled her weapons out of the ground. I rushed at her, grabbed her around the waist with one arm, and kept running. Before she had time to react, I slammed my free fist against the side of her helmet—feeling absolutely sick about hitting my friend—then pulled my arm back and threw her semiconscious body high into the air.

I crouched, braced my feet against the trunk of a tree, then leaped after her.

As I cleared the treetops, I saw Thunder flying toward Abby.

Thunder's greatest weakness was that he was still in love with her. If it had been anyone else, he'd have had the presence of mind to use his powers to catch her. Instead, he went after her himself, briefly forgetting about me.

He was only a few yards from grabbing hold of Abby's limp arms when he realized I was coming down right on top of him. The look on his face was almost worth the beating he'd given me.

He tried to dart to the side, but he was too slow. I grabbed his leg and, as I fell, started swinging him around my head like a lasso, as fast as I could. "How'd you like *that*, huh?" I yelled.

Thunder didn't like it much at all. I felt his muscles tense and flinch, and then he threw up, spewing a wide arc of aerial vomit over a very large section of the forest.

Just ahead of me, only a few seconds from crashing face-down through the trees, Abby regained consciousness, saw where she was, and put the brakes on. Another mistake: That put her directly in my path.

I couldn't help myself: I hit her with Thunder's swinging body. The impact knocked Abby clear across the forest.

I crashed down through the trees, still swinging Thunder over my head. I figured he was unconscious by now, but I didn't want to take a chance.

I landed heavily, my feet sinking deep into the forest floor. As the twigs and leaves drifted down around me, I dropped Thunder to the ground and propped him up with his back resting against a tree.

He was groaning, his face spattered with vomit and his eyes rolling. I leaned close to him. "Hope you're awake enough to hear me, Thunder. . . . Don't come after me again, got that?" I held my hand up in front of his face, pulled my middle finger back with my thumb, and flicked him in the forehead.

His head smacked back against the tree trunk, and he passed out.

My intention was to travel north and cross the border into Canada, but first I had to make a detour.

It was dangerous, I knew, and probably unwise, but I had to do it. I went east, into Vermont. It took me three weeks to reach my destination.

The house was in the middle of a sprawling estate. Thousands of identical homes on identical streets. I reached the edge of the estate early in the afternoon, and had to wait until darkness before I could venture out.

Finally, long after midnight, I left the cover of the woods and walked through streets I hadn't seen in eight years. I passed the First Church of Saint Matthew half expecting it to have been demolished, but no, it was still there, looking somehow smaller and much less significant.

A few minutes later, I stood outside my parents' house, egging myself on and at the same time telling myself that this was a bad idea.

Ma and Pa slept in the bedroom upstairs at the back of the house, so I carefully stepped over the gate and walked around to the backyard.

The old swing was still there, slowly rusting away, the seat now tied to the frame. I noticed that the grass under the swing had grown back—it had been a very long time since it had been used.

I'd expected the crab-apple trees to have grown much taller, and perhaps they had, but it was hard to tell, as I was considerably taller myself.

I took a few deep breaths, steeled myself, and gently knocked on the bedroom window. Voices stirred inside, faint murmurs that I instantly recognized, and again I felt like running.

But I knocked again, even more gently this time.

My father, sleepily: "What? What *is* that?"

"Don't open the curtains," I said softly. "Please. Don't look out."

A moment of silence, then Ma's hushed voice: "Call the police!"

"No, don't!" I said. "I promise you, you're safe. Just listen, OK?"

More silence.

"Are you listening? Say something if you can still hear me."

Pa, his voice quavering, said, "We can hear you."

"Good. Now . . ." I paused. I hadn't actually planned what I was going to say. "Um . . . When your son was six years old, he painted the stairs. Remember that? And when he was ten, he didn't talk to either of you for about a month because he came home from school to find that you'd thrown out all his comic books. And you used to tease him about Kristi Janveski, who lived in number eighty-eight, remember? You'd pretend that you and Mr. and Mrs. Janveski had made an arrangement that Gethin and Kristi would get married when they were eighteen. He'd get so mad about that."

My mother said, "Gethin? Is it you?" I saw the curtains twitch and I ducked down.

"Don't look out!" I said. "Please!" I used the back of my hand to brush away tears I hadn't even realized were there. "Yes, Ma, it's me. I didn't die that day in Saint Matthew's. Instead, I . . . I *changed*. I couldn't talk at first. Couldn't make anyone understand me."

I glanced up at the window, and was relieved to see that the curtains were still closed. I stood up again. "I couldn't come back before now—the people who took me threatened to hurt you. You could still be in danger, and if so, I'm sorry. But I—"

There was a sound below me, and I looked down to see the back door opening.

My father, wearing the same old bathrobe he'd worn every morning when he went out to pick the paper up off the lawn, stared up at me.

"You'd better come in . . . um, if you can."

It wasn't easy, but I managed to squeeze through the doors and into the sitting room. It had been redecorated, but it still felt like home.

I sat on the floor—I figured that the new sofa wouldn't be strong enough to take my weight—and Ma and Pa plied me with cookies and cake while I did my best to explain what had happened.

"But the newspapers are saying that you're one of the criminals," Ma said.

"Well, they're wrong. I've never committed a crime." Then I thought for a moment. "Well, OK, I have committed a *few*, but only when I really had to. I promise I've never hurt anyone who didn't deserve it. I've tried to be a hero, but . . . It's not always that straightforward."

"Everyone told us you were probably dead," Pa said. "But we never gave up hope. Not even when that woman on the psychic hotline told us that you'd been killed and we'd find your body in water. Seven hundred bucks, she charged us!"

"Don't tell anyone I was here," I said. "Promise me! If the authorities found out, they'd . . . Well, they'd probably take you away. Try to use you as bait to catch me."

Pa said, "We won't say a word." He pulled a handkerchief

from his pocket and blew his nose. "Well, we might mention it to Pastor Cullen because he—"

"Not him!" I said. "That guy . . ."

"But the pastor has been very kind to us," Ma said. "Every year, on the anniversary, he holds a special service for you."

"He's a coward. No, worse than that. If he's kind to you, it's only because he feels guilty. After I changed, he begged me not to hurt him. He told me to 'take the boys instead.'"

Ma shook her head. "No, you're wrong. He's a *good* man. He's a man of God!"

"I'm not wrong. And he might be a man of God, but he's still just a man. I can sort of understand the way he acted, and I can even forgive it, but I can't forget it. Ma, he's been telling everyone I'm a killer! He's caused me more trouble than anyone else!" I rolled forward onto my knees. "I should go. I don't know if I'll ever be able to come back. . . . Certainly not as long as I'm like this. But there's a man who once claimed to have the power to turn me back to normal. If that happens . . ."

Ma said, "But what if something happens to you? These other superheroes . . . One of them might hurt you. They might even *kill* you. I don't think I can go through that again!"

Pa stood up. He reached out and patted me on the shoulder. "There's so much a father should tell his son about being a man. You're twenty years old now, Gethin. You've got a life we can only barely imagine. I know it's not going to be easy, but . . . You have to be a *good* man. You have to always do the best you can for other people."

I left them soon after that. There were awkward hugs and assurances that they wouldn't tell anyone I'd been there. Ma made me promise that I'd keep out of trouble. I told her that trouble seemed to find me no matter what I did, but I promised her anyway.

I spent the next few years in Quebec, Canada, on the western edge of Lake Manicouagan, living on leaves and strips of bark.

In the trash cans in the public parks I'd sometimes find old newspapers that kept me informed about what was happening in the rest of the world. Max Dalton's empire expanded, Titan's reputation grew. Pastor Cullen published a book about me—it made a big splash when it came out, but I don't think it sold many copies. Ragnarök and his people carried out a whole series of attacks on military bases and laboratories, each time disappearing without a trace.

Of Abby—or Hesperus, as she was known to the public— there was little mention, though Thunder and Apex had formed a team and an ax-wielding woman was one of their members, so I guessed that was her.

Then one day I found a newspaper that was dated July 27th. My birthday. I was twenty-three.

That discovery brought with it the realization that, barring unexpected illnesses or accidents, I probably had sixty or seventy more years of life—unless I turned out to be immortal, which was something that *really* didn't appeal to me.

I knew that I couldn't spend the rest of those sixty or seventy years living in caves and eating bark. I had to return to civilization. But I wanted to do so on *my* terms, not Max Dalton's or anyone else's.

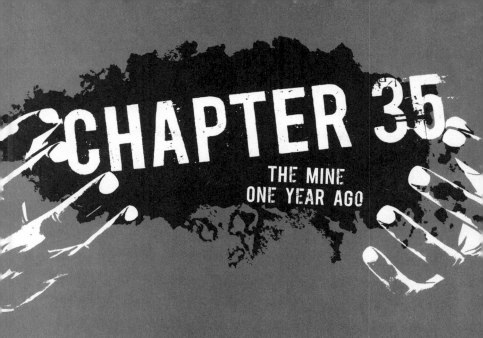

CHAPTER 35

THE MINE
ONE YEAR AGO

"THEY'RE BRINGING IN AN EXPERT," DePaiva told me as we surveyed the now barely profitable mine.

When speaking to me, DePaiva had taken to saying "they" to mean the guards, and "we" to include himself with the downtrodden workers. It didn't fool me, but I pretended to accept it, and I did the same, because it told me that he knew which way the wind was blowing.

I could have been reading too much into it, but I liked to think that DePaiva knew that the mine's days were coming to an end. Perhaps he thought that once it became unprofitable, the prisoners would be shipped elsewhere, and if that happened, it would only be a matter of time before the truth about this place was leaked to the public.

And then . . . Well, then there would be a mass outcry of rage at the inhumane conditions, and all of the guards would be arrested and put on trial. By ingratiating himself with me, DePaiva would be spared.

OK, yeah, I was *definitely* reading too much into it. But it still didn't hurt to have at least one of the guards pretending to be on our side.

"What sort of expert?" I asked. For months the mine had only barely been processing enough ore to keep it open. If this had been any ordinary mine, where the workers had to be paid, it would have been abandoned long ago.

DePaiva shrugged. "Some geologist guy, I think. Thing is, though, he's not coming in as a surveyor or anything like that. He'll be an inmate. Until a couple of days ago he was locked up somewhere in the States."

"So it's another mouth to feed," I said. "I hope he's good at his job. What do they expect to achieve, anyway? We've pretty much picked the land clean."

"Last hope, I reckon." He glanced at his watch. "Copter should be here any minute."

"Right." I gave him a friendly nod and headed off to where my friend Edmond was replacing a drill head.

"Don't know why you bother talkin' to that bleedin' slimeball," Edmond said, straining to lift up the massive drill so he could turn it over.

"It's always good to have a man on the other side," I said.

"Right. That's how he sees *you*, y'know."

"Yep." I picked up the drill and held it in place while he extracted the splintered head.

Edmond looked up at me for a second, then returned his attention to the drill. "A few of us've been talkin'."

"It's not gonna work," I said. "You know where we are, right? Lieberstan. There's not a single village for three hundred miles in any direction. We're more than a thousand miles from the nearest sizeable body of water, and that's the Caspian Sea—it's landlocked. Where would you go?"

"Anywhere that's not here."

"Edmond, we've been through this before. You can ask anyone who's ever tried to escape from this place. You won't get much of an answer, though, because they're buried outside the dome."

"Better to die in the mountains as free men than to die here as slaves."

"No, it's not. As long as you're here, you have the hope of being rescued. But when you're dead, you're dead."

"I've been here nearly eighteen years, Brawn. Imyram's been here fifteen. Our daughter's spent her whole *life* in this place. I don't want her to die here too." He hoisted the heavy drill onto his shoulder.

"Let me—" I began.

"I got it." Without another word, Edmond turned and walked away.

I heard the low roar of an approaching helicopter, and looked over toward the dome's western entrance. DePaiva and Hazlegrove saw me and beckoned to me.

The expert climbed down from the copter with some difficulty: His hands and feet had been tightly chained. He looked to be a few years older than me—in his forties, maybe early fifties—with thinning dark hair and bronzed, weather-beaten skin.

"You show him the ropes," Hazlegrove said to me as he unlocked the man's chains. "He's gonna be with us a long time."

When Hazlegrove and DePaiva left, the chains dragging behind them, the new prisoner looked around slowly. "Platinum mine, huh?"

"They didn't tell you?"

"Didn't tell me nothin'. Judging by the age of the machinery, it's been here, what, thirty-five, forty years? How come I never heard of this place?"

"They don't let the outside world know about us."

"Figures." He looked up at me. "Also figures *you'd* be here. Man, we had some times, huh?"

"Do I know you?"

"What? Sure you do. Leonard Franklin. *Lenny.*" He spread his arms as far as his chains would allow. "It's me. The artist formerly known as Terrain. You remember. We worked together a coupla times, with Ragnarök's crew. We were there when everything went south."

I nodded. "Right. Didn't recognize you. So that's why they brought you in, because you're an expert in geology?"

"I kinda got a feel for it back in the day." He looked over the mine again. "Man, time was I coulda extracted all the platinum outta the ground in one go, just like *that*." He snapped his fingers. "Can't do anything like that now, but I can kinda remember what it was like. The warden said I gotta look at the last survey scans. That's what they got me to do in my last place."

"That was a mine too?"

"Nah, it was just a prison. But they'd bring in satellite photos and ground scans. You know, sonar images. I've got a knack for reading them. I can tell you where you're most likely to find new deposits."

"All that's kept in Hazlegrove's office," I said. "I'll show you."

As we walked to the office, we passed three other prisoners straining to lift a recently repaired cart back onto its tracks. I lifted it up and set it down single-handedly.

We resumed walking, and Terrain said, "You're still pretty strong. Didn't you lose your powers like the rest of us?"

"I did. But my muscles are eight times the size of anyone else's."

"So, you're some kinda trustee, right?"

"Something like that."

"Well, what are you still *doing* here? Man, with your strength you shoulda been outta here years ago!" An expression of disgust appeared on his heavily lined faced. "Don't tell me you *like* it here. You got it easy or something?"

"I hate it here," I said. "And I definitely don't have it easy. I work sixteen hours a day, every day. But I can't leave."

"Why not? You've been—what's the word?—institutionalized?"

"If I leave, Hazlegrove will order the execution of the other prisoners."

"So he says. But if he loses you, he won't wanna lose anyone else."

"I can't take that chance. He's already had more than a

dozen other prisoners killed, some of them just because they knew me."

If anything, Terrain's expression of disgust seemed deeper. "Right."

His opinion of me made no difference. I didn't care if he thought I was a coward any more than if he thought I was a ballerina.

Back when we still had our abilities, Terrain—like so many others—saw me only as a thug, a giant blue brute who specialized in destruction. I like to think that was just the media's portrayal of me, that those who knew me were aware of the truth.

But the fact is, for a while I *was* like that. Shortly after I returned to the USA from Canada, certain events collided and triggered a phase in my superhuman career that I'm not proud of.

It started in New York, when I put my fate in the hands of the public.

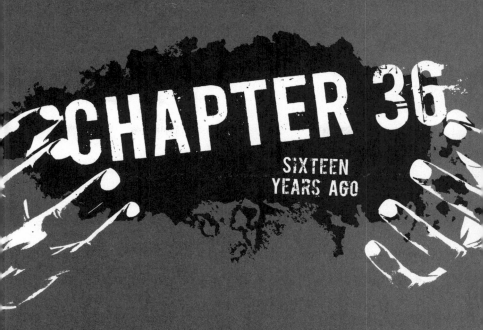

CHAPTER 36

SIXTEEN YEARS AGO

IT TOOK ME SEVENTY DAYS to reach Manhattan from Canada. More than two months of traveling only during the quietest hours of the night, moving as fast as I could and with each step praying that I'd find somewhere to hide out until the next night.

The last night was exhausting: I'd traveled south through New Jersey—coming far too close to Max Dalton's base for comfort—and then took to the water. The Hudson was cold and not particularly clean, but it was safer than the streets and I was much less likely to be seen.

I wasn't a strong swimmer, but—as I had learned in Norman Misseldine's fortress—I could hold my breath for a very long time.

It was almost dawn when I reached Pier 86, and my first

instinct was to hide out for the rest of the day, but that would have defeated the point.

So I hauled myself out of the water and began to walk east, along 45th Street.

Early-morning commuters stared, and there were a few gasps, but far fewer screams than I'd expected.

A crowd formed behind me—at what they imagined was a safe distance—and I had to force myself not to smile as they all bumped into each other when I stopped to use the crosswalk on 9th Avenue.

A police car pulled to a stop ahead of me, and the two officers jumped out and crouched behind their doors with their guns aimed at me.

They didn't shout a warning, so I ignored them and kept walking.

The crowd grew, many of them coming within a few yards of me. Cameras flashed and car horns beeped. Then there were more cop cars, some with their lights and sirens blaring. The police tried to keep the crowds back, but they had little hope of that.

By the time I reached Times Square, the crowd must have been several hundred strong, blocking the traffic and generally causing chaos.

It was a little awkward, because I hadn't expected to get that far without being questioned by the police, so I just stood there and looked around while the police quickly and nervously erected barriers and attempted to herd the crowd in.

Then, finally, a police officer felt brave enough to attempt communication: From across the square he used a bullhorn to blare out, "You are causing a public disturbance!"

"Me? What have *I* done? Not my fault if these people are following me!"

"What do you want?"

I couldn't resist it: "What have you got?"

And then the press came: helicopters, TV vans, lone reporters armed with cameras and microphones.

A TV reporter and her camera crew darted up to the officer with the bullhorn and started badgering him with questions. "What are you going to do? Will this man be arrested? What's the NYPD's official position on blue-skinned people?"

The officer scratched his head with the edge of the bullhorn. "Uh, right now I'm not prepared to comment. Please, get back behind the barriers for your own safety."

"Brawn is a known supervillain—why aren't you arresting him?"

"Don't have cuffs big enough. Now get behind the barriers!"

"Can I say something?" I asked.

It seemed like the whole square fell silent.

I crouched down and beckoned to the reporter. "C'mon, I don't bite."

She moved about an inch closer, and I figured it was the best I was going to get.

"You're recording?"

"We're going out live."

"Live? Wow. Hey, everyone watching, sorry if this interrupts your cartoons or your sports bulletins or whatever. I just wanna say that I'm tired of running, tired of hiding. And sure as anything I'm tired of living in forests and eating leaves."

"So . . . What is it you *want?*"

That caught me out. "Um, a job? Somewhere to live that has walls and a roof? What does *anyone* want?" I looked straight into the camera. "I'm twenty-three, didn't finish high school, can't drive, and have no experience. But if you need anything *heavy* lifted . . ."

Then a loud voice from above said, "Coward!"

I looked up to see Titan floating above me, his arms folded to better show off his muscles, his blue cape gently flapping in the breeze. He always did know how to make an entrance.

"You bring the fight to one of the most crowded cities on the planet—using the public as human shields!"

"*What* fight?" I shouted back. "What have I ever done to you?"

"You freed Ragnarök!"

"Yeah? Well, he wasn't Ragnarök *then*, was he? He was just a guy. But he was Ragnarök all the times you fought him and weren't able to catch him! So don't blame me for *your* failures, you overhyped jerk!"

Another voice, deeper and stronger, laced with authority, seemed to come from everywhere at once: "Everyone—clear the area. Now."

I was amazed to see that it worked. Almost immediately, the crowd began to disperse. Some of them took a few last photos, and quite a few of the reporters retreated several dozen yards. Even the police fell back.

Titan touched down on the street in front of me. A blur whipped through the air, and then Quantum was standing next to him.

They were joined by Energy, drifting down from the sky with crackles of electricity sparking from her eyes and fingertips.

"So," I said. "It's going to be like that, is it? Where's your other pal? Where's Paragon?"

Energy said, "Paragon is otherwise engaged."

I nodded. "Maybe because he knows the truth."

"And what's that?" Titan asked.

"He knows that I'm not who you all think I am. I'm not a monster."

The deep voice came again. "Oh, you *are*." I realized that the voice was coming from behind me, and I turned to see Thunder—his build was even bigger than last time I'd seen him—standing next to Abby and a dark-haired teenage boy who looked vaguely familiar.

"Six against one," I said. "But you're going to have to throw the first punch. Which you probably will if Dalton has your brains sufficiently scrambled."

The young man frowned and said, "If I *what*?" and I realized that he must be Joshua Dalton, Max and Roz's younger brother. The last time I'd seen him, he was ten. But that was seven years earlier. I couldn't help wondering what power he had developed.

"Josh, right? You've grown up. So, where's your sister and brother? They decide not to play today?"

Abby said, "Brawn, stand down. This is your only warning."

"How can I stand down when I haven't done anything yet? If you want to talk, Ab— I mean, Hesperus, then we'll talk. You and me. Thunder will listen in anyway."

She drew her sword and her ax, and walked toward me.

I sat down cross-legged on the ground. "This isn't a fight, Abby," I said softly. "I've come to make peace."

She stopped in front of me. "Peace. After what you did?"

"This was the only way I could think of to get your attention without being arrested. The cameras are still rolling. If you and your friends attack, the whole world will see that I'm not fighting back." I smiled. "Max won't be able to mess with *all* of their minds."

Her grim expression melted. "Brawn, you've got it so wrong! Max isn't like that. He never was. Can't you see? You spent hours talking to Ragnarök that night—*he* got inside your mind, not Max!"

"I don't think so," I said.

Abby came closer still. "All these powers, all these things we can do . . . It doesn't change who we are deep down. You're still just a kid, aren't you? You're still twelve years old—you never had the chance to grow up."

"Have any of us?"

"Yes! Yes, we have! You've had practically no human contact for the past seven years. The rest of us . . . We're adults now. Thunder has—"

Thunder's voice interrupted. "Don't tell him *anything* about me!"

I sighed. "Privacy is a thing of the past, isn't it?"

Abby continued. "I've moved out. My brothers are all

in college. My sister's getting married next year, to Sol—"
Abby stopped herself. "To someone we know. Heck, Lance
is *already* married! Time has moved on for everyone except
you!"

"You moved out? Who's looking after your mom?"

"She has a new boyfriend. She moved into his house."

"And what about you? You seeing anyone?"

Abby nodded. "Yeah. For the past five months."

I glanced toward Thunder. "Tell me it's not *him*."

"Definitely not. He's not my type," Abby said, and then
smiled, and I realized what she meant. "You'd like Quinn, I
think. If we can find a way through all this, you should come
to dinner."

"Maybe. Are you happy, though?"

"Yes. Very."

We looked at each other for a few seconds, and then I said,
"We don't have to do this. I don't want to fight anyone. I never
have."

"What *do* you want, Gethin?"

"I want to be human again. I want a normal life."

Thunder said, "And you'll stop at nothing to get that,
right? Hesperus—back away."

I stood up, stepped around Abby, and towered over Thunder. "Man, he really did a number on *you*, didn't he? I'm the
only one of us Max Dalton can't control. Now, I came here
peacefully. If you can't accept that, then leave. Just go. But if
there's any part of you still in there who can see me for who I
really am, then we can get past this." I hunched down in front
of him and extended my right hand for him to shake.

I don't know what Thunder thought was happening, but I saw his eyes widen and his muscles tense a split second before he attacked.

A sonic bolt hit me square in the face, knocking me back onto my heels. It was followed almost immediately by another to the chest, hard enough to lift me a foot into the air.

Titan crashed into my back, locked his arms around my neck, and pushed me forward, slamming my forehead hard against the ground. I reached up and grabbed his arm, pulling him away.

Then Quantum was on me, zipping around almost too fast for me to see, his punches relatively weak but relentless, a barrage of flickering images that rained against my head, my arms, and my chest.

As I tried to swat Quantum away, Titan flew at me again and crashed shoulder-first into the side of my head. I staggered sideways, reeling from the pain, and reached out to a lamppost to steady myself.

Someone shouted, "He's going for a weapon!" and the lamppost disintegrated into a white-hot spray of molten metal.

The air was heavy with ozone, and I knew that Energy had blasted the lamppost with a lightning bolt, but I had little time to consider what would happen to me if she hit me directly: Another tsunami of sonic blasts from Thunder smashed down on me, pinning me to the ground.

The sonic blasts eased for a second, but before I could rise, I realized why: Titan and Quantum struck simultaneously, Titan's powerful fists hitting me like cannonballs, Quantum's blur of kicks and punches pummeling against my torso, as unremitting and unpredictable as an avalanche.

I held my ground, tried to resist without hitting back. Then Thunder hit my eardrums with a pinpoint high-pitched shriek that sent me reeling, my head spinning. I was barely able to keep upright. And still the onslaught continued: Thunder, Titan, and Quantum all hitting me at once.

I broke out in a sweat, and at first I thought it was the friction of Quantum's mercurial attack, but my body heat continued to rise. My mouth went dry, and the skin on my back and arms began to blister.

Four of them now, I realized. Energy had joined the attack, using her powers to channel heat into my body.

Thunder switched to a low-frequency sound that actually caused my skull to vibrate, and then I found myself lifting into the air, spinning and tumbling, as though I had been wrapped inside an invisible, incredibly strong net.

It felt like Roz's telekinetic shield, but I hadn't seen her. . . . If she'd been there in Times Square, she wouldn't have remained hidden. It had to be her brother, with a power similar to hers.

He slammed me down onto the ground, hard enough to crack the asphalt, and held me there, trapped, while Thunder bombarded me with sonic pulses, Titan flew at me again and again with his clenched, iron-hard fists, Energy scorched the air around me, and Quantum was a circling, whirling haze of kicks and punches.

Don't let go, I told myself. *Hold your ground!*

And then, through the haze of pain and the desert-dry

heat, I saw Abby running at me, her sword and ax gripped tightly in her hands. She pulled her arms back, ready to swing both weapons at once.

"Enough!" I shouted. "I surrender!"

But my voice never reached anyone else's ears: Thunder had blocked the sound.

I raised my arms at the last possible moment. A second longer and Abby would have buried the ax and sword deep into either side of my neck.

Instead, my forearms took the damage: The ax almost severed my left hand just above the wrist, and the sword completely pierced my right forearm, its blade scraping against my radius and ulna as it passed between them.

A spray of blood shot out and hit Abby in the face. She jumped back, shocked, as though only just aware of what she'd done.

The others stopped too, almost at the same instant.

I fell back onto my butt, cradling my arms, my entire body feeling like it was held together only by pain. Bracing myself for the agony, I shook my left arm, knocking the ax free. It clattered to the ground, the noise echoing around the now-silent Times Square.

Then I grabbed the hilt of Abby's sword with my left hand and—with clenched teeth and more courage than I ever imagined I possessed—pulled it free.

There was a buzzing, murmuring sound all around me, and for the first time I realized that the crowds had come back, that every window in the square was filled with shocked faces, that the enormous TV screens hanging over the square were all showing my face.

I looked at Abby's sword for a moment, then wiped its blade clean on my shoulder, flipped it into the air and caught it by the blade, and offered it to her, hilt-first.

She was unable to look me in the eye as she took it, then stepped back.

Thunder was the first to speak. "Oh my God. What have we done?"

No one seemed to know how to answer that.

I tried to keep my legs from shaking as I got to my feet. "I'll tell you what you've done, you little *punk*! You attacked me for no reason. Again."

The other heroes closed around me.

Quantum began, "Look, Brawn, we—"

"Shut *up*! When you people get home tonight, when you're cozying up with your loved ones in your warm and dry apartments, watch the news. And watch it carefully. You'll see that I didn't make the first move. I didn't even throw a punch." I turned to Titan. "You. C'mere!"

He floated toward me. "I'm sorry, man, I don't know what—"

"Turn around!"

Tentatively, he did as I instructed. I reached out and pulled the cape from his back. I tore it into two strips and tied one around my left wrist, the other around my right forearm.

"I want to know *two things*," I roared at them. "Why you did that, and what made you stop!"

A voice from behind me said, "I can answer both of your questions."

I turned to see Paragon walking toward me. To his left and about a step behind was Max Dalton.

"Thunder," Paragon said, "I want a sphere of silence around us."

Thunder nodded, and instantly the noise of the crowd was hushed.

Paragon put his hand on Max's shoulder. To anyone else watching, it would have looked like a friendly gesture, but it was clear to us from Max's expression that Paragon was putting a lot of pressure into that grip. "Our friend here did it. He came here with Josh, and watched from the rooftops."

I stood over Max and peered down at him. "You've gone too far this time. They would have killed me!"

Calmly, Max said, "You didn't fight back. That's really remarkable. But none of this was entirely my fault, Brawn. They're all scared of you. Terrified that one day you'll turn against them. They know how strong you are. All I did was nudge them a little."

Paragon pulled his hand away from Max. "What are you saying? That *you* did this?"

Energy shook her head. "No way. That's not Max's style."

I sighed and looked at Max. "You're doing it again, aren't you?"

"Yes. Paragon here realized what I was doing, and threatened me with some pretty serious consequences if I didn't make them stop. If I hadn't been too busy focusing on the others to notice him coming, this particular scenario would have had a much different ending. You probably owe him your life."

"Wait, wait . . . ," Paragon said. "Max, are you saying that you played some part in this?"

Max smiled. "In a few minutes all that they'll remember is that you were about to attack them and they retaliated. Maybe you were under someone else's control. Yes, that'd be a nice irony."

"What's to stop me from tearing your head off right here and now?"

"You're not a killer, Brawn."

"I'm willing to learn."

Paragon said, "Hold on. . . . Something's going on here. Max, do you know more about this than you're saying?"

Thunder clapped Joshua Dalton on the back. "You did good, Josh. If you hadn't figured out that an adrenaline rush would break Ragnarök's hold on Brawn, he might have leveled the city."

Max's smile grew. "And that's the official story. That's what it's going to look like to everyone watching, once my public relations people start doing their magic. You can't beat me, Brawn. You have to acknowledge that. I win. You lose. That's the way it's always going to be. I'll always come out on top, and you'll never be anything but a giant, blue, *pathetic* freak of nature."

He shouldn't have gloated. If he'd just walked away, it all might have ended there.

But he *had* to keep pushing, had to rub it in that he had won.

I flicked out my right arm, caught him with a backhanded smack in the middle of his smug sneer.

That was a mistake. I should have hit him harder, should have knocked him clear across the square. Instead, it wasn't much more than a light tap. Just enough to break his nose and hurt like crazy, but not enough to knock him out.

If he'd been knocked out, the others might have let it go. But Max glared up at me, his own blood spattered over his costume.

That was when all hell broke loose.

CHAPTER 37

TITAN STRUCK FIRST. He slammed into my side, locked his arms around my waist, and kept going, lifting me into the air. We were already above the rooftops before I knew what was happening.

Energy and Thunder came streaking after him. Thunder hit me with a rapid-fire stream of sonic blasts so strong that it felt like my muscles were tearing away from my bones.

Energy roared at Titan to let me go. For a second I thought she was on my side, but the instant he let go, she launched a lightning bolt that struck my chest and emerged through my back, only inches away from my heart.

Titan grabbed me again, this time from behind with his arms around my neck, trying to choke me as he dragged me upward and eastward.

I caught a glimpse of Paragon below me, flying upside

down, and again I had a moment of hope that was shattered as he launched a volley of small missiles straight at me.

Titan let go once more, and Paragon's missiles struck home, exploding against my torso, wrapping me with clinging fire: napalm. Even through the searing agony, I could hardly believe that Paragon had used napalm against a living being.

The fire coursed over my skin, triggering every pain receptor in my body. Then it reached my face, but I couldn't scream, couldn't open my mouth, because I knew that if I inhaled, the fire would be sucked into my lungs.

I arced through the air, a burning, flailing figure that trailed thick black smoke and rained fragments of charred flesh over the East River.

Even as I was falling, the assault continued. Thunder's sonic blasts hit me again and again, some from below, some from the right, and through the blistering agony of the napalm I understood what he was doing. He was steering my fall.

I opened my eyes long enough to see that I was coming down into the largest rail yard I had ever seen, where directly ahead of me more than two dozen trains were at rest, parallel lines of train cars and engines that weren't going to be much use to anyone in a few seconds.

Thunder must have realized the destruction that would cause, or perhaps one of the others warned him, because at the last moment I felt myself being shunted to the right.

I cleared all but one of the trains: My flailing legs clipped the roof of its engine, flipping me over so that I crashed down face-first onto an empty track.

The napalm had almost burned itself out, but the damage

it had already done, and the impact with the tracks, left me weak, breathless, every square inch of my body in blistering agony.

With shaking, blackened arms I pushed myself up onto my knees and forced my charred eyelids open. I looked to the west and saw them coming: six flying figures rushing toward me.

Titan and Energy led the charge, with Thunder, Abby, and Paragon close behind. Joshua Dalton—perhaps not quite as experienced with his powers as the others—trailed by some distance.

But no sign of Quantum. He couldn't fly, but then he rarely needed to. Not seeing Quantum was the worst: That meant that he could be here already.

And he was. He materialized right in front of me. I braced myself for another assault, but instead he just stood there, his face twisted in confusion and torment.

"This is . . . This is wrong. You won't die here today, Brawn. They're going to need you, at the end. I . . . His voice is in my head, telling me I have to fight. I can't. . . . He doesn't *understand*. He only wants what's best." Quantum reached out and gently touched my arm. "Do not step into The Chasm."

Then he was gone, leaving nothing but a slowly settling line of dust across the rail yard.

The others established a wide ring around me, each of them floating several feet above the ground.

"Surrender!" Titan yelled. "Carrying on this fight is madness, Brawn. It's *suicide*!"

Thunder said, "He's right. You can't defeat all of us. You know that."

I stood up, wincing at the fresh surge of pain as the blackened skin on my legs cracked and split. "Surrender? No. No, I *don't* surrender! You started this—I'm going to finish it!"

I leaped straight at Titan. He darted up and out of reach—just as I'd expected. I came down in a crouch next to another track, my blistered hands on one of the rails.

He came at me from behind and I spun to face him, ripping the rail away from its sleepers. I slammed the rail against the side of his head. The blow sent him reeling, crashing to the ground.

Abby darted in, her sword and ax spinning. I spun again, and swatted at her with the rail. She jumped up over it—but I immediately swept it back and up, colliding with her ax in a shower of sparks and knocking it free from her grip. Holding the rail in the middle, I spun it around and the other end struck hard against Abby's left arm.

I carried the movement through, whipping the rail behind me to hit Thunder in the stomach as he was preparing to attack.

I rushed forward and jabbed the end of the rail hard against Paragon's armor with enough force to split open his chestplate. As he staggered back and stumbled to the ground, I turned to face Energy, ran straight at her.

She blasted me with another lightning bolt, but I slammed one end of the rail into the dirt ahead of me, using it to block the lightning bolt and disperse it into the ground—and kept moving, using the rail as a pole to vault right over Energy's head.

As I passed above her, I slammed down with my right foot.

It connected with Energy's shoulder, pushed her hard against the ground.

I came down next to Joshua Dalton, saw the terror flare in his eyes a half second before my fist connected with his face.

The hook from Paragon's grappling gun missed my head by less than an inch; I whirled around and grabbed hold of the line, jerked my hand back, and pulled him off his feet. I quickly gathered up the slack and pulled again; Paragon hit a release button and the cable came free.

Abby—her left arm hanging uselessly—rushed at me with her sword. I whipped the cable at her: She slashed at it and missed. I looped the cable around her sword arm, then jumped up and over her, the force pulling her off her feet. As I reached the apex of the jump, I pulled harder still, with both hands on the cable, and Abby soared into the air.

I landed with my feet on either side of Paragon and immediately began to spin, swinging Abby around me on the end of the cable. She crashed into Thunder as he was getting to his feet, and he screamed as her flailing sword raked a diagonal line across his back.

Titan grabbed the fallen rail and tried to rush at me again, but mistimed his attack and got caught up in the cable. It slowed him down long enough for me to hit his jaw with the most powerful punch I could muster.

I felt his nose shatter under my knuckles. His jaw went slack and his head reeled, his eyes rolling. I hit him again, just as hard, and then a third time, and he finally went limp, the rail crashing down to rest across Paragon's armored back.

Screaming with rage, Energy darted at me from behind, blasting me with fire and lightning at the same time.

I stamped down hard on the raised end of the rail: The other end shot up and smashed into Energy from behind, moments before she reached me. At the same time, I lashed out with my fist and hit her square in the face.

Energy collapsed to the ground, groaning.

Nearby, Thunder was once again trying to get to his feet. I strode over to him, locked my hand around his head, and lifted him up. His arms and legs twitched.

"Can't defeat *all* of you?" I roared at him. "You wanna re-think that one, Thunder?"

I threw him to the ground.

"You started this!" I shouted at them. "Remember that—*you* attacked *me*! And if you come after me again, I won't go so easy on you!"

I turned away.

And stopped.

Four people were standing in front of me, one woman and three men.

"Now, that was quite a fight," the woman said. I recognized her instantly: Slaughter.

The first man I also recognized: Casey Duval, now considerably more muscular than the last time I'd met him.

Beside him stood an ordinary-looking man wearing a plain shirt and faded jeans, and next to him . . . a nearly naked man whose red-blotched skin glistened wetly in the morning sun. He was covered in sores that looked like the worst case of acne ever. The sores dripped a thick, clear liquid that left tiny smoking craters where it hit the ground. I remembered him from Harmony Yuan's lectures: This was Dioxin.

Casey said, "So. They turned on you, just like I said they would. You should have stayed in Quebec."

"You knew where I was?"

"I've always known. Ever since you and your friends attacked Tremont's base in Pennsylvania. You remember the robot? It planted a little something inside your chest. A tracking device that showed me your location at all times."

"Get it out of me!"

"It's already gone. Energy's lightning blast destroyed it— that's what drew my attention. These people don't want you around, Brawn. You'll only ever be a freak to them. Join us."

"Are you *insane*? You're a thousand times worse than they are!"

"According to Max Dalton's propaganda, maybe. But when have you known him to tell the truth?"

Dioxin said, "Ragnarök here is working on a cure. He's gonna reverse what happened to us."

"Let's not jump the gun," Casey said. "There's a long way to go before that happens. But if there's anyone who can do it, it's me. What do you say, Brawn? I've got a place that Dalton will never discover, and you're going to need time to heal."

I looked back at the slowly stirring bodies behind me. So what if they were under Max's control? They'd still attacked me. And they'd keep on doing it, keep attacking until I was dead. "All right," I said to Casey. "You owe me anyway."

Casey smiled, and turned to the ordinary-looking man. "Terrain, a dust cloud will obscure our departure."

"You're Terrain?" I said. "You almost got me killed! Remember Norman Misseldine's fortress? The trap they paid you to set?"

The man frowned for a second. "Oh, right. That was, what, eight or nine years ago? Yeah, that was a pretty good trap. How'd you get out of it?"

Casey said, "Guys, we really don't have time to play 'How've you been?' right now. We need to leave."

Dioxin said, "Whoa, wait. . . . We're just gonna leave these creeps here? Dude, we're never gonna get another chance like this! This is like, five of the toughest superheroes around, *and* Dalton's little brother! I say we finish them off right here and now!"

Slaughter said, "I'm with you. Especially *that* little cow," she added, pointing to Abby. "Stabbed me in the stomach during the battle with Krodin!"

I said, "I remember that. She didn't stab you—you fell onto her sword. Your fault, not hers. And if any of you lay one hand on them, I'll break every bone in your bodies." I looked at Casey as I said that. "Are we clear?"

He nodded. "We're clear. Despite what you might have read, Brawn, I'm not a killer. And I certainly wouldn't kick someone when they're down. We'll leave these folks to lick their wounds and think about what they've done." He extended his right hand. "Are you in?"

I reached down and grabbed his hand, and shook it. "I'm in."

CHAPTER 38

THE MINE
EIGHT MONTHS AGO

LEONARD FRANKLIN—TERRAIN—had determined that there was a small but potentially profitable seam of platinum ore on the western side of the compound, two hundred yards beyond the dome.

Hazlegrove decided that it was worth mining, although without the dome to shield the prison from the outside world, he first ordered temporary covers to be erected. We planted poles, stretched huge canvas sheets between them, and painted the sheets a dull gray to match the concrete.

And so began a new phase in the mining process: At the start of every shift the workers were chained together and led out through the doors by a line of guards. The work outside was slightly easier, though only because of the fresh breeze that carried away some of the dust. In the older shafts the dust remained in place, clogging up our lungs, getting into our eyes.

The new shaft had been in operation for a week when the mine received its latest inmate. He was scarred from head to foot, but looked strong, and that was what counted.

The first time the stranger saw me, he stopped and stared until one of the guards jabbed him in the small of his back. "Keep movin'! You never seen a giant blue guy before?"

The stranger said, "Just one."

Imyram, standing just in front of me, pointed back toward the doors. "Look."

At the doorway, Swinden was escorting a prisoner out. She was an older woman I knew only as Francine. I'd never spoken to her. "Where are they—?"

The guard said, "Prisoner exchange. Not your business, Brawn."

Three days later I was called to take a look at the crusher, which had jammed up again, and saw the scarred stranger staring at me. He caught me looking back and said, "You don't recognize me, do ya?"

"Should I?"

"Yeah. You should." He was shirtless, and came close enough that I could clearly see the hundreds of scars on his face, torso, and arms. "Time was, you and me were partners. Kinda. But then Ragnarök hadda go and spoil everything."

"Dioxin?"

"Used to be, yeah." He smirked, his face a contorted mess of badly healed wounds and a patchwork of different-colored grafts. "You been here all this time, Brawn? That's, like, ten *years*."

"That long already, huh? Time sure flies."

"Ragnarök's dead, did you hear? Man, he sure left some mess behind. The world's changed out there, Brawn. Guys like us, we don't belong there." He looked around. "Not sayin' we belong *here* either."

Two guards approached. "You two freaks—back to work! Brawn, they need you over at processing."

"Got a lot to tell you," Dioxin said. "Lotta stuff you need to know. Gotta tell you about Wagner and Cooper and the others!"

The guards grabbed Dioxin, taking an arm each.

"We're gonna get out of here!" Dioxin shouted as the guards dragged him away. "We were a team before—we can do it again! Terrain's here too, right? We just need Slaughter. We'll get out and we're gonna make them pay for this! Are you with me?"

I was already halfway across the compound. I didn't bother to answer.

Dioxin was wrong. We had never been a team. What we'd been was a collection of bitter, disillusioned superhumans who occasionally united under Casey Duval's leadership.

Dioxin had worked with Casey a lot more than I had, but I wasn't entirely innocent. I'd helped them plunder bank vaults to fund Casey's research, and I'd stood with them against Dalton and his friends on more than one occasion. But part of the reason I was with them was that they were too scared of what

I'd do to them if they killed the good guys. They'd seen me lose control and single-handedly defeat six of the world's most powerful heroes: There was no way they'd be able to beat me. And I think Casey always knew that.

At the processing station the mechanism that drove the crusher was jammed. This happened a couple of times a month, and all it usually needed was a hard thump in the right area. For months I'd been asking Hazlegrove to take the crusher off-line so that it could be given a complete overhaul, but he'd always refused. That would take three or four days, and as it was, the crusher was barely able to keep up with the workload.

I had just reached the crusher when something in its drive-shaft snapped.

A chunk of rusty metal shot out from the crusher's mechanism. It streaked across the compound, right into the midst of a bunch of kids who were lining up with their bowls to receive their midday meal.

There was a scream, and by the time I reached them, the cook had torn strips from his apron and wrapped them around the little girl's arm.

It was Estelle, the daughter of my friends Imyram and Edmond, the same little girl I'd helped deliver nine years earlier. Beneath the ever-present grime of the mine she was pale with shock, cradling her arm as blood soaked through the crude bandage.

I scooped her up and ran to the office where Hazlegrove and DePaiva were both leaning over a giant ledger. "We need the doctor!" I shouted through the narrow doorway.

Hazlegrove didn't look up. "Doctor's not due for another two weeks."

"Hazlegrove, we need the doctor right *now!*"

He set down his pen. "That's *Mister* Hazlegrove. And I told you, the doctor will be here in about two weeks."

"Then pass me a first-aid kit or something!"

He looked at the girl in my arms. "What happened?"

"Something flew off the crusher. Hit her arm."

Hazlegrove jumped to his feet so fast he knocked his chair over. "How bad is it??"

"Very—I think it might have hit an artery. She's losing a lot of blood!"

He rushed out past me. "No, you idiot! The crusher! Is it still running?"

"Give her to me," DePaiva said. "I'll take a look."

I passed the trembling girl to him, and he carried her into the office and gently sat her on the desk. "I need to have a look. . . ." He peeled back the bandage, then quickly rewrapped it and turned to me. "It's not an artery. She'll be fine."

"DePaiva, call the doctor!"

"He won't come, Brawn. Once a month, that's the arrangement."

"Call him!"

DePaiva hesitated. "Hazlegrove will have my guts for soup if I . . ." He shook his head. "No. I can't. Look, she might be OK."

Estelle raised her head a little and looked up at me, tears spilling from her eyes.

"She's a *human being*, DePaiva! A little girl!"

He glanced briefly at the phone on the far side of the desk, hen shook his head again. "No. Any call like that has to go through the warden, and there's no way it'd be approved."

"Give me the phone."

DePaiva's hand inched toward the pistol on his hip. "No."

The office doorway was too small for me. I pushed in anyway, the frames snapping and splintering.

DePaiva pulled out his gun, aimed it at me with his hand trembling and his eyes wide. "Get back! I swear, one more step and I'll shoot!"

"Won't do you any good. I've been shot lots of times." I bared my teeth. "Now gimme the phone!"

He swallowed. "Get back!"

There was a loud *crack* from the wall as I forced my shoulders through the doorway. "Last chance, DePaiva!"

His hand still shaking, DePaiva lowered the gun to his side . . .

. . . Then raised it again, the wavering barrel only inches away from Estelle's head. "Please don't make me—"

I jabbed at his face with my clenched fist. He crashed through the back wall in a shower of dust and splinters and rolled limply to a stop somewhere on the far side.

I didn't care whether DePaiva was alive or dead: I grabbed the phone and almost immediately a woman's voice said, "What is it, Hazlegrove?"

"Get the doctor. Now."

"What? Who *is* this? Where's Hazlegrove?" I threw the phone to the floor—I knew there would be no help coming.

Estelle said, "Brawn . . ."

I turned to see Hazlegrove and Swinden in the doorway, their guns aimed at me. A dozen other guards were behind them.

"If DePaiva is dead," Hazlegrove said, "so are you. I don't care how many bullets it takes to bring you down."

Moving slowly, I lifted Estelle off the desk and set her down on the floor. "Go find your mom and dad, sweetheart."

She looked up at me and nodded, then carefully squeezed past the guards.

"Hazlegrove . . . I've only ever lost control a couple of times before. Trust me when I say you don't want it to happen again."

They opened fire. I didn't even feel the first few bullets striking me. I leaped at the guards, smashing the door frame completely out of the wall.

I reached Swinden first, grabbed his gun arm, and pulled back and down, wrenching it from its socket. Then I picked him up and threw him overhead into three of his colleagues.

I dropped to a crouch and spun, sweeping my outstretched leg into Hazlegrove. He flipped up and over, and landed on his back. I ended the spin directly over him, and jabbed down hard on his chest with my elbow. The cracking of his ribs was immensely satisfying.

Over at the gate I saw two of the guards raising their rifles, but they were running toward a group of prisoners.

I grabbed Hazlegrove by the ankle and threw him in their direction. I missed, but they skidded to a stop as their boss's whimpering body awkwardly slammed into the ground in front of them.

All of the guards were running at me now, firing wildly. One shot caught me in the face less than an inch above my left eye; another actually passed in through my mouth and out through my cheek.

I knew I wasn't going to get out of this alive, so I made the decision to cause as much damage as possible before I went down.

I threw myself backward into Hazlegrove's office, picked up his filing cabinet, and heaved it out through the ruined doorway. It shattered as it hit the ground, scattering the mine with hundreds of files.

Then I straightened up, forcing the back of my head and my shoulders against the low ceiling. When I heard it crack, I swept my arms up, completely tearing through the roof.

I kicked out at the front wall and split it into two jagged fragments that shot out across the compound, one of them moving so fast, it swept up a guard and carried him with it.

And all the while the barrage of gunshots continued. My skin was peppered with bullet holes.

I crashed through the debris and raced at a quartet of guards standing between me and the main doors of the dome. They held their ground, firing over and over, and dodged aside only at the last second.

As I passed, one of them shouted, "Target his knees! And keep shooting until you hear the clicks!"

I heard the remaining guards rush up to join them just as the first shots hit the back of my legs. I stumbled, tried to get up, and was hit again and again.

I collapsed facedown on the ground, my body twitching as they unloaded their handguns and shotguns into me.

The dirt beneath me darkened as my blood soaked through it.

Then, directly ahead of me, I saw Terrain looking at me with horror. I forced a smile. "They're all outta ammo now, Lenny. . . . You're never gonna . . . get a better chance to run."

I woke up in darkness and agony, my hands and legs bound with chains so heavy that I could barely lift them.

A woman's voice said, "I always knew you were strong, even without your powers, but I had no idea you were *that* strong."

I looked around. All I could see was a thin, bright, inverted T-shape.

"You've caused a huge amount of damage and crippled eight guards. Mr. Hazlegrove will probably never walk again. DePaiva and Swinden . . . They'll live, but it will be *years* before they recover. You're going to be chained for the rest of your days, Brawn, and these chains are utterly unbreakable. We've constructed this special cell just for you. You will be supervised at all times, and you will never again have any contact with the other inmates."

"Who are you?"

A shape passed in front of the inverted T, and I realized what it was: the outline of two closed doors that faced the sun. "I'm the warden. I've been in charge of the facility for two decades, and never once have I had to actually *visit* this godforsaken place. You've embarrassed me in front of my superiors. This will not happen again."

"Hazlegrove tried to punish me, to torture me, but he failed. If you think this is punishment, then you don't know me at all!"

"But I *do* know you, Brawn. I've known you for twenty-seven years."

And then I understood. "Harmony."

CHAPTER 39.

THIRTEEN YEARS AGO

THE POWER STRUGGLE BETWEEN Ragnarök and Max Dalton was always fought on two levels: physically and strategically.

From Casey's point of view, he was always at least one step ahead of Max. He once told me, "I set up the pieces like dominos and that idiot just keeps knocking them down, exactly the way I want. He thinks he's clever, but the fact is, all he can do is channel other people. . . . He's an idea vampire, at best. I don't think the man's had an original thought in his life. He can't *create*. All he can do is react."

Casey had built an empire of his own, albeit one that was so wrapped up in secrecy that I'm sure he was the only one who fully understood its extent. I was pretty sure he was supplying money and weapons to groups like The Chain Gang and The Hive, but I never learned why.

I also knew that he was in regular contact with guys like The Shark and Metrion, but the exact nature of those relationships escaped me. The Shark was said to be invulnerable—and I mean actually invulnerable, not just really hard to kill like me and Titan—and very definitely had his own plans, and Metrion was . . . Well, I'm not a psychiatrist, but I think I can safely diagnose Metrion as "nuttier than a bucket of squirrel droppings." He once went on a rampage through the north of England hijacking ice-cream trucks and demanding that they take him to the nearest pub.

In some respects, Casey wasn't much better. There's a thin line between genius and madness, and sometimes I got the feeling that Casey was using that line as a jump rope.

In the caverns that served as his main base in Pennsylvania, Casey gathered Slaughter, Terrain, Dioxin, and me. "First up, I'm gonna need some more DNA samples from each of you."

"Again? What's this for?" Terrain asked. "Is this gonna go on a chart or something? So you can see how our powers develop?"

"A chart? You really don't know how DNA works, do you?" He took a swab from inside our cheeks—he had to use a special swab made from gold thread for Dioxin—and stored them away. "In seventeen hours The High Command will be escorting a transport convoy bound for Washington. It's going to pass within sixty miles of here. We're stopping it."

"What's the cargo?" I asked.

"A prototype microprocessor."

Slaughter raised an eyebrow. "A computer chip."

"Yes. But not like any other. My spies tell me it's a function-ing quantum processor."

"Seriously?" I asked.

"Apparently so. A couple of years back a team at JPL made some real progress and decided not to keep it to themselves. They started working with dozens of scientific institutes to perfect the idea. And three days ago they successfully created the first working prototype. But it's not hooked up to anything yet—they need to ship it to a research team in Washington that's built a motherboard fast enough to accommodate it. And we're going to take the chip before it gets there." To the others, Casey said, "Imagine a machine capable of computing the most complex calculations instantly. And I mean, *instantly.* The fastest computers in production today can decipher a ge-netic code in a couple of hours. A fully operational quantum-processing computer would be able to decipher the genetic code of every organism on the planet in less time than it's taken for me to explain that."

"So it's worth a lot of money, then?" Dioxin asked.

"Dioxin, that chip is the single-most precious object the human race has ever created."

Slaughter asked, "What do you need it for?"

Casey grinned. "Something I'm working on." He looked at me and Dioxin. "The cure."

Casey analyzed the convoy's route provided by his spies, and we quickly pinpointed the best location for an ambush.

The transport convoy comprised two armored cars in front,

a large panel truck in the middle, and two more cars at the back.

As we watched from the hillside, Slaughter said, "They might as well have painted 'Top Secret Convoy' on the side of the truck."

Casey didn't respond. He was busy climbing into his powered armor, a complex framework that very much resembled the robot he'd built when he was working with Gordon Tremont. I'd seen him using it a couple of times already: It greatly increased his strength and speed. Not to the point where he was a match for someone like Titan, but it certainly put him on a level with most of the superheroes.

Dioxin said, "We could just destroy the whole lot of them. Be a lot quicker and easier than trying to find a single computer chip."

"No," Casey said. He flexed his right arm and the motors of his powered armor whirred softly. "It'll be a much more effective message if they know we have the processor."

"Yeah, but we could—"

"I said no." Casey turned to face Dioxin. "Understood?"

"Sure, yeah. Whatever."

"And *you* don't come within ten feet of it, you get me? It's the only one of its kind, and if your acid splashes on it . . . I'll rip off your own arms and feed them to you. Now, you and Brawn get down there and cause some damage."

As Dioxin and I raced down the hill toward the convoy, Terrain collapsed the road directly beneath the two armored cars at the front. Behind us, Slaughter carried Casey in a high arc.

The truck swerved to avoid the crashed cars, went off the road, and smashed through a wooden fence into a field of wheat before it shuddered to a stop.

With a loud *whoosh* the walls of the truck instantly melted into a spray of white-hot fragments and I skidded to a stop to avoid being caught in it.

I had half a second to see Energy floating in the smoldering ruins of the truck, her skin crackling and glowing, before twin bolts of lightning sprang from her outstretched hands directly at me. I threw myself to the side at the last instant, pivoted on my hands, and launched myself at her feetfirst.

But Energy was too fast: She dodged my kicks and zipped around me in a wide circle with fire spilling from her hands. In seconds the wheat was ablaze, a growing ring of fire with me trapped in the center.

They knew we were coming! I closed my eyes and raced through the flames, then vaulted the fence in pursuit of Energy. She saw me and doubled back, her hands glowing with a built-up charge of electricity.

I saw her prepare to launch the first bolt and dropped down into Terrain's crater next to the crashed armored cars just as the bolt seared the air around me. But I wasn't fast enough to avoid the second: It hit me in the chest, so powerfully that I could feel my flesh boiling.

I ripped the roof off the nearest armored car and threw it at her like a Frisbee—Energy ducked below it, and was preparing to fire again when she suddenly stopped in midair, hesitated for a moment, then darted away.

I looked down and saw two of Max's Rangers—Lash and

Ollie—desperately trying to free themselves from the wreckage. If Energy had attacked again, her lightning could have killed them.

"Hi guys," I said. "Stay put and you'll probably be safe."

I hauled myself out of the crater in time to see Roz and Joshua Dalton launch themselves from the rear armored cars, both of them heading straight for Terrain. That made sense: Physically he was the weakest of us, but his power made him the most dangerous.

Overhead Energy was streaking toward me, and just beyond I saw Titan dropping from the sky like a meteor.

Slaughter yelled, "Brawn! Catch!" I looked up in time to see her let go of Casey and alter course to intercept Titan and Energy.

I raced forward, leaped high over the crater and plucked Casey out of the air, then landed in a half crouch on the road.

"Four of them, five of us," Casey said as I set him down. "They don't honestly think they'll *win*, do they?"

Beyond the rear cars, Terrain was bombarding Josh Dalton with a stream of dirt and rock that flowed up from the ground around his hands and hit Josh's telekinetic shield like the world's largest sand blaster.

Nearby, Roz had Dioxin pinned flat against the ground with her own shield. Drops of his acidic venom pooled around him, burning through the road's surface.

Above, Titan and Slaughter were grappling in the air, beating the living tar out of each other, while Energy zipped around them, unable to get a decent shot at Slaughter.

Casey said, "Huh. I've got a bad feeling we might have been outmaneuvered."

"A trap," I said.

"You think? Yeah, it's a trap, and they're not finished yet." He took one last look around. "We're outta here."

But by then it was too late.

Paragon soared over the hill, followed closely by Abby and Thunder.

Apex came bounding along after them, his powerful muscles enabling him to leap forty or fifty yards at a time.

Then Impervia soared in from the other direction, wearing a jetpack identical to Paragon's.

Octavian came next: He was a relatively low-powered guy that I'd heard had worked with Abby and Thunder on occasion. He carried a skinny young man I recognized as Thalamus, who was supposed to be even smarter than Ragnarök.

More of them came: Inferno. Zephyr. The White Wasp. The five members of Portugal's Poder-Meninas team. And a dozen more whose costumes I didn't recognize.

A twenty-strong squadron of Apache gunships roared over the hills to our east, and moments later at least twice as many were approaching from the west.

Above, Slaughter and Titan broke apart and hovered in place, while on the ground Terrain relaxed his assault on Josh, and Roz retreated to allow Dioxin to get to his feet.

I spotted a cloud of dust on the horizon, and then Quantum was standing in front of us. He looked from Casey to me, and said, "Surrender."

"Give me a couple of minutes to talk to the troops."

"Two minutes, and that's it." Instantly, he was gone.

Casey pulled out his communicator. "Guys . . . We've got an untenable situation here. Gather round."

Slaughter dropped down out of the sky just as Dioxin and Terrain reached us.

"Didn't see *this* coming," Casey said. "You'll notice that there's someone missing from their ranks. If you're listening, Max—and I think it's a pretty safe bet that you are—well played. But we're not going to surrender. And we're not going to fight. You're going to let us go." He smiled, and winked at Slaughter. "Reckon we're going to have to play our one-time-only Get Out of Jail Free card."

He detached a small device from the depths of his armor. "Max, what I'm holding here is a powerful little transmitter. It's got two buttons. The first one—which I've just pressed— summons my craft. You'll allow it safe passage from this location. The second button, which I've also just pressed, has activated a software bomb that five years ago I planted deep inside the code of the computers that control this country's entire nuclear arsenal. That software bomb is now counting down. When the counter hits zero, it's going to start launching missiles. How's *that* sound? Interesting? Scary? By now you're already sweating and desperately ordering your minions to find and disable my little patch. I figure it'll take them maybe six hours. Far too long. The counter will hit zero in fifty-eight minutes. I can disable it, but not from here. What I *can* do from here is trigger it to activate instantly. So for the next fifty-eight minutes, if any of your people attempt to stop us or follow us . . . Boom! That's it for life on this planet."

I felt a knot twist in my guts. *No way*, I said to myself. *He wouldn't do something like that!* But even as that thought ran through my mind, it was met by another: *If anyone* could *do it, it's him.*

A few seconds later, Quantum appeared before us again. "You're bluffing."

Casey said nothing. He just slowly shook his head.

"Ragnarök, this is insane! This is *not* how the world ends. . . ." Quantum frowned. "Even *you* wouldn't . . ." He stepped close to Casey, right up to him so that their noses were almost touching. "There is more to come. Much more. The future has shown itself to me. You're not part of it."

Casey smirked. "Man, you're really losing it, aren't you? You've gone over the edge already, Quantum. Sooner than I predicted."

Quantum shook his head briskly. "Do you understand? The future does not belong to you!" He hesitated for a second, then added, "It does not belong to any of us. The future belongs to those who'll come after us. To the superhumans not yet born. To the new heroes."

"*Right* . . . Well, *you* tell—"

But Quantum was already gone.

Terrain said, "Is it just me, or is everyone else creeped out by that guy? He is *not* normal."

"And we are?" Dioxin asked.

Casey looked up. "It's here." From directly overhead, a

bulky silver aircraft was descending. I'd seen the plans on Casey's computers: It looked like a large helicopter without the rotors. I'd no idea what kept it aloft, but it moved in almost complete silence.

Louder, Casey said, "Clock's still ticking, Max. Are you going to let us go, or will you allow your pride to destroy the human race?"

Thunder's voice boomed all around us. "Ragnarök, Max Dalton's military contacts have confirmed the presence of your software bomb. So go. But this isn't over. You've put the lives of every human being on the planet in jeopardy—there's no going back from this. No forgiveness. You understand what I'm saying? Sooner or later we *will* find you, and when we do, you're dead. All of you."

Thunder's words seemed to hang in the air for a moment, then Casey shrugged and gestured toward the craft. "Should be plenty of space inside for all of us. Dioxin, there's a square lined with gold leaf. Stand on that and try not to dissolve *too* much of the craft before we escape."

The others climbed on board and I squeezed in after them. Before the craft could rise, Slaughter nudged Casey and pointed back out.

Casey said to me, "*Your* friend, I think."

I looked out to see Abby slowly walking toward us. She'd put her sword and ax into their scabbards on her back, and was approaching with her hands up. "Wait, please! I just want to talk to Brawn!"

Casey idly fiddled with the trigger device in his hand. "Sure. Why not? But we're not hanging around. You'll have to fly alongside us. If you can keep up—this thing moves pretty fast."

The craft lurched into the air, and in seconds the heroes were just dots on the ground. Abby launched herself after us, flying in parallel with the craft. "Brawn, you've got to come back to us. These people are killers!"

"Six of you attacked me in Manhattan, Hesperus! *You* tried to kill *me!*"

"It was Max. You know that."

Casey leaned past me and said, "Of course it was. It's *always* Max. Hesperus, when are you going to learn that he is much more of a threat than I am?"

"Shut up," she said. "This isn't about you. Brawn, please. Come back. We'll sort everything out and we can be a team again. When I freed you from Oak Grove prison, I took a chance on you. Now you have to do the same. Trust me. It's not too late."

Slaughter peered out the other side of the craft. "We've got a couple of folks on our tail. Titan and Energy, I think. Pretty far back, but they're matching our speed." She pulled her head back in and nodded at Casey, grinning. "Goes against the rules! Do it! Set the missiles flying!"

Casey shook his head. "No can do. I was bluffing." He held up the device. "The software bomb exists, but all it will do is shut down the missiles. There's no way I can launch them remotely. What, you really think I'm *that* crazy?"

Abby looked at him for a second, her eyes wide, then darted away.

"Slaughter!" Casey yelled. "Stop her!"

"No!" I screamed. I made a grab for Slaughter, but I was too slow.

She launched herself out of the craft, straight down at Abby.

Abby didn't see her coming.

Slaughter swooped down and pulled the ax free from Abby's back.

Far below, Energy saw what was happening and zoomed up toward them.

Abby turned in midair, but Slaughter was fast, and stronger.

Energy blasted Slaughter with a lightning bolt so powerful that for a few seconds there was nothing but a blinding glare.

And when my vision cleared, Abby was falling, her own ax buried deep into her side.

I saw Energy catch my friend in her arms. But she was too late. Nothing could have saved her.

At the age of twenty-four, ten years after I met her, Abigail de Luyando died because she tried to save me.

CHAPTER 40

TWELVE YEARS AGO

TEN MONTHS LATER, in the enormous cavern deep below the base in Pennsylvania, I was helping Casey's people assemble one of the giant engines for his latest project, a mobile fortress that—when completed—would be more than a hundred yards long and completely bristling with weapons.

As I stepped back to check my work, a voice behind me said, "Hey."

I felt my blood turn cold, and I forced myself to keep calm as I turned to face Slaughter.

She hovered in the air in front of me, a slight smile on her starkly beautiful face. "So . . . I understand why you were mad about what happened with Hesperus."

I walked toward her and she floated back, maintaining the same distance between us.

"Brawn, listen . . . She would have told the others that Ragnarök was bluffing. They'd have come after us. . . . We were outnumbered, outgunned. I *had* to stop her!"

"And you thought that killing her was the *only* way to achieve that?" I snarled. "You're sick. Twisted."

Casey came running, skidded to a stop between us. "Stand down, both of you! If you're going to fight, you're not doing it in here. I've worked too long and too hard to have it all destroyed because you can't set aside your differences!"

I glared at Slaughter as I addressed Casey. "How much longer?"

"Soon. A year, maybe two." To Slaughter, he said, "Leave us."

As she darted out of the cavern, I said to Casey, "It had better work."

"I can't promise you that. I'm certain I'll be able to permanently strip the powers that make someone superhuman. But . . . I don't know if I can change your appearance back to human."

"Then what's the point of me even being here? I've spent the past *fifteen years* like this." I sat down on the ground so our eyes were more or less on the same level. "I want to be able to walk down the street without people running and screaming. I want to be able to go into a store without having to crawl on my hands and knees."

Casey nodded. "I know. There might be another solution. I'm thinking that maybe I can give you another body. A clone. I've already had some success in that field. Problem is, I haven't yet found a viable way to accelerate a clone's growth. So if we start growing one now, it'll be another eighteen years

before it reaches adulthood. Of course, we'll need those eighteen years to find a way to copy your brain patterns to the
clone."

"Suppose you *could* do that," I said. "Then what happens
to me? To this body? There'd be two of us, right?"

"We'd dispose of your current body."

"That'd be murder."

Casey shrugged. "That's one way of looking at it."

"And if the clone body reaches eighteen years, well, it'll
have a mind of its own. So wiping that mind would also be
murder." I shook my head. "No. We're not doing that."

"Then you'll have to resign yourself to remaining the way
you are now. It could be worse, you know. You could be in
Dioxin's situation." Casey walked around behind me and put
his hand on my shoulder as we looked over toward the skeletal structure of the mobile fortress. "This is costing nearly
every cent I've stolen in the past decade, but it'll be worth it.
It'll bring the so-called heroes running. The more of them we
have in one place, the more energy we'll be able to siphon
from them."

"They'll try to stop us," I said. "They're going to throw
everything they have at us."

"It's the right thing to do, you know that."

"It'll be all-out war."

"I know," Casey said. "It's going to be *great*."

EPILOGUE

THE MINE NOW

EVERY DAY AT DAWN the guards wake me. They release the mechanisms holding my chains to the wall, then the massive doors rumble open and they escort me out.

I work for eighteen hours, hauling the raw ore from the new mine shaft, without a break. I receive food and water only when my shift is over, and only if I have surpassed my quota of ore.

Sometimes, I think I could snap through the chains if given enough time, but I am watched every moment of every day.

After my rampage through the mine eight months ago Harmony Yuan told me, with glee in her eyes, that I would die here. I am certain that she is right.

Around me the guards are assembling, preparing to once again take me out into the daylight, and I remember one of the last things my father said to me: "You have to be a *good* man. You have to always do the best you can for other people."

It kills me that I've let him down, that I was so willing to follow Casey Duval, to believe his lies. He used me, just as Harmony and Gordon Tremont used me. Just as Max Dalton did.

For all his faults, at least Max was working to make things better for everyone. Though he was greedy, and vain, and misguided, ultimately he put the human race above himself. But the ends do not justify the means. Despite everything he did, that did not make him a good person.

And I wasn't a good person either. I'd been selfish. I wanted to be cured. . . . I wanted a normal life, but now I see that I did little to deserve that. A normal life is not a *right*, it's a privilege that each of us must earn, by helping others, by putting their needs ahead of our own desires.

Harmony said, "Whatever you think about this place, Gethin Rao, you *do* deserve to be here. You sided with Ragnarök when you knew that he was evil."

She was right.

The mechanism in the walls whirs into action, and the strong metal loops that bind my chains to the floor slowly open, allowing me to move.

I stand and stretch as much as my chains will allow.

Ahead of me, the crack in the doors widens and my guards tighten their grips on their guns.

The last words Harmony said to me were "The age of the

superhuman is over. Many of you are dead; all of you have lost your powers. You were an aberration, a temporary flaw. You should never have existed."

Whether that is true, I may never know.

All I know now is that I cannot escape this place, and that my rampage destroyed the last chance I had to redeem myself. While I was working in the mine alongside the other prisoners, I did whatever I could to help them. It wasn't much, but in small ways I made their lives better.

But not now, not anymore.

Outside, I hear the workers from the night shift heading back into the dome, their chains clinking, their bare feet scuffing the dust-covered concrete. I desperately want to help them again, to fight for a few concessions from the guards.

I've lost that chance forever.

I'm thirty-nine years old, and I've been a monster for twenty-seven of those years.

The doors open wider and I see them, my fellow prisoners. They don't look at me anymore.

Once, they looked to me for salvation. They saw the punishment I'd withstood under Hazlegrove's rule, and it gave them hope: If I was able to endure that, then they could endure their own suffering.

Not anymore. We work until we die.

All hope is gone.

Last night, during a temporary lull in the noise from the mine, I heard wolves howling in the mountains. The sound took me back, instantly, to the Antarctic blizzard, to the friendly huskies leading my Argentinean rescuers.

But that was a long time ago, when I was young and strong and still superhuman. Before I allied myself with Casey Duval and stepped onto the path that led me to this place.

I once told Abby that if I could go back in time to the day I freed Casey from Max Dalton's cell, I would do it again. And even now, after everything that's happened to me, I would still make the same choice. Regardless of his later deeds, back then Casey was innocent. And the innocent should never be imprisoned.

My belief that I made the right decision is a small consolation, but it's the only thing I have left. The only thing that's mine.

I am certain that I will never see Max again, but I like to think that sometimes he lies awake at night, haunted by the memories of his actions. And maybe, every now and then, he remembers me and feels a twinge of guilt.

Wordlessly, the guards gesture with their guns, indicating that I should emerge from my cell.

They back out ahead of me, always alert, fingers on triggers. Looking only at me.

They don't see that some of the other prisoners have turned toward the electrified perimeter fence.

They don't see the sparks from the fence as something tears its way through.

But they hear the panic of the prisoners, and finally they turn.

A boy, not more than thirteen years old, is racing toward us. Moving fast, faster than I've seen anyone move in more than ten years.

His hands are glowing, twin balls of energy forming within them.

He leaps over the line of prisoners, and the guards swing their weapons in his direction.

The boy blasts the guards with his lightning.

I cannot remember the last time I laughed, but I'm laughing now.

Harmony was wrong. The age of the superhuman is far from over.

Lance slammed the door behind him, ran through the musty office and out to the front. He jumped onto his bike, slung the backpack onto the handlebars, and began pedaling like crazy. He couldn't help grinning. *I did it! I got away!*

He zoomed around the corner and onto the main road, shifted up a gear, and increased his speed. It was tough going with the heavy jetpack on his back, but he wasn't going to stop for anything.

Then he heard the roar of an engine coming up fast behind.

He risked a glance back: A large white panel truck was bearing down on him. Two black-suited men were in the cab, the passenger gesturing wildly while the driver sat with a grim, determined look on his face.

Lance took a sudden right into another narrow side road, almost coming off the bike. The driver had to hit the brakes to make the turn.

The road was closed off at the end, with only a narrow pedestrian passage leading through the gap between two buildings. *They'll never be able to follow me through!* He mentally pictured his route home. *If I cut through the church grounds I can . . .* He stopped himself. *No, can't go home. Not with all this stuff. I have to hide it somewhere.*

As he was considering the best place to stash his stolen goods where they wouldn't be found, he cycled out of the business park and onto the street. The rush-hour traffic was long gone, but the street was still busy.

He slowed a little as he approached the crossroads, weaved in and out of the waiting cars, then turned right, heading toward the mall. There was a dense clump of bushes at one end of the eastern parking lot—he'd often hidden stuff there before, and it had never been discovered.

At the next junction he jumped the red light and almost collided with a white truck that was turning the corner. He pulled hard on the brakes, put his foot down to steady himself, and glared at the driver. His face fell. *Oh no. . . .*

The two black-suited men looked as surprised as Lance did. The passenger shouted, "That's *him*! An' he's the same kid from the accident! He musta got Marcus's briefcase!"

Lance jumped back onto the bike, darted around the truck and down the road, knowing that they'd have to make a U-turn to follow him.

He heard a loud *bang* and something shattered a mailbox as he passed. "They've got guns? Oh, this just gets better and better!"

Another *bang*, and Lance felt like something had thumped

him in the back. *They hit the jetpack! OK, that's it. I quit.* He slowed a little, steered the bike onto the pavement. *I'll say I'm sorry and hand it all back and when their hands are full I'll run like mad.* A hundred yards ahead was the pedestrian entrance to a housing estate. *Perfect. Stop there and—*

There was a third gunshot. Lance changed his mind about stopping. He hunched forward, keeping his head low, and pushed as hard on the pedals as he could. There were two more shots, and before he even heard the second Lance found himself racing forward, as though he had just crested a steep hill.

But the road was almost flat, and still his speed was increasing. It felt like someone was pushing him from behind. Then a familiar whine reached his ears, and he knew what had happened: The last gunshot had somehow activated the jetpack.

He zoomed out onto the road, his knuckles white on the juddering handlebars. *I'm gonna die!*

He knew that he couldn't slow down or jump off the bike. With the jetpack still thrusting him forward he'd have no way of stopping. He couldn't even lift his head more than a couple of inches.

Lance rocketed across an intersection, overtook a guy on a motorbike, narrowly missed a deep pothole. He could steer the bike, but it wasn't easy—at this speed, the slightest nudge on the handlebars sent him weaving all over the road. *The fuel in this thing has to run out sometime. Need a good long stretch of road . . .*

Ahead, the road branched to the right: the on-ramp for the freeway. He knew that bicycles weren't allowed on the freeway, but figured that in this case the traffic cops might make an exception. Besides, he didn't have any other option.

There was a line of cars at the end of the ramp waiting to pull out into the busy traffic. Lance zoomed past the surprised drivers and cut in ahead of a white Toyota.

The speed limit on the freeway was sixty-five miles per hour. Lance knew from being in the car with his dad that most drivers regarded sixty-five as the minimum speed, not the maximum. He didn't know how fast he was going now, but he was overtaking everything else on the freeway. The bike shuddered and rattled over the asphalt and he prayed to the god of cycling that he didn't blow a tire.

He tried to remember exactly what the newspaper article on Paragon's jetpack had said about its range. He had a horrible feeling that there had been something about Paragon being able to make it all the way from New York to Chicago without the need to refuel. *And he's a lot bigger than me too. Plus he's got all that armor. This thing might not run out before I reach the end of the freeway!*

Lance's back and shoulders were aching from the strain, and he desperately wanted to sit back. He knew that if he did, the jetpack would launch him into the air, bike and all.

Paragon had spent years developing his jetpack. He knew how to control it, how to land safely.

Lance didn't even know how to undo the clasps.

ACKNOWLEDGMENTS

Six novels, one collection of short stories . . . that's over half a million words so far! And none of this would have been possible without the support of some very talented and hardworking people.

First and foremost, my adorable wife, Leonia, who is far more giving and generous than I deserve. It's no lie to say that she is in many ways the heart of the Quantum Prophecy series: Leonia reads every book the day after I've finished the first draft (which, of course, also means that she gets to read all the bits that later get taken out!), and it's her reactions to that first draft that shape the final book.

My fellow writers Harry Harrison, Michael Scott, and John Higgins, who have always been there with their liberal feedback and wise advice.

My friends—too numerous to list, but they know who

they are—who've been behind the books one hundred percent. In this instance, particular thanks must go to Danielle Lavigne, Vicky Stonebridge, Richmond Clements, Dave Evans, and Paul Tomlinson—all of whom are far more talented than I am, but don't tell them I said that.

My loving family—my parents, sisters, nieces, nephews, and in-laws—even though *certain people who shall remain unnamed* still haven't got around to reading the books.

The all-too-often thankless people who work behind the scenes to guide and guard the books on their journey from the author's imagination to the readers' bookshelves: my remarkably tolerant editors Matt Morgan, who started the ball rolling, and Kiffin Steurer, who ably and deftly carried the ball to where it is now. The publishers, copy editors, designers (special thanks to the artistic genius Shawn Martinbrough for the covers to the prequels!), sales and marketing people, bookstore staff, librarians, teachers, and reviewers. Without all of these fine people, books just wouldn't happen!

Then there's you, the readers, whose e-mails and letters have helped keep me going during the difficult times . . . because I'm not writing this series for myself—I mean, *I* already know what happens—I'm writing it for you. This is *your* adventure: I'm just the pilot. I hope that the journey we're taking together has been fun so far!

And sticking with that metaphor . . . please buckle your safety belts and hold on tight, because from here on, it's going to be one heck of an exciting ride!

Michael Carroll
Dublin, Ireland, 2012